A GAMBLER'S
Summer of 1...

By
William Gerald Hamby

Keith Publications, LLC
www.keithpublications.com
©2016

Arizona
USA

A GAMBLER'S FEAST
Summer of 1969

Copyright© 2016

By William Gerald Hamby

Edited by Ray Dyson
www.raydyson.com

Cover art by Elisa Elaine Luevanos
www.ladymaverick81.com

Cover art Keith Publications, LLC © 2016
www.keithpublications.com

ISBN: 978-1-62882-146-8

If you are interested in purchasing more works of this nature, please stop by
www.keithpublications.com

Contact information: keithpublications@cox.net
Visit us at: www.keithpublications.com

Printed in The United States of America

I am not what I think I am, I am not what you think I am,
I am what I think you think I am
— James Cooley

Dedication

For Tressa, Peter, Patrick and Michael. Who else...

Acknowledgements

Without the love, vision and support of many, this novel would not exist. It's a daunting exercise attempting to distill them into a list. But you know who you are, and what you did for me. This is a small tribute to those still with us who helped, and also to the ones whose fingerprints are all over me and the characters who populate my story who are no longer here.

Thank you:

Tressa and our boys, my heroes; my parents, G.F. and Gerry, my brother Larry, the one with the real talent, and his equally smashing wife, Deb.

Jim and Jan Starnes, with me and for me with love from the beginning and throughout the process.

My agent Diane Nine, who believed in my story, and Dave Smitherman, who started the dominoes falling in the first place.

Todd Culbertson, Cynthia Paris and Bob Rayner at the *Richmond Times Dispatch,* who gave me space for my words while the novel was coming together.

Deb Jacobs Hamby and Michael Rhodes, very special people who provided me with writing work when I needed it.

Mary Keith and my exceptional editor, Ray Dyson, at Keith Publications.

James River Writers and the *Best Unpublished Novel* recognition, and Susan Cokal, whose editorial advice was key. The National Press Club Fiction Contest, whose recognition provided welcomed confidence.

Adrienne Stuttaford, my first reader, Mary McBride, my first copy editor, and Hiram Cuevas, generous and crucial.

Finally, my three kings:
Jim Weiss, Ted Levino and Frank Getlein.

Chapter 1

1969

We woke up to Vietnam all at once. The whole fraternity. It was something. Every damn one of us, I think there were fifty-five including the latest pledge class, went to Voorhees' funeral. I had been in my apartment making a collage from *TIME* magazine covers, skipping an English Lit class when I got a call from one of the brothers that Voorhees had been killed. "Took a mortar shell in the upper body, Vic," he'd said. And he named some war zone I'd never heard of. Voorhees was the first real person any of us knew who had actually gone to Vietnam and seen combat. Most of the guys, fraternity brothers and others, had managed to get deferments of one type or another. They got into grad school or med school, flunked their physicals or just lucked out with a high lottery number. Or if they went, managed to get assigned to Germany, or got into the Navy. And nobody I knew could name anyone who'd split the country, evaded the draft. One guy from Indiana whose father had political connections got him into something called the Stenographers' Corps in the Army. He got to type letters for old generals in Washington, D.C., which we thought was cool. But still, in our little world, Vietnam had not touched us until Voorhees got blown apart. Vietnam, that fucking war, had only been six o'clock news until then.

His funeral was in a church in a small town outside Cincinnati. We drove as a caravan from the fraternity house as if going in one large group would make it easier to handle. It was early spring, still cool, trees about to bud. The sun was out. It made the little Methodist church a brighter white.

I wasn't close to Voorhees and only knew him for a year: his senior, my freshman, my pledge year. But I liked him. Everyone liked him. And he stood for something, unlike my sorry ass. He was one of those energetic, go get 'em guys the Sixties couldn't grab. He was really a Fifties' kid in my mind. He thought antiwar demonstrators should be arrested, hippies were idiotic, and a freak band named The Lemon Pipers at Homecoming was a "weird" choice. He was enthusiastic, positive, patriotic, ambitious, headed to grad school, and planning to marry the long-time TRI Delt sweetheart he was pinned to. He was going places, honor roll kind of guy. And funny. A Greek Week cut-up. Short but tough. He volunteered rather than be drafted, went to OCS. Got a commission. All that and then he got blown up the second week over there. Freaky. And fucked up.

The minister said God was sad too, and things about, "The flower of youth, God's plan, mysteries, being taken too early, unaccomplished goals and mountains not scaled..." and other shit. We all listened and looked at his coffin with the flag on it, his smiling picture in uniform propped against it in the curve of a rack of flowers. We held our hands in our laps, fidgeted and listened to the organ music. We stood, sang, and prayed as we were told and tried not to cry or look at each other. Shoulder to shoulder in the first five pews, every one of us trying to come to grips, to make some sense of it, counting the seconds until we could leave. Escape.

His mother kept her head bowed, shaking as she cried. His dad, bigger than Voorhees, wrapped an arm around his wife, dabbing at his own eyes with a white handkerchief. The minister wore purple and black robes. Old people and friends we didn't know from his childhood, other adults and parents in their dark clothes worked to be strong. The too-polite

2

funeral home men in their shiny black suits hovered. The cop on his motorcycle yo-yoed back and forth past the line of cars on the way to the burial, stopping traffic at intersections, blasting his siren. The blowing wind at the cemetery flapped the tent over the grave hole and made the minister raise his voice and wave his hands. His mother hugged the folded flag, really crying. His dad was stone faced there, but still squeezed the damp wad of a handkerchief, like a crushed little flag of his own. Voorhees' fiancée, Linda, the TRI Delt, collapsed into a ball at the edge of the grave. Taps was played from somewhere but no one turned; a funeral official raised his eyebrows and nodded and eight grab-ass fraternity brothers carried Voorhees on their shoulders, swaying, trying to stay in step, their faces tight in confusion and pain and too much responsibility.

I drove Palmeri's VW bus slow out of the cemetery on curvy, skinny lanes, past old, neat graves and headstones and every once in a while a mausoleum, and another burial ceremony in progress. The VW whined in low gears, the sound like sand filling up the interior where six of us rode not talking. As I made the main road back to campus, running as fast as possible away from Voorhees and the funeral in fifth , I was wasted and numbed to a point where all I could do was turn up the radio as loud as I could stand it and hope for some ideas, some direction. Any distraction at all.

I just drove.

Most of us went to Crow's and got shit-faced after we got back to campus. One of those cold spring rains started while we were inside, and by the time the last of us left, it poured down like pellets. And I thought of the mound of fresh dirt over Voorhee's grave as I ran to the VW and wondered if the

3

rain would pack it down tight.

****

Elbow to elbow at O'Hare, we stood drinking beer. He was with Hunsinger, a buddy of his from the plant, on the way to Idaho for a meeting. They were waiting on their flight. I was just in from Cincinnati myself, waiting on a connection to take me to Reno, the next to last stop before a cab ride, bus or something to Lake Tahoe to meet Carl Turner, my wacky friend who'd moved to San Jose, California, with his family when General Electric transferred his dad. My parents loved Carl. They had no idea how crazed he really was though. He'd worked in Tahoe the summer before, had a blast and convinced me I should try it out. He'd said there was work all over the place at the casinos and the restaurants. Tons of college kids our age. "Totally bitchin," was how he'd summed it up long distance. I could imagine his maniac smile over the phone.

It was totally chance I would find myself this far from home and have a layover that more or less matched his. Even more meaningful...almost unfathomable and fucking unbelievable to be truthful...I would be socializing with him, be accepted by him as a drinking buddy in the middle of all the other travelling businessmen at an airport bar. The year had been amazing enough already with shit like riots and demonstrations and schools across the country closing early. But as we drank draft beers and watched the little wet slips of receipts pile up on the table in the concourse just off the bar, people hurrying past on the way somewhere, flights being announced, others standing and sitting, killing time...I could not believe I was having a beer with my Dad, the one

4

I'd positioned myself against for so long now, like Richard Nixon, the Government, the Army, the Corporation, the Man, the Conformist, Patriarch, Disciplinarian: Dad. For some reason I'd noticed he had recently undergone a change of opinion about me. I didn't know if this had more to do with where he was in his head or if he just finally opened his eyes and realized I was grown, almost out of his grip. Maybe I'd finally worn him down. Who the fuck knew. It might have been different if he knew I had flunked out and lost my II-S deferment. But right now, with these two middle-aged, middle-level executives, drinking at an airport bar, I was pumped with a strange new sense of change and freedom.

Hunsinger was one of those big, crew cut, broad-faced German people who were all over Cincinnati. He had big hands and when he shook mine he pumped it hard up and down in three quick jerks. I didn't really know him, but had heard his name from Dad over the years.

"Going to Nevada, Vic?"

"Lake Tahoe," I said. "Going to get a job in a casino or restaurant or something for the summer." Dad pulled on a cigarette and looked at his watch. He was huffing and puffing like only he could because United couldn't upgrade them to first class.

After a lecture about, "...the strictly from hunger service these days," he said, "Your mother is worried. That's her. You know," and he waved at the waitress and held up three fingers. She winked back and leaned into another table for an order. Dad looked back at me as he drained his beer mug and asked if I had enough money.

5

I said, "I guess. Turner says I'll get a job as soon as I get there." But I really had no idea what I was getting into.

"Hold onto your money," said Hunsinger. "Remember the odds are always with the house. If you play, play dice...craps. Tricky game, but the odds are the best you can get."

I looked at Dad and he nodded in agreement, and I wondered if he'd ever gambled for real. I had no idea what he did out on the road on business trips. The only gambling I'd ever seen him do was penny ante poker around the kitchen table, gloating when he beat Mom. Getting her goat. The only gambling stories I'd ever heard him tell were about the "old days" across the Ohio River in Newport and Covington, Kentucky.

"Things were wide open then," he'd always say when he brought it up. The implication was he'd done something, but I couldn't see it in him. It was wicked over there. He was a deacon in the church.

I have guilty childhood memories from the newspaper and television news of a former football hero turned political candidate named George Ratterman who got drugged and photographed in a motel room in Covington, the Tropicana, I think, with his pants around his knees and a hooker or a stripper named April Flowers in his arms. It was a setup by the Mafia or so the story went. Or that's the way my memory wants it. Anyway, when I was a kid, and Newport or Covington were mentioned, it was usually about stuff the adults smiled and whispered about.

The waitress came over and put down three mugs. She was

6

still smiling and blushing from a customer at the next table who she said was flirting and had said something fresh. Her accent sounded foreign when she said, "Thank you, gentlemen." And for the first time I saw my Dad look at another woman besides Mom with what I thought was more than a passing glance. At the same time, I was shocked and sort of proud, and then I thought of Mom and took a quick gulp.

My Dad gave me his look and said, "Remember the peanut man?"

I said, "You mean the old black guy at Crosley Field? Sells peanuts?"

"Wears a top hat and a tuxedo," said Hunsinger. "Hope he's going to be at the new stadium on the river."

"Been there for years," said Dad. "Remember the first time you saw him?"

"I was little. One of my first games."

"Remember what you said about him?" Dad asked. He exhaled smoke from his nose and drank some beer.

I remembered the cool tunnels under the stands, the green grass opening up in front of me when I got up to the last step holding my Dad's hand. And the big laundry building over the right field wall and the tool company behind left field with the broken windows from home runs, but I had no idea what I could have said about the peanut man.

Dad looked at his watch, then Hunsinger, and said, "Guzzle

it up. We better go." As Hunsinger lifted the mug to his mouth, Dad said, "You don't remember?"

"I don't. Nope."

He rubbed out his cigarette, cocking his head away from the smoke in his eyes and said, "You asked me if he got to eat all the peanuts he didn't sell."

"Really. So what? Why do you remember that? Why bring it up now?"

Hunsinger shook my hand again and picked up his briefcase. He said, "Hold onto your money, Vic. And good luck."

We didn't hug in my family, so before he picked up his briefcase, before he scooped his Kools and his lighter off the table, Dad shook my hand and said, "Good luck, son. Be careful. And call your mother." And he dropped some money for the beers on the table.

I stepped back from him, smelling his smell, the Mennen, the Listerine, the beer, the Kools, and I said, "Why did you bring up the peanut man?"

"I thought I would never forget that moment," he said. "But I did until right here, right now. It just came back." And then he gave me a little salute and turned to Hunsinger and said something I couldn't hear. Then they were off to catch their plane, leaving me at the table.

I dreamed on the airplane, pretty much drunk, falling asleep against the window staring at a white full moon that lit up the tops of the clouds. I had beery dreams. One was of a baseball game at Crosley Field. I was at bat and as I looked over the left field wall, I could see all the windows in the Standard Electric Tool Company building had been fixed. Not one pane was broken. The Reds were in the field and that was bad because it meant I was on the other team and it didn't make sense. So I looked over my shoulder to the dugout and on the top step was my Dad. Hunsinger was next to him. They both had their arms folded and were chewing tobacco and spitting.

Turner was in the on-deck circle with that madman smile of his, hopping up and down. He swung two bats at a time. When I turned back to face the mound, the pitcher had become the framed, drugged, political candidate Ratterman, and he was winding up for the pitch, but it was a football. When it got over the plate I swung as hard as I could, connected and the football exploded into a shower of peanuts. I ran to first base anyway, but was stopped about halfway down the line by the hooker or the stripper or whoever had been with him in the Tropicana. She wouldn't let me go and turned me in circles around and around, kicking up the dirt and messing up the chalk line. As I spun, I saw three things: The first was a baseball stitched and white, spinning slowly and arcing high, breaking a window over the left field wall; the second was my Dad on the steps of the dugout hugging the waitress from the airport; and the third was the unreal sight of the peanut man, pushing his cart out from second base toward deep center, marching over perfect grass to the rising terrace below the 420-foot mark, his shiny silver cart reflecting the afternoon sun, pushing slow for somewhere.

Chapter 2

The taxi driver wore a black cowboy hat, the band a strip of
an American flag, and he was going on and on about,
"Isness, man. Isness is where it's at." His eyes were on me
forever in the rearview mirror, barely watching the road. He
scared the shit out of me as he drove through the night. The
interior smelled like incense, or clove, pot and cigarette
smoke. Halfway to Tahoe he told me he'd been up two days
and nights speeding on methedrine. We probably stopped
six or seven times so he could piss because of it. "Asians
accept what is there in front of them and we Westerners
have to look behind what is there all the time. Can't let it
alone. Can you dig that, man?" He went on, making his point
with a stoop and a stare from the road before he got back
into the cab, zipping his jeans after pissing in the wash of the
headlights that lit up a strip of asphalt, scrub and rocks
beside the road.

I said, "Sure," but as we accelerated and drove on,
somewhere between the airport and Tahoe in the dark, my
duffel bag leaning against the other door of the back seat, I
worried if the twenty-buck deal I made for the ride was a rip
off or not. I didn't bring much money, didn't want to ask my
parents for any. I was tired from the flight, hungover, and
while I felt good about getting to see Turner, I was whipped
and had traveled enough to be edgy with what was around
me. The ranting cab driver didn't help. I was hungry and
couldn't think clear or calmly. The hot night air whistled
through the four open windows and wired me up about
getting to Tahoe before all the jobs got snatched up. The
driver, Dave, fussed with the radio when he wasn't lecturing,
tuning in rock music I'd never heard. The new *LIFE* I'd
bought at the airport flapped on the floor at my feet.

Dave was a tall, bony dude dressed in jeans and cowboy boots. A faded, drab green Army fatigue jacket like the one I had in my duffel, the kind we wore on campus, had been tossed across the hood of his cab when I first spotted him. On the door in red writing were the words: Princess Cab Co. of Nevada, and the numbers 411. The car was white. He wore a flashy tie-dyed T-shirt with a major turquoise and silver necklace around his neck that hung halfway down his chest. But this guy was no college student. That was my guess as I walked up to him, the second of three cabs in a line. He was leaning against his car, smoking, rocking and hyper, looking at the crowd, and changing hands to smooth a black goatee when there wasn't a cigarette between his lips. Straight black hair fell on his shoulders under the cowboy hat with the flag hat band. The Flag. The Flag, I thought, as I stood for a moment in the hot, dry, Nevada night, getting a sense of it all, checking him out. This nervous acting dude had actually ripped up a real American flag and was using it as a hat band. Took balls, I thought. They'd arrest you in Ohio for that. Shit, put you under the jail. Even pissed me off vaguely for some reason I couldn't put my finger on.

The automatic doors from the terminal area opened and closed behind me as I stood at the curb. Each slide open let out a cold gust of air mixed with the ringing of slot machines into the night, adding to the cacophony...to use one of Dad's words...of airport noise, traffic and shouting, the jet fuel smell that was everywhere. I had never been in an airport like the one in Reno. Off the plane and inside, it felt more like a hillbilly bar. It smelled like stale beer, with country music, cigarette smoke and guys with cowboy hats and jeans and big belt buckles. And the slots. That blew my mind. It was definitely new turf compared to Cincinnati or Chicago.

Finding slot machines in an airport was a trip. I knew gambling was legal in Nevada, but I was just plain unprepared for the sight of people perched on stools, pulling handles, feeding quarter after quarter, fishing them like popcorn from cardboard cups killing time, while they waited for flights or arrivals. I'd watched a woman while I waited for my duffel bag to arrive at the baggage claim. She chain smoked while she played, had tight white curly thin hair and wore a powder blue leisure suit that rolled at her waist, with shiny white, strapped shoes and a wide belt that matched. She was propped instead of sitting on the stool, one leg on a rung, the other on the floor, and swished her head from side to side between pulls on the handle like she was on the lookout for a bandit waiting to jump her claim. I never did see her win anything big, but every once in a while what looked to be two or three bucks' worth of quarters would clang into the tray. She'd yell, "Sock it to me," and let them pile up until the coins in her cup were gone. Then she'd scoop up her winnings and start all over. As I picked up my bag, she called out to a girl wandering around making change for players. She exchanged a bill for a new roll of quarters and went back to pulling her handle. Never left her spot.

The airport was being renovated, and carrying my green duffel I walked in a crowd along skinny halls with nailed-up plywood walls. I'd stopped long enough to buy gum and the new *LIFE* with Rowan and Martin on the cover. An old woman behind the counter of the newsstand gave me change for a dollar, smiled and said, "Thank you," and her manners made me feel better. I put the change in my jeans and said, "Bye."
But the flimsy walls made me feel weird and the muttering of the others just made it worse. By the time I got to the curb, I was tense and jumpy. My left eye fluttered fast as

hummingbird wings. I made the deal with Dave and we were off.

I'd walk to him at an oblique angle, cautious or something, and asked, "Isn't there a dispatcher guy or somebody to handle all this?"

He'd snatched my bag and barked, "The admirals don't run the Navy, man. Let's roll.

Dave tuned in a station from Reno for a few minutes that was playing music by a band that sounded sort of like jazz, then rock, then South American. It was cool, different, and I'd never heard anything like it on the underground station in Cincinnati. The drummer was great; lots of long drum breaks, and even longer guitar solos pushed the music. Dave pounded on the dashboard to keep the rhythm and bobbed his head up and down until we lost the station in a buzz of static and interference. "Bummer," he said, and turned off the radio. "We're out of it for a while." Then he looked at me in the mirror. A semi passed us and I felt its sucking power as it exploded by. The car rocked and Dave asked, "You never heard of Santana?"

I said, "No. That them?"

"They're bitchin', really bitchin. Catch 'em sometime." And he leaned over to the glove compartment, took out a joint and passed it back to me and said, "Here, man." He had it between his thumb and index finger. He wore a big ring with a skull. "Toke up. I gotta take a leak." We slowed down, first to the side of the road, then bumped completely over into what looked like desert, or scrub from what I could see. He jumped out of the car and ran in and out of the headlights into the dark, the car still running, and radio still off, the only noise a cricket whistling churning the night.

I looked up at the full moon, the same one that had followed me from Chicago, the one I'd watched from my airplane window, and I remembered another, last spring, a year ago. Dave was taking forever, so I leaned over the seat and grabbed some matches on the dash and lit the joint and took a deep drag.

****

The Calhoun Street Riot, as it eventually became known by the Cincinnati papers, *The Enquirer* and *The Times-Star*, had happened under that spring moon. It had netted Baggo and me in its glow, too. The warning sounds were hard to make out at first, coming and going in the dark as we got high and drank in the park. We tried to make out the noise and decided it wasn't a fraternity party from Upshur Street. The pieces of voices came to us from somewhere else. It reminded me of being grounded on a Friday night and not being allowed to go to the high school football game, but every once in a while being able to pick up the excitement because the wind sneaked the sound of the band or the crowd or the public address announcer to me anyway, past my parents, defying them, too. But this night breeze blew in no pep band and cheers. We got back to the joint and six-pack.

I had found Baggo at Crow's Bar, next to campus. Baggo earned his nickname because he was, or seemed to be, constantly drunk. He railed against pot because he said it made his heart race, "Like a GTO with the needle pinned...I

14

ain't a hippie...and besides, it's illegal." He'd lost the privilege to drive months ago because of his drinking. Baggo wasn't a close friend. Hell Week and getting blitzed were all we shared. By himself as usual at the round bar, he was drinking Maker's shots and chasing them with Crow's twenty-five cent Schoenling Draft. He was dragging on Camel straights and melting swizzle sticks with his Zippo. The plastic smoldered with the cigarette smoke from him and the rest, and together with grease from frying burgers hanging in the bar lights, the stale smell of spilled beer, and sweat from the students packed together, it was stifling.

One generation away from hunkering on a front porch next to a washing machine and putting cold cigarette ashes in his pant cuffs, Baggo was just a simple drunk, a young hillbilly transplanted from northern Kentucky to the western part of town, a credit here, a course there, on his way...maybe...to some kind of degree. Baggo faced up to nothing, especially himself, at least on the outside. He was definitely not the king of hillbilly self-reflection.

At Crew's I hoped I could find Elaine, a Jewish girl from Cleveland I'd been dating.

A pay phone call yelled over the juke box only got me a quick and futile conversation with Kay, Elaine's roommate. She told me Elaine was at a new John Cassavetes movie. Kay had something about her that interested me, but she was all business, for sure wouldn't fool around with her roommate's boyfriend. She was as passionate about nursing and medicine as Elaine was about filmmaking. But she was intriguing. Something was going on there. She had a piece of my dream girl.

Baggo and I had walked to Burnett Woods, a city park near

campus. We sat on benches, and weren't worried about being interrupted because *The Enquirer* and *The Times-Star* had just reported the rape of a student from Dayton, and UC kids were warned not to go into the park at night. Our two benches were part of a hub to paths that met at a statue of some famous Cincinnatian, frozen in place, his bald head and shoulders spackled in pigeon shit.

I drew deep on a short joint, held my breath, then exhaled. I leaned back and looked up through the tree limbs and buds to the full moon. The limbs made a map of veins against it.

"That reefer do anything for you?"

I nodded, holding my breath, arms folded across my chest.

Baggo made a loud belch, and droned on about all the different ways he'd heard you could beat an army physical. He stood and then stretched, and sat on the backrest of the bench, his feet on the seat. He swigged his beer and tossed the bottle over his shoulder in the trees. He uncapped another Weideman, put the opener in his pocket and went on. He told me about a dude he knew who had held a bar of soap under his arm for an hour before they took his blood pressure. It made it so high they rejected him. "I-F. You can drink a pot of coffee too. Same deal."

We heard crowd sounds again. Baggo looked around. I leaned forward as I exhaled, my lips blubbering, and had to take a couple quick gulps of air. The sounds ran away. Baggo broke the silence again with another belch. Then, "I gotta piss."

I watched him waddle to a tree next to the walkway, his

shirttail half out as usual.

He talked over his shoulder as he stood. He asked about two fraternity brothers who'd enlisted. "What the hell is the deal with Voorhees and Kettering?" he asked. He came back to the bench. It was incomprehensible to him. "Those guys had it dicked. Both accepted to med school. Could've got deferments. Where'd the gung ho come from?"

I said, "Got me...", and told him I'd heard somewhere they were already out of basic training. But that was the last news I had. "Who knows?" Voorhees, friendly to me at the house, tried to be a real role model. He steered me best he could. Finally threw his hands up because I couldn't get focused. My defensiveness. That was the major problem he'd told me. I tried to tell him I was confused. He wouldn't buy that.

Baggo kept on about their volunteering for Vietnam as he drank. "And, they both got engaged before they went." He said Kettering had confessed he'd been banging his girl, Cynthia, for the last year. I told him Voorhees had confided to me he was going to wait until he returned before he did it with his chick, wait till they got married. Baggo shook his head. "Damn," he sighed. "As my Uncle Ban would say, 'I am clucking over every petal and stem of that tidbit.' "

I said, "Whattaya mean?" I felt my cheeks warming from the grass.

"He always says that when he hears something he can't believe. It's his thing."
And Baggo went on to mimic his uncle in a nasal twang: "Them two boys got the whole dang world goin' for 'em...education, good looks, pretty girls, and they up and join

17

the damn Army when they ain't got to. They Lord, I am clucking over every petal and stem of that story." But Ban knows about war though. Came home from World War II in a full body cast. Went ashore in the first wave at Normandy. Never been the same. Been living on disability ever since. Has a big comic book collection, too. Trades 'em. Hundreds, probably thousands of them stacked in his room." Baggo turned a bottle cap between his fingers and studied it. "We favor one another my Mom says." He looked at me with a face and said, "In looks, asshole." And he threw the bottle cap at me, bouncing off my chest.

He kept going about Uncle Ban. "But he is a smart, old coot. Knows stuff religious, too. Been singing hymns since he was six."

"No shit?" I had to admit, at least Baggo had some stories compared to my starchy life.

He drained his beer and said, "Still don't get Voorhees waiting till he gets back to get laid. Hell's bells, he might get his balls shot off. I bet he gets some chink pussy in Hong Kong or some place on R and R."

Now there was no mistake, it was definitely the chants of voices coming from up by Crow's. Real excited, Baggo said, "It's a demonstration, Vic. Hell. We got our own little peace rally right here in the Queen City. Damn. I am clucking."

I watched Baggo gulp the foam out of his bottle. He dropped it in the bag and left it on the bench and slid off the seat and weaved to the path. "C'mon, man..." And he belched again: I put the cool roach in my pocket.
A real antiwar demonstration in Cincinnati? It'd be news to

me. The real mayhem was happening in Washington, New York, Yellow Springs, Berkeley, Madison, San Francisco, and Boston. Places like that. The sit-ins, the riots, the bombings, mass marches, tear gassing, arrests; the real deal was going down in other places. Protests only existed at U.C. on television and in the newspaper like the war itself. No committed antiwar students here, a tiny minority, maybe. They handed out leaflets at the SDS table, mostly poli sci majors and pseudo artists. They tried to act like deep thinkers, and posed as intellectuals. Everybody else really, they dressed the part, costumed into trendy self-righteousness, influenced by the news film of others wearing beads, flowers, granny glasses and Army surplus. But they really didn't give a shit. I knew. Their business was drinking, getting high, music and partying; good enough grades to avoid parents, work and the war. I knew them. I was one. Baggo puked from somewhere up ahead. He was cussing and snorting.

Cincinnati was good at keeping trouble and "disturbances" away. It was a proud conservative bastion. The Queen City kept the wagons circled against disorder, simply would not stand for the "unseemliness" of a demonstration; would not want that picture in the paper; would never give into to the antiwar movement; would not stand for it. Never. Period. Verboten, another of Dad's words, simply verboten.

Baggo stumbled out of a row of bushes, wiping his mouth, and we walked through the trees to the sidewalk across the street from Crow's, campus at our back, and met up with some others, watching. To our left milled a hundred or more people, massed but stalled, some with signs, others with American flags flying upside down on poles. At the front, a big bearded guy carried a huge wooden cross on his shoulders. Pictures of people were stapled on it and I couldn't figure that out. Students in Calhoun Hall leaned out dorm windows and cheered like they were at Mardi Gras. The marchers shuffled. They alternated their chants between, "Hell, no, we won't go," "Stop the killing" and "Make love, not war." A guy in a green Army fatigue jacket ran around the edges of the crowd and tossed out buttons that read, "Give UC the Finger." I turned it over in my hands then slipped it into my shirt pocket with the roach.

Facing the marchers were the police. Some were still arriving. They formed a barricade of cars, mounted horses and foot police at the end of Calhoun where it ran into Clifton in front of Hughes High School. Twenty, maybe, by my count. Their white parade hats picked up the red from the flashing cruiser lights. Some smiled, some were grim faced and asked questions of bystanders while they held radios at their ears, but with no guns visible. Others cops shook their heads and looked over the crowd. Neither group seemed to me to be a real threat to the other. The demonstrators held their ground. The cops looked confused and disorganized. Tension froze everyone in place including me. This was like a festival. To me a vibe snaked through these people on Calhoun Street, connecting them all for the moment, including those drinking and cat-calling out on the sidewalk in front of Crow's. Normally it was illegal to let that go on along this street of bookstores, shops, restaurants, bars and dorms. Not tonight. The authorities declared an amnesty. The Queen City's finest had changed the rules. Temporarily they had a different kind of trouble to manage.
Baggo pissed me off with another one of his hillbilly expressions. "Well, touch me."

He held onto the last two beer bottles like they were gear

shifts. "I hope the cops kick their hippie asses." And he did a waddling little dance step on the sidewalk.

As I looked over things, I could see no one knew quite what to make of this or how to finish it off. Someone threw a rock through a store window, but it only made the demonstrators yell louder and got the watchers into it. The demonstrators still didn't advance. A police horse stamped and was reined sideways. A student photographer I knew showed up, weaving and crouching through the scene. Music from Crow's juke box came out the door and added a soundtrack to the happenings.

My eyes went from a topless girl waving from a dorm window down to the demonstrators, and across them to the police. I was about to tell Baggo I was leaving to go find Elaine when someone from the walk in front of Crow's dropped the cross bearer with a beer bottle trailed by a comet tail of foam. The cross bearer buckled at the knees from the hit, the cross pinning him to the asphalt. Baggo smiled a lizardy smile, and we both watched as the restraint dissolved on Calhoun Street.

I looked for the moon, but it had been blocked by the spotlight from a police helicopter. It held a circle of bright light on the chaos. Wind from the rotors blasted trash from an overturned garbage can. A film crew from a local TV station drove up at the back of the police cars. The music from Crow's was gone in the chop. I tried to calm my left eye with a hand and turned away.

The next day I picked up the *Cincinnati Enquirer* and read about the riot. The large headline said, *First Local Antiwar Demonstration Results in Riot, Arrests.* Below, a smaller headline said, *University Officials Suspect Outside Agitators.* Under the headlines a photograph showed a thin girl, hair straight to her shoulder, swinging a stick or a pole at a police officer. He held his hands out in defense, his white hat on the ground. The caption beneath the photo that covered most of the page above the fold read, *2nd Precinct Police Officer Defends Himself from Assailant During Last Night's Student Anti-War Riot.*

I decided to skip class and use the newspaper to make a collage.

****

I was halfway through the joint when Dave jumped back in the car.

"Good shit, huh?" he said, sounding very proud, grinning. I handed it back and he said, "C'mon. Ride shotgun."

And I did. And we smoked another joint and stopped at least three more times so he could piss and were eventually able to get an FM station from Sacramento that played really good records.

Dave kept on the subject of "isness." And jabbered about, "...being focused on what is there and that if you go to church it didn't really matter which one because every church is a little door that opens to the big door of spirituality." At one point, he took his eyes off the road as another truck was coming and said eighty-five percent of the brain's work is negative. "Did you know that?" The truck driver blew his air horn and Dave got back into our lane in time, then looked back at me and said in a very calm and even way," "Positive thoughts increase energy, man."

I just looked out at the road as it took forever to run under us. Everything had slowed: travel, time, the car, sentences...and a Stones tune I had never heard kept going and going. And I was starving.

Chapter 3

Dave said, "The new Stones record is far out man, but do you really get what you need? I don't think so."

I opened my eyes from a half awake, half asleep, and dreamy somewhere. My throat was raw from the grass. I was dying of thirst. The Rolling Stones record had just ended. "We listened to them all the time in 'Nam."

That made me think of Voorhees and a mental picture album I'd collected of him came to me in a rush. The underground station we were listening to started to play the new Youngbloods album. Jesse Colin Young was singing about darkness, and I felt sad and disoriented and confused. The moon was gone, behind a cloud or something at the moment.

"We'd get all blasted up and listen to those boys nonstop," said Dave. "Kickin' out the jams with the Stones. Yessir. That's how we got through it. What a bunch of shit."

I had a memory of Voorhees' mother walking away from the grave site in my head, her husband at her elbow, and how she cradled the tightly folded American flag, that hideous, triangle memento of his sacrifice and her sadness.

"I had a friend killed in 'Nam." I said it to say it, to try to connect with Dave and his status as a veteran, maybe, for some impulsive reason; to lift myself from the college boy ranks, maybe. I was just talking.

"Where?" he asked. "What branch? Grunt?"

"Army. Lieutenant. I don't know where," I said. "Took a mortar round was all we heard. Never had sex with his fiancée either. Was waiting till he got home."

Dave didn't say anything.

I said, "I'm I-A now. The draft board didn't like my report card."

"You're gone then." He bobbed his head.

"I'm gone," I said.

"You're fucked," he added.

"Yeah. I'm fucked. Something along those lines." And Dave drove and I looked out into the night. And I thought back to a day three months back and the memory that wouldn't leave me alone.

I had tried to hang a parachute in my apartment bedroom, but it came undone from the ceiling and fell on me. I felt like a monkey in a trap on Wild Kingdom. I'd watched helplessly from my mattress on the floor as the chute, in betrayal, on purpose it seemed, undid itself, one corner at a time, and captured me as I lay stoned. I had a sultan's tent planned, a womb inside my royal blue bedroom. Brand new paint. Now the atmosphere was lost. Destroyed. Hopelessly wrecked like me. Direct sunlight, now unscreened by the parachute, filled up the room with my reality. Another Victor Sinclare day, another class skipped, another joint smoked. Another unaccomplished day of trying to do Elaine.

I said, "Bummer," through the muslin, and imagined the word

breaking into pieces, sieved, and sprinkling about my pad like sleet. On its way down, the parachute had also collected a wine bottle layered in candle wax and dragged the stylus across my new Creedence Clearwater record on the turntable. My karma had been officially nuked. My left eye tremored uncontrollably.

I had sighed in defeat, peeled the chute away, and began to fold it in my arms, when in the process I managed to snag several books from the shelf at the end of my bed. I'd finished most of them: *The Story of Sidhartha, Future Shock, On the Road, Been Down So Long It Looks Like Up To Me*, and something called *Psychology and Art* from an elective course a semester ago. I'd finished Kerouac's *On the Road*, straight through, in a day. Never got out of bed. Putting the books back, I made myself look at the small card I'd half hidden in the hollow oval of one of the cinder blocks holding up the bookshelf. My new draft card. My new status, I-A.

It had come one week earlier in the official, windowed, Selective Service envelope.

I'd read the letter, studied the card with its little boxes and typing, then put it by itself in the small cavern of its own on the bookshelf. To me it deserved its own little tomb. "The hell with them. The hell with him. The hell with the war," I'd yelled at the walls at the time. I rolled a joint, cranked up Jimi Hendrix on the stereo, opened a beer, slumped on the couch and had tried to picture the next nine months, project into the fall. It was all so unknown and vague. The letter said I was to report for my physical in October. That would be either the end or the beginning of something, I told myself. The draft board, in its wisdom…wisdom?…had decided I was not making "satisfactory progress" at school and, therefore, was eligible for the draft. Right on. Sure, I thought, eligible to cut your hair, wear a uniform, go to the jungle and shoot some peasant motherfucker who's squabbling with his Goddamn neighbor about the price of a chicken or something. I couldn't even vote yet. Fuck that, I'd fumed. Nixon, the asshole, could take his wisdom and jump out of a Huey and save all of us the time, and a few lives while he's at it.

I'd stuffed the parachute in the closet and walked barefooted down the hallway of my one-bedroom apartment, one of a box of twenty named Valley Vista stuck out on a steep Oxford Street five blocks below campus and overlooking the Mill Creek Valley. It was the first space in my twenty years I'd had complete and total control. It wasn't home, but it wasn't just a crash pad, either. A beaded curtain and day-glo Monterey Pop and Hendrix posters and my big Janis Joplin collage lined the living room. I sniffed at the incense. Small. Yes. But it beat the hell out of living at home with their rules, the bickering, or the fraternity house, what with roommates and all the other bullshit. Food at regular times was all I missed about that place. I still cruised through there once in a while, but they treated me differently.

Fraternity. Fraternity. I said it out loud, over and over. Fraternity, Fraternity, Fraternity. The more you said words, the more ridiculous they sounded, lost their meaning, their role, reason for being.

But it should be part of a guy's college days, I'd thought, like basketball games, pranks and pussy. Of course I had to admit as I stared inside the empty refrigerator, that was what I believed to be true before this insane, dumb-ass war and political bullshit and demonstrating and hippie, peace-love stuff broke over the country like the Tsunami I'd read about

27

in *Time*, washing away logic. I compared the feeling to the scary experience some high school surfing buddies of Turner's had in California the night after high school graduation. Turner had told me these guys got drunk and high and went surfing at night off Santa Cruz. The tide came in, covering the beach as they paddled out, and then they got trapped. They had to ride their boards all night to keep from being pulverized on the rocks. They were scared shitless. There were times, I felt, the whole world was waiting on a new tide, only there seemed to be a surplus of dumb shits who were willing to risk the wave ride in. And the munchies were driving me to distraction so I'd decided to go downstairs and see if Palmeri had anything to eat.

Palmeri was a marketing major but didn't look the part. He was on track to graduate in the summer and at the moment was a proud holder of a II-S student deferment. He was also the assistant manager of Sunshine and Clouds, a hippie clothing store on Calhoun Street and self described "Part time dealer...to pay some bills." At his door he looked at me with head-cocking curiosity, like I was glowing. "Wow...man," he said. "It's you? Enter."

I got off on Palmeri's astounded welcomes and thought he was funny. When he answered his door, he usually gave a wide-eyed, head shaking, disbelieving and bewildered hello you usually only saw when people are surprised by a long lost friend or family member showing up, not someone you'd gotten wrecked with the night before. It was a performance given over and over and one I never got tired of. He said, "Enter. Enter," with an exaggerated bow and sweep of his arm.

And Palmeri could do an apartment. I stepped by him into an

28

environment that, as far as I could remember, had never seen the sun. Sweet and musty with incense, light came from somewhere which made the apartment always so dark and misty it seemed everyone, everything, floated. He had created the ultimate pad, the coolest setup, not a thing or a pillow higher than your knee, except two columns of stereo speakers and some palm plants that thrived, somehow. My aborted parachute hanging, even had it worked, would never have compared to his magic touch. Then Dew glided by, into and out of the kitchen. In the low light she was ghostlike. And nude. She had recently added a Monarch butterfly tattoo to the left cheek of her butt, and as I eased myself into a big soft pillow chair, I tried to see it. From her I usually only got a big, turned-on smile interspersed with insipid hippie babble. But, man, what a trip. I wondered, as Palmeri chained the metal door with the Jim Morrison poster pasted on it and shoved a towel in the space at the bottom, what it must be like to have a beautiful nude housemate. A naked ghost. Your own psychedelic Playboy Bunny. What a trip.

Palmeri, he had thick black hair that fell way past his shoulders, was wearing an embroidered caftan he claimed was from Morocco, and he tugged at his ear, a habit. His wrist was circled by a wide leather band. Most of his fingers had rings with silver and turquoise, a peace symbol the size of a chocolate chip cookie hung around his neck with a leather strap. He was growing a mustache. I was jealous of these Italian guys. They could grow yards of hair in the time it took to roll a joint. Palmeri could do a Jesus thing real easy if he had wanted; could have stepped into this room from a Peter Max poster.

"You holdin'?"

"No, man. But I'm starving. Let's scarf a Five-Way at Skyline."

Palmeri said, "Can't," as he walked across the room, sat in front of me on a fringed Oriental carpet and folded his legs under him. "My sister ran away from home again. My parents called, completely freaking out. She told them she was coming to see me, so I have to stay and wait for her and her friends and try and get the ditz to go back to Youngstown. At least till she finishes high school. Man, that's going to take some serious salesmanship."

"What grade?"

"Tenth."

"Why?"

"Rules, I guess. Dunno. Does it more and more. Hand me that stash, my man," he directed with a flourish. "Used to be a cheerleader, for Chrissake. Been to Washington on a peace march already."

I handed him a cookie tin painted with yellow and orange sunflowers. He took some Zig Zags, a baggy, and rolled a joint. I waited and watched him work, known as a master roller, and we listened to Rod Stewart on the stereo. He kept swiveling his neck on the lookout for Dew. As hip as he thought he was, I knew Palmeri still had some adjustments to make with a nude and unpredictable Dew when company was around. And I knew clothes weren't the only thing Dew was trying to get rid of. "Do you ever forget and call her Helen, man?" When I first met Dew she was just Helen McNeese from Erlanger, Kentucky.

30

"Sometimes, when I slip," he said. "And she really gets pissed," and Palmeri rolled his eyes.

"What's the deal with your sister?"

"Her boyfriend's a dropout," he went on, licking the rolled joint. "Doper. Dad would like to kill him. Mom says Novenas for him." Palmeri rolled another number fast, licked it, set it aside, picked up the first one, lit it, then inhaled deep, held his breath, coughed and said huskily as he handed the joint to me, "Anyway, I have to do inventory in the morning. Dew's going to help. That oughta be a gas. We have to be outta here early. New goods coming in. Really far out. Come scope it. Great prices. Real value. Stop by."

We traded the joint back and forth without talking until it was too short to hold. Then Palmeri got surgical scissors from the cookie tin and clipped them on the roach. I was gone. My face buzzed, my hands were heavy. Palmeri poured me a glass of red wine from a gallon jug that had appeared from somewhere. Rod was no longer playing, Palmeri's new Miles Davis record, *Bitches Brew*, was on the turntable, loud. My head was spinning, my stomach was grinding and I felt uptight. My eye, that for a while had stopped its constant fluttering, was at it. The music was aggravating.

I heard myself say, "This is excellent shit, man. Expensive?"

Palmeri nodded. "Should be twenty-five a lid. I get it cheaper. Goin' to let it go for fifteen. Score some?" My try at an answer was stopped by banging at the door.

Palmeri pushed himself up. I propped on an elbow and caught a look at Dew slipping from the bathroom through the tie-dyed curtains to the bedroom. I was still blown away that you could create an environment as theatrical as this in a space identical to mine. It blew my mind. Of course, I had no Dew, or Helen for that matter. I watched Palmeri look through the peephole which was Jim Morrison's right eye, then turn and beat the air with his fists like a boxer hitting a speed bag. He tiptoed toward me and whispered, "It's the cops. We're screwed."

I mouthed the word, "Shit." Palmeri and I looked at each other and shared the obvious problem. I was frozen. Palmeri, worry and high anxiety all over his face, suddenly reminded me of El Greco's *The Repentant Peter*. The painting flashed through my stoned brain somehow from an art history course.

My heart banged along with the whacking of what had to be a baton or billy club on the metal door. Wide as my eyes could get, I squeaked, "Well?" but he had his hands over his eyes in a mysterious, helpless, completely useless, see no evil pose. He rocked in fear. I covered in my mind the inevitable results of being busted and exposed as a druggie: the legions of people, past and present, I would disappoint. Led by my parents, then followed in columns by teachers, self-righteous fraternity brothers, old friends, neighbors, girlfriends...everyone who had believed Victor Sinclare, "could have done anything he'd wanted to..." All the world would now know Victor Sinclare, with expenses and tuition paid by his parents, a dropout, (although not announced to anyone yet, but that was inevitably to be resolved soon with the notice home), was busted. Yes, pathetic, on the dole Victor, unfocused and confused with a cloudy view of tomorrow, would be, at twenty, history. Victor, I thought, you have finally offed yourself, you risk-taking asshole.

Dew popped up between us, and said, "I'm going to buy organic rice." Then as if the hammering at the door had just blipped her ditzy radar screen of consciousness, she said, "Phew. Who's at the door?" Palmeri kept his hands over his eyes. I looked at Dew, wearing a flowered granny dress now and sandals, her hair, wiry and long, spiked away from her head like sandy lightning bolts. "Well?" she demanded.

Palmeri, lowered his hands. "You can't go now, Dew. Cops..." and he gestured at the door. She glared at me, then swung her attention back to Palmeri. She squinted at him as the pounding boomed in the apartment.

"Please?" Dew questioned Palmeri. "Excuse me?"

Palmeri repeated, "The Man, Helen...Dew," and he flinched like a cherry bomb had gone off under his caftan at an especially loud bang. But that wasn't as scary as the explosive look Dew lobbed at him. Dew said to Palmeri, "I don't have time for this, and I need my organic rice and the only way to get it is to go through that door..."

Palmeri whined, "Dew, you can't..."

I pulled my legs up to my chest. I locked my fingers at my shins and rested my head on my knees. I wanted to vaporize. I looked up at, "Wrong..." as Dew pushed off that chock of a word and brushed by Palmeri. She looked through the Morrison peephole, then back at the two of us, then turned to the door and said, "Yes, officer? Can I help you?" She pressed her head against the door, then said, "Of course, officer" Dew spun around and said, "Turn down the stereo, imbecile," and Palmeri hurdled the low table at the couch, caftan flying, and turned the music off. "Somebody is complaining about the noise." She folded her arms and turned and leaned against the door. Then, after we all stared at each other for a minute...all you could hear was the humming of the filter in Palmeri's tropical fish tank...she looked Jim Morrison in the eye and said, "Phew. I'm outta here. Catch you later." And she kicked the towel away, opened the door and left. She was some chick.

Palmeri shook his head as the door slammed and said, "Color her gone, man," then the phone rang from somewhere. Palmeri tugged his ear, tossed his hair, jumped up and parted the tie dyed curtains to the bedroom. He said, "Hang on," over his shoulder.

I stretched out on the pillows and wondered when we were going to get something to eat. Then I fell asleep.

I dreamed I was running, gaining speed, air flowed all around me. I accelerated and leaned into a warm, dry wind, naked, my arms at my side, my hair was long now, straight, flowing, in this dream. I felt myself lifted up. I smiled as my feet left the ground.

I was flying.

Up, fast now, ascending to an altitude where I could see below me great patches of color. Purples and greens and reds rolling by. Not an airplane view of normal landscape; no houses and clumps of trees and meandering rivers, my view was swirling, kaleidoscopic, liquid. Somehow I watched myself from somewhere doing all this.

I was free to perform any maneuver I wanted. With a thought I dipped, swooped, glided, climbed and vectored over and near lakes of orange, canyons of dark purple, down waterfalls running royal blue along rocky cliffs of yellow as bright as cockatoo feathers.

But just like that—just like before a bad thunderstorm—the air cooled, color drained from the terrain and the world became as gray as slate. I stayed airborne, but the flying was no longer effortless and I began a gradual and unavoidable descent, closer to the ground, and not happy with pigment and hue, but dull. Flat light. No shadows.

Over a rise, ahead on a road below me massed columns of people. From a distance they at first seemed clumped anonymously as a group, but as my descent got me closer to them, they became more recognizable. All were standing ramrod straight, heads tilted back, with expressionless faces, and arms extended over their heads—every one of them—pointing up at me, silent in their collective accusation. I passed over Mom and Dad, my brother, my grandparents, the Kellys, Eisens and Chambers, neighbors and family friends since birth, Reverend Shaw, Coach Bud, Voorhees and Kettering, and pledge classmates in their beanies. The road was filled to the dim horizon with rigid faces and pointing fingers. And silence.

I began to fall. I wobbled and was terrified my crash would impale me on their spiked fingers. I thought of them as pungi sticks. And as I was fighting with everything to pull out of my fall, pulling hard to clear the road, I heard high voices. First one. Then a response. Then another. One more. A shout. A chorus. Then as I dropped low and at an angle above a class of twelve year olds, I recognized with horror they were the faces of my Confirmation Class. I grazed their fingertips and tried to scream as I fell into them, but could get out nothing but a dry and silent try at a howl.

I woke up with a jerk, against the wall. I coughed and blinked and tried to erase my dream images. I was still on Palmeri's pillows. Someone had covered me with a fatigue jacket. I touched the crease of a scar on my cheek left by the jacket zipper. I was thirsty. I had no fucking idea what time it was.

Voices murmured at my back. People were bargaining. They seemed to rasp at each other. I rolled and saw Palmeri talking real serious by the door with three people. They gave me quick, blank glances when I moved. I rubbed my eyes and gave them a dull stare. One, a freckled, light-skinned black guy with an orange afro did all the talking to Palmeri. The other two, white guys in bulky sweaters, hung behind him, leaning against the Morrison door. The talker passed something to Palmeri. Palmeri gave him something back. I sat up as Palmeri said, "Done." He opened the door for them. Fluorescent light from the hallway got in the apartment. The three looked me over again fast and left. Palmeri closed and chained the door. "I had some crystal meth to unload. I don't like havin' that item laying around," he said.

I shook my head, not so much to agree, but in stoned understanding.

"Look man, while you were crashed, my sister called. I have to meet her and her boyfriend at the Skyline at Clifton and Ludlow and talk her down off the ledge. You stay if you want." He pulled on a leather shoulder bag. "Dew'll be back sometime. I never know when." Palmeri said, "Later," and left.

I yawned, stretched and looked around. I'd kill for a cheese Coney. I stared at Jim Morrison. He stared back. I heard Palmeri's VW bus grind, start and go under the window spewing oil exhaust like I knew it would. My dream was still clear and real, and I didn't like being by myself. I thought about waiting for Dew and getting her to go eat at Skyline with me, but just as fast decided not to because it would have to involve a long, one-sided lecture about eastern religion, health food or the war. All that or more. I didn't have the energy. Anyway, her easy nudity excited me, and she was way out of bounds. I got up to leave. "Being free. Being natural." That was her answer for the unaffected willingness to parade around in front of Palmeri's friends at the apartment. With Elaine, that was a totally different case. Totally opposite. I couldn't get any of her clothes off.

I let myself out. Through the glass double doors at the end of the bright hallway I watched the traffic on Oxford Street for a while. Someone on the hall was cooking spaghetti sauce. I felt susceptible and didn't want to go back to my place. A feeling of some kind settled on me quick and was gone like that, but whatever it was left me wanting a simpler, safer, little boy time. I couldn't put my finger on it, but wished at that moment I could be stretched out on the braided rug of my parents' living room, leaning on my elbows watching television with my brother, my Dad in his chair behind us snapping the newspaper as he turned the pages. The vacuum cleaner whining from a room. I pushed on the smudgy doors into the cold spring night and started walking up the hill, getting caught by headlights once in awhile. The dream still rattled and clattered in my head, and I picked up my pace to find some people to be with.

That night, that dream, or nightmare, I could not shake it. It clung and would not leave me alone. The hot night wind that blew through the cab in Nevada carried it to me and painted me in its disturbing pictures. I could rationalize it, figure out where it came from, but that was not the issue. It was the indelibility of it. The permanence. It was a sentence; a punishment I couldn't outrun.

Dave said, "We're about there. Where you going again?"

"It's called the Y. Know where that is?"

"It's just over into California. Past Stateline. Got an address?"

Turner had just told me to go to the Y and to look for a small grocery store. "The apartment is supposed to be over a place called the Tahoe Sierra Market, I think. Know it?"

"We'll find it," said Dave, who hadn't talked much during the last half hour, hadn't stopped to piss for a while or picked up again with the "isness" stuff either. He'd gotten sullen and tired it seemed. And then I saw for the first time the neon lights and casinos as we rolled through South Lake Tahoe. What a trip.

"Some scene, ain't it?" said Dave, in slow traffic. As we drove past more casinos and restaurants, looking at the tourists and others lit by the glary lights, he started talking about a guy he'd known in Vietnam. The guy was named Prather, and he and Dave drove a supply truck back and forth from Saigon to Long Binh once a week. "Well one day Prather finally had had enough with 'Nam and all the bullshit and he just snapped," said Dave, becoming more animated, stroking his chin, getting into his story. "About halfway back from Long Binh, he pulled our truck over to the side next to some rice paddies and shit and jumped out the door. He rolled up the back canvas, crawled in and opened up a box of Purple Hearts, then started throwing them out the back down to the slopes like they were those coins they throw to the drunks at Mardis Gras." Dave leaned back and laughed. "The Gooks started coming around like geese after corn. They were chattering and reaching and catching them in their hats even. And after Staff Sergeant Prather had emptied the last box, he put a Purple Heart around his own neck, stood at attention at the back edge of the truck, pulled his sidearm from the holster, said, "Ooh la la," put the barrel in his mouth and blew his head back to Saigon. Didn't even look at me before he pulled the trigger. But I had him all over me." Dave said, "Still do."

It made me think of Voorhees again and my eye pulsed and flickered. For some reason I said, "So man, how do you think the parents and relatives of guys like that feel about people like you tearing up the flag and wearing it on your hat? Isn't it disrespectful?"

Dave opened his eyes wide like the road was about to open up and swallow us and said, "I say fuck 'em. I was there getting my ass shot off while they were here doing whatever it is they do..." And with that, Dave suddenly pulled the car over to the curb just past the Sahara casino with its big red glittering sign. He turned to me and dropped his hands into his lap, sighed slightly and held my eyes with his. He was composed, but in an ugly way. In a lowered voice he went on, "...and I was getting my ass shot off before you knew how to blow your nose, motherfucker. That's what I say." Then he yelled, "Get out."

I looked at him and thought about arguing but instead said, "What...?"

"Get your ass out of my car, you pantywaist cock sucker. Now."

He already had my twenty dollars. I had no idea how much farther I had to go, where the Y was, the Tahoe Market or Turner. But I got out anyway, opened the door to the back, pulled out my duffel and picked up *LIFE* from the floor. Dave peeled rubber away from the curb, made a U-turn right there, bouncing off the curb in front of Harrah's casino. He went through a stoplight still accelerating, bobbing his head and stroking his chin.

I found a pay phone and called Turner, who came to pick me up on a rinky-dink Honda 150. He hadn't changed a bit except his hair was longer. It hung pin straight over his ears. He kept having to shake his head to get it out of his eyes. I told him the story about Dave ditching me as we were figuring out how to get the two of us and the duffel on the bike, and all he said was, "That is far out, Vic. Really bitchin'." And we drove to a place called Tippy's Tacos and pigged out.

Chapter 4

"Get it on, Victor," Turner yelled up the outside steps that led to the apartment.

He'd told me the night before they were still taking applications at The Mine Shaft but I had to move. So, even though he was working the three to midnight shift, we both climbed back onto the Honda in the morning when we got up. He couldn't tell me who the bike belonged to. Said it was the "...apartment bike" and let me drive it. I wish my parents could have seen me. I popped the clutch, we lurched and wobbled with traffic and Turner yelled, "Shit, man." He held on, his arms around my waist as I kicked at the gears with my boot toe, but we made the fifteen-minute trip back across the California/Nevada line, through town and got to the kitchen door of the casino around ten. I almost lost it as we skidded to a stop in the gravel parking lot. Turner laughed and yelled, "Shit, man," which he always said when he got excited. "Shit, man," he said again, sliding off the back as I got the bike under control. "What a rush. Man, you almost dumped us."

"Yeah," I said. "No shit," and turned the key off and tossed it to him.

He made an exaggerated show of leaping to catch it, which was typical. Any quick move like that made his hair fly around, and then he looked even jumpier than he already was. He went through the metal door to the kitchen and came back in a couple of minutes with a one-page application in his hand and an apron over his shoulder. He told me they were mopping the floor so I had to go around to the main entrance and walk through the casino to the back where the restaurant was, find a table and fill out the form. When I was finished, he told me to leave it by the cash register and it would get to the right place.

"And," he said as he handed me the page, "Tony, he's the chef, he asked me to stay and work through to my shift since I was here. Some asshole didn't show up. Shit, man. Tony's a mean little bastard. I can't tell him no." Turner pointed at the motorcycle. "Wanna take the bike?"

"Nah," I said. "You're gettin' off at midnight. I can hitch back when I'm done." I felt responsible for trapping him at work.

"Sure?"

"Sure."

"All right. Bitchin'. I'll try and stick my head into the restaurant while you're out there. It's slow right now. They just broke down the breakfast line," he said, holding the door open, drumming his fingers on it. Just inside, over his shoulder, I could see a mountain of greasy pots and pans stacked up at a metal sink. "Later," he said and ducked inside the door.

"Later," I said to the door.

Then he popped his head back out as I was turning to go and said in a loud whisper, "Vic..."

"Yeah?"

"Be sure and mention you've got some restaurant experience..."

"I can make pizzas…"

"Dress it up a little. You know." And he shook his head and gave me that crazy, full of teeth grin, then slammed the door.

The ringing of the slot machines. The sound from the Reno Airport. When I pushed through the glass double doors into the small outer lobby at the front of The Mine Shaft, where there was only a cigarette vending machine and a couple of pay phones on the wall, the first thing I heard was the ringing of the slots, muffled from where I stood.

I pushed through heavy double doors covered in riveted red leather at the back of the outer lobby. Inside the casino the jangle of ringing bells and handle cranking surrounded me. I faced an aisle walled by two parallel rows of slots, about thirty on each side, four or five Twenty-One tables and two dice tables arranged to the right and a windowless draped wall beyond them. A bar lined with stools ran away from me along the tables to the right. A mounted television looked down from above. Office doors of some sort, a short hall and a caged teller window were at my left. Behind the cage a woman counted out bills into neat stacks. Mostly slot players dotted the smoke filled space. In the middle of it all, an older man, alone, played dice at one of the tables, and shouted with each throw. An idle dealer from the other table nervously tapped his croupier stick on his leg and chatted with the bartender who rolled a lemon back and forth along an open palm. The only others at the bar were two men at the far end. They passed some papers back and forth and sipped drinks. One, a gray dress hat tilted over an eye, brushed cigarette ashes from the lapel of his suit, the other, casual in a V-neck sweater and open collar, wrote something down and passed it over. A really pretty blonde dealer stood and slid cards across the curved table to two men in flannel shirts. She seemed bored and looked past her players and through me as she waited to deal the next card. I walked along the gauntlet of slots to find the restaurant.

I came to a cash register on a counter. A sign read, *Welcome to The Famous Smorgasbord! All You Can Eat: $1.99 24 Hours A Day.* A long cafeteria line stretched behind the register. Steam leaked along the edges of empty pans. It reminded me of National Geographic pictures of tiny geysers. The restaurant looked the same size as the casino. No windows in here either, or clocks. Booths lined the walls decorated with picks and shovels, lanterns and panning trays. Tables filled the open area, set with salt and pepper shakers, ashtrays and napkin holders, all embossed with *The Mine Shaft.* More old mining tools and framed, yellow tinted pictures of cowboys and miners were displayed on beams of wood meant to look like the entrance to a real gold mine. It dominated the center of the room. Banks of neon numbers wrapped around the top of the fake mine shaft, and could be seen from anywhere under the words: *Play Keno.* I guessed it was another come on. Casino noises bounced down the hall and mixed with big band music played over the in-house sound system. The restaurant, bacon grease and coffee smell still in the air, was empty except for one old couple at a booth. A young kid who looked Mexican and wore a red smock ran a sweeper over the flower patterns in the carpet. I walked to a table and sat down and even before I felt my pockets, I knew I didn't have a pen or pencil. An ashtray with *Play Keno* stenciled on its side had a short pencil with broken lead and Mine Shaft matches.

I was about to get up and grab a sharp pencil from another table when a short, dark man wearing all white came past the register with a much taller man in a ball cap and work clothes, and a girl about my age in jeans and a University of Tennessee VOLS sweatshirt. The short guy had heavy black framed glasses and was bowlegged, frowning in an annoyed way in a cloud of cigarette smoke that hung around his face, but couldn't hide the deep lines across his forehead. Looked like he could have stepped out of a Dick Tracy comic. The couple had a hard look too and could have been a father and daughter. They were damn skinny, but had a tough way of moving. I watched them follow the little guy to a booth across from me where he sat them with a chop of his hand. Both carried what I guessed were applications like mine. He said, "Leave 'em by the register. If we can use you, someone will call."

The couple looked back and forth fast like they were worried. The father, if that was who he was, looked back up at the little guy and said, "We ain't got a place yet. Can we run by here in the mornin'?" His accent was twangy. He sounded like those hillbillies from across the Ohio River. "We just hit town," and he nodded and smiled big.

The little guy looked at them a moment with a look I couldn't read. The girl, real plain I thought, with longish hair that needed to be washed, caught me eavesdropping and I looked down at my application. The little guy just said, "Come to the back door around ten tomorrow. We'll see." He acted like it was a pain in the ass to listen. Like it was killing him.

He turned on his heel and looked down at me like I just appeared and I asked, "You got a pencil I can borrow?" I could make out the Lucky Strike logo through one shirt pocket. He had a pen in the other one. But he showed me the same blank face he'd given the other two and just walked across the room toward an alcove that might have been the kitchen entrance at the end of the cafeteria line. On the way he stopped and pointed like he was pissed off to a spot on the floor and the Mexican kid ran over and worked the sweeper back and forth under the little guy's stare. I watched this, then looked back at the couple who were grinning over at me.

The father said softly, "Gawd almighty."

The girl shook her head and said, "Lordy, lordy, lordy. Don't say much for him, now does it?"

"Mean little feller, ain't he?" said the father. "Ain't no cause to be that way," and he smiled over at me. The smile on his leathery face showed a gold-capped front tooth that seemed to punctuate the fact the little guy's bad manners didn't faze him in the least. On the other hand, my eye had twitched when he gave me that "piss off" look. The man pulled a cigarette pack from the pocket of a thin and wrinkled khaki shirt, shook one out and held the pack to me. He had a homemade looking tattoo down on his forearm that read, "Sugar Tit."

"Nah. Thanks," I said. I was trying to quit cigarettes. I was sticking to pot. I looked at the girl looking over the application. She moved her lips and head as she read.

The father flipped the top of his lighter open with a one-handed snap. I'd never seen that and I don't think he was doing it for show, as easy as he did it. And while the smoke was still in his lungs he said to the girl, "That banjo-legged little wop is about as big as a minute, ain't he, Kathy?"

46

The girl grinned a smile that gave her an instant look of intelligence and also made her prettier, which totally caught me off guard, and she said, "What is he, five foot nuthin? Looks like he fell off a damn key chain." That made the man laugh so hard he started coughing deep and the girl punched him in the arm and said, "Give that boy your pen, Daddy. We can share."

The father, wheezing into a fist, now that I looked closer, had a hard red face and real blue eyes that sized me up over his closed hand. His cheek bones were high. Deep lines ran down from them to his jaw. He hadn't shaved lately. While I was filling out the one-sided sheet under *Related Experience,* I crammed a few words on a short line about working part-time at La Rosa's Pizza...which was a total lie. The father talked nonstop about how amazing the upcoming moon shot was going to be. "Ain't it the berries, though," he said, leaning back in the booth, hat back on his head, dragging on his cigarette. "A damn man is going to be walkin' on the moon here right quick and we're down here just tryin' to get through the damn day. It's a damn miracle if they can pull it off. Hell's bells, it'll be a damn miracle if I can pull my own life off down here," and he started laughing and coughing at the same time. His daughter looked over at him out of the corner at her eye with a serious look. He turned away from it, crossing his legs in the aisle and hacked smoke across the restaurant. He had scuffed work boots on and pumped one foot up and down.

And he kept going on about the Apollo II program and the moon and must have said, "So forth and so on," and, "What not," about ten times before I finished the application, gave him his pen back and said thank you. "You're welcome, son," he said. "Don't let your meat loaf...and don't be making that little wop mad." And he turned to his daughter and asked, "What'd you put for an address?"

I dropped the application at the register even though there was still nobody around.

Yelling came from the kitchen while I was standing there and I recognized the little guy's voice, and he was giving somebody hell. The Mexican kid was pouring a big bucket of shaved ice onto a section of the food line. He stopped and looked up. I heard what sounded like a plate crashing, then someone yelled, "Idiota," and just then Turner came busting from the kitchen through the swinging doors to the head of the line with a stack of plates he put in a rack on top of some others. His eyes were wide and he was smiling his crazy smile. "Tony just eighty-sixed a dishwasher for smoking reefer," he said. "If you're wired you're fired," Turner giggled. "Tony has spoken."

"Get your ass outta here," I heard him scream.

Turner flinched. "He's really pissed. Going to be a long day." I looked over at the father and daughter at the table, both shaking their heads and looking our way. The busboy emptied his bucket fast and headed down the hall in the direction of the casino. Turner watched him go and said, "That little Mexican kid is scared to death of Tony. His name is Beaner. Look at him vamoose." The old couple who had been sitting at the booth were investigating The Mine Shaft memorabilia. They seemed oblivious to the ruckus. The sound system was playing "In the Mood." I knew it from a 78 Dad played over and over. The old man tapped his toe and leaned in close to look at a picture, bracing himself on a beam.

Turner told me he was going to put in a good word for me and went back into the kitchen. I said, "Sounds groovy," and left. I was going through the outer lobby on the way out to hitchhike to the apartment when the guy in the suit and gray hat I'd spotted at the bar earlier asked me for a match. "You got a light, babe?" he asked softly. He smelled like bourbon and sweet cologne. On the floor by his side a briefcase, nice but scuffed, leaned against the cigarette machine.

I said, "I think," and felt around in my jeans for a book of Mine Shaft matches I had taken from the ashtray.

After he lit his cigarette, he handed them back, winked, and said, "It's a beautiful day, kid, and all the cats on the fence are meowing." He picked up the briefcase and said, "thank you," like he meant it, and went through the doors ahead of me around to the parking lot. I watched him from across the street while I waited for traffic. He walked real slow, strolled, to a big green Cadillac, got in, checked himself in the mirror, then drove off in the opposite direction from the Y, tires spitting gravel. He slouched as he drove, cigarette dangling, straight arming the steering wheel, elbow out the window like a movie bad guy.

While I waited for a ride, I looked at the front of The Mine Shaft. It was nothing but a cinder block building, squatty under the pines at the bottom of a mountain and incredibly blue sky, with a semi-circle blacktop driveway in front. And if it were not saddled with the big neon sign running the length of the roof facing the road, that even in the middle of the day was turned on and streaming like crazy, it would be invisible competing with the glittering signs of the Sahara, Harvey's, Harrah's and even Barney's, right down South Lake Boulevard. A smaller sign under the big one said: *Famous*

24 Hour Smorgasbord: All You Can Eat: $1.99 *24 Hours A Day.* That was The Mine Shaft gimmick; selling cheap food. The big casinos used free entertainment, lounge acts like Vicky Carr, or The Four Preps. Turner had already hipped me to that come on. As I stared and wondered whether Turner would come through, whether putting all my job hope eggs into his basket had been a good idea, an old, rough-running, primered Ford with Tennessee tags stopped in front of me and I jumped, still holding my thumb in the air. I said, "Right on," out loud and had taken a step to the car when I saw it was the father and daughter from the restaurant. The roof was packed with boxes tied with rope. More boxes and piles of clothes filled the back seat. The rear of the car nearly scraped the road. The girl was driving, her dad sitting shotgun. "How far you goin', college boy? Need a lift?"

"You got room?" I said. His gold tooth flashed in the outside light, and I had the feeling he was playing with me.

The door popped open and he jumped out, jerky and quick like Turner. He looked at me real direct, serious, and said, "A working man never passes up another working man." Then he laughed. "Shit, son, but in your case I'll make an exception. Get on in." I slid across the seat. The upholstery had been taped, the dash had heat cracks. A miniature forty-five disc record hung from the rearview mirror. His daughter stared out ahead. When we drove off he said, "How far you going?"

I said, "The Y. Know it?"

"I don't know nothin' from nothin' about this place, buddy. We left out of Knoxville four days ago and been here about four hours now. We've applied at three places so far. Tryin' to catch on somewhere for the summer. Goin' to Seattle after. This here is a port in the storm, Bub. That's the deal. We're the Shanahans. I'm Mic." He stuck out his hand. His grip was strong and his skin was rough like tree bark. "That's Kathy." I turned to say hello and thank her once more for the pen because that's all I could think of, when she slammed on the brakes and I braced myself on the dashboard and the father yelled, "Whoa," and we fishtailed some, skidded and stopped as a dog ran in front of us.

"ShitDevilDickDamnPiss," the daughter screamed. "I shoulda hit him. Boy, that curdles me." She sighed once, heavy, relaxed her grip on the wheel, then looked sideways at me and said, "Sorry. That's all the cussin' I do. I string together all the bad words I know and use 'em at once. Just like my grandma." Then past me to her father, "Daddy, check the roof."

"I'll take a look see," he said. He hopped out and walked around the car, got back in and said, "It's the berries up there, honey. Go on."

She said, "Pull the door to," and started the stalled car and we kept going.

"Coffin nail, son?" Mic shook out the cigarette pack to me. This time I took one for some reason and I wondered if he could tell my eye was shuddering. I reached for the car lighter. It wasn't there. Mic said, "The old lady stole it," and he lit mine with the boxy little lighter from his jeans pocket. Then he lit two at once and passed one over to Kathy. We got to the front of the Sahara, about the spot where Dave had kicked me out. A bad feeling came over me when I remembered the suicide story. And Dave ranting about the war as he drove off.

Mic started, "Kathy's momma—"

"Daddy." Kathy jerked her head at him. "Be still."

Mic leaned into my ear. I smelled sweat, smoke breath and beer. He whispered, "Her momma didn't have sense to pour piss out of a boot."

"Daddy…"

"Sorry, honey, but it makes me tired when I think about her."

"Not her fault…"

Mic didn't say anything right back. Then, flipping a cigarette out the window, he said, "Okie dokie, honey. Let's get this boy…what's your name son?"

"Vic Sinclare."

"Let's get ole Vic here home and be on our way."

We were back across the Nevada/California line and not too far of a walk from the apartment, so I asked them to drop me where we were. I half expected them to ask if they could crash at the apartment if I let them take me all the way and was worried about that. I didn't want to be too open to these two, friendly as they were being. I couldn't explain it, my selfishness, I guess. I fought the impulse to ask them if they had a place. I told them they could drop me anywhere.

I didn't ask where they were going to stay the night and had the feeling they had been sleeping in or around the car by the way things looked. Mic mentioned in a matter of fact way as we slowed to a stop they could sell their spare tire and wheel for food, cigarette and gas money if they had to, if they didn't, "...catch on quick," but I didn't get the idea he was hitting me up for money.

I slid out and said thanks. Mic shook my hand again and said, "I think there's work here in this Lake Tahoe patch, buddy. Maybe we'll see you in the mornin'."

"See ya'," I said. Kathy gave me a half smile and a limp wave when I looked at her when Mic got back in.

When they drove off, Mic flicked a cigarette ash out the window and a backhanded salute goodbye. As the Ford pulled away, I read a bumper sticker on the back below where the fat rope held the trunk to the bumper. It read in big black letters against a white background: *Jesus Christ Is Lord Over Knoxville,* just over the tail pipe, inches above the pavement.

Before I went up, I stopped and looked at the empty lot next to the apartment and Tahoe Sierra Market. I stood on the bottom step on the outside staircase, the busy road at my back. The lot was unpaved, just packed dirt and pine needles. An old Volvo was parked next to the staircase, pointed to the road. Four tall pine trees made splotches of shade. Turner had told me they were Ponderosa pines. Just like the TV show. They made the clean air even sharper. At the back of the lot, in a row, three little cabins needed work and painting. All three had *No Vacancy* signs on the doors. Their white siding was peeling. Pine needles clogged overflowing gutters and were falling onto the small porches down below. I didn't see any hope for them. An untended bed of yellow blooms shot up between our building and the last cottage, making the sad little area seem friendlier. I looked at them through rectangle sections made by the open red steps while I climbed to the apartment door and wondered why the cottages were in such bad shape.

Turner hadn't given me a key but said not to worry. The door was never locked. I went in and took the time to look over the place in the daylight. The night before I'd just smoked a joint with him after Tippy's and crashed on a bare mattress covered with magazines at the end of the hall. I'd been too tired to argue when he told me that was going to be my bedroom.

I leaned on the wall by the door and surveyed the barely furnished apartment in the daylight. A light brown wood framed couch and matching chair with thin cushions looked sad and uncomfortable. A cheap-looking, scratched coffee table with uneven legs sat in front of it. A single end table, its mate missing, took up space against the opposite wall, a plain lamp and shade on it. A poor reproduction of a farm scene in a yellow plastic frame leaned against the wall next to the end table. I guessed it had once been on the wall where someone had hung up a big, day glo orange astrology calendar, with each astrological symbol illustrated by a couple in a different sexual position. I studied Aries a second then went through the year.

To the right of the wall where the poster hung, a small kitchen entrance opened up and I could see a metal table that could seat four, but chairs were missing. I saw one by a window. The back of the Tahoe Sierra Market sign above the market entrance downstairs partly blocked the view of a laundromat across the street that looked busy. The road held a steady flow of traffic in both directions. I stared and felt tired. Jet lag weighed me down. It added to a huge feeling of detachment and loneliness as I walked around this afterthought of a place to live, knowing it was going to be my home all summer.

There were two bedrooms off a hall to the left as you came in the door from the outside. One, then a bathroom, then the second, locked and used for storage, I'd been told. My mattress was just past that second door. Across the hall a window looked out at the laundromat and the back of the Tahoe Sierra Market sign, a slightly different angle of the kitchen window view. The apartment ran the whole second floor of the building.

I kneeled and picked up a *TIME* with a cover story about Nixon's Vietnamization plan. I licked my finger and was about to turn a page when I heard noise from the front bedroom, the clear sound of two people getting it on big time. I straightened back up with the magazine in my hands and listened as a guy and a girl's voice went up and down together. All at once I felt like an intruder and wondered why in the hell Turner had not told me others might be at the apartment. I had no idea what to do except split. I snuck past the bedroom door, nervous, but at the same time trying to imagine pictures to match the sounds. My heart was pumping. I got out as quietly as I could and walked down into the sun. The Volvo was still the only car in the lot. I had no idea who was in the apartment. But I was starving, tired and bummed so I went inside the market, trying to visualize the rooms above. I got a can of Olympia beer and a pepperoni stick from a cold case under what I figured was our bathroom. I walked out to the bottom step of the staircase and flipped through *TIME* and tried to figure out what to do next.

In about a half hour, when I went back up, there were no voices, but I smelled grass and heard sitar music coming from the bedroom. Quiet as I could, I walked to the end of the hall to the mattress covered by magazines where I'd dumped my duffel. I swept off the magazines, and using my duffel as a pillow, lay down and let the exhaustion take over. I wanted to sleep and made the decision to not make a big deal out of having to sleep on the floor. It was against the bare wall, out of the way for me and my stuff after all, and I fell asleep, listening for more action down the hall.

When I woke up, I was disoriented. It was dark, I was chilly, and laughing and music came from the living room. I knew I had been dreaming, but only felt the remnants. I had no clues. The music sounded like the Santana band Suicide Dave had told me about. I looked at my watch in the light coming down the hall and saw it was around ten. Too early for Turner. Still half asleep, I stayed where I was and tried to decide what to do. Turner had been hazy about who else might be sharing the apartment when we first talked. Details sometimes got lost with his kindness and "Mr. Good Guy" intentions. He was loose about the nitty gritty and always said the future would take care of itself. It was his mantra. It all came and went through my head as fast as the car light that for a second streaked through the window along my wall. And for no good reason, I decided I didn't want to invite myself to the party. I had no idea if whoever it was out there knew if I was even in the place. I was being a chicken. I knew it.

I guess I fell back asleep because when I opened my eyes

again I was staring at Turner who was about six inches from my face and shaking me. "Vic. Vic. Shit, man. Wake up." I focused on his face and up close it seemed as big as the moon.

"What time is it, man?" Music was still playing, but I didn't hear any voices.

"After midnight. I just got here." He straightened up, stretched and said, "Looks like you missed a party, Victor. C'mon, man, I boosted some roast beef from the job."

I followed him into the living room. More chairs had appeared from somewhere. A cheap turntable and speakers were strung along the top of the coffee table. Album covers were scattered on the floor. A few of the records out of their jackets were stacked next to the turntable. The new English band, Led Zeppelin, played and I'd never heard a white singer with a voice like his except Janis Joplin. A full ashtray with a roach and clips and cigarette butts sat on top of a speaker. I stopped short there because someone, I couldn't make out if it was a guy or a girl, was passed out or asleep on the couch, curled up, long hair covering the face, a big Indian-looking sweater pulled up under the chin. Tall, brown, scuffed, square toed boots were on the floor. "Turner...who's that?" I asked, trailing him into the kitchen.

"A friend of Sara's," he said matter of fact over his shoulder.

"Sara?"

"She's a friend of mine." He and I stood at the kitchen counter. He pulled apart a package of white butcher paper, and said, "Sara and I are ballin' buddies. She was asleep when we got here last night. You didn't meet her today?" He spread open the butcher paper. Sliced rare roast beef was piled three inches high. He was gloating like it was a saddlebag full of silver from a train robbery. "Walked out with it under my shirt," he shook his head. "Tony didn't have a clue." He took a slice and said, "She's a change girl at Barney's. Today's her day off. Met her last week thumbing. The Volvo is hers."

We ate with our hands. "Vino, Beano?" he asked, and reached for a half-full gallon jug of red wine on the counter next to a tinny looking toaster. "Red Mountain, Vic. Dollar twenty-five a gallon." And he drank from the jug and handed it to me. "Staff of life, man."

"Where 's Sara now?" I asked.

Turner wiped his mouth with the back of his hand and said, "She's in the bedroom with the guy she came here with." He pointed in the direction of the couch on the other side of the wall in the living room. He saw my confused look, so he said, "Sara and the dude that came with her"...and he nodded toward the couch again..."they hit it off so they decided to get it on. He and Sunshine...I think she calls herself...are taking off in the morning. It's cool. Let's make a sandwich."

I drank some wine as the record ended.

"You don't give a shit?"

"I don't care, man. Shit, they're just ballin' because they dig each other. That's all."

"How about the girl on the couch? Whatever her name is."

58

Turner said, "What about her? She's just crashing."

"I guess she doesn't care either," I said. "I mean, are you going to get it on with her?" I looked around the corner, and she was still in the same position.

He leaned back on the counter and folded his arms across his blue T-shirt. The refrigerator started humming. He smiled at me and said, "Where are you at, man? Shit." Turner looked at me with a confused expression, his eyebrows bunched together, and I thought about how some people at home would deal with all this. Like Dew. Maybe Dew could handle this scene. But the others, I thought, no way. Palmeri would freak. Elaine would be disgusted. And Baggo would want to kick somebody's ass, and probably, if he thought he could score, try to screw one of the girls when he got looped. And my parents? Their nightmare come true.

I didn't or couldn't answer Turner because I was flustered and didn't know what I was trying to say. I went to sit in the chair at the table by the window so I could sort out where I'd been, where I was, what was happening and how I felt. I could see the steamed-up window across the road at the laundromat. The windows in my life were getting even more steamed up, I thought. I asked Turner if he knew anything about me and a job.

"Oh yeah, I forgot," he said. "You go in with me tomorrow. I knew there was something."

I punched the air and said "right on" exactly at the moment a scream ripped through the apartment like an ambulance siren. It was like my air punch had cued the yell. I jerked my head at it and it came again. Turner pushed off the counter, bumped me and we stood looking into the living room. The girl on the couch bolted up, pulled her hands to her mouth and whimpered. She looked at Turner and me standing at the entrance to the kitchen, then at the direction of the scream coming from the front bedroom. At that moment, the door swung open and slammed the wall. A naked guy exploded out and howled again. Without the door to get in the way of its throw, his new scream ricocheted in the apartment like a panicked bird banging the walls and windows for a way out. "Motherfucker," said Turner, eyes wide, backing up as the guy stopped in the middle of the room, screamed, started turning in circles and looking wildly around, not focused, long curly hair in tangles. A speaker crashed on the floor when he spun. "Shit, man. He's trippin'." And the guy ran down the hall toward my mattress. All the girl on the couch did was whimper some more, but louder. Turner yelled, "Sara?" and stepped to the bedroom as a girl, short and plump, pulling hair from her face, wearing an oversized, tie-dyed T-shirt that hung to her knees, came out and said, "Bummer. I think he got some bad acid, man. He just freaked out. Thinks his skin is melting." She went over and sat on the couch with the other girl. They both pulled their legs up under themselves. I heard the guy banging into the wall and wailing and then he was back in the living room with us. He looked around, but I don't think he saw people. He breathed hard, lapping like a dog, then began crying in gulps. He clenched my blanket he'd grabbed from the mattress. He held it at his throat and looked up at the ceiling and back down in an instant, almost invisible it was so fast. Turner said, "C'mon, man...C'mon." and took a step forward. "Calm down, man, you gotta come down, you gotta come down," he said in a quiet, steady voice. "It's okay..." But the guy squealed again as if he was being skinned alive, ran at the door, yanked it open and was gone. For a second I was scared he was going to jump over the railing, but I heard his feet on the steps and he hollered in pain as he ran down. I couldn't imagine what nightmares the acid had cooked up in his brain.

"Jesus Christ," said Turner, and he jumped across the turned-over speaker and chased after him out the door into the night.

I didn't know what to do next. Sara patted the girl on the back and the whimpering quieted down. Then they held onto each other. It reminded me of two reunited sisters I'd seen at a gate at the Reno airport. I went outside. At the top of the steps, I leaned with both hands on the railing and looked down at Turner stalking the freak, who had dropped my blanket. He was standing in the lot on the pine needles with his hands held up and his head thrown back. He turned in a bowl of light coming from a street pole. Turner reminded me of a matador, using the blanket like a cape as he crouched and got closer to the guy. I closed my eye to stop the involuntary twitching, shivered and wanted bad to block out the awful yodeling. I felt exposed, sure the weirdness would attract trouble. A car slowed down on the road heading out of town, and my heart jumped because it looked like a cop car at first, but it was just a cab, roof light glowing red, and it picked up speed and was gone. I turned just as Turner hit the nude freak like the linebacker he used to be, threw the blanket over the guy's head and dove on top as if he were smothering flames. Inside, one of the girls had started playing the Led Zeppelin record again.

Chapter 5

Turner and I got to the casino the next day on time. But barely.

We'd both been up all night with Sunshine's boyfriend. His name was Alex. I'd helped Turner wrestle the guy back up the steps and inside. We used the blanket to wrap him, and with a rolled up sheet, tied his arms to his chest and wound a belt around his ankles so he couldn't kick. But in the process, he got me in the balls and I yelled louder than he had when he imagined he was melting. I wanted to kick the shit out of him, but he was bundled up, helpless and pathetic. I sat on a chair in the kitchen doorway and let the other three finish the job. We had to keep a red bandanna in his mouth until Sunshine, Sara and Turner soothed him enough to keep him from screaming whenever it was pulled out. That was about the time the sun came up. We drank the rest of the Red Mountain while he was laid out on the floor of the living room, smoked a few joints and staved off the munchies with a stale loaf of French bread we shared that was hard as a rock. The roast beef had been gone for hours. Alex's eyes quit jerking back and forth about mid-morning and he crashed for a while. He got so still I worried we'd choked the fucker to death. Sunshine bent over him to listen for his heart and smiled like an idiot. She pulled the bandanna out of his mouth. Alex opened his eyes then and didn't yell, instead, smacked his lips and said hoarsely he had to piss and would we please unwrap him?" When he was untied I was happy to watch him limp to the bathroom, glad the freaking out had stopped. But now I was wasted. Even Turner, who seemed to never need sleep, was a zombie, sprawled on the couch. Sara dozing, mouth open, was leaning on his arm. I caught myself being jealous and horny at the scene. Sara had nothing on under the T-shirt. I'd seen her big boobs and a perfect shaped, heavy butt during all the rolling and tumbling needed to restrain Alex during the night. She was as unselfconscious and natural as Dew.

Later, they all hugged at the bottom of the steps, even Turner, and that blew me away. "Peace," said Alex and Sunshine at the same time.

"Peace, man," said Turner with energy from somewhere.

"Peace. Be happy," smiled Sara, hugging herself, turning her face up into the sun.

I said, "Later," and gave them a wristy, belt high, peace sign waggle Sunshine mistook for sincere, and she stepped to me and threw her arms around my neck.

Alex said, "Right on, brother," as Sunshine got back to his side. And by two o'clock, Sunshine and Alex, hair hitting the top of their back packs, were walking away from us, north to the Y, hoping to catch a ride to Emerald Bay where Alex said he knew someone. Then he said they were going to go to Petaluma where he claimed he was going to score some righteous hashish. We had twenty minutes to get to The Mine Shaft, and hadn't slept a wink.

Fresh air blowing in my face on the back of the bike helped wake me up. I hoped the wind and a shower I'd had would help me through my first day on the job without falling asleep. I really felt like shit.

The first person I saw when we came through the back door

of the kitchen was Mic Shanahan. He wasn't wearing his ball cap, but he had the same clothes on I'd seen him in the day before. He had a white apron around his waist and he was bent over a mop, covering the floor in short hard strokes. He stood and said, "Watch your step." Then he recognized me and said, "Hey now, whattaya say, college boy? I told you there was work in this Lake Tahoe patch." Turner looked at me, and before I could explain anything, Mic squinted and I guess saw we were pretty messed up and said, "Fellers, your eyes look like piss holes in the snow." Then he splashed the mop into the bucket on wheels, squeezed it out leaning on the short handle and headed off past a huge stainless steel pot with a big lid and singing some corny song. I was glad to see him and wondered where Kathy was.

Turner went into the small stockroom at the back of the kitchen and got me an apron. It was frayed, but starched stiff and creased from folding. I half thought I'd get some formal welcome or maybe even training, but instead, while I was slipping the apron strap over my head, I heard Turner say in that dingy way of his, "Hi, Tony."

I looked up and Tony, same white clothes, cigarette, scowl and bad mood from the day before, was standing in front of us. He gruffed at Turner, "Get two boxes of Iceberg from the walk-in and rinse and chop it. Salad's low. Okay, kid?" He asked it like a question, but there was no mistaking it was an order.

Turner said, "Sure, Tony." And he bounced off on the balls of his feet, swinging his arms, and said over his shoulder as he was under a metal ceiling rack strung with hanging pots of different sizes, "Vic's a good guy. Tony..." and he laughed his laugh. But if he thought it as a way to soften up Tony for

64

me, it wasn't. I think he already had me made as an asshole. I crossed my arms, looked down and pawed a seam between two tiles of the red floor with my boot. I saw a stain of grease from somewhere on the new rawhide. "I need these," he grunted and pointed to the stack of big pots and skillets on top of the sink next to where we were standing, the sink I'd seen the day before from outside. There were more and they were greasier than they'd seemed from outside. I don't think anyone had touched them since then.

"Sure," I said.

"The two big ones first. Now." And he walked back to the front of the kitchen past a dishwashing machine to an alcove that led out to the dining room. When he got there, he said hello to the guy I'd seen driving the green Cadillac, and another man I was pretty sure was the same one he'd been sitting with at the bar yesterday. The guy, the one who'd been writing at the bar, was dressed casual in a mustard colored sweater and matching turtle neck and maroon slacks. He had smooth hair and wore shiny loafers. They all strolled from the alcove like they were on a tour. The slick dresser acted in charge and was waving around a hand with a cigarette like he was showing off the kitchen. He put his hand on the shoulder of the Cadillac guy, who put the briefcase down and pumped Tony's hand. Then they all three turned and went back out into the restaurant. I started filling the sink and tried to shake the recurring lyrics from the new Rolling Stones song I'd first heard in Suicide Dave's taxi and thought, what do I really need? And when the sink was full, I let the biggest pot from the stack down into the hot water, took a stiff brush off the back of the sink and started rubbing, but not before I burned the shit out of my hands.

I had to change the water after only two pots. The soap evaporated into a scummy grease slick in no time because the pans were so scorched and burnt with food. After a while, Turner came by with an armload of empty cardboard boxes to throw out the back door. When he came back in he said, "Havin' fun yet, Vic?"

I said, "I'm just burnt...and this is a shit job, man."

"Don't worry. This is where everybody starts. If you can stand this, Tony'll move you up. Get you at the Hobart, washing dishes, or cook's helper. Hang in." Then he said in a low voice over the running water, "Lou Colini, Sweet Lou, that Perry Como looking guy that was walking around...he's the casino manager. Supposed to be Mafia. I heard he hired a new chef for this shift. Tony's gonna move to days. Petty sure that's what's going on." Turner went into the stockroom just inside the door a few feet from my sink and came out grunting with two big boxes and said, "Cans. Tomato sauce for Tony's lasagna. It's really bitchin'," and he walked past the vat and put them on a long counter and went back to his side of the kitchen. My mind was on pleasing Tony. I got the pots he'd asked for done as soon as I could and walked around the kitchen looking for him, or a place to put them. I walked to the alcove past the dishwashing station on my left where Shanahan was spraying and sorting dirty plates, glasses and silverware from plastic tubs. Beaner came by me with one on his shoulder and bounced it down next to the one Shanahan was emptying. "Keep 'em comin', Pancho," he said to the kid, who smiled. Then Shanahan turned the nozzle of the snaky black hose on me and said, "How's your hammer hangin', college boy?" He winked and I ducked and wondered if I had gotten in earlier maybe I could have been doing dishes instead of standing at a greasy sink. I went right, going by two big silver ovens, one stacked on top of the other next to an even bigger black stove with eight burners and a flat part. Another oval rack hung from the ceiling above the oven with all kinds of kitchen tools: whisks, ladles, tongs, sieves shaped like dunce caps and other stuff. A counter stretched along the wall to the left, a big double sink dividing the working spaces. Turner and one other guy with their backs to me were busy. Turner had a big knife and was chopping heads of lettuce and scraping the chopped leaves into a sink next to him, using the blade of the knife to push with. The other guy, a blond haired kid I'd seen earlier, was on the other side of the double sink pulling what looked to be frozen chicken parts from water in the sink and prying them apart and laying them out on large shallow trays. It all looked infinitely better than what I was doing. "Put 'em there, kid." Tony surprised me from behind and pointed to the top of the oven. I put them on top of two unlit burners while he bent to open one of the lower ovens, first wrapping a towel around his hand. When he opened the door, he squinted and the mixture of cigarette smoke and steam made him go back on his heels and he said, "Shit," and the door slammed shut. He faced me with fogged glasses which gave him a goofy look, but I held back. With one hand Tony pulled the cigarette from his mouth, with the other he took his glasses off. He blinked at me. I waited a second for a thank you or something, but instead he said, "Do the roasting pans next."

"Roasting pans?"

"Roasting pans," he said for the second time. He put his glasses on and looked at me like he was in pain. "Come," he ordered, and we walked around the island in the middle of the kitchen made by the section of ovens and range, and long counter top and a big vat behind them, back around to my sink. He pointed to five wide and deep pans, probably the dirtiest, stacked at the bottom of the pile. "I need 'em," is all he said, and he walked away.

I daydreamed as I scrubbed. I thought about whether I should call my parents, but didn't want to have to talk about flunking out. I thought about Elaine and for sure how different her television station internship in Cleveland was from this. Dew rode in on some of my thoughts for a second for some reason then vanished. I thought about how the cool late May weather here in the Sierras was different from the stifling summer humidity in Cincinnati. And I always got back to the fact I was expected to report for my physical in the fall. I pictured myself going through with it. I pictured myself running away from it. Turner had shared his draft plan with me. It was pretty ballsy for sure. I guess. Mostly my scenarios were vague and noncommittal. I denied my future and got busy on scraping Tony's roasting pans and humming music.

A parade of people came and went through the alcove as the night went on. I saw Kathy copping a smoke and a quick word with Mic, whose station at the Hobart put him as a gatekeeper of a kind when anyone came into the kitchen. The good-looking blonde Twenty-One dealer came in a couple of times to smoke, and I watched her rub her neck with one hand while she leaned on the wall. Other girls with white blouses, black skirts and short aprons at their waists stenciled with *Play Keno* jumped in and out, drinking coffee and Cokes and gabbing. Beaner was all over the place, bringing in bus trays, grabbing mops and booster seats, smiling his nice smile. Every once in a while Turner or the blond kid would go through swinging metal doors to the line with full trays of food, coming back with empties they dropped on me, laughing. I was a million miles away, my arm weak from rubbing, when I heard a light knocking at the door behind me. I dried my hands and opened it. A tiny man, scrawny, red and shivering, said, "Can I see Lee? Get Lee..." and he coughed a deep cough that rattled. "...Lee...the chef...Tell him it's Georgie, please..."

I didn't know what to say or tell him. "I don't know him. I just started. Who?" His answer was another cough at the grease barrel by the door. He turned, leaned on it and hacked in shoulder-shaking heaves. When he turned back to me, his face had lost color and he curled his lip like he was fighting off pain. "Hang on," I said, and Tony was at my back. I said, "Do you know..."

And Tony elbowed around me in a flash and said, "Beat it. Get the fuck out of here." He leaned at the waist and yelled, hands on his hips. He waved him off in a way that reminded me of someone shooing a dog away from a garbage can. I leaned back on the sink and watched. "I don't need any drunks or winos in here. Go way, g'wan." And he pulled the door closed and turned around. His face was red. He fumbled for a Lucky from his pocket. And with it in his mouth he said, "Chrissake. The last thing I need in here is that rummy." His hand shook as he lit his cigarette and said, "Listen, kid. If that little pot licker shows back up again you get me quick, hear?" and he brushed past me and headed back to the front of the kitchen. I looked at my puckered fingers. I stared at the door and wanted to look out. And I wondered what a pot licker was.

At the sink, the shift wouldn't be over for about four more hours. I ran new water and stretched while it filled up the tub. I stared at the never-ending stack of pots and pans. The blond kid who was trying to grow a mustache came over with a pan half filled with uneaten lasagna and said, "Where do you want it?"

"Anywhere." I shrugged as the guy in the hat, the green Cadillac guy, walked past me from the back door.

He said, "Hey, babe," not so much like he recognized me, more like a hello, and he went into the stockroom carrying the briefcase in one hand and rolled up white clothes or something under the other arm. I pointed to the floor as an answer to the blond kid. He shrugged his shoulders and dropped it with a clang and split.

When the stockroom door opened and the hat guy came out, he was wearing white chef's clothes, white apron tied at the waist, a dish towel folded into the draw string, a tall white stovepipe-looking hat and he was still carrying the briefcase. He winked at me and said, "The cats are meowing, babe," and he went over to where Turner and the blond kid had been chopping lettuce.

Around midnight, when the shift ended, after I'd gotten the extra lucky job of regular floor mopper, Tony rounded us up in the front of the kitchen by the ovens. Me, Shanahan, Turner, the blond kid and Beaner. The new chef, his name was Lee, sat by the sink rolling his knives in towels and putting them into his briefcase. Tony told us real quick while he was pulling on a short black rain coat over his whites, that because the season was about to get busy, there were going to be two chefs, one for the day shift, eight to six, and one for nights, three to midnight, "Or whenever." Tony said he would run the day crew. Lee would run the night crew. Lee turned around at the counter, crossed his arms and legs and winked at us when his name was mentioned. The night crew would keep the dinner line full and prep for breakfast and the lunch rush. The day crew would manage the lunch rush and start prepping and cooking for the dinner crowd. Everyone would get one day off a week and they would be staggered. "But you knew that already? Right?" We'd all be told our day soon. It would be posted by the back door. "Just show up when you're supposed to," he said. "You new guys, just so you know, we get paid in cash every two weeks." Tony said he and Lee would overlap from three to six, "...or whatever," but the crews wouldn't, and the night crew wasn't going to hire anymore unless he and Lee decided more help was needed. He said, "All right," like it was, "Goodbye," and walked past us to the back door. I smelled bacon and sausage frying and assumed a guy I'd seen a few minutes earlier whisking a big stainless bowl of eggs and dressed in whites, tall hat, and red scarf, was on the other side of the swinging double doors getting the all-night breakfast going at the grill on the line. I was dying for the baked chicken Turner told me he had wrapped up in his coat and stashed in the stockroom. I found myself wondering what the connection was between the new chef and the little drunk. Shanahan pulled me over when we broke up and said, "That little dago ain't half bad, but I'd just as soon not have to be around him a whole shift. Bet that."

"Yeah. I agree," I said. "The new guy seems pretty cool, though."

We watched Lee stroll, carrying the briefcase, whistling, to the stockroom. "I don't figure we're going to be in too much hot soup with that one," said Mic. "Don't look too excitable." I hoped the baked chicken Turner had stashed in the stockroom was hidden good since it looked like it was going

71

to turn into Lee's closet. Shanahan lowered his voice, at least for him, and said, "I hope you boys hid that yard bird good..." and he smiled as Kathy came in from the alcove wearing a faded blue car coat over her Keno outfit. I wondered how in the hell Shanahan knew about our chicken.

Kathy said, "Hi," to me with a try at a smile and, "If you're going to the commode, Daddy, do it now so we can get goin.' I'll start the car" She went to the back door, and I wondered again about the two of them.

"Okay, honey, but watch your step," he said to her back. "College boy," he put his hand on my shoulder, "you left some wet spots when you was moppin'." He flashed his gold tooth again and said, "This floor's slicker than owl shit when it's wet. You could bust yore ass," and he slapped me on the back and went out through the alcove to the men's room down the short hall between the cashier's cage and the casino.

Tony was long gone, but the rest of us pulled out of the parking lot about the same time. The blond kid, Redding, drove off in a brand new, red VW bug. Mic and Kathy, the Ford still packed to the gills, were giving Beaner a lift somewhere. I was on the back of the Honda, the bag of chicken wrapped in heavy foil between me and Turner. Lee, back in his street clothes, gunned the Cadillac and headed out. Everyone turned into the traffic and headed into town down South Lake Boulevard under a black sky loaded with stars, but by the time Turner and I were across the line and at the place where the lake bows the road, everyone had scattered. I was burnt but glad the day had ended and hoped some hippie wasn't going to be melting when we got to the apartment.

And after first day on the job, May 25th, a couple of days before Memorial Day, things pretty much got into a groove, at least for the next month or so. I stayed stuck on the pots and the pans, and, because Tony decided I did a great job mopping the floors, I got to do it three times a shift. He'd come around squinting behind his glasses, and say something like, "C'mon, kid. Give the floor a go 'round. It's starting to look like shit, you know..." like I cared. But I went around once when we got to the kitchen at three, then once again around seven after we'd taken a break to eat something and hide the food we would smuggle out at the end of the night; and then one more time over the red tile before it was time to split. I figured I was going to be stuck a while because Shanahan was making a name for himself as a dish washer on the Hobart. Tony didn't seem like he gave much more of a rat's ass for Mic than the rest of the crew, but he did give him some leeway the way he acted around him, maybe because they were closer in age. But Mic did do a kick ass job. No question about that. He slammed, banged and sprayed and kept those clean plates, forks, knives and glasses coming. And I did take it as a good sign when Tony gave Redding the nightly job of taking apart and cleaning the radial slicer. It was nasty duty. Little pieces of gristle and flecks of meat got stuck in the hardest to get at places. And handling the sharp blade unscrewed from the works gave me the willies. It tightened up my asshole. Tony said the slicer was where the *stronzi* from the health department would look to stick us. He was obsessed with the slicer. Almost as much as the floor.

But the work had a rhythm. I was off at eleven or midnight, back at the apartment to get high, drink Red Mountain and listen to records if we didn't stop by one of the other casino lounges to listen to free music and try the slots, which

73

usually just meant I ended up crashing on my mattress later into the night. Sometimes there were people there at night, sometimes not. And I got to like my thin mattress at the end of the hall, with my magazines and old Army blanket. At least it was out of the way.

Turner and Sara must have told everyone they ever met they were invited to hang out or crash at our place. It made me crazy. I was convinced that sooner or later some weird space cowboy was going to get us into trouble with drugs or something else. Off and on speed, hash, grass, acid, mescaline, peyote and psylocibin got passed around, dropped, smoked, traded and sold; usually with the music cranked and the windows wide open with people coming and going. The parade of freaks and the drug bazaar didn't faze Turner. He didn't do anything but smoke pot and drink Red Mountain. Sara was about the same, but could be talked into anything once. They were incredibly laid back. Enormous space cadets.

During that month I got to know the others better, too. Redding was the son of a tomato farmer from northern California, on his way to grad school at Berkeley. He wanted to be a novelist. He thought he could get some material for a book working in The Mine Shaft. He didn't live with us, but started hanging out there anyway when he found he had a market for his stuff. Redding was interesting. I'd never met anybody who wanted to write books. And I'd never known anyone willing to risk so much when he didn't have to. He sure didn't need the money from working at The Mine Shaft. His parents had plenty. But once a week or so he drove down to Berkeley to score and came back with his stash. He specialized in opium and hash, but he could get anything. To me, his pale, one or two shades away from being an Albino skin and invisible mustache, didn't give him the face of a drug dealer. He had fine hair, the color of oats combed down low across his forehead, liked western shirts and cowboy boots with riding heels that tilted him forward when he walked. But he had a way with people, for sure, and he was a super friendly dude. Once in a while we would drop by his place, a one bedroom in a motel-looking complex called the Mountain View with doors that opened to the outside. There was a pool. His spot was nice compared to ours. He lived by himself. Redding could afford it. He was making lots of bread.

We got paid every other Wednesday, which ended up being my day off, and in cash, just like Tony said. They gave it to us at the cashier's cage: a brand new one-hundred dollar bill and a crisp twenty for two, six-day work weeks. Along with the money, we got two free drink tokens per day until the next payday. Turner hipped me to the fact it was just one more way for the casino to get the money back as fast as possible. I learned the hard way the first payday. I got paid at the cashier's cage, traded a toke for a Seven-Seven, got two rolls of quarters from a change girl and sat at the slot machines until four in the morning until I lost almost sixty bucks. Some woman at the next machine hit three cherries twice in five minutes and won a big jackpot. Bells rang and lights went off over an avalanche of coins and I waited forever for her to get off that machine and give me a shot, but she was still there when I went into the restaurant to eat fried eggs and bacon and try to sober up. I walked almost all the way to Stateline before some drunk in a pickup gave me a ride to the Y. I had to turn out lights and step over three people in the living room to get to my mattress.

Lee was the coolest, though. It was great to watch him

manage Tony. Tony would grab him as soon as Lee came out of the stockroom in the afternoon in his whites. He'd spend the two or three hours their shifts overlapped listening to Tony talk about the menu or ordering stock, his opinion about the kitchen operations and the crew. Whatever. Sometimes they would go out front and sit with Sweet Lou in his regular booth, drink coffee, smoke and talk. Lee just nodded and got along with Tony. When Tony went home the whole place relaxed and we had a lot more fun, but things still got done. Food got cooked and out to the line. People got fed. The crew liked to perform for Lee. His style was smoother. He called himself and the rest of us, toodler's, whatever the hell a toodler was. I think he made the word up. And he was off on Wednesday's like me.

Wednesday nights he'd usually go to Reno to the Moonlight Ranch, a new legal whorehouse all the guys talked about, and meet an old prostitute he had a relationship with. About Friday, when he usually felt good enough to talk again, he'd start telling stories. "Never gets tired of telling me she's a personal friend of Johnny Paleo, babe. You know, the little guy in the Harmonicats?" Lee would tell me this every time he mentioned her name, which was "Karlene with a K," then he would laugh like it was the funniest thing in the world. "She's a worse actor than Tom Ewell" usually got stuck in the story somewhere. He normally went with his friend Skin, an Art Carney lookalike from the Sahara who ran a lobby concession stand there.

"Skin." Lee had told me one night while he was standing and smoking at the back door looking into the parking lot. "Skin use to drum for Tempest Storm."

"Who?" I said.

"Tempest Storm. The burlesque queen? Big time stripper, babe."

"I only know April Flowers."

Lee gave me a quick look and said, "You know, I think I caught her act once at a club on Broad Street in the city."

"What city?"

"The city. San Francisco. There are a couple more that come close. One that's better."

I unplugged the sink and thought it was cool we'd linked with strippers. I loved his bullshit.

"Go on."

"Tempest Storm," he said, looking back across his shoulder at me with a curvy grin and a raised eyebrow. "Tempest Storm is a great one kid." He said it like I needed the information to be a better person.

"Well, Skin traveled the world with her, Havana to Berlin. He was her number one man." Lee flicked his cigarette into the parking lot and added, "He also did all her sets and props. Skin is a craftsman. A very talented toodler. Very talented. Not just a rim shot guy."

I saw Lee and Skin all duded up one Wednesday night at The Mine Shaft when we were picking up our pay at the cage. I said, "You guys look spiffy."
Lee said, "All the cats are meowin', babe," and he turned to Skin and said, "Let's roll, Skinny:' and they went out the front

past the bar. They both wore hats, Skin may have had on spats. I couldn't tell. But they shuffled in step through the heavy leather doors.

Shanahan was covering for somebody that Wednesday and was at the bar getting something for the kitchen and watched Lee and Skin leave. He stubbed a cigarette out in an ashtray and shook his head and walked over to me. He ran his hand over his hair and said, "Look at those two will ya? Nigger rich, and dressed up like clap doctors. Jesus Christ, what a fucking sight."

"He's going to see Karlene."

"With a K" and we said it at the same time, and I laughed but could see Shanahan was somewhere else.

"I wouldn't want to be on the road between here and Reno tonight with those two feller's on it." He stared at the back of the doors a second. "Remind me to tell you a story sometime," and he walked away carrying an aluminum bowl of oranges back up the hall to the restaurant alongside the line waiting to get at the smorgasbord. Something told me he had a bunch of stories, probably missed something or someone bad and Kathy was what kept him straight. And I'm sure she had her work cut out. I could have been wrong, but my guess was Shanahan would have loved to be on the road with those two toodlers and not in the steamy kitchen scraping plates on the one night of the week, "The little dago," pulled a double shift to cover Lee and was especially cranky.

During that first month I also started a tiny relationship with Rennie. Rennie was the blonde who dealt Twenty-One I had spotted on the first day. She copped smokes and yakked with the Keno girls in the alcove three or four times a shift. She was beautiful and looked older than me. When I saw her talking with Sweet Lou it intimidated me enough to figure she was out of my league. So in a way it gave me the excuse I needed to not try to get to know her better. But even so, she was usually nice to me and always smiled for what I took for genuine when I could catch her eye in the alcove or in the casino when I would pass through, when she wasn't shuffling her deck or hitting some asshole with a card. But as nice as Sweet Lou was...he was real smooth and suave in a James Bond way to me...and learned my name fast...I wasn't about to try to get to know Rennie better if he was the competition. But she was sexy when she walked, and I was turned on by a small scar on her tanned forehead, a ding of imperfection I'd noticed when we talked a minute together on a break. I looked for her every day. Turner almost cut his finger off gawking at her one night. Rennie stopped the kitchen dead when she showed up with her cigarettes and tan.

My one luxury, a habit I brought from home, was to spend sixty cents a week on *LIFE* magazine. I felt like the magazine was a part of my life; had been since I was born. It was always around. The stack of magazines and old newspapers left in the hallway when I got to the apartment included lots of *LIFE*s. I threw away a pile of old Rolling Stones and a campus paper called the Berkeley Barb and sorted through the *LIFE*s. They went back almost to the first of the year. It was a trip to look back at all those covers: Sirhan Sirhan, Nixon, Woody Allen and Bogart, Ben Gazzarra (Elaine's favorite), Sex and the Arts, Nixon again, Campus Riots, Mae West (fat and doughy), Judy Collins, the Pueblo; cool cover pictures. I'd been experimenting with collages for a while and so I kept the *TIME*s and *LIFE*s in stacks by my mattress with the plan of using the pictures as material. Slamming images together at odd angles, overlapped and pasted on a surface to form something new, fit my frame of mind and had for over a year. But I needed a space to work and I needed to make the time. My one daily reach for discipline was getting off the mattress and out the door to the kitchen. But when I lost most of my first payday at the slots, after paying rent and Red Mountain and a lid from Redding, I was broke. So I borrowed some money from Sara and bought a cheap pair of scissors, glue, paste and tape. Every day, even if I had a minute before I crashed or when I woke up, I started cutting out pictures and headlines and tossing them in a box.

One night at work, about seven, on a break, the line just reloaded with pounds of what Lee laughingly called, "Tony's best work..." I was outside the back door flipping through the new June 20 *LIFE*, with Joe Namath on the cover, when Shanahan and Turner interrupted me. They were arguing about Vietnam.

"Face it," snarled Shanahan. "You're a pussy."

Turner was anything but a violent person, hated confrontations unless he was throwing offensive linemen out of the way to kill the quarterback. He was always polite. When Shanahan watched Turner kowtowing to Tony, he'd said, "That boy's so nice he wouldn't say shit like he meant it if he had a mouthful." But they were at each other when they got to the parking lot.

"But, Mic, you don't get it. I have a right to disagree with the system. I think it is a dishonest war. We don't belong there, and I am not going to be part of a system that is killing and napalming innocent peasants and children." He stood with his hands on his hips in front of the grease barrel.

"You're a pussy, plain and simple." Shanahan leaned on somebody's red Buick that was nosed up close to the back door. "A yellow one to boot."

"C'mon, Mic. This isn't about you or me." Shanahan reached in his jeans and pulled out a Case pocket knife, called it his frog sticker. He always carried it with him, not as a threat or a weapon I didn't think, more of a tool, just something he liked to have in his hands when he was thinking or talking. It was sharp though. Could shave a row of hair off your arm with an easy swipe. He'd done it to me one night. Turner watched him unfold it and Mic started to clean his fingernails.

Mic didn't look up, but said, "It sure as shit is about you and me. Do you think the USA would be getting ready to land a damn man on the moon if people like Mic Shanahan didn't risk their fuckin' life in Korea? Shit, buddy, I seen our guys hangin' from parachutes gettin' shot up like pigeons by commie bullets and fellers with their toes and fingers frozen so hard you could snap 'em off like a dead switch. You ain't got no room..."

I stood and brushed off my butt.

"Mic," Turner was pleading, his arms out wide, "the moon shot doesn't have anything to do with Korea or Vietnam." "The hell it don't," said Mic, and he wiped the blade of his knife on his jeans.

"You're a draft dodgin' pussy, son." He still hadn't made eye contact with Turner.

"No, I'm not."

"You goin'? No you ain't goin' are you? At home we call that a draft dodger."

"No. There's where you're wrong. I am going to play by their rules. I'm already drafted, Mic."

Shanahan finally met Turner's eyes then looked over to me with a question on his lips. I could tell Turner, always the optimist, felt he was making progress. He stepped toward Shanahan. "Listen. I got my notice: I-A. I took my physical. I passed." He flexed and giggled. "Shit, man. I got my induction notice and I'm supposed to report to the Oakland Induction Center in two weeks."

"So, you're goin'?" Mic looked skeptical.

"Where? 'Nam or Oakland?"

"Vietnam. Goddammit." said Shanahan. "Viet-fuckin'-nam."

"No. I am going to Oakland like they want. I am going through with everything they want me to do. I am going to hold up my hand and be a good American boy and all the other shit they ask you to repeat, and then, when they ask you to step forward, step across that line," he looked back and forth at the two of us, "I am going to refuse. I'm playing by their rules. I am staying within the system. But I am not going to step forward. I'm not running. I'm refusing to be inducted. Got it?"

Shanahan just stared at Turner, whose eyes were wide, hoping he'd made Mic understand. Then Shanahan pushed up off the hood of the Buick and looked at me and said quietly but firmly, "Don't say much for him, now, does it, college boy?" And he walked past Turner and the grease barrel into the kitchen humming one of his Fifties songs, folding the knife closed with a click and slipping it back in his pocket. He didn't say anything to Turner, and I was incredibly glad he hadn't asked me what my plans were for the war. I was a confused collaboration of one, and when Tony came out to go home with his black coat over his arm, I didn't need him to tell me to give the floor another go around.

Chapter 6

One Wednesday afternoon, my day off, broke and nothing to do, I started taping and pasting cut out pictures and headlines from *LIFE* and *TIME* magazines on the wall above my mattress. What I wanted was a collage that would cover the whole wall at the end of the hallway. Turner and Sara thought it was cool and didn't think the landlord would bust us. The place was pretty much a dump anyway. Sara had wandered down the hall and sat cross-legged on the floor next to the mattress and sorted and cut with me. That she wasn't wearing underwear, and that she had such a lack of self-consciousness about it, was a cool distraction. Reminded me of Dew's attitude. As she scooted and cut, her skirt hiked up, and I caught myself staring every time I turned to pick out a picture. It was a turn on for me, but she was absorbed in the magazines. She just rattled away. She thought a wall collage sounded like a "bitchin' good idea." Her hair was washed and pulled back with an embroidered leather cinch, she wore black and white just like the Keno runners and the change girls at The Mine Shaft. On her feet, the only shoes I ever saw her wearing were white Keds. She'd just washed them across the street at the laundromat. They were clean and smelled like bleach, the rubber soles puckered at the edges of the canvas tops. For the job, Sara wore red lipstick, loud as the neon in The Mine Shaft sign, and no other make-up, but I could smell baby powder. Her legs were shaved, but under protest as a rule of the job, but not her underarms. Earth Mother Sara walking around Barney's making change for old ladies, drunks and bus tour groups was a sight I was going to have to check out. Still, she hated to wear a uniform.

"I hate this costume."

"You look fine."

"I look like a bimbo is what I look like," and she shook her head and flipped through a *LIFE*.

"It's just a gig, Sara," I said. "Better than washing pots and pans." And she was quiet.

But for sure, Barney's Sara wasn't the girl I'd seen dancing by herself in the flower garden downstairs one night, barefoot, bare arms, red dress, whirling in circles, eyes closed, smiling, bright paint smeared in circles and streaks on her face and down her arms and probably all the way down her front, bunches of yellow flowers in each fist and a single bloom in her hair. She was oblivious to anything and anyone except the pot and wine stoked choreography jangling in her stoned head. She was pouting over *LIFE* like the white blouse and black skirt and Keds she had to wear for eight hours were a straightjacket and manacles.

She showed me a page with a flat-chested, skinny model who had long hair and white eye liner and matching white lipstick wearing a lime green micro miniskirt. Then I watched while she turned and cut along the edges. She was proud of the job and held it up for my inspection. "Huh?" she questioned, waving it like a paper doll back and forth. "Some chick," she added.

"Cool," I said, dropping my eyes from the cutout to her thighs and back in a flick. "That'll work."

"Turner wants me to go with him to refuse to get drafted next week, but I can't." She dropped the model into a pile on the mattress. "Gotta work," she said and lit a big roach from a jar top on the floor I was using as an ash tray. I kneeled on the mattress and took it from her when she held it out. Neither one of us said anything, and we held what was left of Redding's lid in our lungs. We exhaled together, me coughing and pointing at an almost empty Red Mountain jug. I swigged and handed it to her. Sara shook her head. "Can't." She stretched her legs straight forward up onto the edge of the mattress and, bracing with her arms straight and her elbows locked, leaned back and threw her face up at the ceiling. "I'll get fired. Can't smell it on my breath. I'm fine," she said grinning. "Just looking for a small buzz, puddin' head." It was her name for people she liked, and that seemed like everybody. It was the first time she'd called me puddin' head. She'd cooed it to the trussed up and gagged Alex when she was trying to calm him down.

Redding always had the best stuff and half a joint got us both good and high. We toked some more, down to nothing until I dropped the ember into the jar top when it burned my fingers. "Why don't you go with him, Victor? He really wants someone to witness it all. It'll be bitchin', for sure," she said.

"How's he going to get there?" I leaned against the wall and imagined Turner and that goofy, wide open, all American face saying, "No, thank you, sir. I am not going to step across your line, sir. Your war is unjust and illegal, sir. But I am here to deny you and this country honestly, sir. Within the system." It just seemed silly.

And I was ripped.

Sara nodded and giggled, said, "Yeah, man," like she knew what was going on in my head. "He's going to use my Volvo."

"It loses reverse doesn't it?"

"Yeah," she went on, "you have to know how to baby it," spinning on her butt, crawling. She snapped her ponytail over a shoulder and it covered the Barney's name tag pinned to her blouse. "You gotta be there at seven in the morning. To report," she growled. "Gonna have to leave sometime after midnight to get to Oakland on time, puddin' head." This time she drew out "head" to "heaaaad"...and pulled the cinch off her pony tail. Then she crawled onto the mattress and said matter of factly, "Victor, I'm hungry and I'm horny, and I don't have to be at work for thirty minutes. And I can skip the food." She was in my face and her bottom lip pursed in a mock challenge, and in an instant, her blouse was over her head and she unhooked a frayed bra and tossed it onto the floor, the black skirt bunched up at her waist like a belt. And she said, "Let's get it on puddin' head." And we both tore at my jeans and T-shirt, and whatever guilt I had about being with Turner's girl crumpled like the magazine pages we rolled around on.

When we were done all I could say was, "Wow...you're loud."

Sara relaxed her grip on my hands, pushed the hair out of her face and looked down at me and said, "What?"

"I don't know. Just..." then I noticed a cutout picture of Richard Nixon, his arms raised in victory, plastered to her thigh and I started to laugh, hard enough that, since she was still on me, bounced as I shook.

Sara peeled the president off and made a face and said, "Oh, God. Ugh. Tricky Dicky," and tossed the picture in the box and rolled off me, picked up her clothes and hair cinch

87

and took off down the hall. From the bathroom she hollered over running water, "Try and go with Turner to Oakland, okay? And see if you guys can get some more of that grass from Redding." She trotted out of the apartment buckling her change belt at the small of her back as she went. She called over her shoulder, "Later, Victor," and the door slammed.

I stretched out on the mattress, my hands behind my head, and tried to figure out how I felt about Turner. I wondered why I didn't feel bad about screwing his old lady. It felt more like an accomplishment, really, something I needed to do to get into this scene. And if guilt was lurking, it hadn't slithered close yet. I wondered if it would happen again. It was definitely a groovy thing, fast as it was. I decided to leave it up to her, but got excited again when I pictured her naked, especially her big brown nipples, bold as Sara herself.

I followed the path of sunlight that streaked from the front window across the floor out into the hall and across my mattress kingdom. It ran over my bare leg and chest and disappeared in a point at the collage wall. I was sliced obliquely by it. And I wondered about Elaine, no doubt triggered by Sara, and thought about the movie she'd made as an assignment about her immigrant grandparents in Cleveland, both deaf. I thought about the screening she'd had last year. And from nowhere, my eye began flickering like sixteen millimeter film, loose and fluttering in a projector gate.

Elaine was playing a Stephan Grappelli record. She wanted to wild track her Cinematography 301 class movie assignment with jazzy violin music. The fiddle playing reminded me of black and white cartoons from the Saturday mornings when I was little. I'd stood by the door in Elaine's apartment, the lower half of a chopped up old Victorian, carrying a bag of ice cubes leaking puddles on the floor, and remembered black and white cartoon images of a fat and bald farmer in overalls chasing armies of animated mice into a hole in the wall with a broom. Very clearly I could see myself and my brother in corduroy pants on the floor of the living room, transfixed, eyes locked on the small TV screen, Dad in his chair rustling the newspaper, smoking his Kools, Mom cleaning up the breakfast dishes in the kitchen. Sink water running.

Elaine picked up the stylus and waved me to the kitchen with orders to pour the ice over bottles of white wine in a cooler in the corner. I did as I was told, and as the ice rattled over the bottles, Elaine stopped and started the music, and I had a feeling of gratitude for her direction. More aimless than even I thought I could be, I had reached a point where making the most basic decisions was becoming difficult, confusing and agitating. I emptied the ice and freely admitted to myself that in Elaine's presence, where lists were made, plans were planned and schedules met, I felt safe. Her structure gave me a sense of protection from everything else.

This willing and sudden self-awareness confused me though, since among other things, I could not square it with the fact I had not reached my goal of having sex with her. She had teased and frustrated me, and we had both said we wanted to do it, but as naked and excited as we could both get, she always stopped just short. But I didn't give up. I knew she really had it for me, and I just figured if I could wait her out by being a nice guy I would win. Still, how could this other feeling have crept up and begun to wage a successful battle while I had worked hard at the one job of keeping emotion out of it, sex my only serious ambition?

I wadded up the plastic ice bag and dropped it into a garbage can and knew the same hopeless and circular thought process blocking all logic in my head would not be able to add up this situation either. But I felt good around her anyway. I couldn't deny it.

I got pretty caught up as the apartment gradually became organized. "We're dressing a set, Victor," was how she described the rearranging, fussing and cleaning.

As I set up the screen and the projector signed out from the film department, she arranged flowers in vases and put them around her apartment. "Zinnias, Victor. Zins are my favorite." The Stephan Grappelli music had a sophisticated sound that kept me with it and fit somehow with the bright flowers. I'd never known the fiddle to be anything but an instrument hillbilly bands scratched on that *Midwestern Hayride* TV show.

"Victor," from the kitchen, "thread the projector, will you? The can's by the door on the table with the phone." I was at the bay window blocked by the film screen looking out on the back yard of the house. At the middle stood an empty stone bird bath with a gray squirrel in it. I thought about how grown up...that was the only way I could describe it...this party was going to be compared to the laid back and last minute parties, if you could call them parties, I usually was around. The floor of Palmeri's, where the main action was pot, sopers, wine, music and nodding out, was all I was experienced with these days. Her screening was going to be a wine and cheese party. Elaine would not tolerate dope. And comfortable as I was with her, I was worried if I wasn't high. I didn't know how I would do chit chatting with strangers and professors, more than one who had been asking of my whereabouts. As the squirrel was chased from his spot in the bird bath by an identical looking challenger, I started to worry about how I was dressed. I knew in myself a nagging need to be liked and accepted. I wanted to be different, but not embarrassed, but shook off the thought, hid from it, to be straight, and went around the screen to the apartment door and picked up the silver film can. The can, the size of a plate, an inch thick, was sealed around the edge with white tape in dark ink with Elaine's writing. It read, "Ruth and Red."

I threaded the projector and cued up the record on the stereo. Elaine was in her bedroom. I said, "Who's coming, anyway?"

She popped her head out. Thick black hair pulled away from her face which gave away its round shape. She had on jeans, sandals and a bra. It was a come on, a classic Elaine. I smiled and she ticked off the invitation list while she messed with something at the back of her head, "Doctor Davison and his wife, a neighbor from upstairs, a guy Kay met at the hospital, that SDS girl that's so nice and anyone else from my class who wants to." She stepped back into her room. "Any of your friends coming? Did you invite Palmeri?"

Elaine liked Palmeri, had run into him on campus a few times and been in his store on Calhoun Street, but had never seen his pad. I just couldn't trust Palmeri not to bring Dew, who might take her clothes off, or he might show up with the two teenyboppers who'd shopped in his store that I just knew he was balling. Baggo would've likely thrown up on somebody or slipped and made a slur about "Hebes or Kikes." I couldn't risk it. Not those two. They'd be scary surrounded by zins, Brie, jazzy French fiddle music and a student movie about an old Jewish immigrant couple who'd both been deaf since birth.

"Haven't had the time..."

Elaine came out of her bedroom, hair still up, apologizing for the curlers that looked to me big as storm drains, wearing an oversized Cincinnati basketball T-shirt. On the way to the bathroom at the end of the hall with two bobby pins in her mouth, she shot a look I knew was to be taken as one of amazement I could claim to be too busy to make a phone call. Time, I thought: too much of it, too little of it, getting through it, waiting on it, sleeping through it, just thinking about it for some reason made me crazy. Elaine was right, of course. I had the time to do anything, any damn thing I wanted to do. And right now I decided I wanted to get high.

"I'll be back in a half hour. Everything's ready out here," I said. She stuck her head out the bathroom door with a toothbrush in her mouth and said, "Be on time. I need you to synch the music with the film, okay?"

I said, "Cool," and left the house, undecided if I had time to walk to my apartment and get back before it all got going.

When I got there, for some reason my key wouldn't fit into the door lock. Then with a rush of surprise, fear, then anger, I saw the handle had been crimped with large pliers or something like that. The door wasn't latched and I pushed it open. From the doorway I saw right away my stereo was gone, the only thing of value that could be fenced in the entire place. I wheeled and on a dead run got to Palmeri's door in seconds. Palmeri answered wearing his Moroccan jilaba.

"Somebody ripped me off, man...in broad daylight." I involuntarily glanced to the window even though the time of day in Palmeri's pad was indecipherable at all times.

"Wow, man, what'd they get?"

"My stereo..."

"They take your records?"

"No. They can't fence those..."

Palmeri pushed his hair back with one hand and said confidently, "Junkies. Spooks or junkies, man."

"Should I call the cops?"

He said, "Let's smoke a joint and consider this." He pulled me inside, picked a rolled joint off a small round table draped in a fringed cloth. "I'm not so sure I would call the heat in." He lit the joint, inhaled, passed it, and when he had exhaled, said, "I'm not sure you want the pigs snoopin' around. They don't give a rat's ass anyway."

As I started to buzz from the marijuana, everything started to seem more unreal and bizarre than usual. The combined effect of the grass, the break-in, and my messed up life, made me want to get extremely high or drunk or both. A big time vacation from reality.

"Do me a favor," I said. "Come upstairs with me and let's take a look around. I didn't even go inside."

"What if there's a crazed junkie or a spook with a gun?"

"C'mon, man. C'mon…" After a short look around my place—Palmeri armed with a small knife I'd seen Dew peeling onions with—we sat on the floor and drank shots of tequila and smoked some of his special hash. With the stereo gone, and no music, smoking and drinking was the entertainment, and it sucked any genius for small talk, so we just stared off between the ledge of blue smoke folding back on itself in the room. Voices in the hallway scared us, but it was only dope paranoia, and they passed by. And I thought once more about time passing, and that the only thing left in this place worth stealing was time from ourselves. And we were doing one helluva job grabbing that. I remembered a Richard Brautigan line about teachers being time stealing bank robbers, or something close. As the hash and tequila robbed me of my senses, I had the thought I could have ridden with the James Gang and all those teachers. Made a big contribution. Could've boosted saddle bags of the stuff and ridden off to the cave with him and Cole and the boys. Made him proud. And I slipped into a delicious sleep.

At the screening, the first thing that went wrong was the Stephan Grappelli record started to skip and even for a wild track, the music didn't fit. Then the film got stuck in the gate and the lights in the room came on, and I was freaked to see Palmeri and Dew, both smoking enormous joints, and the teeny boppers, giggling and holding hands, and next to them Baggo, drunk and laughing and puking. I started to freak because Elaine, who for some reason still had her hair in curlers, was crying and shrieking, "Victor, Victor, Victor." And I looked down and saw I was naked and tried to act normal and ignore all the attention being focused on me. Dr. Davison, the head of the department, was smiling his condescending smile. Dew, also naked, gave me a grin of understanding, Kay and her boyfriend were taking notes, and the two squirrels from earlier in the day were tearing around the apartment in mad circles, coughing and knocking over the zinnias and grabbing nuts from a bowl. The SDS girl from Elaine's class was lifting her granny dress over her head. She had a peace symbol tattoo on her stomach.

"Victor," Elaine hollered again, and I realized I was trapped in a dream so I shook my head to clear it out and woke up in my apartment on the floor. It was night outside. Palmeri was gone. The door was still open a crack. The screening over for sure. I sat up and blinked my eyes in a waking up process that would take some time. A real long time, probably. Maybe forever.

I decided not to put my clothes back on and went back to the collage. I remembered a joint in my fatigue jacket and I got lost in the work. The newest *LIFE*, by the bed, still not cut up, had a black and white cover photo of a soldier, a guy who looked about my age. As I started to flip through it, about halfway in, checking it out before it became part of the wall, I was stopped by pages of pictures of people, all military, laid out in row after row, like pictures in a yearbook. Sailors, Marines, Air Force and Army, some smiling, some staring, most lost in a pose, they went on page after page. I looked at them, some closer than others, looked for names I might know, or someone from Cincinnati, and then flipped back to the first page of the section. Then a rolling sensation, a slow rush of awareness, and I realized every one of these people I had been looking at so close was dead. Killed in Vietnam. Killed in Vietnam in one week. Last week. I held in my hand *LIFE*'s scoreboard of dead. Pictures as tombstones. A visual cemetery. All killed in seven days when I worked six, where the most important thing I had to do was get to a sink of water by three p.m., the most dangerous action, crossing the damn road or getting into the wrong car hitchhiking. I spent the next hour, maybe two, pouring over every face on those pages. Every one. My eye twitched, and I got so high I had to put the magazine down after a while and just listen to the whiny buzz in my ears and the beat of my heart. And later, when I cut up those pages, those faces, I knew I was making a decision to do something. I just didn't know where or when. But I had crawled under the wire and was inside some kind of perimeter somewhere now. That much I knew. And I felt huge relief. I made the cover of the magazine with the picture of that dead soldier the bullseye of my collage.

I was still focused on the impression *LIFE* had made on me the next day at the kitchen as I worked through the pile of lasagna pans. The dead faces wouldn't leave my mind. I thought about it when I bummed a cigarette from Shanahan and went out back and talked and smoked with the grease man. He usually came once a week to collect the barrel of old fry grease and to leave a new empty one at the back door. I was fascinated by that greasy little man who wasn't much taller, but almost as wide as the barrels he wrestled with. I just got off on his energy and determination, his pleasure in finishing off a simple job. He roared in and out of the lot in his flatbed, full of life and motion. The grease man gave me energy. I looked forward to seeing him. He was habit forming and I began to depend on him. He took my mind off the war and the impact of the *LIFE* pictures.

One day the motorcycle was gone and we had to thumb to work. Turner didn't seem fazed about the bike, but that was no surprise. Nothing seemed to get him. We got a lift in a VW bus with a bunch of freaks who wanted to sell us some "genuine" Owsley acid. "The purest shit, man," a guy with hair down to his ass kept saying. We piled out in front of The

Mine Shaft and they headed on toward Carson City. When we got to the kitchen, Shanahan was jumping around with news, in addition to the usual jabbering about the moon shot. He caught Turner and me at the back door and told us Kathy had been promoted to the job of hostess, a clear step up from keno runner as far as Mic was concerned. He called the new job "a PR type thing." She's gonna work the line and keep all them people happy while they's waitin' to eat our grub. Chat 'em up. Get 'em to the tables. It's a perfect job for her," he said. "Them yahoos out there will take to her like a speckled puppy, she's so damn cute."

Then he told us as he dragged on a cigarette, that starting tomorrow he was moving to the day shift. Somebody got fired or just didn't show up. "You get to move up to the Hobart on nights, college boy," he said and he punched me in the arm. "Hey boys," he said. "What's long and hard on a black guy?"

Turner and I looked at each other.

I said, "I'll bite. What?" Turner just shook his head.

"The third grade." And he laughed and punched me in the arm again. He smiled wide with his cigarette clinched between his teeth, satisfied with himself.

I said, "But who says I'm moving up to the Hobart, Mic?"

"The little dago says."

"Shit, man," Turner said, and he popped me in the other arm. "I told you if you did a good job for Tony you'd move up. See?"

97

Just then Lee came out of the stockroom. Shanahan said, "Chef, tell the boy he's taking my spot."

Lee tugged a clean towel through his apron string and looked at me and said, "The Mighty Wurlitzer, Rosa Rio. You're moving up," and he strolled away. But I wasn't going to believe it until I heard it from Tony, who just then was walking down the back aisle.

Shanahan, who mostly could get away with talking to Tony any way he wanted to, said, "Tony, ain't this college boy graduatin' to the shiny dime Hobart? Gonna be yore new stoker?"

Tony's answer, squinting through his cigarette smoke, first at Mic, then at me, was, "You're still doing the floors, kid. They ain't clean three times a shift your ass belongs to the gypsy's. You fuck it up, this hilljack's back on nights, and you're gone." And he turned around picking at his ear. Over his shoulder he snorted, "Get your aprons on."

"Hear that, buster?" said Mic, giving Tony the finger behind his back. "Don't mess it up or yore gonna have a mad little dago and a madder mountain man on your college boy ass like stink on you know what. I'm due for some nightlife, fellas. Been awhile, don't ya see." And he went to the Hobart whistling "Tall Paul" on his last night shift. He looked like a guy ready to cut loose.

I could not believe people would line up to eat our food like they did. Right at Memorial Day, like a cannon went off, the line seemed to never quit, off tour buses, out of the parking lot, waiting patiently to get at the $1.99 *All You Can Eat* bargain we whipped up for them seven days a week. When I

98

would leave the kitchen to go to the men's room I'd pass alongside the line. There was every type of person you could imagine. Every day, especially at two different peak times, the line backed up into the casino. First, just before noon at about eleven thirty. Next, about three-thirty, our shift, and it stayed that way until about ten. Whatever else they spent their money on in Lake Tahoe, the Famous Smorgasbord at The Mine Shaft had to be the best deal, odds wise at least.

The food along the steam line was the same every day. With almost no changes, there was lasagna, tuna noodle casserole, ham salad, chicken salad, baked ham with fruity sauce, baked chicken, sliced roast beef, sliced ham, sliced turkey breast and something I had never seen...tongue...a big bowl of chopped Iceberg lettuce on ice surrounded by three dressings and croutons and always some kind of soup. The soup was about the only thing that changed. I think Tony and Lee did different soups to keep from going crazy. They also took turns cooking special things for themselves and Sweet Lou and his friends who would come by. It was kind of a competition between them. Tony tended to make lots of bean soups and his "special" minestrone, and to me they always tasted about the same because Tony just threw in leftovers with a ton of garlic and oregano. Lee had a different touch and made creamy soups. They were great. He created tastes I'd never known. Their different approaches to cooking pretty much said what those two guys were about in more ways than one.

I found out later that Lou, Tony and Lee had had a meeting at Sweet Lou's table to figure out the hostess job. Sweet Lou felt there needed to be someone paying attention to the line as the season heated up. And there seemed to be a waiting line all the time. It made sense to me because we were really busy. It was just that Kathy seemed an odd choice. Tony's idea was a blonde with big tits. But I guess Lou saw something in Kathy and overruled him. It didn't matter to Lee. He didn't sweat about much, it looked to me. Lee told me Sweet Lou liked her "authenticity." And they even gave her a little bonus money to buy some hostess clothes. Lou looked out for her for some reason. I couldn't figure.

Even though Kathy looked better in her new clothes, and Sweet Lou seemed to like the way she was working the line...even getting lots of them into the casino to the tables and the slots while they waited to eat, I noticed a trace of something in her face, concern maybe, I hadn't picked up on before. And I usually noticed it when the second shift crew came in. She and Mic would hug after he took off his apron, then walk into the parking lot and talk before she handed over the keys to the Ford. I couldn't hear them ever, but when she walked past me at the Hobart on the way to the front of the house, her smile was phony, distracted and far away.

Chapter 7

It was time for Turner to reject the draft and he wanted me to ride all night with him to do it.

"Sure you want to go through with this?"

"Positive. I'm thinking very clearly. I'm clear. I feel good about myself."

"Well I'm scared for you. I'd be scared."

"Let me ask you a question."

"Shoot."

"How do you feel about yourself?"

"Like what…"

"Like what do you think about the way your head is these days?"

After a minute or so I said, "Well actually I guess…I think I'm pretty fucked up. You know. Confused about all kinds of shit. Who isn't. So what?"

He looked at me and said. "Right on. I agree. You think your head is fucked up."

"So?"

"So, it's like this. Because you think your head is fucked up and that you're confused, when you look out you see confusion." Turner paused, leaned with a turn in the road, over the summit, coming down off the hill in the Volvo. "Too heavy?"

I didn't say anything. I just looked at the silhouettes of the pine stands that walled the road against the night sky.

"My head is clear. Me? I look out and I see clearly," he said.

"I'm trying to follow." I blew on the window and drew a peace symbol in the fog.

"Now try this on. I don't think you're that fucked up."

"Yeah..."

"So try acting like I see you. Like that."

"What?"

"We think Lee is cool. Hip, right?"

"Yeah..."

"And he keeps getting cooler. Right?"

"Right."

"Tony's a maniac. Mean ass Italian."

"Sure."

"Right. Sure. And he's more that way every day. Right?"

"I guess."

"Guess, shit. We feed him, he feeds off what we think of him. Ya see?"

"Okay. So what?"

"Well, you see me as crazed, taking a risk, standing for something that could get me in trouble. Right?"

"Right. Go on."

"So, Victor, Victor, you dope, don't you see that pumps me way, way up? Makes me even more willing and set to motor on? Tell the silly Army no way Jose? I am acting like you see me." He looked over and said, "Try it man. Try it." Then he stuck his fingers into the breast pocket of one of the dozen identical blue Penney's T-shirts he owned and handed me a rolled joint. "Here. Fire this up."

I'd lit the joint with the cigarette lighter, taken a hit and passed it back to him with my lungs burning and bursting, and I swear to God I'd wanted to explode right then and there.

I'd wanted to spend my day off working on the collage. Plus, I was tired. But I said I'd go. Mid July, it was the peak of the tourist season. And the kitchen crew, more or less, was stable with not too much turnover, and the lines to eat our stuff were steady and long. We were cranking. Most of us were in a routine and were aware of everyone else's patterns and habits. And moods. The balance and tone of the kitchen revolved around a loose connection between Sweet Lou, the boss, but kind, Tony, simple and crude and capable of volcanic tantrums, and Lee, quiet, talented, a lady's man and big time drinker. As a threesome, it somehow managed to work. But when one of them was absent or overstepping their role, it could get weird. Like once when Redding accidentally poured a pound of salt into the fruit in the big saucer instead of sugar, I thought Tony's head would explode. He was pulling a double shift for Lee who didn't make it in after his day off. Tony would have fired Redding on the spot, but help was tough to find in peak season. "Chrissake," he fumed. "Wadareyou? A moron? An idiota?"

"Sorry, Tony," Redding brushed at the hair on his forehead. I swear I thought Tony was going to have a heart attack over about fifty cents worth of salt.

"Dump it. Start over. I'll bring you the sugar. Show you what it looks like, you dumb ass." And he walked off muttering about "imbecile college kids," and some other words in Italian I didn't understand. Redding watched him turn the corner then stuck his finger into the sauce. He screwed his face up and shook his head at the taste. He straightened up when Tony came back with the sugar and acted very attentive as Tony supervised the restart on the goopy, pink fruit sauce we served over the baked ham. It had the consistency of cold motor oil. The idea Redding was going to be in grad school at Berkeley in a couple of months and Tony would still be here on the hill gooping up the ham was a righteous thought.

But Redding watched reverently when Tony gave him his "see stupid?" look and dumped a bag of sugar into the new sauce. From Redding's face you'd think he'd just seen an atom split. Tony shook his head in disgust at Redding over the kettle, Lucky between his lips, as he stirred the sauce with a spoon the size of a canoe paddle.

Another time Turner caught Tony's wrath when he carbonized three full trays of baked chicken breasts because he forgot to set the timer. He was lecturing Redding and me about the immorality of the war, or staring at Rennie smoking in the alcove, and didn't turn the timer to fifty-five minutes. Tony had showed all of us, even me, in case I got called into chicken panning and baking action. All you had to do after spreading the thighs and breasts and legs on the big baking tray was, "Put some water in the bottom of the tray, shake with salt and pepper...paprika is for color, but don't put too much on, and then put the trays in the oven at three-hundred and fifty degrees for fifty-five minutes. That's it, idiotas. I could train a retarded circus monkey to do it." On a busy night, we baked about twenty trays of chicken.

But Turner forgot to turn on the timer and the chicken got incinerated right when it was needed at peak rush, and the front of the house was popping. Tony got so mad at Turner he screamed at him in Italian for ten straight minutes. Made me think something else must be eating at Tony to make him go off like that. He made Beaner carry the blackened parts to the dumpster out back. Then he sent Redding into the walk-in for new boxes of chicken parts. We all had to pitch in and thaw them in the sink, pan new trays, get them cooked and out to the line. It's a tribute to Turner that he could stand there and take that kind of shit from Tony like he did. He was peculiar and cool in that way.

Turner had made it clear he wanted to leave The Mine Shaft as soon as the shift was over at eleven, but I got us sidetracked because Rennie had finally agreed to have a drink. I was committed to Turner's escapade, but had been working on getting to know Rennie, so I convinced him to wait until midnight before we took off for Oakland so Rennie and I could have a quick cocktail at the casino bar. "Shit, man," he sighed. "Okay. But please meet me here at midnight. I'll gas up the Volvo. Sara put some munchies together for the ride."

"Will it go in reverse?" I asked.

"At the moment," he smiled. "But I won't. See you in an hour. Later." And he threw his apron at the hamper at the back door and went out into the parking lot.

Since Rennie worked in the casino, she was friendly with Danny the bartender, who we all figured was gay, and she got us free drinks, which was good because I'd spent my drink tokens already. I'd learned a little about her in short talks in the alcove when she was taking a smoke break. I knew she was about ten years older, didn't go to college, had a small baby home in Tucson with her Mom, and a shithead husband who'd bailed out on her. On the surface she was a confident girl, coping with a completely different set of worries and problems than I had. I felt, and that was all it was because I knew no different, that if there was a similarity between us, it was that she was also confused and wandering. But she seemed to mask it in a more organized and better way than me. That was my hunch.

She had worked a full night shift like me, but still smelled fresh even though she complained the smoke after eight hours had saturated her uniform and hair. I felt like a stinky mess, blasted by the steam from the Hobart every time it cycled a new rack of dishes. But we sat and talked about the characters in the casino and the kitchen, and made fun of the customers and the tourists with Danny. We drank Seven and Sevens and smoked, which I was doing more and more of.

The action behind us at the tables was still busy and every once in a while somebody would whoop and the bells and clanging would start. One dice table was hot, and there was a big crowd around it. The other craps table was empty and the croupiers leaned on the rails and talked with the box man and watched the scene. One dealer used his stick to scratch his back. Rennie was tired and didn't care about what was happening behind her. She told me Sweet Lou had called security earlier because some guy at her table was caught counting cards.

"They eighty-sixed his butt in a heartbeat," she said. "Sent for Butcher." As a reaction, I craned my neck to see if Butcher, Lou's assistant manager, was still around. He scared the shit out of me. His nickname was really The Butcher, but he answered to just Butcher. He doubled as The Mine Shaft bouncer. I didn't want to know why they called him that.

"He cheated?"

"No, not exactly," and she gave a small wave and dipped her head as a hello to a waitress taking drinks from the service end of the bar to the lucky dice table that was getting noisier, completely surrounded by players, two deep around the rails, yells and groans rising and falling with each throw of the dice. "No, card counting is not cheating. Sort of," and she bit her lip and looked at me for understanding and then sucked on her cigarette. I could feel the looks Rennie was getting from other men at the bar, but she ignored them and paid attention to me. I hated the idea I was going with Turner to Oakland.

"But he got thrown out for it. I'm confused."

"The house doesn't like it. It's not fair. They catch you, they eighty-six you. Put your name in a book and don't let you back in. Ever."

I started to ask another question, but a loud cheer exploded at the craps table.

Someone yelled, "Thank you, shooter. Thank you." Danny looked up from drying a glass. Then the table quieted down.

"Tell me now," she tapped her front tooth with the end of a red fingernail, "what is he going to do again? Dodge the draft?"

"Nope," I said, watching Danny scrub and rinse bar glasses from soapy blue sink water to clear, then onto a rack. "Turner is much more moral than that."

"Moral like what?"

"Like he would never dodge the draft. He thinks that's the coward's way out. He's accepted the system, but since they give you an opportunity to not cross the line, he's going to go that far, then say no. I mean, they do ask you a question. He has a right to answer." I sipped my drink: and watched her tap her tooth and think it over. "Otherwise they would just say, c'mon, guys, get on the bus. Let's go napalm some people. Turner is just going to give them an answer they don't usually get face to face. See?" Danny was eavesdropping, but when I caught him, he looked over my head while he shook a martini for a short older guy on my left with a Boston accent who was asking Danny if there were any hookers around. He kept leaning forward and trying to make eye contact with Rennie.

"He's high minded then," she said finally.

"Yeah, high minded. That's Turner," and I asked Danny for the time and he said it was five of midnight. "Shit. I gotta go," and I slid off the bar stool. "What are you doing for your day off?"

Rennie smiled and said, "Sleep, sun and errands," and she dropped a Mine Shaft five dollar chip on the bar, put her cigarettes into a small purse and clipped it shut. "Nothing as dramatic as telling the United States Army no thanks. I think his idea is for the birds, but good luck to you two." She said goodbye to Danny, who thanked her for the tip. "And you know he's probably going to ruin his life. Going to follow him around. Sooner or later some government goon is going to eighty-six him. He's counting cards," and she reached for a mint from a bowl next to Danny's cash register. "Remember who's got the odds, Victor. Chiselers always get it in the end," and she waved her arm at the gamblers and the room and blew a kiss to the pit boss, who winked back and waved a fat hand. She went out through the red front doors of the casino. Danny watched all this without changing his expression, even though I searched his face and wondered whether I should ask him to put in a good word for me with Rennie. But he went back to wiping down the bar, and I headed down the hall to the kitchen. On the way I passed the steam line set up for breakfast; pans of scrambled eggs, bacon and ham drying out under heat lamps. The new breakfast fry cook, I hadn't learned his name—it seemed we got a new one every week—was breaking two eggs at a time with one hand, then beat them in a large stainless bowl with a big wire whisk. The last fry cook called scrambled eggs ship wrecked eggs, an expression my Dad used.

When I walked out into the parking lot and saw Turner waiting in the Volvo, I was thinking about Rennie's ideas about card counting and what she'd said about Turner and his future. I started to fret about all the risk I suddenly sensed out there. Turner had the heat on in the car, and the Stones were singing that song again on the radio. He gripped the wheel, looked at me and said, "Well, what did Marilyn Monroe have to say?"

"She said you'd be better off on your one day off getting some sleep and running a few errands and lying in the sun than telling Uncle Sam thanks but no thanks. Your idea is for the birds."

"He laughed and said, "Ah, shit, man. Is that verbatim?" Then, "Go back in and get some road coffee."

We were nodding in Sara's Volvo in the huge parking lot of the Oakland Induction Center, U.S. Army, Oakland, California, at six a.m. Wednesday. We were early. And to be safe, we had parked so we wouldn't have to risk putting the car in reverse. The sky was flat gray, like a sheet of wax paper. The sun hadn't broken through yet. It fit my mood. And sleepy as he seemed, you would have thought Turner was going to a big free concert instead of being about to decline, however politely, the chance to serve his country in a foreign war. I was consciously suppressing the very real fact that in a few months I was due to make a decision I knew had to be made. I just didn't know what it would be yet. I didn't see myself in this scenario. I was capable of the big impulsive decision, right or wrong. But I wasn't designed for this kind of theater, this East Bay, crack-of-dawn drama Turner had been preparing and rehearsing so long. I tried to talk myself into a better mood by remembering the way I'd felt when I'd made the decision to put the dead soldier at the center of the collage.

While we waited, Turner told me about a passive demonstration against the war that was getting popular and designed to harass the San Jose draft board, his local.

"You may want to think about this," he smiled.

He said he had subscribed to the *New York Times*, including the Sunday edition, in his name and given the draft board's address as his. "They have to keep everything you send them in a file," he laughed, head against the window. "Phone books, magazines, letters, yearbooks, cans of food, everything." The *New York Times* idea was actually the inspiration of a high school friend of his who had burned his draft card way back and disappeared into Mexico, or Canada. "Or, he's probably right here in the Bay Area," Turner said and stretched. "What he really wanted to do was get a gig as the janitor at the Fillmore or the Avalon Ballroom. Figured he'd get to see all the acts for free. He's a Mike Bloomfield freak."

We were not far from the building where he was supposed to report for his swearing-in. It was gray as the just-before-dawn sky. A blue metal sign alongside the concrete walk that led to twin sets of revolving doors said it was Building II, with the subtitle: United States Army. As it got near seven o'clock, Turner got firmly back into his energy crazed role and said he wanted me to go with him as far as they would allow. "You gotta witness this, Vic."

"Are they going to arrest you after you tell them no?"

"No," he said. "At least I don't think."

"What if they do?"

"Then they do." And he turned and rummaged in the back seat for a big envelope he said he had been instructed to bring along to the swearing-in. A few empty beer bottles, paper cups and bags Sara's cookies had been in cluttered the back seat. He found his envelope with the official-looking postmark and turned around. "They won't though." He opened the door. "You with me?"

"Sure. What the hell."

He grinned his crazy grin and hopped out, slamming the door. "Solid, brother," and he stepped out across the asphalt to the walk at Building II.

The night before as we'd passed the apartment on the way down off the hill at the Y I could see a bunch of people who looked like they were partying. Strange cars filled the lot at the foot of the stairs. I told Turner I sure as hell hoped no one would mess with my collage. It was almost covering the whole wall at the end of the hall and it had taken on a definite antiwar theme. At least that was what I was trying to achieve. LIFE's dead cover soldier was right in the center, and as I added pictures and words, I wanted it all to relate to him, his empty stare, his death. I'd also sewn a small American flag on the sleeve of my fatigue jacket, upside down. I would get stares sometimes but it was my small public statement. Like it or leave it. It pissed off Shanahan when he saw it, but he wrote it off as stupid college boy horseshit. He told me I didn't have enough sense to come in out of the rain. But the truth was that ever since he had gone on days I wasn't around him that much, and when I was he seemed different somehow from when we first met. Wasn't quite as talkative and loud. Couple of times when he said hello to me, I thought I smelled booze. Earlier in the summer, he was always drinking a Coke or coffee. Always had a glass of something like that in his hand. But shit, everyone drank something in that kitchen, until you got nailed, then it was your ass.

I caught up to Turner just before the revolving doors. "I'm starving, man. How long do you think this is going to take?"

"How long does it take to say, no, thank you." And he pushed through the door and was gone. I let one section spin pass, then jumped in and was spit out into a large, plain marble-floored lobby with a metal desk. It was flanked by an American flag on a stand on one side and the California state flag on the other. Behind, centered on the wall, a framed picture of President Nixon. That made me think of the magazine picture that stuck to Sara. And I felt a little shame, but it passed and I was overtaken by an urge to have sex with her again. Turner and I had never talked about what had happened between Sara and me. I don't know if Sara ever mentioned it to him. A couple of times when we were together, I hoped she would come onto me again, but she didn't. Never even got close. Like nothing ever happened.

113

"You gentlemen here to be inducted?" A large black woman with a badge, not military, behind the desk looked up from a magazine.

"Well, yeah," I said. "Sort of."

Turner practically yelled, "I am."

The woman looked back at me, bored but curious. "You are? You ain't? Which?"

I said I'd like to watch my friend go through the process. She told me I couldn't go all the way, but I could get close. "The hall. You can hear, maybe see some."

Turner hugged his big envelope and walked up to the desk. "Which way?"

"Down the hall to the left, then two halls down to Room 202. It's on the right. Someone will direct you. Sign here first," she said. And she spun a black notebook around. "Both." Turner signed his name, the time and date, and I immediately started to worry that if he did get in trouble today, they'd know who I was and that I was an accomplice to the whole deal. I remembered the name of one of the soldiers from LIFE and wrote his name down on impulse and somehow felt like I'd stepped into a new life. I felt deceptive and it felt good.

Other inductees had come in while we were in the lobby. We'd seen others go in while we waited in the car. Everyone carried the big envelope. You could tell some of the guys had new haircuts and their self-consciousness was painful to watch, the way they walked and the angle they held their head, like the lack of hair knocked them off balance.

There were some real freaks, too, and at least ten black
guys who hung together. Nobody was smiling or cutting up.
One or two came with someone else like parents or a
girlfriend. One skinny girl who reminded Turner and me of
Kathy had to be pried off her boyfriend's arm where two
soldiers in uniform stopped anyone at the door to 202 who
wasn't being inducted. Benches along the wall were hard
and uncomfortable. The skinny girl went into the bathroom
down the hall, and I could hear her crying and the toilet
flushing. When she came out, she looked down at me a
second with a beaten look, then bent over a water fountain
and didn't drink, but let the water bounce off her lips, and
then she left. A black woman in a long brown coat holding a
big purse clamped by both hands, and her husband, wearing
a San Francisco Giants cap, tried to see around the soldiers
at the door, but were persuaded they should, "...find a seat in
the hall area if they would like to remain." The soldier's flat
direction showed no emotion. One of the soldiers, I think he
was a sergeant, said to the father, "Sir, once they are sworn
in, they will not be able to talk to you. They will be exiting out
a different door to the bus."

The husband looked at his wife who, looked like she was
about to faint. "Honey," he began and reached out for her,
and she looked at him as if he was speaking a different
language, or had lost her hearing. They both turned to the
sergeant. Their open confusion made me cringe. The soldier
stood stiff, hands at his back, feet a shoulder's width apart,
and I wanted him to give a little. The woman pulled a tissue
from her coat sleeve and held it to her nose.

"Sorry, sir." he said, "Sorry, ma'am."

He looked across at me on the bench as if he was expecting a question, or maybe daring me to ask one. For some reason I chirped, "Solid, brother," then avoided his eyes and looked down the hallway wall lined with formal portraits of past Army secretaries. Their perfect spacing, the perfect row, reminded me of the dead soldier pictures in *LIFE*. I wondered how many of these guys were still alive. As he'd challenged me with his stare, the guard squinted at my upside down flag. I thought about Suicide Dave, my own reaction to his hat band, the irony of my situation at the moment and how this soldier's eyes reminded me of Suicide Dave. The mother started blubbering and the husband held her a long time. Then, finally, the two of them went back down through the hard hall, her wails bouncing off the marble in the glare. It was tough to watch something so sad, and I wished I could have softened up the walls and floors so her sadness could be soaked up somehow instead of being amplified. The sentries locked their eyes on a point somewhere on the wall over my shoulder.

I had no interest in pissing off the guards by trying to see into 202. But I figured there must be a total of about fifty guys inside. The milling about and the noise of chairs sliding across tile and the pieces of conversations came to a stop and was replaced by one authoritative sounding voice, sharp and definitely in control. I tried to picture Turner, of course on the edge of his chair, chomping gum, his eyes wide, leg pumping like he was working a loom, anticipating the moment when he could say, "No." In my mind, the other guys in the room were slumping, resigned, dreading the coming moment when they would be ordered, "...on the bus in double time, your asses are mine now."

The soldiers at the door weren't much older than me, I

guessed. And if they weren't in the position of having to play the roles of guard dogs at the moment, I wondered if they might not be all right guys, okay if we had met in different circumstances. It was like my Prince Charles, David Eisenhower game. There were two guys my age, but clearly from different places, means and experience. But they were my exact age and every once in a while I'd wonder what it might be like if we checked in on each other every five years or so, say to throw a ball around the back yard or shoot the breeze. What we might find in common, if anything. Like, "What did Ike tell you about World War Two, Dave? And Charlie, what's it like living in a castle?" You guys want to hear about my first Redlegs game?" Now I'd probably ask them about 'Nam. But there was about as much chance of me playing Pickle with David and Charlie as there was shooting the shit with these two to kill some time while I cooled my heels waiting for Turner. I did wonder a second if I might be wearing a uniform in a few months myself, and what I would do at this exact moment if the tables were turned. But I ran from that thought.

While I waited for Turner to come out, since it was Wednesday, I thought about Lee and Skin and their weekly visit to the Moonlight Ranch. Right now I knew Lee would still be asleep, passed out, just in from a post-shift drink 'em up somewhere on the hill. Once when his brother was in town from Sacramento, they got so hammered his brother got on the wrong Trailways bus trying to go home and ended up in Reno. They shook him awake and threw him on the next bus going the other way. I couldn't believe you could get that smashed. Lee was always in some stage of being drunk, but for the most part, he functioned. I knew his patterns. Thursdays he was really in pain. He didn't talk, wasn't his usual jive self and his hands shook badly. And no amount of after-shave could cover the sweat, the sweet, smell of alcohol coming out of his pores. He was in the bathroom lots on Thursdays and usually sent me down the street to the drug store to get him paregoric. Most of the time on Fridays he was back to normal, teasing Tony behind his back, joking about his bow legs and telling stories about Karlene and the Ranch. He started talking about taking me to Reno with him and Skin, which both excited and scared me to death. But I couldn't tell if he was joking. By the time the end of the shift came the next Tuesday, he was all excited, whistling jazz tunes while he cooked, answering questions about anything with, "Pally, all the cats are meowin', now what can I do you for?" He told me once I was as nimble as a wedding photographer the way I zoomed around the kitchen with the mop.

Pulling out of the Induction Center, Turner was sky high. "Well?" I asked. I looked over my shoulder, half expecting to be followed.

He was pounding the steering wheel. "Oh shit man, it was so bitchin'," was all he could say for blocks before we found an Orange Julius and pulled into a space.

He sucked half of a large one down before he talked. He had an eggy white mustache on his lip that made me think of the one Redding was trying to grow. "Vic, I felt like the only kid in class with the answer to the teacher's question. I couldn't wait to jump up and tell them I wasn't going to go."

"What happened?" I said, "Tell me what everybody else did."

"Quick. It was really quick. An officer got us to line up in rows of eight. All the black guys stood together, made rows of their own. We had to put our hands over our hearts while he read some stuff about defending the country, responsibility to serve if asked kinda things..."

"Were you scared?" I asked. "You know, trapped, like nowhere out?" The fog had burned off and the day was starting to heat up. A damp salt breeze off the bay blew through the open windows of the Volvo. And I realized we were nosed into a parking place, cars on both sides.

"Man, my heart was pounding. I'm surprised you couldn't hear it in the hall. Then when he was done, he said with a step forward we would become United States Army. He was polite, actually."

"What happened?"

"Everybody stepped forward," and Turner tipped his yellow and orange cup back, slurped and looked over at me and said, "but me."

I said, "Yeah," and tried to imagine the moment.

"Well, first, everyone in the room turned and looked at me. The guy behind me stepped on my heels. It's crazy, but in an instant, I felt like I could read just about all their faces. A couple of them were mad looking, one or two of them laughed kinda nervously. I think the black guys and some of the others got pissed when they realized too late that there was another way to beat this shit besides faking a physical or leaving the country. But they all stared, spun around just looking at me standing at attention with my envelope at my side."

"What did the officer do? What'd he say?"

He said, "Sir, with this failure to step forward and accept your responsibility to be inducted into the United States Army, you will be prosecuted to the full extent of the law. At this time, you still have the opportunity to be inducted at no jeopardy."

Turner looked at me and yelled, "Can you believe that?"

I said, "Right..."

"Actually it musta happened before, he didn't seem too pissed."

"What then? This must have been at about the time that the two guys guarding the door looked in to see what was going on."

"Well there was some quiet, and they were all still staring and I just said, No, no thank you. I was very polite. I said, I played by the rules. No, I refuse to be inducted. Then he yelled at the others and told them to go out the rear door of the room and get on the bus that was waiting to take them to Fort Ord. At that point he was pissed, but I think it was for their benefit. You know, show. He didn't give a fuck about me. His whole attitude was way out there," said Turner. "I feel sorry for those guys."

"That was it?"

"Yeah," he said. "By the time I came out into the hall, they were already gone out the back."

I said, "Those two guards at the door didn't quite know what to do. You messed up their heads, man." Turner had just looked at them when he came out and blew them off with one of his wide open, "How can you not like me" smiles. For a second I thought he might try hugging them. I had hopped up off the bench and went back down the hall to the front door feeling like we had skipped out on a check at Tippy's. And Turner, playing by his rules to the end, insisted we sign out with the lady at the desk. I couldn't believe it. He was still smiling and minding his manners. The woman looked us over without saying anything with an expression I couldn't pin down, then we went through the revolving door back out to the walk.

At Orange Julius I asked him again, "You're not worried? You know, the future. Jail. That kinda shit," thinking at the same time we had a more immediate problem if Sara's Volvo wouldn't shift into reverse.

Turner smiled. "Remember, I am very clear about myself, Victor. I've envisioned my future." And he straightened and turned the ignition and spoke to the windshield. "You know, Vic, when you are feeling good about yourself, thinking clearly, then everything you see when you look out, in the future, the past, now...it's all very clear, too. I feel fine. Shit, man, I feel fucking great." And he looked at me. And before he shifted the gears, he said, "And when you're feeling great, things work for you. And to prove it, I'm gonna make this car go backwards." And with that and a goofy shoulder shake for drama, he dropped the Volvo into reverse and put his foot on the accelerator. We sat and listened to the engine rev. It sounded like the grease man's lift gate straining to hoist a barrel of old fry grease to the truck bed. "Shit..."

I said, "Shit"...and I looked out to my right at the gooey face of a thirtyish woman pulling hard on an Orange Julius through a straw, watching us, wincing at the sound of the Volvo whining.

On the way back to Tahoe, after we'd pushed the car out of the space, I kept thinking about Turner and what he'd said about being clear about yourself and seeing things clearly, mainly because I was as confused as ever and definitely headed south on the clear thinking map. The way I saw it, the world was fucked up and so was I, and I didn't know who to blame. What I knew at the moment was I wanted to see Rennie again and I wanted to work on my collage. Both were drawing me in, becoming very important. That was as far as I could go. On those two scores I was not mixed up.

For the moment.

As we crossed over the summit, The Youngbloods were on the radio singing about helplessness. I said, "Perfect," and turned up the volume.

Chapter 8

Turner and I had managed to spend most of the day and early into the night getting back from Oakland. We made a stop on Telegraph Avenue in Berkeley that turned into a major event when he tried to find some special Thai incense Sara had heard of. We watched a big rally against the war in People's Park, with a bunch of freaks and speeches, and all kinds of crazy shit. I didn't see any Black Panthers. Turner had to check it all out. At the rally they burned an American flag and hung President Nixon in effigy, but the cops didn't seem to care. The ones I saw just let things happen. The Calhoun Street riot flew in and out of my mind and I smelled pot, musk and candle wax everywhere we walked. Wind chimes hung in doorways, music came out of windows, and musicians crowded the street playing for coins. I threw a quarter into a hat case and got a big bow from a crazy-looking guy playing a flute, who wasn't very good.

When we got back to the apartment at the Y, we were both burnt. I was dead on my ass and fell onto my mattress, crashed, and didn't wake up until it was time to go to work on Thursday. I never even took off my jeans. The last thing I looked at was the soldier on the collage. And I made a mental note to buy the latest edition of *LIFE*.

At the end of the shift on Thursday, I was still wrecked, but Rennie had suggested we go down to the Sahara and have a drink, catch the free lounge act and use up some drink tokens a player had given her as a tip. I couldn't pass on that. She wanted to know how it all went in Oakland. Talking to her in the alcove earlier in the shift, I caught Lee, Redding and Turner standing in the corner near the walk-in, heads together, checking the two of us out. I loved it. Redding and

Turner were smiling, and Lee had that day after the Moonlight Ranch sick look. If Rennie noticed, she was cool, never gave it away. Blew them off.

Later, Kathy came in from the dining room and said, "ShitDevilDickDamnPiss. There are some of the ugliest people I have ever laid eyes on in my entire life out there today. There's a fat man—you can barely see his little BB eyes in the folds—with a skinny old wife with her mouth hangin' open. They are so hideous they should have signs around their necks." She lit a cigarette and dropped the match in a half filled coffee cup in a full bus tray I was emptying. She went "ssssss," as the match died in the cold coffee. "And you, college boy?"

"What, me?" I said, seeing that sometime in the last few weeks Kathy had put on some weight and didn't look as homely as she had when I met her and Mic. I figured Sweet Lou's attention was helping somehow. She also didn't look like someone who'd been sleeping in a Galaxie. I think she seemed happier, too. She had her head cocked and was studying me. "What, me?" I said again, scraping chicken bones into the garbage can next to my Hobart.

She held her cigarette between two fingers out to the side of her head. "You know..."

"Know what?"

"You and that gal from Tucson. The dealer, Rennie," Kathy said, and raised her eyebrows.

"What's that mean? We had a drink the other night." Beaner plopped another full bus tray on the counter. Some forks clanged to the floor. I turned and closed the door on the machine and hit the knob and started a cycle. Redding and Turner were sliding chicken trays into the oven and arguing about what was the best Blood, Sweat and Tears song, but between them and the Hobart, I had to lean over to hear what Kathy was saying.

"Oh, it don't mean nothin'. Just Danny boy told me the way you was lookin' at her. Said you had the face of a dyin' calf in a hail storm." And she smiled. "My words," and she dropped her cigarette into a plate of cold macaroni and cheese and turned to go back through the alcove. She blew smoke to the ceiling.

"Where do you get that stuff?" I said. "What the hell does a dying calf got to do with anything, anyhow?" She wiggled her butt at me as an answer and was gone. Beaner saw that and shook his head as he lugged a stack of plates out to the line.

The grease man showed up during my break. We talked about grease. We stood on the stoop at the back door after he'd loaded the full barrel and rolled a new one in place and discussed all the pickups he had to do in a day. His route took him all over the area, Douglas County, over to Carson City and Reno, North Shore. "All over," he said. "All over."

"Where's it go? What do you do with it?"

He wiped his hands on his apron, then mopped his face with his forearm. He had streaks of grease, like war paint, on his cheeks. "Make stuff. Clean it up and make new stuff." And he slapped me on the back, jumped in his truck and gunned out of the lot leaking a stream of something from the bed onto the gravel as he went up the road toward Reno.

Rennie had a three-year-old Chevy Nova, and we rode down to the Sahara after work, down South Lake Boulevard and parked next to it in the huge car lot. A dozen tour buses were lined nose to tail down near the lake. We went in the same door Suicide Dave had dropped me in front of the night I'd come to town. I couldn't believe I'd been around almost six weeks. That night was still with me.

Inside we sat on bar stools along a railing that circled the audience for the lounge acts, the free entertainment that pulled the gamblers in. You could pay to see the headliners like The Four Freshman, Neil Diamond, The Fifth Dimension, Jerry Vale or others like them for the dinner show, but that was a two-drink minimum and real dough. In the lounge were small tables for the audience, glass globes in the middle. People talking and laughing, hanging out, half listening to the acts. The crowd was about the same as it was at The Mine Shaft, just a helluva lot more of them. Slots and tables and people jammed the main floor area on our other side. It seemed as big as a football field compared to our casino. And noisy as a jet engine. I had to yell at the waitress when I ordered our Seven and Sevens. On stage a band and five black guys in red sequined suits sang Motown tunes. They were pretty good, one guy always out of step, but the audience was pretty much with them. Waitresses balancing trays over their heads would swoop in as hands were raised to call for more drinks or the check. People stood around the sides smoking, holding drinks, swaying or bobbing their heads at the music. Red light flooded everything. I felt self-conscious dressed in my fatigue jacket, hair getting longer, sideburns down to my jaw line almost grown in. I'd learned by now Tahoe was about one thing: money. And money was all about control as Lee had preached to me. And a lot of that has to do with the way you look. He'd also said, "Control and surprises don't mix, babe. Surprises upset the apple cart and you and that flag jacket could surprise some of the wrong cats." He'd warned, "The apple cart up here on the hill is filled with money that all these chumps who eat our food leave behind at the slots and the tables. So be cool. Watch your toodling ass." I knew security at all the casinos in Tahoe was tight, and I looked around to see if could spot the Butcher of the Sahara.

Rennie and I leaned close so we could hear each other, and I tried to tell to her what had happened in Oakland. She complained about the smoke in her hair, but to me, that combined with the smell of her hair spray was so toxic it almost made me high. When she listened, she tapped her tooth and up close I could make out that tiny scar on her forehead. I focused on it while we talked. We ordered two more drinks she paid for, and she dropped five Mine Shaft dollar chips as a tip. "So? What do you make of it?"

And I pulled myself out of her face after I finished the Oakland story. She looked over the crowd as the band finished a set and looked back at me. I could read her lips over the applause, but asked her to say it again anyway.

"He's a high minded boy," she said again. "Like I said the other night. I hope his little merry go round keeps turning. Why's he got to be such a nonconformist anyway? What's his hang up?"

But right then, something happened across the lounge, exciting people against the opposite railing. A small group, hard to see, pushed along the inside of the railing perimeter. Heads were turning. A couple flash bulbs went off. Someone began shaking hands with the crowd. Whoever it was creating the excitement, the crowd was fighting to touch them. I said, "Can you see?"

Rennie said, "Nope."

Then I said, "Look. You know who that is?"

"Nope."

"It's Fats Domino." And I spun around on my stool to watch him and his entourage as they came our way. He autographed a napkin. He kissed a woman. He waved. He let a guy stand next to him and have a picture taken. His guys, both at least a full head taller, were all over him like secret service guarding Nixon. He reached and shook more hands.

Rennie said, "He's so little."

"Yeah," as I thought about what I could get him to sign. "But he's cool. I love New Orleans."

"Been there?"

"Want to..." I started to hum *Walkin' to New Orleans* as he got closer. Then I remembered the two dollar bill my Dad had given me on my thirteenth birthday. "For good luck, son. Don't ever spend it." It was so out of character and creative for him. After I'd gotten over the initial shock, I tucked it into the corner of my wallet. I'd carried it ever since. It had been washed by accident, and lost for periods of time, almost been spent more than once out of desperation. I had no idea whether it had ever brought me, or would bring me, good luck, but I had managed to hang onto it anyway. I'd shown it to Lee one day and he'd said it'd be a toodlin' idea to get signatures of important people on it. "If you ever meet any," and he'd broken up laughing and pointed at Tony who was pissing and moaning about something or other at the time. So when Fats got to me I shoved the bill at him with a, "Would you mind?" He grinned real big at Rennie who was calm enough to realize he needed a pen and she handed him one from her purse and gave him a smile. And Fats looked at her forever. And I looked at him. He had on sparkly rings on stubby fingers with shiny pink finger nails, and ruffled cuffs. His eyes were happy, and you could see Rennie made them happier. He held her hand with the pen for what seemed like an hour, then turned to me, winked and signed the bill, holding it against the back of one of his guys as he wrote. The sequins on his powder blue Edwardian suit reflected the red lights. His hair was conked in tight waves, and his sweet cologne smelled like flowers. He gave Rennie a short bow, blew her a kiss, gave me a thumbs-up and moved on like a little king with his guys.

I looked at the bill and read, *Luck! Fats Domino!* The signature was big and loopy, *Luck!* above Thomas Jefferson's head, *Fats Domino!* under it. I watched him climb three short steps to the stage and then disappear and was pissed when the lounge band came out and Fats wasn't with them. Before they began their second set, one of the band, now wearing lime green jump suits and matching shoes, acknowledged, "The thrill of having Mr. Domino in the audience tonight at the Sahara."

Rennie said, "He's cute."

I said, "Please sign," and gave her pen back and focused on the scar on her forehead while she tapped her tooth and thought about where to write her name on the bill.

Later, Rennie asked me back to her apartment and it surprised me as much as having Fats Domino turn up from nowhere to sign my two dollar bill. And I thought of Lee and what he'd said once: "Surprises, Vic. Always be on the lookout for surprises."

He told me that the same day he warned me, "Never look in the mirror when you're drunk."

We didn't talk first. I put some wine we'd bought on a table by her front door. She put her keys on the same table, kicked her shoes away and turned to me. She stood on her toes and put her arms around my neck. She sighed into my neck, then pushed back slightly and just looked at me. I loved her smell and had to catch my breath. Light from a pole on the far side of the parking lot came in through the blinds, past a lamp and a dried flower arrangement and threw a crisscross shadow in front of our feet. She wore an oval turquoise ring where her wedding band used to be and I could feel it against me. When I looked at her, she held her mouth open some and looked back at me like I'd just shared a big secret. Part of the shadow covered her eyes like a mask, and for a second she was blindfolded, and I buried my head in her neck and forgot where I was.

The next night was a carbon copy without Mr. Fats Domino. And the next. Every night for the next week we left the casino together and went to her apartment. Gradually we fell into a routine there, and at work. At work, besides the usual small talk in the alcove, she was all business no matter how hard I tried to get her attention when I had an excuse to be in the casino, like when Lee sent me to fetch a bottle of wine.

But when we were away from The Mine Shaft and the bullshit, we couldn't get enough of each other. There was so much heat. I'd never known it. And, old as she was, she acted like she'd never let go like she did with me. I loved it. It was a dream having Rennie to look forward to after eight hours of scraping Mine Shaft leftovers off plates and shoving racks through the Hobart.

Usually we would take some food I'd boosted from the kitchen and go to her furnished little one bedroom up one of the side streets not too far from The Mine Shaft. We'd drink cheap wine then put some records on and smoke a joint, eat, than get it on. White Bird always seemed to be playing. It was her favorite.

But first she liked to talk. She needed it, used it to relax. Had to revisit Mr. Asshole and the way he had treated her, and talk about her daughter and her weekly calls to her mother. We tried not to talk about work. In between sips of wine, she would hold a gulp of pot in her lungs and blow it out, then, in between little hacks wonder how she could have been so dumb to marry a jerk like him. Swore she'd never marry again.

"Ever."

"Oh, c'mon."

"Oh, no, I don't think so, Vic." She said. "I attract assholes. I'm a damn asshole magnet."

Sometimes she cried. She let me hold her, but I got the feeling she felt that was a sign of weakness. But she said once she started, "I can't stop."

Eventually, she would slow down though...wind down...run her finger up and down the side of the glass stem, try to smile her "bad girl smile" and say, "I'm having impure thoughts." She said she used to be a Catholic. "Sex was never very good with him," she said. "Never. It hurt. Couldn't get excited. I didn't enjoy it until you and I started doing it. I didn't get it."

"I love doing it with you."

It was the anytime, anyway, no rules nature of our sex that really turned me on. She asked for nothing. Nada. She loved doing it and would try anything. At her age she didn't act as experienced as I thought someone who'd been married would be. She sure wasn't as rough and selfish as Sara, and played zero games compared to Elaine. Truth really was Rennie made herself available, left it all up to me. But she didn't make any judgements or demands...except to leave her alone at the casino...and she was just willing all the time. Just wanted to do it. That was the turn on. No games. No jive.

After, propped on an elbow, sooner or later she would always say, "Is this the part where we fall asleep then wake up and do it again?" It was like she was acting out things she had been thinking about for a long time. Or reading about. I didn't care. I was learning with her. I was hooked.

"I'm glad you know how to do this," she once told me as we did it in the back of her Nova in the parking lot at one a.m. after work. We couldn't wait to get into the apartment. It was scary and exciting. We had to stop quick and duck as a guy scuffed through the parked cars. I felt like a jewel thief.

The July 2nd issue of *LIFE* had a strange picture on the cover. It showed a tiny Dustin Hoffman as Ratso Rizzo standing on John Wayne's head from the new movie, *Midnight Cowboy*. The Duke was dressed as a cowboy. The story was about heroes, new ones, old ones. But it was perfect for my collage. Sara was always telling me how groovy she thought the collage was. But she didn't seem interested in getting it on with me anymore. By my count, since we had screwed that afternoon a few weeks back, she had banged about five different guys, not including Turner. One of them was a scary-looking black dude she met hitchhiking. She brought him to the apartment and let him spend the night. I woke up on my mattress the next morning with the two of them standing naked over me, checking out the collage.

"Just showing Damu your work, Victor. He digs it. He's an artist, too. Works with metal. A welder," she said looking down.

"Right on, man," Damu said. "Super righteous," he said very seriously, taking in the collage. He looked about nine feet tall, had a dick as big as a beef tongue from the kitchen and a smoldering joint in his hand that seemed the same size.

All I could say was, "Thanks. I don't know when it will be done though."

"Oh, you'll know," said Damu. He took a hit on the joint and offered it to me. I said, "Nah," and he handed it to Sara. He draped an arm around her neck, and with smoke tunneling out his nostrils, he said very emphatically, "You will know when it's done. It will tell you, or you will just stop. Either way it will be done."

133

I just wanted to catch a few more Z's. All I could think to say was, "Cool. Thanks."

He smiled down on me and Sara took his hand and they walked back down the hall. I listened to them rustling around in the kitchen, and I managed to go back to sleep.

****

For the life of me I don't know why Tony hired the big ape. I guess things were just so busy in Tahoe in the middle of the summer and the job pool was so thin that if you could stand up and say your name you could get a job in a casino kitchen. That had to be the case with Big Ed.

When I saw him for the first time walking behind Tony from the kitchen door out to one of the tables in the restaurant between lunch and dinner service to fill out an application, it looked like a guy in a circus leading out the big dumb bear to hop around on a stool in one of the rings. Tony should have had a leash.

Tony put him on the pot and pan sink. It was like he had voices, or music, in his head that made it bob up and down all the time. Then he would stop the bobbing and jerk his head to the side and stare off, like he was being called. He was real tall, bald except for a ring of hair, dark and Italian looking with super long arms. And he did not talk. We figured he was crazy and was cut loose to drift around in the world for fucking something up somewhere. So we made a game out of trying to guess what he had been before he screwed up and landed in our kitchen. He looked to be about thirty. The only thing he uttered was, "Jesus Christ," which was all purpose in the kitchen, in English, Spanish and Italian. Every way except reverently. Kathy even ended ShitDevilDickDamnPiss" with "Jesus Christ" once in a while.

Lee thought Big Ed was entertaining and used to stand and try to talk to him while he slogged through the pots and pans. Big Ed would smile a goofy smile, bob and dunk pans and never really make eye contact. Lee leaned over the counter at the Hobart once and said, "Seems like a harmless cat, pally. Just a smidgen over cooked, maybe," and he winked and walked off sipping from his coffee cup. Big Ed didn't seem harmless to me, and I stayed away from him. When I ran the mop over the kitchen, I stayed away from the pot and pan sink and his crusty shoes. But he showed up every day for work, giggling his giggly laugh. He freaked me out. And I hated the way he looked at the girls when they came into the alcove or the kitchen.

One Thursday Lee was in worse shape than normal. He was at work, but he looked like hell. He didn't do much after Tony went home but sit on a stool and direct the rest of us in getting the chicken panned, and the lasagna and the goopy ham sauce made, and the other stuff that had to be prepped for the line. I made the run down to the drugstore at break time and cut through the casino to catch a glimpse of Rennie, who had a full table. She didn't look up. Butcher was hanging nearby watching the action. Danny gave me a wink and I winked back as I passed. After I bought the paregoric, I got the new *LIFE*, dated July 18. The cover was a hippie family and friends. They wore beads, beards and buckskin and granny dresses. The story was about communes. One of the girls in the picture reminded me of Sara. I wondered if this girl banged every guy she met.

Back in the kitchen Redding came over to the Hobart and said he needed me to help him chop lettuce. We both checked out Big Ed at the sink holding a sauce pan in front of his face, studying it like he was looking in a mirror.

"He's a crazy fucker," said Redding.

I said, "No shit. Put him in your book."

Just then Shanahan, who'd been gone since three, came in the back door. He more or less fell through it and stopped and looked up at Big Ed, who still had the pan in his hand and that silly look on his face. Shanahan was weaving and looked to be pretty drunk. I'd never seen him like that. He had his arms shoved into a short denim jacket, his ball cap low on his head, and he was working a toothpick over good. He looked up at Big Ed and said with a wide grin, "How's yore hammer hangin', Bigfoot?" Big Ed just rocked back and forth and grinned back at Shanahan.

I yelled, "Hey, Mic." But he just kept smiling at Big Ed, who looked back, the pan still in his hairy puckered fingers.

Then he turned slowly to me and I could see his eyes were lidded heavy and he said, "Hey, college boy, how's yore hammer hangin'?" Then he said, taking a wobbly step toward Redding and me, "Ya'll boys do me a favor, will ya? Go fetch Kathy. I need to talk to her. I ain't been able to run her down lately."

Redding pushed me a little and said, "I'll get her." I asked him if Sweet Lou was on tonight?"

"No," he said. "Butcher."

"Shit," I said. Redding took off through the alcove.

Lee wandered over with his coffee cup. His hands jittered like the floor was being jack hammered. He could barely get the cup to his mouth without spilling the wine. Shanahan said, "Lordy, lordy, Lee. Don't start me to lyin', but you look like forty miles of you know what."

"Well, thank you, babe," trying to be blasé through his hangover. "The shift is about over, and as soon as these toodler friends of mine, and you if you'd care to, help me find my car, I'm going to Inka Dinka Doo myself to bed so I can get my beauty sleep, get up, throw up and then come back for one more day of polishing this turd of a kitchen."

"Weeoohwee…touch me and *touché*," was what Shanahan came back with.

I shot a look at Lee. Nobody…not Redding or Turner…nobody had mentioned anything about hunting for his car tonight though we had done it before.

"How 'bout it, pally?"

Rennie was on my mind. But I felt obligated to the guys and Lee. "Sure. Okay. Got any ideas?" Turner shook his head.

More than once Lee and Skin had lost the Calais on one of their Moonlight Ranch drunks. They'd park it somewhere in or around Tahoe and forget where. They wouldn't have a clue. We found it once at the marina at Zephyr Cove almost in the lake. Another time it was in the woods off Route 89 on the way to North Shore. Lately it was becoming a Thursday ritual to try to find it. Shanahan hopped some to his left to get his balance. "I need a drink."

I said, "You know Butcher's on, Mic."

"Fuck some Butcher." He reached for Lee's coffee cup as
Redding and Kathy appeared in the alcove. Redding kept
coming. Kathy stopped between the ovens and the sink and
looked at us. She stared at Mic, his arm still out.

"Hey, baby..." Shanahan said. Kathy didn't budge. "I been
tryin' to run you down, hon. I need a favor." Then as if he
was noticing the change in her looks for the first time, said
"Boy, you look scrumptious..."

"What?" Her arms folded, hip stuck out.

"It's embarrassing in front of you boys," he apologized to us.
I felt bad for him. I saw Big Ed checking out Kathy. I was
worried Butcher was going to show up. My eye started
jittering for the first time in weeks. Mic leaned and lowered
his voice like none of us would hear and said, "I need a few
simoleons, sugar. I hit a bad streak at the dice table down
the street." His gold tooth flashed. "Whattaya say, hon? Toss
me a penny. Payday's in a week. I'll make it good."

Beaner came walking by Kathy, ignorant of it all and yelled,
"Lee, some guy is complaining that the tongue is gone. Got
anymore? We eighty-six on..." Then he saw he was in the
middle of something and turned and went back into the
restaurant.

Kathy stared at her dad, narrowed her eyes at us, then said,
"Daddy, I ain't givin' you money to gamble and drink." She
stamped her foot and said, "ShitDevil..." then stopped and

burst into tears, spun and went back to the restaurant. Big Ed started to chuckle his insane little chuckle and before I could get him, Shanahan had pulled his knife out of his pants pocket, pried it open and swung it at Big Ed, who didn't mean to use the sauce pan for a shield, but Shanahan's drunken swing was so wild he hit it by accident. The knife fell onto the floor. Redding and I grabbed Shanahan by each arm at the same time, his feet gave on the slippery tile floor around the sink, and he brought all three of us down. Lee backed up and said, "Jesus fucking H Christ," and looked toward the alcove.

"I'll cut yore head off with this frog sticker, buddy, and pour that scummy sink water down yore neck, you crazy piece of shit. Don't you ever laugh at me..." Big Ed grinned down at Shanahan.

Lee said, "It's almost midnight, Ed. Take off. Go on. It's all right." Shanahan was still fighting us to get up off the floor.

Big Ed splashed the sauce pan back in the sink water still holding that silly look on his face, took off his apron, neatly let it fall into the hamper and went out the door. I focused on the hair that grew up his back, out of his shirt into the hair at the base of his neck.

Shanahan watched him go and when the door closed said, "This floor's slicker than cum on a door knob, you pussies. Lemme up. Help me, dammit."

We got Shanahan calmed down and gave him his Case back. Turner put together a roast beef sandwich, and we made him drink some coffee out back where Butcher wouldn't see him. Kathy didn't come looking, and Mic said nothing else about her or money. He did swear he'd kill Big Ed if he crossed him again though. Said, "That retard'll be gurgling that little laugh for the Lord if he don't watch himself." He said he was dyin' for barbecue, even though he said the roast beef sandwich was, "Dick in the dirt good. Ain't eaten all day. Been at the tables." Then, like he was letting us all in on a big secret, he said to Redding, Turner and me while Lee changed in the stockroom, "Quiet as it's kept, fellas, if you put vinegar in a skillet, fried ham will taste just like barbecue. Let's get Lee to try it sometime. How 'bout it?" We were shivering in the night air and we said, "No, shit? Really?" and "C'mon..." all at the same time.

"Bet that, buddy," said Shanahan.

The door opened and Lee came out in his suit and dress hat. He had his knife briefcase. He said, "The gout is killing me," to no one in particular.

"Where should we start looking? You got any idea?" I asked again. I was hoping to get this over with then get somebody to drop me at Rennie's. Turner must have been reading me.

He said, "Going to Rennie's, huh?"

"Yeah."

Shanahan took that in and said to everyone but me, "College boy probably never had anything that good before," and everyone laughed. Then he winked at me.

"Fuck you, Mic." I said.

"Fuck me," he laughed and lit a cigarette.

Redding said, "I'll drive," and trotted off to get his new Volkswagen. He was so proud. Turner said, "Will we all fit?"

Shanahan said, "I ain't goin'. Good luck," and went over to the Galaxie, got in and turned on the engine, but didn't go anywhere. When we drove out he was listening to the radio, leaning back, cigarette smoke curling out the half opened driver's window.

We drove all over Tahoe, the four of us, Redding at the wheel. Lee, briefcase on his lap, rode shotgun, Turner and me in the back seat. We met Skin in the drive-through in front of the Sahara. He was no help. He leaned in the window and told us the last time he saw Lee and the Calais was when he got dropped off at his girlfriend's house. Skin, who I was pretty sure was older than Lee, looked even worse than Lee from their night off, and I couldn't imagine what his "girlfriend" must look like.

Lee said, "Get any, pally?"

"Irma la Douce wasn't home. I jimmied the back door," he said. "I was knee walking blotto and she was mighty agitated with me when she came in." He leaned into Lee's ear, big spotty hands on the door frame, and raised his voice, "But I managed to accommodate the old girl." And he fell back, cackling, and brushed the front of his brown, double-breasted, pin-striped suit. It had padded shoulders and he had a white flower in the lapel. He was looking around like he wanted to brag to someone else.

Lee's head popped back like he was impressed. "Ah," to the windshield, as three drunks in suits with their ties undone tripped and stumbled across the drive. A long limousine had to brake to miss them. "What a toodler you are," he said. "How nice of you, Skinny. I'm sure she's grateful." I watched the limo pull out onto South Lake Boulevard, the lights from the big Sahara sign above reflecting onto it like a stream of sequins. Redding pulled out behind it and left Skin yukking it up with one of the door men. We looked in all the usual spots where we'd found the Calais before. It wasn't at Zephyr Cove or any of the casino parking lots, so after about an hour we gave up. We promised Lee we'd come by his place in the morning before work and look some more.

On the way to drop him off, Redding asked him if we ought to try Tippy's Tacos. All Lee said, drumming his fingers on his briefcase, was, "Mexican food's hard on me."

I couldn't help myself. "Hey, Lee. How do you lose a car?"

"Sorry, kid. I'm buffaloed. Just can't answer that. Just don't know."

Pulling up in front of his small apartment building, Lee started singing, *"Oh, where, oh where has my little Caddy gone...Oh where oh where can it be...?"* Then as Redding yanked the emergency brake and shifted the VW into neutral, Lee turned to us and said, "I think I could do with a short nightcap. Say what, fellas?" Opening the door and easing himself out he said, "How about a little scotch and milk before beddy bye?"

All I wanted to do was to get to Rennie's. It was about one-thirty already. Redding made a face in the rearview mirror and mouthed, "Scotch and milk?"

Turner pushed the seat up and jumped out and got in front

142

and said, "Shit, man, Lee. Cannot do that. We'll come by tomorrow around noon. All right?" He smothered Lee's invitation with Turner energy.

"Turned down by my toodlers," he winked. "Well, well. But thanks for the recon and lift anyway, boys." And Turner pulled the door shut.

"Easy," said Redding. "This thing's new." Turner looked at him like that was the most ridiculous thing he'd ever heard.

Then Lee tapped on the window and Turner rolled it down. "Got a match?" Redding pushed in the lighter before Turner could, and while he waited for it to pop out, Lee looked around the night, working the unlit cigarette up and down in his lips like a tiny, sawed off conductor's baton and sang through his teeth, *"Oh where, oh where has my little Caddy gone..."* And Turner held out the lighter.

"Careful," he said as Lee aimed the cigarette at his hand.

"There we are," said Lee as he dragged, and he straightened from the car and saluted us and limped away singing his ditty. Redding shook his head and pushed hair out of his eyes and said, "Scotch and milk. Really?"

I said, "Can you drop me at Rennie's?"

Turner looked over the seat at me, and said, "Oh, shit, Victor. You going to accommodate her?"

I woke her from a deep sleep after some loud knocking. When she opened the door she had on a plain blue T-shirt and her hair was flat against her head. I hugged her. She smelled like soap. "You're hot," I said.

"I was buried in the bed," she said back. Then she took my hand and we walked to the bedroom. "Where've you been?"

I squeezed her shoulder and said, "Looking for a Cadillac. Wanna get high?"

Redding picked us up before noon and we let Turner out on the boulevard on the way to Lee's so he could look through the parking lots of Barney's and the Sahara in daylight. Lee's one-room apartment was a shoebox. A tiny open kitchenette at one end, a closet at the other, a fold-out couch for a bed against the wall. The place smelled like fresh paint and fried chicken. Lee was sitting at the edge of the bed over a carton of milk and a fifth of Usher's Green Stripe Scotch on the floor, cigarette in his mouth. The bottle had about two inches of liquor. An old hi-fi on a kitchen table was playing a jazz record. Trumpet music. The room was bright from the glare of a pie plate-sized fixture in the ceiling.

The first thing he said to Redding and me when we came through the unlocked door was, "Hey there, fellas," like he wasn't expecting us. "Either of you cats ever notice how well Lawrence Welk's suits fit him? I was just thinking about that." He sipped what looked like watery milk from a tall glass. "They lay on him like his own skin." And he smiled like he was picturing what he'd just said. Then, "C'mon in. What's up?" It was the first time I'd ever seen Lee without a hat. He was slick bald on top except for a few gray wisps that sprouted from a spot high on his forehead and a ring of fine hair the same color on the sides. He saw me looking and immediately pointed at his dress hat at the end of the bed. "The fedora, pally." I got it, handed it to him and he put it on.

Somehow he managed a cool look even though he was wearing an undershirt and white chef's pants. His bare feet were on two packages of new bed sheets still in the plastic wrap next to a bowl of ice cubes. The ball of his right foot was red and swollen. He was using a taped-up packing box as a bedside table. On it was an ashtray, an open carton of Camels, a wind-up alarm clock and a pair of dice. "What brings you toodlers by here? Can I ply you with booze?"

I said, "Your car, man. We're gonna help you look."

He picked a piece of tobacco off the end of his tongue, inspected it, then flicked it in the direction of the ashtray. "What about it?" He leaned and picked up two ice cubes. He dropped one in his glass and rubbed his sore toe with the other. "Gout," he winced. "Can't lay a sheet on it, hurts so much." Redding and I looked at each other. He was pale and sluggish, and through the smoke I could see Lee was baffled. "I'm buffaloed, fellas..." It was weird, but his confusion made me feel in control of the situation.

I said, "I gotta take a leak."

"It's through there," and he waved his drink at the closet door.

"Tell him, Redding," and I went through a walk-in closet to the bathroom. In the closet there were three suits hanging, a bundle of laundered chef's clothes, a couple more boxes and a black Samsonite suitcase. I couldn't believe he'd forgotten about last night. I wondered if the Calais and the stuff in this place was all he had. When I came out, Redding gave me a thumbs up which I took to mean Lee had dredged up the memory to remember his car was lost. "Who's playing?" I asked.

"Chet Baker. Sure you fellas don't want a toddy?"

"Nah. Too early," I said, even though at the apartment the first thing we did when we got up was do a number and drink some Red Mountain.

Lee motioned at Redding. "You?"

"That's okay," he said. "Can we toke up?"

"Reefer?"

"Be my guest. We'll get ourselves ready to go here in a second," and he leaned and picked up the scotch bottle and poured some into his glass with more milk and ice. Redding lit up a joint and we sat on the floor and passed it around. Lee tucked an unlit cigarette behind his ear to free up a hand. He coughed then lit his cigarette and said, "I had a friend, bald headed Jerry, had a reefer habit. And a big juicer. Regular Robert Mitchum, this guy. I tried to save his life, but in the end," and he lifted his glass, "this got him." He smiled down at us and said, "Jerry's big casino was the day he had Tim Tam on top of a superfecta in the Kentucky Derby."

I said, "Cool." My lips were numb. My forehead was tight.

Redding asked where he'd known this guy. "He was a waiter in a white table cloth place in the city. I was the exec chef. He was a helluva captain." Then he said again as the needle on the hi-fi scratched to the next song, "I tried to save his life," and he dragged on his cigarette. The music started. A drummer was riding a cymbal. I guessed Lee had seen some stuff and wondered if he had anything else besides whatever was in the closet, those few boxes and the Calais. He looked at the wall behind us.

I asked him about the dice on the packing box. He seemed surprised we didn't know how to play and got excited at the chance to teach us. He put his glass down, stubbed out his cigarette and slipping to the floor said, "Flip the record, babe," and we got lost in time, learning the basics, throwing the dice against the wall, going for points, fetching the dice for him. We passed another joint, and Redding and I drank some Four Roses and Seven-Up Lee found in a kitchen cabinet. We never went looking for the car, and when we saw Turner at the back door of the kitchen at three, we were all pretty high. And starving. He told us he had found the Calais, "In the lot behind Barney's, unlocked, parked across two spaces. There's barf on the door."

Lee frowned then said, "Thanks, pal. We'll get it after work. I'll buy you a cocktail."

And he limped into the stockroom to change.

"Where you been?" asked Turner. "Don't let Tony smell you."

Redding said, "Gambling," and pulled an apron over his head.

I said, "Getting loaded," and walked to the Hobart remembering Lee on the floor leaning against the bed, knees pulled up, shaking The Mine Shaft dice in his cupped hands, giving us a boozy lecture about the game of craps. "It's risky. Like life," he said. "The risk of living and all that hoo haw. But it's the best odds in the house, boys. If you know how to handle yourself, you can't lose." Once in a while he'd glance at his swollen toe and make a face, then he'd breathe deep and yell, "Shoot 'em, shooter," and let them fly while Chet Baker played in the kitchen.

Chapter 9

"There was a nasty little midget out there in line. Might be a dwarf," sniffed Kathy. Rennie and one of the Keno girls were smoking in the alcove. "Charm bracelet size." She asked Rennie for a light.

I walked over from the Hobart, wiping my hands on a towel, caught up for the moment. I asked, "Which?"

"Which what?"

"Midget or dwarf. There's a difference."

"Like what? What does it matter? On his toes, he could barely put his nose in my business." Rennie coughed on her cigarette. "ShitDevilDickDamnPiss. college boy, I have no earthly idea, but he's a runt with the nastiest mouth I ever heard. I was just doing my thing, talking to the folks, gettin' them to their tables, making sure they knew about our cushy Mine Shaft odds."

Rennie said, "Twenty-One's already two decks at the Sahara and Harvey's, you know."

"Lou told me," said Kathy. "Anyway, I'm yakkin' it up with little bit and he starts to flirt with me and at first I think it's cute. Now, he's really tiny. Barbie Doll size."

Lee walked over and said, "What's up, cats?" He pulled a cigarette from behind his ear and lit it.

Rennie said, "Kathy's pissed at a midget. Or a dwarf."

"Which?" he asked. The Keno girl shook her head, straightened her skirt and went back into the dining room.

Kathy gave Lee a wicked look then shot me the same. "Chef, what does it matter? The little shrimp said the dirtiest stuff to me. He could take a bath in Beaner's bus tray, Lee. He could stand up in the Hobart machine."

"Is he gone?" I asked. "I'd like to scope him out. Least he won't get drafted. There's a height requirement."

"A midget is proportioned. A dwarf is all out of whack," explained Lee. "Big head. I don't know. Maybe it's the other way around. But I think that's it," he finally said, "There's a difference. I'm sure."

"Yeah," I said. I could hear Big Ed banging pots.

"Ever see an albino spade?" asked Lee "How about a ginger-haired, blue-eyed shine? Any of you?"

"Anyway." She was getting pissed. "Let me tell you what happened you all. I'm tellin' you a story about an oddity."

I said, "Go then."

"Do tell," said Lee, nodding to Rennie, who was checking her watch. I was getting horny thinking of her naked. I looked at my watch.

"Well at first the little jerk is pleasant enough, then he tells me he likes regular-sized women like me. Says he can show me a real time of it. Said he used to be in show business. Wanted me to believe he did it with Edie Adams. Like I believe that."

"So?"

"So I am moving up the line with him, trying to mind my manners, trying to do my job the way Lou wants me to, and he says, 'I'd like to shimmy up those legs and shake your fruit.' Well, that stopped me, and I looked at the others in line to see if they'd heard any of that nonsense. And all I could think to say was, sir we'll have you a table in just a minute, and I about asked him if he needed a booster seat." She waved her hand at the baby seats stacked against the wall. Rennie had an ashtray set on the top one. She was edging away, hurrying for Kathy to finish. "But I bit my tongue."

Rennie said, "Gotta go."

"And, he's drunk."

"Least he wouldn't have far to fall," Lee said. "I'll rent my glove compartment to him if he needs to sleep it off." Lee loved his joke and slapped his thigh and I wondered when we'd next be looking for the Calais.

"Wait a minute, Rennie. Listen you all. Listen to what happened. He's enjoying himself, looking up at everybody, smiling, showing his ass, the sawed off wiener, and right when I start to walk away again, he says loud enough for everybody to hear, 'How about you and me get it on?'" "Rennie stopped at the door. "That turned a few heads," said Kathy, eyes wide.

"I'll bet," said Lee, loving the story. "Quite a toodler, this midget." I was distracted by Big Ed and his pans.

"Well, ladies and gentlemen, I turned around and walked over to this pint-size pissant, and with the whole line of folks watching me, I got down on my hands and knees and looked him straight into his eensy beensy blood shot eyes...he smelled like creamed corn...disgusting...and I said, I'm calling security, buddy, and having your little butt tossed outta here, but before I do, minner dick, I'm gonna warn you that if you ever do that to me...and I find out about it. I'm gonna lock you in my train case and chuck you in the lake."

"Heavens," said Rennie. "Nice work. I gotta go. See ya." She made me crazy, winking my way as she split for the casino.

Lee yelped, "Whoa," and, "well, well," and shuffled off in the direction of the walk-in box, rolling his right foot to the outside, shaking his head at another six trays of panned chicken Redding and Turner were sliding into the ovens. It was frosted with paprika. Water from the trays splashed onto the floor.

"So what happened?"

Butcher eighty-sixed him right out the front. He was squirmin' and squealin' like a piglet.

"Nasty," she said. "Just plain nasty. Cussed all the way."

"Takes all kinds," I said as Beaner showed up with another bus tray spilling over with dirty plates and silverware. Some of the plates were still full, the pigs.

Kathy said, "That's for damn sure, and they all come to The Mine Shaft," as Sweet Lou came into the alcove. Kathy and I smiled at his timing and traded looks. I reached too late for a plate that slid to the floor off the bus tray and shattered. Lou said, "Save the pieces." But he wasn't mad. It happened all the time.

He was dressed real slick as usual. He wore black suede loafers that looked extra expensive. The rawhide on my cowboy boots was getting stained darker every shift. Lou's soft shoes wouldn't last five minutes in the kitchen with all the grease, water and spillage if he wasn't careful. They had a loose, little horse bit of gold chain on top where on Weejuns you could put a penny. He was wearing tan colored, beltless pants, flared just some, with a crease as sharp as the blade on the slicer and a turtleneck sweater that matched. He had great hair, that guy. I'm sure he had it razor cut.

I waved and said hello.

He poked the air in my direction, then I heard him tell Kathy, "Nice job with that smutty midget." He was smiling. Kathy shook her head back and forth in an exasperated way, then they lowered their voices and talked while I swept up the broken plates and scraped, rinsed, sorted and ran another load. Kathy raised her eyes once to see if I was watching and I looked away. When I looked back over, Kathy was gone and Lou was strolling through the kitchen, not so much to be nosey, but to check in, say hello. That was his style. The tension was gone at six when Tony left. The only thing recently creating any stress after six now was that crazy ape, Big Ed.

I don't think Lou knew jack shit about the restaurant business. When he walked around or came back to hang around, he always seemed interested though, acted amazed at how the place worked, how food got cooked in bulk and delivered to the line for the customers. He was cool, but we still hid the wine and were on our best behavior when Lou was in the kitchen. He could have been Mafia. That was the word. But who knew. You couldn't believe half the stuff you heard around here on the hill. Shanahan, who seemed to have gotten back on track and sobered up, really believed men were going to walk on the moon in about a week. He ranted for an hour one day in the parking lot that Kennedy was being kept alive at a hospital outside Washington. He also thought the big moron, Ed, had probably worked for the CIA. Shanahan saw conspiracies everywhere.

Lou looked over Redding's shoulder as he did the trick with Iceberg lettuce heads. The easiest way to get the core out so you could chop, he'd said, was to grip it in your hand and slam the lettuce head down on the chopping block right where the stock had been cut. The core in the lettuce would loosen, then you could pluck it out easy with two fingers like a watermelon plug. Redding was grabbing them from a box at his feet, slamming heads and sliding cored ones to Turner, who was chopping them into quarters like a mad man, then pushing the wedges into a sink with Lee's big French knife to be rinsed, drained and carried out to the line. We went through four boxes of lettuce a shift, at least. I came over to watch.

"Get you anything, Lou?" asked Lee, coming in from the line. He looked over Lou's clothes like he approved while he patted his pants pocket. "Smoke?"

"No, thank you," said Lou. "Just wandering. Slow out there. I'm about to go, let Butcher keep an eye on it. Things okay back here?

"All the cats are meowin, Lou. A-okay. Sure I can't make you an omelet, roast beef sandwich? Got some nice pork chops."

He shook his head and said no thank you again. He was so polite. Shanahan said he was classy. Rennie liked him because he didn't hit on her, treated her fair.

"Think I'm going to spring Kathy and take her out for dinner as a thank you for dealing with the problem."

"Yeah, nice move," said Lee. "Handling the midget situation," and he turned my way with a baffled look, "or dwarf."

I said, "Whatever..." Kathy and Lou were odd together. I couldn't figure it out. I wondered about Mic. What he thought, where he was on this.

"No offense, Chef. Need a change of venue," and Lou patted Lee on the shoulder and looked at me for understanding, like he even needed to do that. "White tablecloth place somewhere. You know. A dozen on the half shell and a rare fillet. Maybe a cigar."

"And a couple of martinis. Sounds dandy." I knew Lee was dying to get a drink soon himself.

Someone, one of the Keno girls, yelled, "Hey. Watch out," and we all turned to see Big Ed standing with three sauce pans at the Hobart out near the alcove facing her down. She had her arms folded and was looking away in the direction of the dining room, ignoring him, puffing fast on a cigarette. He turned back and started to hook each of the pans up onto the rack above the oven. His big head was swishing back and forth like a horse as he hung the clean sauce pans on their hooks. He was mumbling. Redding's lettuce pounding whammed behind us. In a strange way, it synched up in rhythm with Ed's head jigging.

Sweet Lou looked at Lee like he wanted an explanation.

Lee's response was, "Squirrelly." Then he called out to Ed, "What's up, babe?" Redding slammed a lettuce head against the chopping block. Ed went on grumbling. I could make out "Jesus Christ" scattered throughout whatever he was saying. He didn't make eye contact and then he went back to the pot and pan sink. He never looked our way.

I said, "He's nuts," as Redding smashed more lettuce and Turner split and raked.

Lou said to Lee, "Walk with me." And they went to the alcove where the Keno girl was smoking. She was new. I'd only seen her a few times. I walked behind and stopped at the Hobart, but was able to hear as I wiped down the counter top.

She told Lou and Lee she had walked into the kitchen just far enough to get an ashtray off the Hobart sink and when she did, Big Ed, who was coming up between the ovens and the Hobart, intentionally veered out of his way and, "Bumped me then blamed me for bumping into him. He's scary."

There was silence while they looked at each other. I would have walked back and fired his dumb ass, but all Lee and Lou did was shake hands, say goodnight to each other like it was no big deal, although Lou put his hand on her shoulder and rested it there a second like a father might do. Then she followed him into the restaurant. Lee came over and said,

"I'm thinking about a sauce, kid. Run out the back around to Danny and tell him I need a bottle of red. How 'bout it?"

I knew the drill. I skirted Ed, who was still mumbling, dunking pans and rocking back and forth at the sink, and got a bottle of wine from Danny, who smiled, and said, "Bon appetite." I glanced to Rennie's table. It was full. She happened to look up while she waited for a woman with hair as high as Lee's toque to make a decision. We made eye contact across the room for a shred of a moment, enough for me, then the woman scratched her card against the felt and Rennie looked down and hit her. I couldn't wait to get off. I heard Danny tell a customer who'd ordered a Chivas Regal and ginger ale that he wouldn't...couldn't...put that in the same glass. Danny looked like he was in pain when he set out the two glasses and poured.

Butcher was across the room talking with one of the pit bosses and they seemed interested in the action at one of the craps tables. Butcher was built like Dick Butkus, with a flat top haircut you could land B-52 on that ended in a widow's peak down low on his forehead. I was freaked he'd eventually catch onto our wine scam and eighty-six us for drinking in the kitchen. All it would take, if it hadn't already happened, was for Danny to give us up, but I just had the sense Danny wasn't going to do that. Maybe it was because of my relationship with Rennie, but I figured if we got nailed, it would be because we screwed up somehow, not Danny.

After pushing the cork using Lee's steel down into the bottle in the stockroom, I poured four coffee mugs, left them on a shelf and tossed the empty bottle into the dumpster out back. I took two cups into the kitchen, one for me, Lee the other, and told Turner and Redding where to find theirs.

They had finished with the lettuce and were teaming up to slice cold cuts for tomorrow. "Prep a couple pans of ham and roast beef and put 'em in the walk-in, fellas." He lifted his mug and said, "Up your kilt," and took a long slug. Then he shooed Redding and Turner in the direction of the stockroom and said, "Get your toddy first, boys. Take a break," and Redding turned off the slicer. It whistled to a stop.

"Don't let Big Ed figure out the wine con," I told Turner, a slice of roast beef dangling from his mouth. "That's all we need." Then Lee asked me if Sweet Lou was screwing Kathy. I told him I didn't know, but her beauty upgrade and the way they acted around each other now was weird. "They don't match. He's married, right?"

"Was."

"He's almost twice as old."

"So?"

"You think Mic knows?"

"I have no idea, pally. So," he asked again, "is he knockin' that off?"

I said, "Got me, but a guy like Lou could get any chick he wanted. I just don't get it." I wondered why he hadn't followed up with Rennie. "He's Mafia, right?"

Lee smiled over his mug.

Beaner came up behind us with a pan of fryer grease. "Hot stuff," he said. "*Muy caliente*, guys. Look out," and we moved and he headed for the back door.

"Well, kid, remember this. In the dark, it's all the same. And she'll always be able to look up longer than Sweet Lou can look down," and he started humming and walking out to check the line. His limp didn't seem as bad.

"How's the gout?"

"Better," he said over his shoulder. "Simmering."

Redding was something for a guy who seemed to have everything in the world. Here he had a deferment for grad school, parents with money, new car, been to all kinds of places like Europe, pleasant personality, California blond good looks, president of his high school class, knew already what he wanted to do with the rest of his life, and he risked it all by dealing drugs. Didn't think a thing about it. Went down to Berkeley every couple of weeks when it was necessary, or when he had to pick up a special order. Drove around the place in his red bug, usually with a trunk full of speed, mescaline, psylicibin, acid, hash, opium sometimes and pot. You name it. He was a regular drug mobile, making house calls, breaking big bills. He became known quickly as the guy to go to in a pinch around Tahoe. And he never really took on a hard core look as much as he tried. Redding was a Creedence Clearwater guy, sometimes we called him Opie after the kid on the Andy Griffith Show, but he took it well. He just did not think he was going to get caught, saw himself as bulletproof in that way, and treated the whole business of buying and selling dope as a game. He had a blast at it. Thought it made him a heavy dude. I think things must have always come easy to him in life, and he just carried it over into his drug hobby. He said the people he was meeting in the drug dealing business would make great material for his book one day. But I never saw him write down one word.

I rode down to Berkeley one Wednesday with him to score some hash from a source he had. It was hot and sunny down there. The difference in temperature between Tahoe was dramatic, it was the California I'd always imagined. He was supposed to meet his source in a big old house off a wide street not far from the campus. It was pink, paint peeling, trimmed in white, a group house, he said, with tall, out-of-control bushes along the street. One tall palm tree in the front yard gave the scene a laid back feeling. Cats were all over as we pulled up behind a VW Bus, a peace symbol on the rear window and a bumper sticker that read: Stop The War. A couple of bicycles leaned against the tree. A birdhouse was nailed to the trunk. The porch eaves were hung with wind chimes, but the day was still, the chimes weren't ringing. A zodiac symbol was painted on the floor of the porch in front of the door. I felt like I was walking on a grave.

Even though the whole scene was low key, I was eye twittery and paranoid, but the guy who let us in, and Redding, were calm as the still wind chimes. He wore dirty bell bottom jeans, a T-shirt with the word "Diggers" across the front in psychedelic balloon letters, a floppy brown leather cowboy hat with a long feather in the band, beads around his neck and bare feet. He was tall and smelled like incense and sweat and slouched when he walked. Nobody mentioned anybody's name or said much. Redding had told me earlier he had done business with this guy for a long time. "Six, seven months at least," he'd figured. "He's cool."

Inside the front door a totem pole, or at least part of one, took up most of a high ceilinged foyer. Love beads hung off the tip of a green and red wing that grew out of a scowling, carved bird face. A couple in the living room to the right were at a card table playing chess. A bare-chested guy with long, yellow curly hair, long nose and pointy chin moved a piece and said, "Checkmate," with a satisfied shout and slowly turned to the three of us as if we'd been an audience pulling for him all along and were enjoying his moment as much as he was. The other player, a woman of thirty or so, wearing faded jeans and a T-shirt, looked up and down slowly through tiny granny glasses, first at the board, then at the man, then conceded the match by knocking over her king with a flick of a finger.

She said, "Satisfied, fucker?" stood and walked past us and up a wide staircase that had something...shoes, newspaper, cereal box, beer bottle...sitting on almost every step.

The guy with the curly hair stood and dropped a Navajo blanket that had wrapped him. He was naked and stooped to pick it up and then pulled it over to his shoulders like a cape, and held it at the front with one hand, said hello to us and went up the stairs.

The tall guy said, "Congratulations, Blanket Man..." then to us, "Hates clothes." He then led us past the staircase down a hall with faded Oriental carpets worn out to the backing, and guided us to the left through double doors into a parlor. Further down the hall I could see into a kitchen and some people cooking and talking. I smelled garlic and oil and it reminded me of the clam sauce Tony made special for Lou sometimes. Funny. Being around food all the time made me lose my appetite at work. But away from the Mine Shaft it was a different story. Music came from somewhere. I asked him who it was, and he told me it was Quicksilver Messenger Service. "Local," he said, I guess having pegged me as someone not from the area. He smiled big, the corners of his Fu Manchu mustache curling to show crooked teeth, the front two overlapped like crossed legs, making me not trust him, and he motioned for Redding and me to sit on cushions on the floor. Then he closed the double doors, walked in front of us and went through another door to a different room. "Hang out," he said.

Quicksilver whoever was another band I'd never heard of. I made a mental note to try to find some of these local groups' records when I got back to Cincinnati. For the first time, just for a sliver of a moment when I thought of Cincinnati, the idea of not going back—never, ever—seeped into my mind. A yellow cat with an attitude and a peace symbol hanging from its neck crept its way close to my leg, but I pushed it away. Maybe I would leave it all behind. For the most part, I had eliminated thoughts about school, parents and Elaine. My summer had become work, getting high and getting laid. I was in a groove with my new friends, my new crazy scene. I was having a good time. But the thread of worry I tried to break wouldn't. I always came back to a hairy rope of a connection to Cincinnati and the draft. They were still expecting me. The yoke on my shoulders was Vietnam. I was trying to run from a decision about what to do, but the more I worked on my collage, which I was finding I had to do, the more I realized I was headed to a confrontation with myself. I knew the time was corning. I knew it was out there, I even think I knew what I would do, but I didn't want to be there yet. I was on the high board, scared to death to jump, I had to admit. I thought about what Turner had-said about seeing clearly when you're clear yourself.

"Nervous?" Redding asked.

"Day dreaming," I said.

"'Bout what?"

"About being strong, about not being strong."

Redding squinted and said, "Dig it, yeah."

Busying myself keeping the cat away let me bury the thoughts in my head. I looked around the room. It was furnished with Salvation Army-type furniture. I asked Redding if we had to stay on the cushions.

"What's wrong with that couch?"

"Got me," he said.

My back was stiff from the ride. "We being polite?"

"Guess so," he said. The cat went to Redding, and he held it in his lap. "Never hurts." The guy came back in the room and said, "I have been through the terrors of the damned to get this, but it was worth it. This is righteous shit, man. It's going fast." He seemed thrilled. "Your timing is sweet." He sat with us.

"Hello, Pineapple," he whispered to the cat. "We think he was a Buddhist monk in a different life. Very perceptive and spiritual, Mr. Pineapple. He can really vibe you." I looked at the cat, curled in Redding's folded legs, purring at his strokes. I wondered what misstep could get you demoted to a cat in Buddha world. For all I knew, it was a promotion.

Shanahan would have a hoot with the idea of Mr. Pineapple, the cat monk. The tall guy was carrying a crinkly ball of aluminum foil the size of a golf ball, a long metal pipe with a small bowl at the end, and a welder's torch attached to a little tank and a thing that looked like an oversized metal clothes pin. Feathers and beads hung from the pipe stem. "My peace pipe," he said. "Got it in Taos from a friend on a commune. It's got some very heavy spiritual shit going on with it. Karmic," he said, eyeing it with pride. The rest of the equipment was piled next to him on the floor. It seemed like lots of paraphernalia for a high.

He unwrapped the aluminum and set it at his feet, exposing a tarry black lump inside. "Where you from?" he asked as he arranged the torch and tank next to the ball of opium.

"Ohio," I said.

"You?" He looked up from turning a knob on the tank. His mustache jumped again as he smiled. He looked across at Redding, still caressing cat monk Pineapple, then back at me and said, "Around here. The Bay Area."

He made me feel defensive and not very cool. For something to say I asked him if he was in school. He thought that was hilarious, and he and Redding stopped what they were doing and laughed. Pineapple hunched his shoulders and looked up at Redding's face. The tall guy put a knife down he'd pulled from a sheaf at his belt and wiped at his eye. "I was, some time ago, a philosophy major. I gave it up. It was bullshit." I decided to stop with the small talk. I did not dig this guy and his arrogance and evasiveness. He carved a chunk from the ball and put it in the pipe bowl. He held it out for Redding, who held the cat out to me, and I said,

"Nope," so he put the cat on the floor at his side and took the pipe. The cat stretched then turned its back and swished his tail like he was giving me the finger and walked away. The guy turned a knob on the torch and it made a thin whistling sound that blew to a whoosh as an eight-inch flame bloomed from the nose of the torch at the scratch of the big metal clothes pin, the spark igniting the gas. I had an instant recall from television of jet engines and Craig Breedlove shooting across the salt flats breaking the land speed record in his rocket car. The cat ignored the action and curled up on the couch. The guy adjusted the size of the flame some and bent forward to heat the opium in the bowl of the pipe. I was trying to figure out how I was going to gracefully say no when it was offered to me. Hash was my limit. I didn't know if I was ready for opium. I knew it was in paregoric, and that Gnossis Popodopolous in *Been Down So Long...* had dipped joints in the medicine and dried them over lamp shades for an extra good buzz. And I'd heard Lenny Bruce used to pry open Vicks inhalers and eat the ball from inside and drink a coke for a quick high. I didn't know if I could get hooked. I knew it was used to make heroin. The heat from the flame made the opium oily and produced a wisp of blue smoke as Redding sucked in short bursts to fire it up, then he took a long drag, closed his eyes and leaned back as the tall guy took the pipe out of his hands. He held it out to me. I hesitated, then said, "Fuck it," and took the pipe.

He goosed the torch flame up an inch or two. I pulled on the pipe like I would a hash pipe, but the draw was hard and I didn't get very much smoke into my mouth. I kept pulling and finally felt the heat and sooty smoke fill my mouth. I drew it into my lungs and held it, fighting to keep it down even though short burps split my lips, until I couldn't hold it any longer. With a heave, I let it go from my lungs, coughed hard, pounded my chest and felt my eyes tearing up from the convulsions. I blinked and looked at Redding, who was evenly releasing smoke from his lungs into the parlor, a room I'm sure had once been decorated with lace and formal furniture at some time in its history. The only thing dainty today, though, were the veils and wisps of smoke hanging light in the air above the three of us, the cat and the smoldering pipe. The tall guy gave me an unwanted crooked smile of fake understanding, then he toked up and held the pipe out to me again, but I shook my head. I hated him. Pineapple jumped back into Redding's lap after he'd fired up the pipe for the dealer.

"Well?"

"Quality. You're right."

"No question. I told you. Hard to score, but worth it, right?"

Pause. "Right."

"All of it?" Pause.

"Half."

Long pause. "How much?"

"Two-hundred. All of it for three-fifty."

Pause "Throw in some grass. A few lids. Deal?"

Long pause. "Deal." And the wind chimes on the porch jangled in a Chinese sounding confusion of clanging, the mustache jumped into a smile and the cat jerked his head along with mine at the window. Redding started counting out bills from the tooled leather satchel he always carried.

Later, before we left, there was talk about Vietnam. I couldn't tell if anybody was high. I wasn't. Redding told the dealer he still had his deferment, was going to grad school at the end of the summer. I said I didn't know what I was going to do, but that I was I-A.

Redding said, "He's confused." I cut him a look.

The dealer, holding the cat in his arms, said, "I was confused once."

I really didn't give a rat's ass about his life, but he went on.

"Wore a tie. Part of the system. But, and I can't quote the dude, but in a philosophy class I ran into an awesome quote from a German philosopher who basically believed that if you could dream it, you could do it. Like, he said, once you make a decision, all kinds of other stuff starts happening and you get set free. Something along those lines, man." He said, "So I made a decision."

Redding was at the car, cowboy boot on the running board. Opium in the trunk. "Let's get it on," he said. I had a foot on the bottom step looking back at the dealer on the porch. The cat was watching the chimes move, jigging its head at the different sounds.

The tall dude said, "Make a decision man," made the peace sign and carried the obnoxious cat monk back into the house. And I thought, sure, right on, like it's as simple as that. I was picturing Rennie, had a scorched taste in my mouth and I was hungry.

****

All July Shanahan couldn't talk about anything but the moon shot. He'd even volunteered to work double shifts on the 20th and 21st so he'd be around a television set and not miss a thing. I thought about him and his running argument with Turner over Vietnam as I stood on my mattress the morning after Redding's opium deal in Oakland. I cut and pasted pictures and headlines on the collage, covering more and more wall. I looked my dead soldier in the face and wondered if his life had included as much confusion, tangled thinking and aimlessness as mine before he found himself face down in the mud over there. Had he been a patriot, clean and simple? Did he question his decision to serve, or had he been pushed or shoved, or obligated out of guilt, not wanting to let everybody down, the ones who said they loved him? Or had he been wandering around like me playing musical chairs with his life that one day left him standing, standing in a uniform in Vietnam. I said out loud, "Who are you?" to the soldier. "Are you me?" I wanted him to answer, but he just stared, far off, the bridge of his nose wrinkled and not making eye contact with the camera.

From the front room, Sara yelled, "Victor. I can't hear you. What do you want?" And I didn't answer. I went ahead and fit a picture of a village on fire into the upper right corner of the wall. Then I got ready to hitchhike to work.

After work, at Rennie's, she asked me, "Where does Lee go every Wednesday?" She was lying on top of me and stretched to reach a glass of wine on her night stand. She took a sip then rested the glass on my chest, rolled to her side, her legs holding my right one in a tight and wonderful crimp, her tanned body close against me.

"Lee and Skin?" I raised my arm slowly to let her head in against my chest. I steadied the wine with my left hand, my right rested on her rib cage, brown under her white chest "They go to the Moonlight Ranch in Reno. It's a whorehouse. It's legal in parts of Nevada now. They get all duded up. Got regular girls over there. Lee's is named Karlene. Talks about her all the time." I brushed my thumb light over Rennie's ribs like I was strumming guitar strings. She shuddered.

"Aren't they afraid of getting something?"

"I guess not. Lee said Karlene had never given him a dose. It's a strange relationship."

"You ever been there?"

"No. Why? Why would I want to? Having you, I mean."

"I dunno. I thought all you guys did it at least once. Like Mr. Asshole."

"We're not all assholes like your husband."

I sipped some wine then tilted it for Rennie, who sipped at an angle, dribbling some onto my chest. She said, "Whoops. Sorry," then licked the drops and said, "Yummy."

"Lee keeps asking me to go. He's teasing me."

"You ought to do it."

"C'mon...you kidding?"

"I'm just curious," she said. "I'd like to know what it's like. Try and understand it, maybe."

"Turner went with them. Crazy man will try anything once." I laughed as I remembered his story.

"What?"

"It's just what he said. About what happened."

"Tell me."

"It's nothing, really. But the way Turner tells things. It's funny."

"Well tell me." Rennie was looking at me with her blue, eyes wide and demanding.

"Well, all it really was, was that when he finally got to the room and he was naked with this girl, well he couldn't get it up. He got scared I guess. Who knows? Anyway, like I said, it's the way he told it to me and Redding when Lee made him tell it."

"Go ahead... "

"You know how Turner talks. How excitable he can be." I rolled my head to her face, our noses almost touching, and the little divot in her forehead pulling at me. He said it was fun and they did it. But before they did, he said, 'Shit, man, you guys, I was worried. My dick was as small as it had ever been. I thought I was going to have to tie a shoestring to it and pull it out it was so small. Like I needed tweezers. It was embarrassing. Then, for some reason it got the idea and got big. Huge. Like it wasn't mine. It was amazing. Went from being as small as it ever had been to being as big as it ever had.' "

Rennie said, "That's the story?"

"It was funny at the time. Him telling it."

Rennie got out of bed and walked to the bathroom. As she walked she said, "I like to watch you get excited." It was almost three in the morning. I was drifting to sleep when she opened the door and came back to bed saying, "Is this the part where we fall asleep and wake up and do it again?" And she clicked off the lamp at her bedside and crawled over to me.

I fell asleep and dreamed we woke up later and made love again, rough, without talking. But in the morning, I wasn't sure if it was a dream or if it really had happened. I felt her warm breathing on my back and went back to sleep and was glad because it didn't matter. Not one little bit. I just hoped my luck would hold.

****

One night I got hot at the twenty-five cent craps table at Harvey's. It was a great spot to get experience. I felt like a high roller turning my ten dollar investment into a sixty-five dollar win, Rennie at my side for luck. Once, I held the dice for thirty minutes. Point after point I made. People cheered and crowded around to get in on the action or just watch.

Lee had said to be ready when you were on a roll and try not to get too excited, but to almost get unconscious, the luck would carry you. You had to be available for the moment he'd said, the day he taught us how to play on the floor of his apartment. So even though the croupier had to correct me a few times when I backed my bets with too much, or tried to hand him dollars instead of first laying the money on the table when I needed chips. But I got into it even though I couldn't figure out how they could compute the odds and remember who was who around the table. My insight that night was that a chip was just a chip. It didn't know what kind of limit the table had. It could be quarter table or a hundred dollar table. What did the chip know? If I could get on a roll at the quarter table, I might as well win some big dough where the chips just cost more. I even put a chip on Eight the Hard Way and won.

We ate huge shrimp and drank white wine with my winnings in a nice restaurant in the Sahara that stayed open late. Rennie ate so much she upset her stomach and had to use the ladies' room. When she got back to the table, I told her I was going to move up to bigger stakes. She tapped her tooth and just said, "Be careful."

I felt like I had nothing to lose and I ordered another bottle of wine. I was on a roll. I felt it. Now I knew what Lee meant when he had compared dice to living. I said, "It's just another risk, Rennie."

When we were through, she tapped her tooth then said, "You're a trip, Victor. A real trip."

I left a nice tip and was surprised the waiter didn't treat me like a bigger deal when we walked out.

Chapter 10

I never saw anybody going to church in Lake Tahoe. Sunday was like every other day. When I got to work on Sunday afternoon, the 20th, the only difference was that Shanahan's Galaxie was parked outside the back door. Then I remembered how he was "itchin" to catch the moon shot. So much that he volunteered to pull a double shift, and again Monday if he had to. I'd completely forgotten this was the big day until I saw the car. It still didn't seem possible, real at all. It was just hard for me to believe you could get somebody to the moon. It felt as out of reach as all the answers to my future.

The grease man was there at the door at the same time. I was glad to see him. We talked after he did his thing with the barrels. The heat of the July sun had the flatbed full of barrels and about-to-be recycled oil, grease and fat warmed to the point the rancid smell, even at ten feet away, reminded me of the stockyards that used to be down by Crosley Field. Windows rolled down in the 1955 Buick Electra on the way to a Redlegs game, holding my nose, listening to Waite Hoyt on the Burger Beer Baseball Network pregame show describing a pitcher who was, "All wind-up and no speed," a phrase my dad borrowed and repeated when he thought somebody was talking, "through their hat." I'd hated the odor and stared at the long low buildings and fences and asked Dad about what could possibly make a smell that bad.

"Porkopolis," had been his answer. "They used to call Cincinnati Porkopolis. We could have been Chicago, son, but we blew it." Even though he'd said it was cruel, I had nightmares for weeks after he'd told me the way they killed the cattle was by hitting them in the head with a sledgehammer. Anyway, if I smelled anything close to that stockyard stench or reek of sulfur that hung over the Mill Creek Valley in my Cincinnati childhood, then the memories came right back.

The grease man and I stood for a few minutes, running through our ritual. He told me he had a friend, a guy named Gayle, who ran a small funeral home and drove a hearse all over the area. Gayle had the contract to pick up bodies for Douglas County, Nevada. He laughed and pointed to his truck. "We both haul used stuff. Last night he picked up a naked guy."

"Dead guy?" I asked for some reason. The grease man just looked at me.

"As a jay bird...and dead." He leaned closer and I had to pull back. "And his car keys were taped to his butt," he whispered. "Camaro keys. Cops found him hung up in a jungle gym on a playground just on the other side of the parking lot of a trailer park up in North Shore." He waited to let that sink in. Then he added, "Had a few big caliber bullets in his back. Real dead." Before he started again, he ran a dirty hand through his hair and said, "Wanna know what happened? You ain't gonna get the full story in the paper."

Lee was crunching over the gravel in the Calais, driving our way.

"A planner apparently," he said. "The cops told Gayle the guy couldn't break a habit of slipping over to this gal's trailer and gettin' a little when her husband was working. Husband's a box man nights over at the Cal Neva, Sinatra's place. She's telling this to the cops, you see. She said her boyfriend was always nervous that her old man would show up, even though she guaranteed him he was working, you know. It's understandable I suppose. You'll have that."

"Yeah..."

"Well, as insurance, or to give himself a shot of courage to perform with this gal, he always diddled her with his car keys taped to his butt...just in case."

"A quick getaway?"

"Bingo," he said. "A quick release I guess you could call it. Figured he'd at least have a ride, I suppose."

"What happened?" I asked. Lee came up and stood next to me.

"What's up, babe?" he said nonchalantly. His face was puffed up and waxy. He had a crescent puff under each eye, a razor nick at one sideburn. He smelled like Old Spice and bourbon.

"Guy got shot. Had Camaro keys taped to his butt..." I started.

"Oh my. One of ours?" asked Lee. "Shanahan?"

I said, "No. Different dude. Does sound like something Mic could get into, though."

Lee said, "Camaro, huh?" I watched him think about that.

"Right, Camaro," said the grease man.

Lee made a pivot and looked back at the parking lot, hand at his eyes. Seemed he was trying to spot a Camaro to remind himself what one looked like. Then he turned from the sun like it had blistered him.

"Surprise. Ha." The grease man pointed an imaginary rifle at Lee's Cadillac. "Boom. The husband came home and caught them mid hump and was able to drop lover boy with his deer rifle scootin' bare ass across the parking lot. He made a run for it though. Dove out the trailer window, slid over the propane tank and hot footed it. Wife was wrapped around the hubby's leg screaming and wailing, but she didn't throw off his aim."

"Plugged him, huh? Just imagine that," Lee said quietly. "Poor fella."

"Guts, feathers and all," said the grease man, grinding his cigarette butt out in the gravel.

Lee winced. His knuckles showed white on the briefcase handle. He said, "That tightens me up." Then, "How 'bout a roast beef sandwich?"

The grease man said, "Can't. Gotta move on," right when Shanahan opened the kitchen door with an armful of flattened cardboard boxes.

Mic stopped and looked at us. "Hell's bells. You fellers are missin' the show. They got them boys landed up on the moon. Why in Heaven's name ain't you in there checkin' it out?" He went over to the dumpster muttering, "Lord, lordy,

lordy."

The grease man got in his truck and rumbled off, but not before he told me and Lee about a dead prostitute Gayle had picked up later on the same night the car key guy got shot. He'd laughed and said at least she'd be on her back for eternity. "You know. Like Gayle said, 'Dreams can come true.' "

On his way back from the dumpster, Shanahan made a face and said, "Son, did you smell of that greasy feller?"

"Yeah..."

"Whooo, he's ripe."

Inside, after a couple of hours, Turner came over to the Hobart while I was grinding the garbage.

"Vic," he said, real excited, talking low and urgent.

"What?" I couldn't hear. "What?" I flipped the disposal switch off and hung up the spray hose.

"You won't believe this."

"I heard the story. The naked dead guy with the keys taped to his butt. Right?"

"What?"

"The grease man's story."

"I have no idea." He looked at me.

"Never mind. I'll tell you later." I said. "What then?"

"I had a long talk with Big Ed."

"Bullshit. No way."

I could hear Ed banging at the sink. When I came in I noticed he was still wearing the same clothes he'd had on the day he'd been hired.

"I had to walk the last mile or so today. Couldn't get a ride. When I got dropped I saw Ed walking up ahead. He was kicking gravel and swinging his arms. Looked like he was talking to himself. I followed him some, then said, what the hell, and trotted up and walked the rest of the way in with him."

I looked over him at Redding coming out of the walk-in with a jar of mayonnaise the size of a waste basket. Lee and Tony were talking and smoking over by the swinging doors to the line. Tony's lasagna sauce, simmering in the big saucer, filled the kitchen with the smell of oregano, thyme and garlic."

You're shitting me..."

"No way, man."

"He actually talked?"

"Yeah. Listen. When I got up to him, he didn't act surprised or anything. Just started talking like we were best buddies."

"About what?"

"I just asked him where he was from. He said Detroit. Then he just started rambling. He said he had been to Vietnam two times. He wanted to go three, but his wife fucked him over, double-crossed him is what he said."

"Like how?"

"Here's what he said." Turner was so excited. He leaned into the aisle and peeped back toward the pot and pan sink. Redding looked over to me and held up his hands like a surgeon washed up and prepped for an operation. His sleeves were rolled up to the elbows and his forearms were slathered in mayonnaise, ground ham and pickle relish. He was doing the job nobody volunteered for. Tony had you mix gobs of chopped, leftover ham butts, the relish and mayo in a big vat to make ham salad. The vat was shaped like a trough and the whole process was disgusting. You had to get on your knees to do it. Redding looked like he was having fun. He caught Turner's eyes that had trailed my glance and yelled, "You're next, buddy." And turned and ran his hands into the vat like he was scrubbing clothes or panning for gold. Tony was bent over an open oven door now, his coat on over his whites. Lee was stropping his knives, briefcase on the counter top next to a coffee mug. Turner said, "C'mon. Let's check out the front. I'll tell you."

Turner and I walked through the alcove to the restaurant. It was packed, every table full, but it still wasn't as hot as the kitchen. I guessed maybe the moon business was responsible. But who knew? These value diners were all kinds. Shanahan was ducking and bending between the people as they moved down the line filling their plates. He was wiping up spilled gravy and dropped pieces of food like a tall, jerky bird, pecking. Beaner, with that innocent look on his face, was smoothing out the ice at the salad station like his hands were on a Ouija Board. I asked Turner if Shanahan had ever told him about the time when he was a Marine in San Francisco when he claimed a pervert had paid him twenty-five dollars to come up to an apartment on Broadway and throw a bag of rotten grapefruit at him while he stood naked against the wall. I didn't know whether to believe him, but since I'd known Mic, I'd heard him tell the story to anyone who'd listen.

Turner smiled and said, "Shit, man, about a million times."

I'd watched when Shanahan had told Beaner the story once. I think Beaner had understood every fourth word, but he smiled and shook his head as if he'd understood, all the time playing with his crucifix at his throat. Shanahan always ended the story by saying, "So I nailed his queer ass and took the money and went to a Giants game and got pickled. Juan Marichal threw a one-hitter in the rain." Shanahan always had a smug, satisfied, Popeye sort of expression on his face when he finished that story, confident whoever he was telling it to would be knocked out by his brassy bullshit. When Beaner heard it he was quiet, a delay while he waited to make sure Shanahan was finished. Then he complimented him with a, "*Si. Si. Si.* Juan Marichal. *Entiendo. Entiendo. Si.*" I don't think he'd any idea what Mic had been talking about.

Mic flipped a damp towel over his shoulder and said to us, "Before you girls cage any drinks out there, how about checkin' with Mr. Cronkite and see how our boys are doin' up there. How 'bout it now?" All shift he had been running back and forth between the kitchen and the casino with regular updates on Apollo 11.

Turner said, "*Semper fi*, Mic," in a falsetto voice and sashayed like a hula girl, hands on his hips.

The deep lines that cut half circles on the sides of Shanahan's mouth when he smiled snapped straight down, and he scowled at Turner like he wanted to slam his head into the fake Mine Shaft beams and we kept moving. Lou and Butcher were at their booth, talking, drinking coffee, looking bored like usual. Keno girls dodged customers coming back for seconds.

We walked past the waiting line and Kathy gave us a two thumbs-up as we went by, then fanned at her neck to show us a diamond on a gold chain Sweet Lou had given her for doing such a good job. She was chatting with two old ladies in identical dresses decorated with blossoms and green leaves. If they weren't sisters they should have been. They both had red rouge splotches on their cheeks, red as the fry cook's scarf, and they were complaining politely to Kathy in southern accents about the air conditioning. One couple argued as they inched ahead about how he had lost all their money at Barney's. The woman kept hissing, "What have you done to us? What have you done to us?" The people behind them acted like they didn't hear a thing. The line snaked almost all the way back into the casino. I could tell by the way the poor, beaten guy was looking around he was tempted to jump out of line to try to win their money back at our tables. And I could tell that's exactly what his wife was thinking; was scared of. If I had to bet, I'd guess they had the price of two Mine Shaft Famous Smorgasbord dinners in her purse: Three dollars and ninety-eight cents and she wasn't about to let him squander it. The casino was like flypaper or a magnet for the ones waiting to get something cheap to eat. But, of course, that was the plan. Lou and Butcher wanted the opportunity for risk in front of you at all times. Even while you waited for our bargain eats. I eavesdropped as much as I could, picking up pieces of conversations. The house sound system was pumping out *Peter Gunn*. As we got closer to the noise in the casino, all those blaring horns started to be drowned out by the action. We went into the casino and hung around by the service end of the bar. The television was on and Walter Cronkite was sitting at his desk over his microphone taking his black rimmed glasses on and off and saying something. I couldn't hear a word. Nobody seemed to be paying much attention. I looked over at the Twenty-One tables for Rennie.

Turner took a mint from the bowl next to Danny's register and said, "Here we go. Ed told me that he had two tours of Vietnam, both combat. Killed a bunch of people. Had friends get killed. He had wanted to re-up for a third, but when he was on R and R in Honolulu at a hotel he called The Royal Hawaiian. He mentioned it a zillion times, always raising his eyebrows and talking about how 'big and titty pink' it was. Well his wife had come out from Michigan to be with him, and he started having terrible dreams and night sweats while they were there. He sort of freaked out. She'd bitched that he was drinking too much, smoking grass and scaring her. He said he was just trying to cope with being in normal life around normal people. But the dreams wouldn't stop. It freaked his wife so much that she got in touch with the Army, and tattled on him; said he wasn't mentally healthy enough to go back, that he was doing drugs. So they didn't let him re-enlist. Big Ed said he spent about one month back in Detroit with his wife then told me, 'Got on Ninety-Four. Got on Ninety-Four. Got on Ninety-Four heading to Chicago. Never looked back. Never looked back.' Just like that. See, man. That war is fucked up. See what it does to people?"

And he waved to the television like there was a news story on right now about Big Ed. But Cronkite was still at his desk. He had one hand at an ear.

"Ninety-Four, the interstate?"

"Guess so."

Danny told us to move so a waitress could grab a tray of cocktails.

She threw a small wedge of lime into each glass and said to Danny without looking up, "Which one's gin?" Then said, "Ah, got it," before he could say anything. "The one with two swizzle sticks. Okay, I'm a dummy." Danny nodded, arched his eyebrows. He held a bottle of Bloody Mary mix to his nose and made a face, then poured it into the sink.

Rennie had a full table. She was smiling and dealing. And for fun I followed the food chain of watchers from three young soldiers on stools at the table studying their hands, to Rennie holding her deck, waiting, to the box man, arms across his chest watching her, to the pit boss leaning on another table watching the box man, to the floor supervisor watching the pit boss, and up to the eye in the sky, the small flying saucer dome in the ceiling watching him and everybody else, and I looked back at Rennie. And for some reason, at that moment, I became aware of our relationship. Became conscious of it, felt I could hold it up and see it. Really see it for the first time. In my mind I pictured it like a broken electrical wire with current jumping and arcing to get across to the other wire, when just seconds before the electricity had been flowing quiet and taken for granted. I thought I caught a hint of strain in her eyes and felt the natural thing between us begin to slip away right on the spot. Something like that. I looked at her really hard again, but saw nothing different and told Turner we'd better get back to the kitchen. I wondered where in the hell that moment of super feeling, if that's what it was, had come from and what it meant. Or if it had happened at all. Anyway, the thought went away as we walked. The moment had been like watching a movie with just a few frames missing, barely noticeable, and practically invisible. Felt, more than anything, like my dream echoes. I looked back at the television and Walter Cronkite was still talking, a picture of a rocket over his shoulder. I asked Danny if there were men on the moon yet. He said, "I haven't been paying attention. Been too busy."

In the restaurant, the couple who had been bickering about the gambling loss were moving down the line, having paid, but weren't talking. Their attention was on the lasagna and the other Famous Smorgasbord shit in front of them. The two old ladies in matching dresses were discussing each selection, backing up the line, their plates dotted like painter's palettes with plops of mashed potatoes, ham, green salad, bean salad, chicken salad, jello, roast beef and rolls. They both oohed and aahed when Redding came through the swinging doors with a full pan of ham salad on his shoulder. Beaner pried up an almost empty pan streaked with low ridges of raked over tuna salad and Redding fitted his pan into the opening. I pictured him making it and said to Turner, "It looks like stucco. You could plaster a house with that stuff." Then in the alcove, I asked Turner why he thought Big Ed wouldn't talk at work.

"Got me. He's a head trip, but I think harmless. He shut up when we hit the door. Like he was at the finish line of a race. I said, 'Well thanks,' and he said, 'You also,' and went in.

That's it."

"He hasn't talked to you anymore today?"

"Nope. Not a word," and Turner shrugged his shoulders and went over to the counter where Redding and Lee were pulling chicken parts out of the sink and spreading them on trays. From where I stood I could see the big ham salad trough jutting out into the aisle from the pot and pan sinks, a big, industrial looking barge of a thing. It was like having to clean a canoe at the sink. You had to change the water right after you rinsed it then dig around in the drain for chunks of ham or the sink would stop up.

When I got back I told Shanahan nobody was walking on the moon as of six o'clock. He straightened up from mopping around the ovens, pulsating, wired up as always, and took in what I'd had to say. Then he said, "Just you wait. This is gonna be a great night for the United States of America and everybody in this damn casino. Just wait." And he splashed the mop on the floor and started singing that dippy Fifties song "Tall Paul" again. I started scraping plates, spraying and hoping he and Big Ed would stay out of each other's way.

I took a break out back about six-thirty and really wasn't hungry. Our food killed my appetite. I didn't usually get hungry until after work. And then, whether I was at Rennie's or at the apartment, I was usually smoking pot and drinking wine and that caused a case of the munchies and then I could eat, really scarf it down. If I hadn't managed to sneak any food out of the kitchen we'd always seem to end up at Tippy's, or if we had to, went to a hot dog chain called Der Wienersnitzel that I really didn't dig. Seemed so stupid. But you could fill up for cheap.

I was sitting on the stoop staring at the growing patches of greased, shiny leather on my boots. I could hear Big Ed's sink sucking and draining through the door. Redding and Turner had made a run down to a record store to see if they could find the new Rita Coolidge album. Redding had the hots for her. I was trying to arrange in my head the different thoughts, people and issues all tangled together in there, when I looked up. Looking down at me was the little red-faced guy Tony had run off weeks earlier, the day I'd started, the one he called a pot licker. He wasn't in any better shape than he'd been when I'd seen him the first time. I pushed up. He was wearing a flannel shirt buttoned all the way up to his flappy neck, and even though it was getting dark I could tell his eyes were as blue as the water of Lake Tahoe at noon. His hands were big for a little man, and they were shaking, red and rough as his face. They were gripped together where his belt buckle should have been. His head was full of thick, white hair, oily and combed straight back off a high and wide forehead that gave him a jumpy, surprised look. And, all told, I guessed his hair was about the only thing he hadn't lost. I assumed he was here for a job. But I was pretty sure he needed a drink worse. I left him at the door and went to see if I could find Lee.

Lee was behind the line watching the customers as they slid their trays along. He had a smile on his face, and now that I knew enough about him from his wisecracks, no matter what the reasons, the fact he'd found himself in what amounted to a cafeteria at this stage in his career was a cruel joke to him. Shanahan was trotting out to the casino to get an update.

"Lee. That guy. He said his name is Little Georgie. He's

asking for you again at the back door." I glanced past the three soldiers I'd seen earlier at Rennie's table as they went down the line, loud and drunk, then over to the house table to make sure Tony wasn't around still. I really thought he would stab that little guy if he saw him again based on what had happened six weeks ago.

Lee said, "Little Georgie, eh?" in the same thoughtful way he had reacted to the grease man's news that the naked guy with the car keys taped to his ass had been driving a Camaro. "Little Georgie?" he said again, a little more focused on me the second time he answered. He flinched when he saw a fat guy with three chins marching two dinner plates down the line. One was covered in chicken legs, the other a plate full of mashed potatoes with a lake of gravy in the middle. Lee was staring at the plates while he said, "Put Georgie in the stockroom. I'll be right there. Let's give him a hand, help him out. Whattaya say, kid?" And he started humming something jazzy, still watching the fat man move his plates down the line.

After I'd brought a bottle of red back from the bar and used the steel to push the cork into it, I set up Little Georgie with a mug in the stockroom. He sat on an unopened box of tangerine nectar cans and sipped at the wine with two hands vibrating, somehow getting it up to his lips. He wore beat up wing tips that were too big, without laces, and thin, dirty white socks loose and low at his ankles. One of his ankles had an ugly scab. Then he grinned at me and tamped his feet in a dusty circle of spilled flour. He grinned and grinned and grinned. At one point he looked like he was going to throw up, but fought it down. Lee looked in on us twice and said, "Hey, cats," in that soft way and I gave Lee a refill and could see over his shoulder to Big Ed with that loopy smile on his face sneaking a look our way. I think. There must have been miles between where he was and where we really were, but after hearing Turner's story about him, I had a small bit of sympathy. I wondered how normal he'd really been before he went, how close he came to finding himself in my collage, on my wall. Lee closed the door and left Georgie and me in our little bunker, walls lined with sauce cans, bags of sugar and supplies, one light bulb over us. If Butcher caught us, there'd be hell to pay. We could all get eighty-sixed. But Lee was laying it all on the line for his friend, and I was impressed by that. And I was willing to help. I'm sure Lee was out by the line, keeping it loaded up, watching the customers, sipping from his mug, looking like he was doing his job, out there on the perimeter keeping a lookout for Butcher.

I left Little Georgie after a while. He still wasn't talking. Just smiling. I went out behind the line to ask Lee if we should put an apron on Georgie, have him do something in case Butcher showed.

"What kind of shape's he in, kid?"

"Shape?"

"Could he shave without slitting his throat?"

"I see what you mean."

Lee reached under his apron and pulled out a ten dollar bill. He said, "Give him a sawbuck."

I took it. "That's nice. It's a lot. But it's nice. Known him a long time?" Kathy came running into the restaurant at the

188

back of the customers in line.

Lee said, "He came here in 1949. Been on the hill since then. Can't seem to get off."

Kathy yelled over the customers and the food: "The Eagle has landed boys. ShitDevilDickDamnPi...." and she caught herself as some people in line turned to see who was yelping and cussing, "...whoops. Sorry..."

Lee reached for a cigarette and said, "Sometimes that girl can be a blunt instrument. Go check on Little Georgie, pally."

Kathy had her hands on top of her head, turning in circles. She gushed a few sorries, and "What was I thinking..." then cut in line and leaned on the counter above a pan of baked beans and said to us as I was about to shoulder through the swinging doors, 'They landed, boys. There's men on the moon. Walter Cronkite said, 'The Eagle has landed.' That's what that means. Come see for yourself. Don't ya see? Daddy is beside himself. I was tired as a stuffed dog tick, but I'm revved up now. I'll keep you posted," and she pushed back from the line as a customer reached under the sneeze glass and spooned a big glob of Redding's ham salad.

When I got to the stockroom the door was open and Little Georgie was gone. Lee's dress suit and fedora were hanging on the back of the door. Our coffee mugs were on a shelf in front of a fifty-pound bag of potatoes. Mine, which had had three fingers of wine, was empty. I opened the door and looked across at Big Ed, the back door, then back at Big Ed. He pulled his head out of the ham salad vat straddling the two sinks. He was humming and bouncing while he scrubbed. I hesitated, then asked anyway. "You see that little guy leave? See him go? Did he say anything to you?" He didn't look at me and I wasn't sure he'd heard me. I repeated myself, "You see little Georgie leave?" He looked at me, but didn't say anything. I shook my head. "Thanks," I said, not close to meaning it. I wanted to tell him he was a real asshole, but didn't want to risk pissing him off. I turned on my boot heel to go tell Lee.

Big Ed said to my back, "You alsoooo." I looked back, but he was busy soaping up the sides of the vat.

I saw Redding and Turner hurrying out through the alcove and figured they were headed to the casino to watch the men on the moon. Lee came in from the line, and I told him Little Georgie had split. He didn't act surprised.

"Flew the coop, did he?"

"Yeah. Gone."

"Took a powder..."

"I guess."

Lee had his coffee mug in one hand, a cigarette in the other. He turned the mug upside down and acted surprised, "Dead soldier," and I knew what was next. "Go tell that toodler Danny we're making a special sauce to celebrate men on the moon. Whattayasay, pally?"

I said, "Sure" and held out his ten dollar bill.

He pushed it back at me and said, "Put it in Danny's hand."

Just then Beaner came in the kitchen from the alcove and yelled, "Lee. Veek. Man on the moon." His gold crucifix hung out over his red smock, and he skidded on the tile as he tore back out through the alcove.

I thought if they could really land men on the moon, it would bring everything to a dead stop all over The Mine Shaft, and everywhere else in the world for that matter. I knew my parents would be glued to the set. The common room at the fraternity house would be jammed with summer quarter goons drinking 3.2 beer. Even at Crow's the summer school students would stop drinking and watch it. But as I walked back to the casino through the restaurant, along the line, down the hall toward the action, things were pretty much normal. I think Lou was ready to make a big deal out of the whole thing if that's what seemed to be called for when and if it really happened. He said he was ready to hand out freebies of champagne if that would keep the players around. But it was a bad time to try to get a bottle of wine from Danny. Both Lou and Butcher were hanging around in the casino. Lou was right at the cashier's cage, just across from Danny's register. Butcher was near Rennie's table, watching her. A few people at tables and at the bar would glance up to the TV once in a while, or ask if anything had happened yet. I still couldn't hear the announcer, and the screen was staying on a picture of the landing rocket, or whatever it was. I could see no one. I couldn't make out if it was a photograph or a live picture of the rocket thing not moving. There were no men walking around on what was supposed to be the moon. Danny switched around for something else, but the same shot was on all three channels. The TV set might as well have been a light bulb. And people kept betting to win while it glowed above the bar. The place was packed.

Lee and Big Ed were the only kitchen help who weren't in the casino. We were pushing it. As long as nothing was happening on the moon, there was no good reason to justify all of us hanging around. Everyone had gotten excited for nothing. At least it seemed that way for now. I asked Danny what time it was and he said it was just before seven. I watched Butcher look at the room and figured he was doing a head count of the kitchen crew. But Lou was standing there for protection. He neutralized Butcher.

I felt Lou's arm loosely around my waist and he said, "Do me a favor, kid. Go tell Lee I'm going to watch the moonwalk in my office," and he tilted his head to the short hallway that ran off from the casino next to the cashier's cage. "Tell him to fix up something nice for a couple of people. Okay?"

"Sure, Lou. Gottcha." It was smart to do Lou favors.

Then he said, "Tell Kathy I need to see her in my office."

I brought her back into the casino and felt Butcher's eyes without having to look.

And when Kathy walked down the hall to Lou's office, I watched him stare at her back until the office door closed, both hands in a loose clinch at his sides.

In the kitchen I told Lee what Sweet Lou wanted, and he sent me to the walk-in for steaks. I was starting to help out with cooking when things were busy, but I hated the walk-in. It always freaked me out. Someone said it was the only thing that scared Butcher, too. No way he'd go in. It was back in the corner of the kitchen on the other side of the stockroom from the pot and pan sink. It was a refrigerator big as a bank vault, a smaller door inside at the back that went to a freezer. Anything that could spoil—lettuce, celery, milk, big bags of hamburger meat, you name it—was kept in there. I had this fear I would get trapped and freeze to death. It wasn't like there was a phone in there. The light switch was on the outside. You'd be safer in a stuck elevator. And there wasn't a handle, a real handle, on the inside. You had to hit a plunger-like thing with your hip or butt if your hands were full, and it always worked, but I still didn't get off having to go in there. It was as creepy as a dark basement. Once we got Big Ed in there for some excuse and killed the lights for a second. He came raging out into the light like a bull, his eyes yellow and wild. Now that I knew more about him, we're lucky he hadn't done something insane.

I got two T-bone steaks, thick and blue, from a dozen or so stacked in a big pan covered with thick foil. They weren't for the customers, and definitely not us peons. They were for Butcher and Sweet Lou or their friends and their special dinners. Redding, Turner and I had talked about lifting a couple, but decided against it because they'd be too easy to miss. I was convinced Tony counted them every day. But they were beautiful pieces of meat.

Lee said, "Let's have a cooking lesson, kid." But first, *"Donde es the vino?"*

I told him it was a bad time. Butcher was prowling. Lee winked, stepped over to his knife briefcase under the slicer table and pulled out a pint bottle of vodka and tipped it up. He handed it to me and I took a swig. He put it back in the case after another. I hiccupped and held my breath. My throat burned.

"Listen up. It's easy to be a good chef. It's tough, babe, tough to be a great one." Then he started laughing like he laughed when he was talking about Karlene or some other gag he and Skin had pulled, but stopped when he reached for a big skillet from the rack above. He said, "And...I...ain't...either...one...any...more." And he banged the skillet, black from a zillion times on the flame, on top of one of the cross hatched burners on the Vulcan. He turned a knob on the oven front and blue flame whooshed and flickered up around the sides of the skillet.

"C'mon..."

"C'mon, my rear. Hand me that can," and he pointed his cigarette like a throwing dart to the big square oil can with the red and green designs that held about a gallon of olive oil. He drizzled a circle of green oil the size of a silver dollar into the skillet, and the puddle right away squiggled to the heat like an image in a psychedelic light show. Lee said, "You know how Tony worries his ass off about the crap we turn out of here every day? Too much sugar in the sauce, too much paprika, not enough paprika on the chicken? That ketchup over there he calls red sauce? It's a joke. Let me tell you. It's a joke. I had a place. I ran five chefs. San Francisco. Fancy food. Real cuisine. First-class crowd. Guess which dish I always had to taste before it was allowed out of my kitchen?" The olive oil, heating up in the skillet smelled good, different from the cloud of Hobart steam and grease that gusted around me most of the time. Lee had the steaks on a platter and sprinkled them on both sides with salt and pepper. As he shook the pepper from a dented tin shaker that was passed around the kitchen and nearly always in need of a refill, he said, "Not even a Goddamn pepper mill in this place." He shook it once more and tossed the shaker to me. "So. You know what I had to taste every night?"

"What?" He dropped both steaks into the skillet. They crackled and sizzled in the hot oil and sent up a spout of steam into the fan at the ceiling. He shook the skillet, towel on the handle.

"The green salad." He shook the skillet some more. "The Goddamn green salad, babe." And I'd never seen him so agitated. "Nope. I didn't have to check the signature dishes: the lobster with ginger, and lime and white wine sauce, never. I didn't have to check the sweetbreads, no, or the souffles, or the Dover Sole." His voice kept going up and getting louder. "No. I had to taste the Goddamn green salad." He'd turned his back to the steaks. He looked at me and said very slow and soft now, like he had when he pulled the skillet off the rack, "Nobody gives a shit about the green salad." It was almost a whisper. He stopped. Then he said, like he was tired more than anything, almost in pain, "But that's the point..."

I wasn't sure if I got the point, so I shut up and just watched him a few more minutes. Then, without looking at his watch or poking much, he turned the steaks with the stainless tongs that hung on the oven handle and put the skillet in the oven. And real fast—before the steaks had come out, and it could not have been more than three or four minutes—he had cut in half and fried on a lower flame two big tomatoes sprinkled with oregano, salt and pepper, melted butter. He skimmed off the foam and sautéed some whole mushrooms in it, and sent me to the line to get two "nice spuds."

"How will you know when the steaks are done?"

"They're done when they're done."

We fixed two plates and set them on the counter next to the double sink, and with a fresh tomato in his left hand, and a small knife in his right, with an exact identical motion, he peeled the tomato skin into one long strip, cut the strip in half, and as neat as I'd ever seen anyone use their fingers, rolled each strip of red skin inside out into what looked exactly like a small rose bud and put one at the edge of each white plate. He said, more to himself than to me, "Presentation. Beats the hell out of a fucking parsley sprig, don't you think?" wiping his hands on his apron.

He seemed to have calmed down from his story about the green salad. I said, "Lee, why don't you get out of here? Do some real cooking again?"

But he kept talking. "This little tomato rose does to this plate what a musician does with a note of music. Adds something. Colors it. Doesn't change it, just accents it. Gives it personality, you see. An edge with the personality, babe. Timbre."

"What?"

"Timbre."

"What's timbre? How do you spell it?"

"T-I-M-B-R-E."

"What's it mean?"

"Like I said. Color in music. Style. Personality."

"Okay…"

He put two metal covers over each dinner and walked over to a stack of trays, took one and set it next to the covered plates. "Pally," he said, "You got four tastes in your mouth. Bet you didn't know that, did you? Sweet, sour, bitter and salty: four. And somewhere along the line, can't explain it, I figured that you get about four shots at life. Seems like a good number. I always bet it. Four times to tune it up and get it right. Well, babe, I've had mine. Take it to the bank." He put the plates on the tray and told me to get some silverware and napkins and take them out to Lou's office.

I held the tray and looked at him. He was walking back over to the briefcase. I said, "Why just four?"

The catches on the case popped open, and facing the wall, the vodka pint in his hand, he said, "My best cooking is way behind me. Way behind. I could never repeat what I've done. I'm finished with the best cooking of my career, kid. I've hit four the hard way already. Hit it too many times." And he held the bottle and studied it a moment, and I felt sorry for him, not because he drank, but because I realized nothing he'd just said was about cooking. Walking through the alcove it made me sad to realize that, even though I could hear him laughing that whorehouse laugh, by himself, alone for a minute in the kitchen except for Big Ed.

Everything had gotten backed up since the false start on the moon landing.

Everyone came back from the casino at the same time and started getting it on. Beaner had piled full bus trays all over the Hobart counter. Lee, slurring his words at times, was getting on us the best he could to keep the line filled. Shanahan was slicing ham and roast beef at the radial slicer like he was sawing logs. He had it flying. He'd told us the piece of finger missing from his left hand was from a sawmill accident, and watching him run the slicer, smoking, talking, looking around, I could imagine how it happened. Turner had an assembly line of lasagnas working, layering the noodles with big splashes of Tony's sauce ladled from a stainless pot. Next to the sauce pot was a tub of cheese Turner was also spooning in with the layers. He flicked it in the pans like he was flipping butter across an elementary school lunch room, jabbering the whole time. Redding was panning chicken and running a relay to the line and back through the swinging doors, taking empty pans back to Big Ed. The place was popping.

Lee was wiping his hands on a towel and crossing in front of the ovens, weaving, and I knew what he was coming to ask me. He'd want me to hit up Danny. He wanted another drink, but it was only a little after seven and I'd never seen him this drunk, this obvious, this early. I always worried about Butcher. But Lee was my man. The Hobart was mid cycle so we leaned together over the counter to talk. His eyes were half closed, his breath had the no-smell smell of vodka, and I waited for him to say what I knew he wanted to say, but he couldn't get it out. His words and thoughts weren't connecting. His mouth moved, but all he did was lick his lips. I said, "Lee?"

"Sauce...time...right?" And he caught himself, shuffling to the right. "Yowser." He was smashed. His face seemed to get grayer.

I said, "I think we ought to get you out of the way." I could almost make a small pony tail with my hair in back and I gathered and tugged at it nervously.

He licked his lips some more, straightened up, and found a Camel pack in his pants pocket. It was empty. He fingered it, dropped it on the counter, then patted every pocket he had and felt behind both ears. He smiled at me. "Got any?" Shrugging. "Seems I'm eighty-six on the fags, babe."

Rennie came into the alcove. I hadn't talked to her all shift. She looked tired, but great. My earlier worry about something, about her, whatever it had been, was gone. She lit a cigarette and leaned on the wall. I nodded in Lee's direction. He was into a slow, unsteady turn, surveying the crew for someone with a cigarette.

She picked up on it right away and said, "Butcher's on the way. I think he's looking for a steak."

Lee heard her and turned. "Hey, darlin', anybody walkin' around in green cheese yet?" Then, leaning on the Hobart counter again, "How 'bout a smoke?"

I said, "Hey, Lee..."

She was holding her hand out with the pack to Lee and he was taking a few careful steps to her, not hearing, or else ignoring me, when Butcher showed up in the alcove and sized up the scene: Lee's hand was wobbling out in the air like he was trying to charm a Cobra. Rennie looked back over her shoulder at Butcher, who winked at her, which pissed me off, then over at me like I was a dirty plate or something, then back at Lee. He swallowed before he spoke and his Adam's apple undulated under his turtleneck and for some reason I thought of a hand grenade about to explode.

We were frozen in place. Nothing was moving except for Lee's wavering hand and my jittering eyelid. Butcher said, "Let me help you out, Chef." And he stepped and took the cigarette pack from Rennie and held it out to Lee, who made a clumsy swipe that knocked them from Butcher's hand. Butcher didn't look down and stared at Lee.

Lee said to me, "Be...be a toodler...pal. Pick 'em up, will ya?"

Chapter 11

"You're stewed, Chef," said Butcher.

Rennie folded her arms and bit her lip. Then she started tapping a tooth with a fingernail. I came from behind the counter, got the cigarettes off the floor and pushed one into Lee's fingers, then stood with Rennie at Butcher's back. Lee had his back to the rest of the kitchen and all the usual action. Big Ed, that walking coma, pulled his nose out of the sink and was walking up the aisle at us carrying clean sauce pans. The bell timer went off on the stacked ovens and Redding came sliding over to pull out the latest baked chicken. He saw us standing in the alcove, but like the rest of the crew, he made it a rule to keep as much distance as possible from Butcher. He went about his chicken business. Big Ed was clumping closer, but he may as well have been on the moon himself, the only person in the kitchen who didn't realize Lee was balls to the wall hammered.

Lee didn't, or couldn't talk. He leaned on the Hobart counter, the edge of the stainless rail catching him just above the left hip. He tried to hold onto a smile I'm sure he hoped would look cool. The unlit cigarette I'd given him was wet between his lips. From where Rennie and I stood, Butcher seemed nine feet tall. Thick rolls of skin covered in short hair at the nape of his neck were coiled like fuzzy worms over the top of his turtleneck. Big Ed walked up close behind Lee and stopped with that dumb ass smile on his face. I shivered to think I was spending so much time everyday so close to those guys. I thought of Sonny Liston and what they used to say about the length of his arms, and what a mean dude he was supposed to be. How he took it to Cassius Clay. Big Ed and Butcher were brooders, like Liston was supposed to be, and probably as dangerous. They were both bad dream material.

"Light, Chef?" Butcher finally moved, and very slowly pulled a silver lighter from his pants pocket and snapped a flame in Lee's face. A thick gold bracelet, guaranteed to be the most expensive thing in the kitchen at the moment, dangled from his wrist.

Shanahan yelled, "Weeeooo" for some reason from across the kitchen.

Butcher teased Lee with the flame. His hand stopped just short of the cigarette tip. Lee leaned forward, still draped on the Hobart counter for support, and stretched his neck to get at the flame. His elbow slipped and he knocked a coffee mug to the floor and it shattered. Butcher turned around and tried to get to Rennie and me with a smile, grinding a small piece of the porcelain mug under his toe. He was having a ball. He could have been a sick kid, excited about the idea of torturing a cat. Then he swung his arm back to Lee, whose head was moving back and forth like he was following a ball in a slow motion tennis match. I sucked in a breath. Rennie said, "Break's over, I..."

"Hell it is, honey," said Butcher. "Stay put." He held us both in place at his back with that. I was totally confused and scared, and I could feel the tension, or fear, or both, coming out of Rennie. Lee was still trying to get the tip of the cigarette into the flame, but couldn't make the reach. It was pathetic.

Then something moved me. Pure impulse. I snatched Rennie's pack, fumbled out a cigarette, lit it with some matches I had in my jeans and dipped around Butcher, and pulled the cigarette from Lee's mouth and stuck in the one I'd lit. It was all over before I knew it. I said, "There you go," and he lowered his head and clamped down hard on the filter. I looked up at Butcher. The only thing I could think to say was, "I gotta get on these dishes," and pointed to a bus tray on the counter.

Butcher clicked his lighter shut and dropped it into his pants pocket, and noisy as the kitchen was, it surprised me when I heard it hit his pocket change. He didn't look at me with any special meanness. He just said, "Take a break, kid. Stretch your legs." Then he wheeled to Rennie like he suspected she'd done something behind his back, and said, "Go wait for me at my table," then he faced Lee. Rennie bit her lip and walked out into the restaurant. Butcher looked at me. "Well? Take a load off." This time his voice boomed from somewhere inside his chest and I left for the back door, bumping right away into Big Ed on his way back to the pot and pan sink. He fell away from the scrape like I had hit him in the stomach with a baseball bat.

"Hey," he barked. "Watch it."

I looked at him like the nut case he was, but was surprised he could say anything intelligible at all, and then I looked over to see if any of the guys were following what was happening. I had my hand on the back door knob about to go outside when I heard Lee say to Butcher, "The kid...the kid got it. The kid brought the booze in here, Butcher." I stood a moment listening to Big Ed clumping down the tile, feeling his psychotic, Marmaduke walk to the sink, but it wasn't as sickening, or hurtful, as what I had just heard. Lee might as well have followed me and buried his French knife up to the hilt between my shoulder blades.

It killed me. Ate me up inside. I could not believe he would betray me to Butcher like he did. And it wasn't even true. Lee was already drunk when he got to work as usual. I was going to get fired. I knew it. Probably Lee, too. I didn't care. I walked in circles outside the back door. I kicked gravel and looked up in the stars to find the moon, and, breathing heavy, heart pounding, felt like I was going to cry, so I took off walking into the parking lot.

I decided to quit. I didn't have any money, hadn't saved any. But there had to be work someplace else in Tahoe. The place was crawling with tourists. I'd find something. I felt like a kid whose best friend had ditched him on the playground in front of all the other guys. I tried to figure it out. Why was I so busted up about Lee lying about me and the drinking? I hardly knew him, really. He was just somebody I'd known a couple of months now. An older guy who was kinda cool, had some style, been around, had collected experiences in his head about living and cooking. I felt sorry for him, but I liked helping him, didn't mind covering for him at all. But what did he mean to me? Why in the hell was I so upset? In my twenty years I had spent just under two months in a hash house kitchen with wackos, drunks, drifters, drug dealers and mob guys for all I knew, but in that short time I had become a part of it, and now out of nowhere, like that coffee mug falling on the floor, my life was broken in pieces again. Like I needed that. So, I said to myself as I walked, what the hell's new Vic? What'd you expect anyway?

I sat on a small mound covered in pine needles and cones at the edge of some trees that rimmed the back of the parking lot. It was cool out. Like most Tahoe nights. The lot was full.

About three spaces in front of me a red and white Ford Falcon bore Oregon tags. Someone had left the door cracked open. The dome light was on, and I knew if I didn't close the door the battery might be dead when they came out. Instead of jumping up, I focused on that decision, whether to take the time to do the simple act of getting up and closing the door as an anonymous favor for what felt like a long time. And the mental exercise became important, and it began to take on much, much more weight than just a pure act of courtesy. In my mind, it became the act on which I was going to decide the rest of my summer in Tahoe at The Mine Shaft. I could leave the door open, leave the people to their own devices, walk back to the casino, throw my apron in the hamper, tell Big Ed to kiss off, and try to have a word with Rennie, collect what they owed me at the cage and split. Or I could get up, brush the pine needles off my ass, close the car door...just close the door...and go back in and deal with it all.

I heard Turner yelling. "Vic. Vic. Where the hell are you? You out here? Vic."

I pushed up off the pine needles and scrambled up the hill behind me a little way and hid behind a tree, hands at eye level like I was going to try to push it over, resin sticking to my fingers, pine scent sharp in my nose. And it was even cooler just a few steps higher on the hill.

"Victor. Victor. Where are you, Sinclare?"

At this height I could look down across and over the tops of the cars parked tight together back to the side of the building and out to the road. It was a patio of roofs. I could see cars going both ways in front of the casino, could hear their tires singing on the pavement. I spotted the grease barrel under the light at the back door. I had a better view of the Falcon's lit up red and white interior, and I wanted to continue to focus on the decision, my choice, what to do about it. I saw Turner getting closer, once going out of his way to avoid a couple leaning on a car, making out. They were getting it on heavy and, of course, I thought of Rennie. Turner's shape, his outline and body movement were familiar to me, but I could not make out his face, but I could picture it perfectly. I knew the exasperated contortion it would be in under that ridiculous hair. A Cougar, maybe a Mustang, pulled through the dark prowling for a space. The windows were down. I heard part of that new Rolling Stones song again and then it was lost as the car turned away.

I liked it in the woods, above the cars, hidden from Turner. Playing hide and seek with him started to seem funny, and my internal debate about the dome light in the Falcon had distracted me from my funk about Lee's screwing me. But just as fast, I got strung out again when I thought about the surprise, shock and confusion, and I was right back at the place where I wanted to quit. It settled on me totally, just like the parachute from my apartment in Cincinnati had done.

"Dammit, Vic....c'mon, man. We need you." He leaned on a car about thirty feet in front of me, and said, "Shit." Then he started walking right to where I was. He stopped when he got to the Falcon. He looked in. I was suddenly alive with a fear he was about to rob me of the chance to work my way through to a decision about leaving it on or turning it off, and I realized my little life game had become super important.

He reached for the handle. Just a hip check, push, a lean, any pressure or firm slam would close a circuit and the light would be snuffed out, the interior would go black. One more decision made out of my control. He was about to steal something very special from me.

"Hey," I hollered from the hill. "Turner." He jerked his head in my direction, but left his hand on the handle.

"Vic?" Then, scuffling through the gravel, he said, "Vic? You asshole. Shit, man. What are you doing up there?"

I said, "Taking a leak," and took sideways steps coming down, surfing down the pine needles. I got to him, hands on his hips. Out of the peace and the dark of the pine trees I felt exposed, almost like I had walked into a roomful of people. The wind kicked up and it swirled in the tree tops and some of them creaked, I thought I heard one pine cone hit the ground.

"Hey, man, we need you," he said, "Butcher wants a steak like Lou's. Sent Beaner in to tell Lee."

"So?"

"So, Lee's out of it. He's bombed. You know that."

I said, "Tough shit. You know what he did? What he told Butcher?"

"Yeah, yeah. Redding heard it all." He punched me in the shoulder. "Get over it. He's all liquored up. He didn't mean it. He won't even remember it in the morning. You know how he is."

"Remind me of that when I'm looking for another job. I'm

quitting anyway. Fuck it. That was bullshit, what he did."

"Victor. If Butcher doesn't get his steak, Lee's gone for sure. Then Tony's our man. You want that? Listen. You're the only one who saw Lee cook the steak. He kept mumbling, 'I showed the kid. I showed the kid. It's nothing.' Shit, man, you gotta do it."

"Turner, I wash dishes and mop the floor. I'm no chef."

"C'mon, man. We'll help."

"Is Rennie still at Sharkey's table?"

"No. I looked. He's there by himself, drinking. She's back in the casino."

I heard a car radio from somewhere near. An announcer or a news guy was talking in a deep voice about Neil Armstrong and Apollo 11. I asked Turner if they were walking on the moon yet, and I looked up to the night sky. He said, "Got me, we've just been trying to get Lee to stand up and walk on earth. Shanahan will know."

We were at the Falcon. Turner was next to it. I didn't have an answer for myself, so when he stuck his butt out and closed the door with the same motion we used to hit the plunger to leave the walk-in, I wasn't even really pissed he had taken an important decision away from me. In a way, the more I thought about it, the farther away we walked from the pine trees and my dark hideout, I was happy he'd saved me from making a choice. He'd bought more time for me to wallow around in confusion. I felt pretty good.

I said, "You know where they are. Get a good one."

It took some hard rubbing over one of the double sinks to get the pine tar from my fingers. I said over my shoulder to Shanahan that Lee had made cooking the steaks for Lou look really easy.

He said, "The great ones always make it look easy, college boy. Where you been?" Then, "What time is it?"

I dried my hands on a towel and said, "Don't know."

He said, "Well, I'm gonna giddyup back out there and see if they're walkin' yet. Damn if I'm gonna miss history." Turner was waving me over to the Vulcan. Shanahan said as he lit a cigarette, "I'll betcha those card tables and them machines are going to shut down when they see them men walking on the moon. They'll be empty as my old lady's head." And he reached and pinched Turner on the butt as he left the kitchen. Turner acted like he was going to throw Butcher's steak at him. Shanahan gave him the finger. Those two really wanted to like each other. You could tell it. Too bad the Vietnam thing was such a big deal between them.

"What do we do first?" Turner held a big T-bone, flopped over two hands. He was at attention at the Vulcan. I looked up at the hanging skillets.

"Where's Lee?"

"Gone."

"What'd you do with him?"

"We're hiding him from Butcher. He got it together enough to convince Butcher to give him a second chance. You too, but when Butcher left he passed out."

"Where?" I reached for a skillet that looked like the one Lee had used, turned on the burner and put the skillet on the flame. I said, "Put the steak on the counter and salt and pepper it. Both sides." I didn't really want to see Lee anyway. I was glad he wasn't around. I just wasn't too sure about cooking the steak.

"How much?"

"Like the chicken. Hell, I don't know. Just do it." I looked for the olive oil, and asked again, "Where'd you stash him?"

Turner flapped the steak on the counter and started shaking it with the pepper and salt.

"We put him in the walk-in."

I had my hand on the skillet handle, could feel the heat conducting its way to my hand. I left it there, feeling the handle warming. I looked at him getting after the steaks like he did every other job, intense, a maniac. I couldn't believe what he'd just said so nonchalantly. "Wait. What? You put him in the walk-in? He'll freeze his ass in there. Jesus Christ."

"It's okay, he's not in the freezer." He flipped the T-bone. "Redding went in with him. It's only been a couple of minutes. Butcher was coming back and we had to put Lee someplace he wouldn't look. We figured he'd never guess the walk-in, and besides, he's scared of it. Lee was passed out on the floor of the stockroom. We had to get him hid. We told Butcher he was getting something out of his car."

"Jesus Christ," I said. "Butcher bought that?"

"Guess so. He just said, 'Gimme a T-bone like Lou's. Rare. Tell him.' He did poke his beak in the stockroom, but that's all."

"Oh you think so?" I really didn't think Butcher could be had so easy, and I started trying to figure out his next move when the door to the walk-in opened and Lee and Redding stumbled out. Lee had one arm around Redding's shoulders. Both wore at least three red table cloths wrapped around their shoulders. Lee's face was as white as his toque. His lips were gray. I couldn't tell if his eyes were open or shut. They were slits. Redding said, "How about a hand, guys?" He lurched with Lee, who I guessed must weigh at least two hundred pounds.

He looked dead. Turner said, "Did he puke in there?"

Redding said, "Nope," as Turner got under Lee's other arm, "but we knocked some of Tony's sauce off the shelf into the ham salad tub. It was uncovered."

Turner said, "I'll stir it in later. Never know the difference. Let's get him back in the stockroom." They dragged him around the corner, Turner saying to Redding, "Get him some soup or coffee. Keep an eye out." I wondered, as he bounced and mumbled at his sink, what Big Ed made of all of this, or if he even noticed.

I tried to picture Lee cooking the steaks for Lou, remember

211

the steps. I guessed on the flame, and knew the pan had to be real hot. When I poured the olive oil, I had no idea if it was the right amount, but I saw again the green psychedelic swirl the oil puddle made as it ran around the hot skillet bottom. And the smell of the warm oil was great. But he made it look simple and he talked the whole time. I felt like a right handed baseball pitcher who suddenly had been told to throw a curve ball with my left. Redding walked across the kitchen from the stockroom through the swinging doors to the line, shaking his head the whole way, rubbing his arms, trying to restore circulation or heat to his body.

"He's getting him some soup." Turner was at my side, fidgeting. "We got him propped up. We made a bed out of sugar and flour bags." He looked at the skillet and said, "How we doing?"

I said, "Who knows?" Then I looked at the skillet. The oil getting lighter in color had started to smoke. It rose up fast. I said, "Shit. Drop it in, man." Turner picked up the steak with one hand and tossed it into the skillet. It sizzled and popped and splattered both of us with hot oil and made the same sound like when Lee had cooked his, only there was a thicker cloud being sucked to the ceiling fan. My forearms stung and I pulled my head away.

Turner jumped and said, "Yow."

I looked at him. "Too hot?"

He said, "Who knows? What next?"

I tried to shake the skillet, holding the handle with a towel doubled in thickness. The steak didn't move. It was welded to the bottom. There weren't any tongs on the oven handle. I decided to lower the heat and said to Turner, as I held onto the handle, "Get me some tongs. Quick." He ran over to the Hobart and grabbed a dirty pair from a bus tray and came back I pried the steak up and checked out the charred bottom and decided there wasn't enough oil, so I poured some more into the skillet and the smoking quieted and the steak moved when I shook the handle.

Turner said, "What do we need?" I decided I wasn't going to try the mushrooms. The T-bone was enough of a challenge.

"Round up some shit to go with it from the line." He got a tray, the baked potatoes, some mixed vegetables, silverware, and had it all ready to go as I flipped the steak and pulled open the oven door. I got ready for the rush of heat escaping from the Vulcan, but it didn't sweep out and surround me. The oven wasn't hot. It had been turned off. It looked as cold as the walk-in to me.

"Jesus Christ," I yelled. "The damn oven's not on." I looked up at Turner. He gave me his big-wide eyed look. "Big help." Redding came to stand with us.

"Lee's snoring," he said.

"The oven's cold," I straightened from a crouch, put the skillet on an unlit eye next to the flame I'd been using.

Turner asked Redding If he knew what Butcher was doing. "Being an asshole and drinking at his table. Waiting."

Turner said, "Well, just cook it on the burner, like the other side. Who cares?"

"You can do that?"

"Why not?"

"That's not the way Lee did it."

"You got a better idea, Chef Boyardee?"

I said, "Fuck it. I'll be glad when this night's over," and put the skillet back on the burner and we listened again to the sound of meat frying, the fat getting brown at the edges, the steak curling up.

Redding said, "When's it done?"

I couldn't help myself: "When it's done." Then, "I have no fucking idea..."

Big Ed walked by with clean trays for the line. He put them in a stack on a rolling stainless rack by the swinging doors with other bowls, sheet pans and roasting pans. He sniffed the air like a dog in a field and stopped next to the three of us on the way back. He hovered over my shoulder and sniffed some more without looking at or talking to any of us, then walked back around the stacked ovens to his sink. Redding made a face.

Turner saw that and said, "Leave him alone. It's not like he's Richard Speck. He's just strung out. C'mon."

"Who's that?" Redding asked.

"Nurse killer in Chicago, I think. Students?" and I looked at Turner.

"Righto," he said cheerfully. Then, like he was threatening the steak, growled, "Let's cut it. We can tell that way."

"Hold on. Wait another minute or two." I held up my hand, and watched him prance over to the cutting board and grab Lee's French knife. He slashed the air like he was fencing.

"Careful, Zorro," I said. "Those are his babies." Then I remembered the tomato skin rosebud and blew off that idea. I just wanted to get this damn steak out to Butcher before he came back into the kitchen. I sent Redding for some parsley. After a couple more minutes I said, "Okay, let's give it a try," and picked up the T-bone with the tongs and carried it over to the cutting board next to the double sinks. Turner snapped the towel at the board to clean some wilted lettuce leaves from it. The steak looked good enough to me, black on the outside, but still juicy and hot when he cut into it with a slit next to the bone.

"Too rare," he said right away. And he pulled the incision open and I could see the meat was still blue in the middle.

"Okay." I picked the meat off the board with the tongs and halfway back to the Vulcan it slipped onto the floor into a patch of sawdust and soap scum Shanahan had spread on a spill of chicken grease. I said, "Jesus Christ." My heart started pounding, my eyelid flapped.

Redding said, "ShitDevilPissShitFuck...whatever she says," and mimicked Kathy turning in a circle with her hands on her head the way she did.

Turner spiked Lee's knife into the cutting board and said, "Aw, shit, man," and started laughing.

I picked up the steak and looked at it on both sides and flicked at a patch of sawdust that stuck to it like iron fillings on a magnet.

Turner said, "Brush it off, Vic."

Redding said, "He'll never know."

I rubbed the steak off as best I could, and thought of Butcher bossing Rennie out to his table and the shit way he'd dealt with us. I saw Rennie being scared and Lee's pathetic attempts to reach the lighter and it pissed me off again. I looked at Turner.

He stopped laughing and said, "What?"

I said, "Go long," and stepped back like a quarterback in the pocket, my butt up against the double sinks, arm cocked, Butcher's steak my football.

Turner's mouth fell open. "Are you nuts?"

"Cool," said Redding. He had a bunch of parsley in his hand and shook it at me like a cheerleader's pom pom. "Gimme a V. Gimme an I. Gimme a C. What's that spell?"

Together Turner and Redding yelled, "Vic, just call me Broadway Vic. C'mon, go."

"Aw, shit, man," and Turner cut in front of me doing a slow, dopey trot across the back of the kitchen, past the walk-in door, along the stockroom wall. He disappeared over by the pot and pan sink behind the saucer.

"I'll hit you when you clear the chicken ovens, at the Hobart," I yelled. Redding jumped as someone knocked a booster seat off the stack in the alcove. I dropped my arm, but only a second. Beaner came in, loaded down with a full bus tray, Shanahan at his back. They both stopped as Turner came open just past the stacked ovens, and I changed my grip on the steak and decided a Frisbee toss was a better way of completing the pass. I bent my knees, wound up and let it go. It carried much better than I expected and barely grazed his outstretched fingertips before the T-bone sailed over his head to the wall above the Hobart sink. It knocked the sprayer hose off its hook as it flopped into the garbage disposer sink. Turner slid on the tile into Beaner and held onto his shoulders so they could both stay on their feet.

Shanahan came up alongside Beaner, almost nose to nose with Turner, and gave him a dirty look, but for once held his tongue. He looked over at the disposer sink, then back at me and said, "Now that will put you off your food." Then with a hand on Beaner's shoulder he announced to us all that, "While you pissants are throwing food around, there's some real men about to take a walk on the surface of the moon. In about fifteen minutes there ain't gonna be a soul in the world not watching the biggest thing that's ever happened." He shook his head as I crossed the kitchen to get Butcher's steak back from the bottom of the sink. "College boy," he said, "I hate to sound whiney," and he looked Turner and Redding up and down, trying to get their goat, "but you and yore dipshit buddies will excuse me if I take a rain check on this foolishness and get back to the business of America, won't ya'?" And he turned and almost ran through the alcove.

"Right on. Solid. Yeah, yeah, yeah," said Turner in a

monotone, and gave the raised fist, black power salute to Shanahan's back. Then he yelled, "Power to the people, Mic."

Redding said, "Like Road Runner. Look at him go."

Beaner hadn't moved, and he looked real close at the steak as I walked by him on the way back to the Vulcan before he moved and found a place on the Hobart counter for his bus tray. I needed to get back to those dishes or I was going to be buried by them. "Let's just do this," I said, and rubbed the steak good with a damp towel and put it back in the skillet. I was starting to feel better, messing with Butcher. It felt good. He was, after all, the one who started the chain of events that led to Lee's screwing me over. Butcher was the bully in the deal. He deserved it.

I arranged the steak on the plate the best I could, picturing Lee at work, making sure the cut side was down, decorating the plate with a hot load of mixed vegetables, cooked to death, steamed into pastels, not one bright color in the corn, carrots and beans. The fresh baked potato, if that's what you could call it, had such a tough, heat lamp wrinkled skin it should have Rawlings stenciled on it. While Turner looked for a better one, I asked Redding for the parsley. He snapped off a branch, handed it to me and I put it across the top of the T-bone. It looked okay. I said, "That's parsley?"

"Oregano," he answered. "I couldn't find any. Looks fine. He's not going to eat it anyway. Who eats parsley?"

Turner yelled from inside one of the swinging doors, propped open with his foot, "Catch. Hot spuds, take your pick," and tossed two new baked potatoes to me. "Best on the line.

Sorry," and he shrugged his shoulders. Neither one seemed better than the other so I picked one and put it on the plate and tossed the other back to Turner, who made a jump shot with it into a garbage can.

"All right. Let's get it out to him." I put the warmer cover over the food. Turner said, "Who's taking it? I'll bust a gut if I have to."

I looked at Redding. He sniffed his oregano like they were lilies. "Nope. No way. I got in the cold box with Lee."

Beaner had gone back to the dining room, Big Ed was out of the question, so I took a deep breath, said, "Sayonara," and picked up the tray.

When I came back in the kitchen they told me they'd watched from the line when I delivered the tray. They wanted to know what he'd said. I said, "It's Butcher. He doesn't say shit. He just took off the lid, looked at it for a second, knocked the oregano off and started cutting and stabbing. When I asked him if I could get him anything else, he just chewed and looked at me. I took that for, 'Get out of my face.' "Turner and Redding looked at each other then busted out laughing. "C'mon, guys. It ain't that funny." Turner snorted and pounded his knee. He lifted his apron to wipe his eyes. Redding shook the oregano at me. "What?" They couldn't talk they were giggling and hooting so hard. "C'mon. What?"

Turner looked at Redding like a signal to give in. Redding had another short spaz attack before he could get it out. Then he said, "Vic, the oregano was pot." And the two of them broke up all over again.

"Grass, Vic. You garnished it with grass," Turner said. "I love it."

"You're shittin' me, right?" and Redding handed me his marijuana bunch. I held it to my nose and even before I got to the swinging doors, I felt a rush of revenge. I looked through the door window and watched him gnawing on the steak bone, finishing his dinner. He'd inhaled it. Butcher leaned back with a toothpick in his mouth, then sat up straight when one of the floor supervisors came running up to his table. They both walked back to the casino in a hurry. I said to myself one of those things Shanahan was always saying: "Well, touch me and *touché*," and still felt lucky, at the same time wondering if there were guys on the moon, finally. But I had to admit that at the moment what I really felt was relief. I closed my eyes to it all. I stood very still.

Because I'd bought into Shanahan's story over the world getting crazy about the moonwalk, I actually expected the casino would be quiet as a morgue, all the action stopped, all the players, dealers and staff riveted on the black and white pictures on the TV. But when Redding, Turner and I got out there, it was all going strong. The usual scene. No way you could hear the announcer, Walter Cronkite, or whoever was talking. The set had the same picture of the rocket or landing ship, whatever it was, just parked there on the white ground. If it was the moon, it was neat.

The three soldiers who had been in the casino earlier, the ones who'd gone through the line drunk and loud, were back at a craps table that was almost full. The pit boss was keeping a close eye on them. I couldn't tell if they were winning, but the waitress was bringing them free drinks so I guess they at least had staying power. I wondered if they'd killed anybody. They looked so young. My age. Like my collage soldier.

Shanahan was pacing up and down the full bar. Danny didn't seem to mind he was leaning into the customers, every once in a while stopping to tap one of them on the shoulder and pointing up at the TV screen. I was sure he was giving them the same patriotic bullshit we were constantly subjected to. We'd told Beaner to stay back and to come get one of us if anything ran out on the line. And we'd told him if Lee woke up, come get us right away, don't let him out of the kitchen. The waiting line had slacked off so maybe we could catch the moon stuff.

One of the soldiers wandered away from the craps table to the bar under the TV and was talking to Shanahan. Like the other two, his hair was cut to the skin on the sides, and I could see now his green pants were tucked into the tops of very shiny, tall laced boots with big rounded toes. His little wool hat was folded square and neat into his webbed belt. Mic was slapping him on the back and pointing to the soldier's chest, admiring his medals. All three of the guys had three stripes on their shoulders. I guessed that made them sergeants. I didn't really know. The soldier with Mic waved to the TV screen with his glass, and it looked to me Shanahan had finally found someone else interested as he was in the moon stuff. The soldier waved to Danny and pointed at Shanahan. Shanahan was insane to be drinking during his shift, especially with Butcher so close. I couldn't believe him sometimes. He was asking for it. Danny didn't care one way or the other; that's the way he was...and made Shanahan a drink and put it on the bar. The soldier threw some money over a woman's shoulder. She looked at him and made a face, and I couldn't tell if she'd been bothered by the brush of his hand over her shoulder or the fact he was wearing a uniform. The soldier reached for Shanahan's drink, handed it to him and they toasted the TV and drank at the backs of the hunched over bar crowd.

Butcher sat at the end of the bar. There was no way he could miss Shanahan. He raised his hand and signaled for Danny, who got to him and leaned over. Butcher said something. I laughed to myself thinking about the T-bone he'd wolfed down, but hoped I didn't have to cook anything for him again. Helping Lee and washing dishes was just fine for the time being. I tried to make some eye contact with Rennie, but as usual, she was all business at her table. I had that odd feeling about her again and looked back up at the TV to lose it.

A man pulling on a handle close to us said it was about fifteen minutes until eight o'clock.

I didn't see Lou or Kathy anywhere and figured they were still in his office. I hoped Lee was sleeping it off in the stockroom. Redding, Turner and I were all still wearing our aprons, so we tried to half hide near the slot machines by the hallway to the restaurant.

"Look," and I pointed to Shanahan at the bar. "Can you believe he'd be drinking right in front of Butcher?" The soldier was wedged in between two customers on stools, trying to get Danny's attention. Shanahan had his glass tipped up, patting the bottom.

"He's crazy," said Redding. "You've heard his stories. If half of them are true he's—"

"He's not afraid of Butcher," Turner interrupted him. "That's the real deal. Simple as that."

Lights on the machine next to us lit up and a bell that sounded like a fire alarm went off. Then the shower of quarters hitting on metal began, and we slipped around to the front to check it out. The man who'd been in line earlier arguing with his wife about losing money at Barney's was jumping up and down, pointing to the money gushing into the tray. It was puking quarters. He got into a crouch and pointed his hands and index fingers at the slot like six shooters. "See, honey. See, honey." She gave him a small smile and seemed embarrassed by the attention, which I found interesting because when she was bitching at him in line she hadn't cared who was listening. But I was jealous. He'd hit big. Three cherries were lined up on the wheel behind the glass. He'd won a hundred dollars in quarters and got on his knees and scooped the ones that had overflowed the tray. He looked up to his wife and said. "Keep our place," and she edged closer to the machine.

She bent over and asked her husband, "We going to leave now?" He looked up, a pile of quarters between his knees. He stopped scraping the carpet.

"What? Cash out? Now?" He went back to scooping the coins and said to the carpet and the money, "We're hot, honey. This is the one."

On either side people were putting coins in their machines and pulling on the handles, glancing over at the hot machine, waiting for their turn, but having to be content for the time at the every once in a while clink of seventy-five cents or a dollar and a quarter into their trays. The row of dime slots was the same scene, but I knew how much even they could kill you. They were just as addictive. The two old ladies in the flowered dresses were playing one of those. One put a dime in. The other pulled.

I could hear Shanahan's voice cutting through the jangling sounds of the casino action. I slid sideways and could see him waving his arms, probably telling one of his tales to the soldier. I said to the guys, "I'm going to tell Shanahan to cool it. He's going to screw this up for all of us."

I came up behind Shanahan with my eyes on Butcher, who had his back turned and was jawing with some people. I put my hand on his shoulder. "Hey, Mic." For an old guy he felt hard. He turned.

"Hey, college boy." And he rolled right into an introduction. "Made a friend," and he used his drink hand to point at the soldier. "Say hello to Sergeant Crawford here. Hunnerdt and First Airborne. Two jumps under heavy fire and he's going back for more. Reports back tomorrow. Yore lucky to shake his hand. You owe him."

I shook hands with the soldier. There was the same distance between this guy like there was at the Oakland Induction Center with those two guards. "How you doin'?" He didn't say shit and slurped his drink. "Mic. You got a minute?" He sniffed, smiled and looked at me. The soldier watched. "I need to tell you something."

"Go on," he said.

He was staying put. I leaned into his ear. "Butcher's right at the end of the bar, you know."

"So what?"

"So he'll kick your ass if he sees you drinking. Fire you."
Shanahan gave the soldier a look that made me feel like I
had worn a dress over to say hello, then turned around to
look at the end of the bar where Butcher was. Then he
turned back and took a long gulp from his glass.

"Finish it off," and Mic handed his glass to me. "C'mon. Don't
be a pussy. Kill it."

The soldier, no older than me, maybe younger, loved it.

"Mic..." He pushed it into my hand. I took it, and even though
Butcher had his back turned, I turned away and drank. It was
Coke. I knew Danny would be watching somehow. He
seemed to see everything, and I looked to my left and damn
if he wasn't grinning at me. I felt Shanahan and the soldier
branding four eyes into my back. I turned around ready for
the shit. "All right..."

"College boy, you think I'd screw up the moonwalk by being
a turkey? You think I'd show my ass now? Of all times?
Here?" And he waved to the TV screen and looked up. "You
think I..." and stopped. A guy in a bulky white space suit was
coming down a ladder from the space craft. Shanahan said,
"Hey...hey...hey, ya'll. Here it goes. Here it goes. Weeeooo."

And the same woman who'd been annoyed at the soldier for
touching her shoulder turned and said, "Please." Right at
Shanahan. And she snapped back from his hard look like his
face had been a clenched fist. The smile lines at either side
of his mouth were ramrod straight like they'd been yanked
down by ripcords.

Chapter 12

I watched the astronaut start backing down the ladder, bulky and unsure in his space suit. He had climbed out of a metal thing that looked like it could have been built out of an erector set. Turner said it looked like Redding's VW on stilts. Shanahan's eyes were wide, the soldier was intense, they were both way into it. It was blowing me away. The astronaut wore a suitcase size backpack and a huge helmet with a visor as big as the TV screen. He was taking it real slow, and it was all pretty amazing when you thought about it. I turned and waved Turner and Redding over. I figured an event this big would be a good enough excuse to hang around a while. Nobody gave us a second look in our aprons and jeans. I said, "Check it out. He's about to step on the moon."

Turner said, "Far out. I'll bet somewhere up here you can get odds on whether or not it's made out of cheese." Nobody answered him. We all watched and tried to listen over the talking at the bar and all the other usual casino sounds.

Redding said, "You know, once he gets down on the surface, he'll be able to jump about thirty feet."

"Cold there, right?" I said.

"Than a witches' tit, or the walk-in," and he faked a shiver. Then, he complained, "I can't hear shit. Gotta get Danny to turn that thing up."

Sweet Lou and Kathy came out of his office across from the service bar and walked toward the register. Kathy whispered something to him and peeled off, heading back in the direction of the restaurant. Lou checked out the ass of a waitress bent over the service bar poking around in a mint bowl, then came over and looked at the TV. He had a big red mark on his neck. If he knew it was there, he wasn't worried. He lit a cigarette with a thin gold lighter and blew smoke over the heads of the people at the bar in front of us. "Big night," he said. He looked back over the casino, glancing up at the eye in the ceiling. "I see the kitchen's all caught up." He grinned and looked around.

"Uh, we're taking a break, Lou. Watching the big event." I didn't think it mattered to him that we were in the casino.

"The players into it?"

I said, "Doesn't seem like it. Can't really tell what's going on."

Redding said, "We're trying to get Danny to turn it up."

"Gonna change the world, boys." He stopped talking, smiled at the action, and then said to me, "Tell Lee the steaks were tops. You can get the trays out of the office whenever. I'm going to go watch this somewhere quiet."

"Sure. No problem."

He absent mindedly touched the splotch on his neck with the heel of his hand and moved down the bar, stopping to talk a couple of times, then all the way to the end where he and Butcher got into a conversation. He seemed even calmer and cooler than usual. He was gliding tonight.

I said to Redding and Turner, "You see his neck?"

"What?"

"Passion mark. Right on the left side of his neck."

"Kathy do that?"

I said, "I cannot for the life of me figure that out. What's he see in her?"

Turner stuck his hands in his pockets and said, "What's so hard to figure out. She's doin' him. That's it."

Redding said, "She ain't the hillbilly she was when she walked through the door two months ago. Sweet's Lou's rehabbed her."

Turner said, "I think it's a great gig for her. She's gung ho for him, too."

"I'm here to tell you guys," Redding said, "that it's not going to end well." I felt the same, but had no idea why.

Lou was patting Butcher on the shoulder. He left him leaning on the bar and came back our way and nodded as he passed, and went to the cashier's cage. While he was doing business with the cashier, Kathy came back down the hallway. She was practically skipping. She had a long coat on. She'd wrapped her pony tail up into a swirl on her head. I could tell from where we were she'd put make-up on. She stood at Lou's side, brushing at something on his shoulder then looked over at the three of us. She gave us a happy, little girl, Mickey Mouse Club wave, then looked farther down the bar. She spotted Mic and the soldier and her face became serious. She dropped her hand. Maybe it was the light, or the angle she turned her face, but the color in her cheeks disappeared for a second, then came back as fast when she looked to Lou. Butcher had both elbows on the bar, swishing a rocks glass in small circles in one hand. His head was down, but he was watching Lou and Kathy. The effort creased his forehead.

I said, "Guess she's got the rest of the night off."

Turner said, "It's Sunday. Maybe they're going to late church." Redding rolled his eyes and stood on his toes for Danny's attention.

When Kathy and Lou left, she was holding his arm. They were strange together, and I really didn't want to make any judgements, and at the same time, felt bad about it. But they walked like they were invisible. Of the two other men who had a real stake in those two, one was watching TV, and one was just watching.

When Danny came down our way, I asked him if he could turn up the sound. He looked at me, then up at the TV. He said, "What's happening?"

Turner said, "Guy's about to walk on the moon."

"Can't hear shit," added Redding.

The expression on Danny's face shifted. "Hang on," and he leaned over to Butcher. I watched Butcher's eyes go to the TV then out over the casino then go back to the TV. Danny came back to us and said, "Butcher doesn't want to distract the players."

"Danny," I said, "there's a fucking guy a billion miles away, and he's about to walk on the moon. Right now. There," I pointed. "Live."

"Butcher says not until enough customers ask." Then he said, "Watch yourself," as a guy chewing on a cigar, wearing a Nehru jacket, who smelled like he had taken a bath in English Leather, slid up beside me and ordered a beer. He gave a half ass "s'cuse me" and tapped a chip on the bar, one foot on the rail, while Danny got him his beer.

I said to Turner and Redding, "Believe him?" The other two soldiers had come over from the craps table and were standing with Shanahan and their friend. They were further down, as close as you could get to the TV. Besides the three of us, they looked like the only other people in the casino who actually cared about what was going on; knew it was the real deal. I could tell Mic wanted to get a couple of guys at the bar behind him interested in the TV, but they basically ignored him and kept going back to their conversation. His head was angled trying to hear the announcer, and he was showing his frustration to his new buddies. Finally he stomped down the bar to me and said, "Don't start me to lyin', son, but in case your head is straight up your ass at the moment I want to tell you that history is being made up there, men are risking their lives, and nobody is paying any damn attention. It's disrespectful."

Redding said, "Well you can't hear shit." He pointed to the astronaut. "What's that guy's name?"

"How in the hell would you know?" Shanahan spit. Then he yelled at Danny over the same woman who'd stared at him earlier. "Danny, damn you son. Turn up the damn sound and tell these people to clam up and pay attention to what's important."

Danny was wiping off a glass. Sometimes it seemed to me nothing ever moved on Danny except his hands. He looked down the bar for Butcher, who'd left his stool. He smiled thinly at Shanahan. "Can't. Butcher says ix-nay, Mic."

Now I could smell bourbon on Shanahan's breath. The woman, whose stacked blonde hair was spun wispy like cotton candy, swiveled around again, and this time, instead of please said, "Will you go away with that howling. I have had it." She sounded plastered. She looked at Shanahan like he was on fire.

A man next to her in a blue suit and a five o'clock shadow leaned back to me and said, "Buddy, here's a hint, take your friend down the bar. He's been annoying this lady all night. Be a sport."

Shanahan looked at Danny, then to the couple having a hard time with him. Turner said, "C'mon, Mic. C'mon." I was afraid Shanahan was going to hit the roof, but instead he let Turner, of all people, pull him back down to where the soldiers were. That group had all the flash potential of a grease fire, so I hoped Turner didn't start preaching about Vietnam. A roar went up from one of the craps tables as they walked away and the whole bar turned like a chorus line to see what was going on. Almost at the same time, two different slot machines hit big, and the clanging, ringing and yelling started. Change girls and waitresses were weaving through the crowd. Some guy with a loser's look on his face left the craps table and hurried to the men's room.

Before the guy at the bar in the blue suit turned back to his drink, I said, "You do know there's a man about to walk on the moon?"

He raised his eyebrows. "Is there?" Then he looked at the woman. She wore a red shiny dress, with skinny straps that cut into her shoulders. Compared to Rennie's smooth skin, hers was spotty and hard looking. Bronze freckles ran down between wrinkles on her chest. "Did we know that?"

She looked across a shoulder at me, elbow on the bar, and said, "I think we did but we forgot to give a shit." Then lightly over to her friend, "But we do need to go to the powder room," and winked at him and laughed, coughing as she did, smoke coming out her nose and mouth.

Beaner tapped me on the shoulder.

"Something wrong?" I said, "Is Lee awake?"

"No," he said, "*Pollo. Pollo. Mas. Mas.* People are asking for more. Cluck, cluck, veek."

"Jesus Christ. Already?" I swore I was never going to even look at, much less eat, baked chicken the rest of my life. I told Beaner to check the timer, that there was supposed to be some up soon. "Listen for the bell. I'll be right there. One of us will," and saw Turner and Redding were in a knot with the soldiers and Shanahan. They were all still glued to the TV. Things seemed under control. I could see the astronaut was still on the ladder. It was taking all day, or night, whatever time it was up there.

Beaner trotted off. The woman with the red dress was sliding off her stool and leaning over to kiss her friend on the cheek when she lost her balance and fell on the floor, bounced on an arm and rolled to her back. One of her red high heeled shoes came off and dangled from a stool rung. Her dress had hiked to her thighs. She was screaming, "I broke my ankle. I think I broke my ankle. Help me. Ooh." Her hair looked like a crushed bird's nest at my boot toes. She made a pitiful effort to reach for her feet. I looked down at her then up at Danny, who had both hands on the bar and was stretching to get a look. His face said nothing. Her friend stabbed his cigarette in an ashtray and jumped down next to her. Nobody at the bar did much but lean and gape, then went back to their drinks and talking.

He said, "You all right? Sure it's broken?" He breathed real heavy, didn't seem to know what to do and looked embarrassed. His tie hung just above her nose.

She moaned, "Pull my dress down...pull my dress down..." reaching for her hem. And he tugged at it, rolling his head to catch me like I was trying to get a peek at her girdle.

One of the floor supervisors was coming over and I did not have a clue what to do, so while she complained, I backed away and went out to the kitchen to check on the chicken. The fucking chicken. The timer bell on the ovens was pinging over and over. Beaner was sliding trays out, splashing the floor with hot greasy chicken water. Big Ed was standing over Beaner's shoulders, on his toes, excited for some reason, looking like a six-year-old about to ride a merry-go-round or something, just watching. I turned off the bell and sent Beaner to the line to bring in the empty chicken pans. Ed stood and bounced, fingertips of one hand pinching the other hand's fingertips at his chest. It was dainty and weird.

I carried a tray of chicken over by the double sink to wait for Beaner and when I passed the Vulcan I saw six perfect red tomato rose buds bunched together in small circle on the counter top. The skinned tomatoes were off to the side, running, Lee's paring knife beside them. I was still staring at the buds when Beaner banged through the doors with an empty pan. With almost everyone somewhere else in the casino, the only noise was the exhaust fan clattering and scraping. Ed was now gone from the chicken ovens, and if he was at his sink, I couldn't hear him.

Before I went back to the casino, I looked in on Lee. Big Ed was out back, standing on the stoop by the grease barrel, still bouncing, looking up at the night sky. I wasn't going to ask him about the tomato roses, but I couldn't figure it out, unless Beaner did it, which seemed impossible, or Lee woke up from the dead and pulled it off. But Lee was arranged sideways, half on, half off the flour and sugar sacks Turner and Redding had laid him down on. I had to laugh. Even asleep, snoring, passed out and dead drunk, his vanity was intact. His bald head was covered by his toque. It hadn't come off in his sleep. I was over being pissed. I just wanted to get through the shift and get him to his apartment.

Beaner and I panned another four trays of chicken real fast and put them in the ovens and set the timer. I left him to watch the line and ran down the hall. Halfway to the casino I realized we hadn't put salt on the chicken. But I didn't slow down, the customers gobbled the food so fast, it didn't matter. Besides, I wanted to catch the moonwalk.

But I had missed the moment.

That was obvious as I cleared the hallway and looked across the room. The astronaut was already walking on the moon. And there were two now. They reminded me of snow men, puffy and round, with their big windshield visors. I really had blown it. The visors reflected everything around them including an American flag standing straight out on a pole stuck into the surface. The flag was static, like it was stitched onto the air, or whatever was up there. I wondered what it must be like to have a view so clear to Earth and back. I couldn't figure out how they were getting the camera shots and I thought of Elaine and all the trouble she went through to set up a shot with her spring-wound Bolex. I wondered where she was watching all of this. I knew she would be, somewhere. Then I became conscious of Shanahan's voice, cranked up, and just as fast glass broke and yelling started. People between me and the bar area started backing up, blocking me, blocking my sight line. On my left the two old ladies were still at the dime slots, but stopped at the commotion and stood shoulder to shoulder. One clutched her sweater at the neck, the other held her change cup tight in two hands. The man and his wife weren't at their lucky machine and I wondered about them, if their streak had ended. A man balanced on the rung of his stool for a view. But most played on, throwing, pulling, getting hit, standing pat, guessing. And as I pushed through to the scuffling, not a soul I could see was watching the men on the moon. Butcher and two of his guys cut in front of me, pushing people, and I rubbed past a group of giggling college girls with tall drinks watching a dice game, and got over to Rennie's table, which was full as always. Of the five players, only one seemed interested in the racket over by the bar. I looked at the pit boss, who was not distracted in the least. He hawked the tables in his area just like normal. Jayne Mansfield and Marilyn Monroe could have come back to life and been dancing naked on the bar and that guy would never quit looking out for cheaters and scammers. Rennie was waiting to hit a guy and looked at me with a scared look. I shook my head and elbowed my way back into the group that had ringed whatever was happening.

As I pushed to the front, I saw Shanahan, blood all over his apron front, take a wild swing at the man in the blue suit who'd given me shit. The punch caught him in the neck, not really a direct hit, no snapping sound like a TV punch, and the man yelled, "Fuck you, asshole, you're crazy," and bent to pick up a bar stool on its side next to the rail at his feet. Shanahan must have hurt his hand because he held it between his knees and crouched as the man got his hands on the legs of the stool, but Mic hopped once and kicked him in the knee. The man fell on top of the stool like he was covering a football fumble. He stayed down and groaned. Shanahan had told me once that real fights were nothing like the ones on TV cowboy shows. He'd said, "Don't try and be Cheyenne Bodie, you bedwetter. In a real fight, pick up anything that ain't nailed down, including nails, and use it. It ain't gotta be pretty, but you got to win."

The woman in the red dress hollered and grabbed an ashtray. Before Danny could stop her, she winged it at Mic, hit him in the ear. It looked like it hurt him and he said, "You old sow," and he came at her, his hand holding his ear.

"Fuck you, you asshole," and she lurched for another ashtray, but this time Danny got to it first. "You're an asshole, too," she snarled at him. Danny just smiled.

She turned back to Shanahan, in her stocking feet, and called him "White trash," then started to hit him in the face and chest with lots of slaps and out of control punches. Shanahan just stood there, ramrod straight and took it. He grinned like a fool at attention and let her beat on him. She

236

had to stand on her toes to reach his chin with her slaps. But whether he was drunk, or out of it for some other raging reason, he suddenly collapsed her with a closed fist to her jaw. Quick as the flip of a hole card and she was on the carpet. I couldn't tell if she was unconscious, but he had hurt her bad. His gold tooth, that at good times helped his oddball sense of humor, just made his face sinister and scary as he stood panting over the still woman.

Shanahan's soldier buddy was being held back by his friends and they were trying to push him toward the lobby. He was cussing and straining to get loose and calling them motherfuckers and pussies and his buddies were saying to Butcher and his guys, "We'll get him out, we'll get him out." But when they pushed him he dug his boot heels into the carpet. Turner and Redding were by the bar, backs to it, watching with others. Turner was twitching like he wanted to do something. Redding smiled; he just watched and chewed on a swizzle stick. Danny was watching, too, wiping a damn glass, having cleared the bar of anything else that could be used as a weapon.

Butcher came up behind Shanahan right when it looked like he might try to do something else to the knocked out woman. Now some people were acting scared, the college girls I'd pushed past were skirting the crowd, going for the door. Once he'd hit the woman, two men in the crowd yelled and got up like they were going after Mic, but they didn't put their drinks down and didn't follow through. Shanahan took his eye off the woman as two of Butcher's guys came at him from behind. As they lunged, I heard myself yell, "Mic," but he didn't turn. Even as I shouted I wondered to myself if I'd throttled back my voice for some deep, cowardly reason, or if I just didn't gauge my warning against all the other noise.

Butcher got him from behind and grabbed him in a choke hold, and just like that, Mic was on the floor, Butcher's knee on his chest. Then Butcher pulled what looked to me like a black leather shoe horn from his rear pocket, and with one sickening crunch of a blow, came down hard on Mic's right temple and his body went limp. Then, siren sounds coming through the door with them, two cops in uniform were in the middle of it all.

One yelled, "Put your nigger beater away, Butcher." He put the leather strap in his pocket and put all his weight on his knee as he pushed up from Shanahan. I knew he wanted to hurt Shanahan, and much as he deserved it, I worried he'd cracked his skull. Butcher's neck and face were sweaty red, boiling out of his turtleneck. One of the cops felt Mic's throat and said an ambulance was on the way, and they yelled everyone back. The cop turned to the woman, who was sitting up, crying hysterically, spitting blood through her fingernails. Her friend in the blue suit looked lost and disoriented and didn't move a finger to comfort the woman. Her ratted hair was now in a ridiculous tilt away from her head, a red ribbon that had been pinned to it was hanging pathetically, about to fall. Butcher and his guys paced and told everyone to calm down, that it was over, and to enjoy the night. He started buying drinks for the house. The cops ignored the soldier for some reason, even though he was still being held by his buddies and muscled to the door. As he was dragged past Turner and Redding he called them "Chickenshit hippies and cowards," and, "...won't even help your friend..." and for some reason, the gang of college girls who'd stopped by the door to the lobby turned on the soldier and his buddies as they dragged him out. All of them yelled and taunted. One kept calling them baby killers.

"You ought to be ashamed," one said. Another tried to spit at the soldier closest to her, but he looked more surprised than mad, even though he laughed in her face and kept moving. It was strange how they jumped on them in a pack like that, like they were taking advantage of the fight and the wildness to say whatever was on their mind.

I watched them heckle and jeer at the three soldiers through the double doors to the lobby. Then they huddled together, and it looked like they were afraid to follow them outside. Mic was rolling on the floor, bleeding out of both ears and his nose on the carpet. Butcher kept telling the cops Shanahan ought to be moved out of the way. The cops said they wanted to wait until the ambulance arrived before they did anything. One of the floor supervisors and a cop were helping the couple Shanahan had banged up. The cop was listening to the woman's story, holding her shoes and trying to get her under control. She was sitting on the floor, back to the bar, using her toe to point at Shanahan. Danny was spacing ashtrays along the bar again and lining up drinks on the house. Except for three or four stools at the bar where the fight had been, people and things got back to normal pretty fast, even though nothing really ever stopped. The brawling seemed like a good fit in the smoke and the gambling action, a bloody and violent floor show.

Butcher walked a circle around Shanahan. "He's bleeding all over my carpet," he complained to the cops, and then he stopped and acted like I had just appeared out of nowhere. Then he saw Turner and Redding hanging around. "Get the broken stool out of here," he said to Redding. "You," to me, "get the Spic out here with the mop bucket," and he looked at Turner and said, "Ain't there something to be done in the kitchen?" And before we moved, he rubbed a finger under his nose, and said, "Say goodbye to Jethro," as two ambulance guys came through the doors and knelt by Shanahan's side. He was now sitting up, a wet bar towel handed to Turner by Danny and relayed to Mic, stuck at one ear. Looking at Shanahan, I felt helpless, and sorry for him. I started to say something, and happened to look up at the TV. The astronauts, those big snowmen, were jerking and bouncing on the moon, having a blast. The surface looked like an albino pepperoni pizza, and they had scattered tinny, foil looking junk all over the place. And for all the people in the world who were watching, and for all the important things the walk symbolized and might mean, it hadn't changed a single thing in this place, had not touched a soul. No one in this casino was about to give up a shred of their time and risk missing the right hand or the lucky roll just to watch a life-changing, history-making event. It was personal and selfish at The Mine Shaft. On the screen, it was all silent and peaceful. It looked like a cool place to be. Dew had always yakked about following her bliss, her dharma. The moon, the way it looked on the TV, seemed like a good place to follow it to. I wished I was up there with them, sealed up and protected, knowing exactly what to do, my next move planned and mapped out. Me and the snowmen leaping thirty silent feet through space.

Before I looked away, I laughed. I said to Redding and Turner, "Check that out." Turner said, "Oh, shit, man. *Perfecto* for tonight."

Redding said, "Beautiful..." On the lower third of the screen were the words: *The Sea of Tranquility.* And when they dissolved away he finished, "...that's what we call irony."

Shanahan said, "Weeeooo" at our backs and we turned. And

240

he smiled at us triumphantly like he had just spun one more tall tale. I think he was looking for praise. His head was bulging over one ear; the other ear was still leaking blood. Like finger paint, there was streaky, rust colored, dried blood on his face. The ambulance guys had cut most of his apron off, but the yoke was still around his neck. What was left of his blood-smeared apron was hanging like a child's bib. He spit down at the floor, then, as the ambulance crew and one of the cops were leading him away, he wadded the bloody bar towel and flung it and hit Butcher in the face. It hung on his shoulder a second and fell to the floor. Butcher just stood there. Shanahan spit some blood at his feet and the cop shoved him along.

The other cop had the couple up off the floor, leading them back toward the restaurant, still carrying her shoes. Without them she was shorter and seemed pudgier. We passed them all sitting at a table in the dining room on our way back to the kitchen. The cop was writing. The woman had the blue suit coat from her friend over her shoulders like a cape. Her head was in her hands. The man was smoking and drinking a beer. He followed me with a mean, dumb look. I told Beaner that Butcher needed him pronto out at the bar to help get the blood out of the rug. He gave me a scared look, crossed himself and plopped the mop into the bucket. I said, "Don't worry."

"Mic all right?" he asked before he left.

"He's tough. He'll be okay." I waved to the alcove, "But you better get out there." His face shifted back to worry, but he put his head down and pushed the mop bucket across the tile out through the alcove into the restaurant.

It was after nine and soon the shift would be over and I couldn't wait. I started on the pile of dishes at the Hobart as the others began prepping for tomorrow and winding down the kitchen. Turner yelled from the swinging doors that President Nixon had declared the next day a national holiday to celebrate the men on the moon.

"Monday, everything's gonna be closed," he said, and he went back out to the line.

It'd be nice if The Mine Shaft closed. Just for a day. But that was a joke and I knew it. Barney's, Harrah's, Harvey's, the Sahara, they'd all be happening. And we'd be back here, too, loading the line. Whipping it up, laying it on the bargain eaters and losers.

Beaner was back after a few minutes and steered the mop bucket past me and was shaking his head and mumbling in Spanish. He went out the back door to empty the dirty water on the ground next to the dumpster like we did. I'd done it a million times. He'd fill up the bucket with the hose at the wall next to the grease barrel and, with soap from the big box at Big Ed's sink, he'd be set and ready to roll again. The routines were endless. Over and over, seven days a week. I slammed another tray into the Hobart and hit the switch and listened to the machine cycle and churn.

Turner was thawing frozen chicken parts in the sink. Redding was back by the saucer wiping it clean. I could hear Big Ed banging. And I wondered what the next cover of *LIFE* might be, but realized instantly it was a cinch: Men on the moon, for sure. How it would work in my antiwar collage; I'd have to figure that out. I thought about one of the classes I actually attended called Psychology and Art, and what the

242

professor told us about Marshall McLuhan's take on artists and their gift to feel the future coming and see over the horizon and to bring it to life with their art. The antenna of society, he'd called them. I didn't know if my collage was art or not, and I didn't consider myself an artist, but as I hosed leftover food into the disposer I had to laugh, because my only wish was to see far enough ahead to know what was going to happen to me in the fall. I might be feeling the future, I might be gluing the future on the wall at the apartment for all I knew, but I didn't know a thing. Not a damn thing except I was I-A. The Army articulated me. Me, I had no response.

I did worry about Shanahan and the fact Kathy might freak out when she heard he had been beat up and arrested. And I worried about her and her relationship with Lou. I pulled open the door to the Hobart and pushed the tray, steam swarming over me, and I worried about Lee. Shit, I worried about everybody it seemed, including myself, I put my hands on the sink and looked up at the ceiling and said in complete and delightful confusion, "Holy shit." What a completely strange and bizarre night this had been, and I turned back around, looked over the kitchen and wondered how in the hell did I ever find myself in a place like this? I was far from anything familiar, in the company of people I never expected to be around, in the middle of random violence, pain and insanity, no real control over my life, lorded over by dimwit hoods and barely able to tell the bad guys from the good guys. But I reminded myself I was free to leave anytime I wanted, but had to admit I really didn't want to. Not right now for some reason. All I could think to say was Jesus Fucking H Christ and I said it out loud again.

I was on my way to check on Lee when the cop who'd left

earlier with Shanahan came into the alcove. He stopped and looked around. He was tall, in a tight gray uniform with a Smokey the Bear hat; every piece of leather he was saddled with squeaked when he shifted his weight. He said to me, "Victor Sinclare here?"

"Yep."

"You?"

"Yep."

"Johnny Cash asked me to give you this," and he tossed me a key on a ring, then a pocket knife. He sniffed once, and I almost asked him if he was hungry, but he turned and left as Rennie and another Twenty-One dealer carrying a sweater and a purse walked into the alcove on either side of the cop. It was a Ford ignition key on a chain attached to a cheap ring with a flat plastic pinup picture of a naked woman in a Forties era, Vargas Girl kind of pose. He'd given me Shanahan's folding knife. I stuck them both in my jeans.

Rennie was worried about Shanahan and said Butcher was being a real jerk out in the casino. "He's been all over Beaner," she said, "got him on his hands and knees scrubbing the blood stains." Rennie lit a cigarette and came in from the alcove, the other dealer had walked out back to get some air and wait on a ride home. Rennie and I stood by the chicken ovens and talked about getting together later. Redding and Turner were breaking down the line, trying to get a jump on leaving. We all wanted out.

I started to bring up Lou and Kathy when Beaner came back in the alcove and slammed the mop bucket into the wall. He ripped off his apron and smock and threw it at the stack of booster seats, jerking his head our way. He was crying, his face a mess of tears. "I said, Hey man..." and took a step, but he came to Rennie and me, wiping his nose on his forearm. "What's wrong, Beaner?"

Rennie touched his shoulder and it seemed to make him cry harder. I asked again. "What's up, Beaner?"

He looked at me and said, "Butcher fired me. Told me to leave. Get out."

"Now?"

He says, "Right away. Eighty-six. Come back tomorrow for my money."

I looked at Rennie. Turner and Redding came out of the walk-in. Turner came to the chicken ovens. Redding leaned over the back counter, eating a slice of roast beef.

Rennie said, "What happened? The carpet?"

"*Si*. Yes, I did my best, but couldn't clean out the blood." He gulped and sobbed hard and said, "I rubbed and rubbed..."

Turner said, "This fucking night can end anytime. Shit, man. What in the hell is going on?"

Redding said, "Men walking on the moon? Who knows? Bad kharma?"

All I could think to say to Beaner was, "You gotta ride?" And he tilted his head and gave me a look that made me feel ignorant and embarrassed, and he managed a smile and said, "Veek, I almost never have a ride." And I realized I never even knew where he went when he left work, and I felt like an asshole. I didn't know anything about Beaner. I didn't even know his real name. I don't think any of us did. Never thought to ask. Redding tossed him a kitchen towel and he wiped his nose. Rennie let out a deep sigh and said she had to get to her table.

She touched his shoulder again and said, "I'm sorry."

"See you later," I said, counting on it, and told her I'd get to her apartment as soon as I could.

She licked her lips after new lipstick and said, "Yeah, we need to talk about something," and clicked her purse closed. The bell timer to the ovens went off at my ear, and I hit it with my hand to stop it and cursed the damn chicken. Redding and Turner moved away with looks that said they weren't about to deal with it. Turner, backing up to the radial slicer, fingers crossed like he was warding off a vampire, said, "The yard bird is yours, buddy." Everybody was sick of the chicken.

I walked with Beaner to the stockroom, where he got the wooly green sweater he wore every day. Lee was restless, but still asleep, snoring. Ed watched us walk out the back door, but he just scrubbed and bounced. The other dealer who'd come in the kitchen with Rennie, a cute girl from Sacramento, was on the stoop, rubbing her neck and smoking.

"I'm done," she said. "*Finito...*"

"Long damn day," I said.

"You can say that again."

I felt responsible for Beaner. Somehow. I saw Shanahan's
Galaxie parked up by the wall and felt in my pocket for the
key. I gave it to Beaner and said, "Wait in Shanahan's car.
He's given you a ride before. Right?"

"Yeah. Some." He looked at the key and grinned at the pretty
girl. I said, "Hot cha cha..."

But Beaner looked at me and said, "Butcher is a mean
fucker. Watch out." And he picked up a piece of gravel and
pinged it off the grease barrel and it ricocheted to the girl's
feet. She looked at us out of the corner of an eye.

"Hang out, Beaner," I said. "I'll see you in about an hour.
Wait in the Galaxie," and I went back in to rouse Lee, get
him out before Butcher caught on. The girl had her arms
folded. She was pulverizing her cigarette butt under a toe.
"You hear what he did to Beaner?"

"Butcher's a shit. I can imagine."

"Yeah," I said and told her good night and left her waiting for
her ride. I went in and opened the door to the stockroom.
Between the stoop and the stockroom I was trying not to
forget about the chicken that was done and still in the oven,
and I was nagged by Rennie wanting to talk. I opened the
door. Lee was on his feet and, except for his suit coat, had
changed from his whites. I was surprised he was so
together. He read my face.

247

"Takes a licking..." his suit coat over one shoulder, he said, "...and keeps on ticking..." Then, "Hey, pally. Call the maid, time to turn the bed down," and he snorted a soft laugh. He slipped his coat on and said, "What's happening?" Then he stopped, a thumb and forefinger pinching each lapel, and said, "What day is it, babe?"

I said, "Sunday night."

"Time?"

"After ten, John Cameron Swayze."

He buttoned all three buttons on his suit and brushed the lapels. "The kitchen?"

"Closing down. How you feeling?"

"Like a class A toodler. My steel?"

"Safe."

"Been busy?"

"You could say that."

"How'd those moon cats do?"

"They got there."

"Nifty. Very nifty," then he looked down at the sacks that had been his bed. He said at them, "I think I'm supposed to rendezvous with Skin. How about a nightcap?"

"Lee, I..."

He interrupted me, looking up from the floor, a question on his face like he was reaching for a memory. "How'd Lou and Butcher like the steaks?"

He was fighting his way back to remembering. I said, "Best they ever had..."

"Well then, now, heh heh, imagine that. The best they ever had..." and he laughed some, I think out of nerves, and rubbed his hands together and started singing, "Fly Me to the Moon," then he stopped. "Let's get the knives, go get Skin and have one. Sounds like things here are tippity boo."

"Yeah," I thought. Tippity damn boo. Lee took a step to me, I turned and put my hand on the door handle, and if the loud scream that made Lee tumble back over a sugar sack on the floor had been an arrow, it would have split the door and pinned us both to the wall. I thought for a second the woman in the red dress was back, but that was impossible. But for the second time tonight, some woman was freaking out. And I smelled the Goddamn chicken burning.

Chapter 13

"I can't believe this day. I can't believe this night. I cannot believe that so much shit happened today. Why aren't I wasted?"

"I know."

"God, I'm wired...I thought Beaner getting fired was the end of it, but I'm coming out of the stockroom with Lee and I hear this awful yell and I jump out and there's Big Ed. He's huffing and puffing and that friend of yours, the dealer, what's her name?"

"Donna..."

"Donna, she's got her back to the saucer, Ed's got pans in his arms and she is looking like she thinks he's about to cream her."

"What'd he do?"

"He bumped her. That's what she said. Said she was coming back into the kitchen to use a phone because her ride was late, and he stepped out of his way to bump into her. Scared the shit out of the girl. She screamed. I would. It freaked her. Then he gets all weird and puffed up like she did something to him."

"Calm down. Here..." Rennie handed me a joint and I leaned my head back on the edge of the couch in her living room, hit the joint and held my breath. The White Bird album was playing. Rennie had taken a bath and was sitting cross-legged on the floor in a T-shirt I'd left behind one night. I could smell her. As usual, she was soapy and clean, and I was a mixture of sweat, kitchen funk, food smells and Hobart steam. I couldn't move. I thought about the last few hours.

Lee had said he'd be okay to drive. He was going to pack up his knives and go find Skin. So he took off. I had Shanahan's car. When I left, I woke up Beaner—he'd fogged up the Galaxie windows—and dropped him off at the Sahara where he said he had a cousin on the cleaning crew. He was going to ask him about a job. He hooked up with his cousin there every night anyway. They all stayed together somewhere with a bunch of other Mexicans in a group house. I never thought to ask Beaner where he lived. I said I might see him tomorrow when he came in to pick up his money, and he told me he was going to go in and get the pay and split. Then he was never ever going to go near The Mine Shaft after that. No way he ever wanted to be near Butcher again.

When I'd pulled under the portico at the Sahara to drop Beaner, I expected some looks at a burnt, hippie looking college kid and a skinny Mexican boy in a smoking, banged up Ford with a roped down trunk. But either the doormen were bored or weren't paying attention, because when I dropped him off, it was a big nada. In fact, Beaner trotted through the front door like he owned the place and went to find his cousin. I was glad. I didn't need another confrontation.

As I'd driven to Rennie's place, I wondered about the moonwalk and turned on Shanahan's radio, but the only station that was clear was playing Henry Mancini. I think it was the "Love Theme from Romeo and Juliet." I turned it off. The Galaxie smelled like Shanahan. There was quilt and a pillow in the back seat.

"Lee was actually a help," I said to Rennie. "That guy can bounce back. It's amazing."

Rennie said, "What did he do?" She sipped some wine from a water glass.

"Well, Fric and Frac, Turner and Redding, they come running and don't do squat but stand and look. I don't really want to take on Ed, but the girl is so scared she's shivering and I feel like I have to help."

"Poor Donna."

"I have no idea what to do, and the burned chicken is getting really strong and that's adding to the tension when Lee pipes up in that jive beatnik way. All he says is, 'Hey Ed, let's cool down. Whattaya say, pal? C'mon, put those pans away daddy.' And damn..." I took another hit on the joint and exhaled and felt a rush. "Damn if, after a snarl, Big Ed didn't just walk to the rack at the front and start putting the pans away. Lee took your friend out to the lobby to use the phone. That was it."

"Do you think she overreacted?"

"Don't know. Don't think so." Now it was catching up to me. I was fading and wanted to get it on with Rennie in a big way, but I could feel my eyes getting heavy, and she hadn't reached that point where she was ready, or willing, to lose control. I'd learned to wait and listen for the right words. I could tell the timing was off and I hoped I wasn't sensing something bad. "I think he's got it in for women. His wife screwed him, Turner told me. Did I tell you that? His wife? Vietnam. Drugs? The guy is a trip."

"I can tell he's strange."

"I've seen him looking at you. Stay out of his way."

We were quiet a while. We went over the fight in the casino. Then we were quiet again. We smoked the joint and listened to music. If one of us said anything, it was me. I dropped phrases and words into the room as they floated in and out of my mind.

"Burned the shit out of the chicken...Feel sorry for Shanahan and Beaner...What a fight...The tomato rose buds...You wouldn't believe Shanahan's car...It's a trip...Butcher's evil..."

Rennie rolled onto her stomach and supported her head on her crossed wrists. She looked at me. I'd crawled up on the couch and stretched out. I was drifting.

"What?"

"Nothing."

"What are you looking at?"

"Can't I just look? I'm looking at you." I dropped more thoughts onto the air as the record ended and the arm retracted, but neither one of us got up to put more music on the turntable. Some of the things I think I said I might have just thought. I was having a hard time telling. I closed my eyes.

"Fucking men on the moon...the moon. Kathy and Lou...Kathy and Lou...My collage is turning into something...Butcher's a prick...What did you want to talk to me about..."

I opened my eyes and she was in the same position on the floor, but she was naked. But strange, her hair was red and all done up like the Vargas Girl on Shanahan's key chain, but it didn't matter. I wanted to have her. I started to reach out, but my arm was lead. Then I tried to slide my leg off the couch and I couldn't move that either. Her eyes were open and inviting, and she rolled up on an elbow and propped her head on one hand. In the open palm of her other hand she held out one of the tomato rosebuds. I tried to speak, but couldn't get a sound out. I felt leaden all over, helpless and scared. I tried to scream and rasped instead, and shook myself out of the dream. I think an echo was still in the room. My throat was scratchy.

I'd crashed. Hard.

Rennie was gone. I went to her room shaking, took off my clothes and crawled in beside her. I slid to her back and held her around the waist. "I'm awake." I just wanted to hold her. "I couldn't wake you," she said to the window, her heels at my shins.

"How long ago?

"Five or ten minutes. No more. I came to bed."

"Let's make love."

"Victor."

"Yeah?"

"I'm going back to Tucson."

I didn't say anything at first. "When?"

"Friday. I have to." She flipped around and faced me in the dark. "It's time to go. I miss my daughter, and I feel like I've got this thing out of my system."

"This thing?"

"This thing about getting away and doing what I've been doing. I'm just tired of it. Not you. Listen. It's not you. I'm just tired of The Mine Shaft. I'm tired of flirting with customers. I'm tired of the meanness. The bullshit. Butcher. I've just had it." She said, "Believe me, it's not about you. I proved to myself whatever it was I had to prove. I did whatever I felt I had to do. Now I have to get it together."

I just started talking. "Rennie, this thing, this thing isn't like a prescription, a pill you take until you feel better. This thing is more than that. What are you going to do there? What about Mr. Asshole?" I said, "What else can happen tonight?" I looked away.

"Victor..."

"What?"

"Vic, look at me."

"What?"

"What did you expect? You knew I had to leave sometime. Right? You're going to leave sometime, too. You've got a future."

"Right...How can it not be about me? You're leaving me." I tried to laugh. "You know what happens. Now we get to be good friends. That's what old lovers become, right? Good old friends, yukking it up long distance listening to each other's new love stories and giving each other advice. That's what happens, isn't it? It sucks."

She said, "Are we lovers? Are you in love with me?" I had no answer.

"Victor, be fair."

I wanted to say nothing is fair. Being in the bed where we had had so many wild times, to be having this kind of conversation just completely bummed me out. I knew I was feeling sorry for myself and knew everything she was saying made some sense. What I didn't want to admit was that I actually respected her for being brave enough to make a decision to move on. But I still hated it. Hated to have this one wonderful part of my life yanked away like a pile of chips raked away across a dice table.

"Well it sucks. It just does."

"Vic, there's another reason."

"Someone else?"

"No." And she slid closer to me. "I'm pregnant."

I felt my face flush and thought about everything I'd just said. We'd never talked about birth control. I figured she was on the pill or something. My eye started to quiver. I couldn't talk.

"It's not you, Vic. I..."

"Who?" I was on my back talking to the ceiling. Rennie sat up.

"I was pregnant when I got here at the start of the summer. I didn't know it. I'm sure now. I missed a period the week I got here. Remember when I got sick at that restaurant in the Sahara the night you got hot on the dice table? It wasn't the food. Don't worry. It's not you, and she grabbed my arm. That's why we never used anything."

"Who then?"

Rennie got quiet and I knew she was about to cry. I looked up at her. "My ex-husband. He came by one night after I'd thrown him out. I caved. We did it for some reason or another. I knew it was a mistake before we did it. But we did it anyway."

"Rennie, what are you going to do." Now she was crying and I pulled her down, and said again, "What are you going to do?"

Her tears were wet on my chest. "I don't know. But whatever it is, I've got to leave here. I'm not doing anything here except getting out." And she cried and cried and cried, and I stared at the window and felt the one more brick in the weak foundation of my world crumbling. We made love. But it was more out of a sense of responsibility. We both tried way too hard. But she did roll her head to the side at the end as always. She fell asleep after that, but I slid out of her arms, insanely awake, and took off.

I started to go to the Y, but instead, took the Galaxie back out to the boulevard and drove to Harrah's. I thought of Lee and how he compared dice to life, risk and luck, and considered, bad as this day and night had been so far, it couldn't get any worse. It was time to turn it around. It's hard to find clocks in Tahoe, but the radio said it was three a.m.

At dawn I was pulling into the lot at the apartment at the Y. I had more money in my pocket than I'd ever had in my life. With more luck than skill, I had managed to turn my last forty-five dollars into three hundred and fifty. It happened fast. When some of the chips started coming my way I hadn't a clue why, but I scooped them up anyway and lined them in the notched canals on the table shoulders. Before I knew what was happening, I had almost four hundred dollars. I would have brought home more, but a guy who said he was Frankie Valli's assistant's personal assistant made lots of money on my rolls so we had some rum and cokes and celebrated when we quit. But for some reason I paid. I didn't care though. I was loaded. Once, I held the dice for almost thirty minutes. I hit point after point and even the croupier had said it was the best action of the night. I said, "Men walked on the moon," and laughed. He slapped his croupier stick on the table and said, "Coming out, shooter. Shoot 'em." Then he yawned. Even at that time of night, the pit boss had his eyes on the croupier. And Frankie Valli's guy was having a terrific time.

Upstairs at the apartment, there was a big, bearded guy asleep on the couch. I needed to go see about Shanahan in a couple of hours, and I had every intention of just closing my eyes for a short nap and then trying to find where they'd taken him. But when I woke up, it was almost noon by the clock on the stove in the kitchen and I felt like I'd been drugged. I looked up at the collage and was pissed to see some of the edges were curling and I made a mental note to get back at work on it as soon as possible. It had developed into the one permanent thing of value to me. The new *LIFE* would be out soon. But when I patted my pocket and felt the cash I felt better until I remembered the talk with Rennie. But I tried to stay focused and knocked on Sara and Turner's door to see if he wanted to go with me to find Shanahan. The knock bothered the guy sleeping on the couch. He opened his eyes and shot me a squeezed eye shitty look and pulled the sleeping bag over his head.

Turner said through the door, "I'm dead. Go on."

I said in a quieter voice, "Where the fuck is the jail? Where would they take him?"

He cleared his throat and said, "The little shithouse place that looks like a small post office, just over the line. I think." The guy on the couch grumbled again from under his sleeping bag. I really wanted to get back to the collage, or sleep, but I had to see what was up with Shanahan.

"See you at work," I said, and just for the hell of it slammed the door to the stairs as hard as I could and left.

The Nevada State Highway Patrol was almost where Turner said it would be, a block off South Lake Boulevard. It was a low, blond brick building, American and Nevada state flags on a pole from the roof fluttering against another bright blue sky, but a light rain had started to fall. It was strange. First I could remember all summer. But Turner was right. The place did look more like a post office than a jail. And Shanahan was gone.

When I'd asked for him, without lifting his eyes, looking for something in a pile of papers, a tall cop behind a counter said, "Mr. Shanahan has been released on bail."

"When?"

"Within the hour."

I said, "Thanks," as a phone rang. Then he looked at me.

Outside at the Galaxie, parked between two trooper cars, I heard, "Hey college boy," and saw Shanahan walking back to me from a gas station at the corner. He snapped his left hand at me like he was trying to catch a fly midflight. I leaned on the car and watched him, listening to the slap clang of the flag rigging on the pole, trying to tell if he was limping, most of all wondering why he wasn't still locked up.

"Hey, yourself," I called back. As he got closer, I could see his face was swollen, he had a thick pad of a dressing on one side of his head, one almost the same size over the other ear, and a stripe of a bandage across the bridge of his nose. His ball cap seemed to have shrunk. Somewhere he'd picked up aviator style sunglasses. "Nice shades, Mic." Then, "You look like shit..."

He got to the other side of the car and rested his arms on the roof. His right hand was wrapped in gauze and tape. "I'll tell you what, son, betcha this mornin' I'm a whole lot easier on the eyes than that blonde floozy with the droopy titties," and he cackled, then winced and licked a split on his lip. "Or her fat boyfriend. If that's the best he can do, he's one sorry feller. He oughtta kill hisself."

"You nailed her Mic."

"Yessir, college boy. Damn right. You just don't walk up to a stranger and start talking that kind of crazy shit like she did. She earned it buddy."

I held up the keys. "You want to drive?"

"G'wan. Knock yourself out." I asked him where he got the sunglasses. He told me there was a lost and found in the jail, "...and I found 'em. Shit son, if I had an Army and a pipe, I could be General MacArthur," and he grabbed the rearview mirror and stuck his face up to it. "These are nice." Then he opened the glove compartment and pushed some maps around, felt around on the seat and looked over at me as I was readjusting the mirror and backing out and asked, "You got any butts? I'm dyin'."

I said, "We'll get you some, General." The rain shower stopped. "That was weird."

"What?"

"Rain with the sun out."

"Devil's beatin' his wife."

"What?"

"You never heard that, dumb ass? What are they teachin' you in college, anyway?"

261

At a waffle and egg place with a black and gold awning up toward the casinos, we stopped to eat. At a table inside with plastic chairs we sat against a big window, the Galaxie on the other side of the glass. There were two Nevada Highway Patrol guys three tables away, hats on empty chairs next to them. They were bent over plates and ignored a walkie-talkie. It sat, screeching with static and calls next to a ketchup bottle. There were customers at a counter and some at tables. They looked like Mine Shaft customers, but I pegged them as locals. They didn't seem to be in any hurry. A little boy in a *Jetsons* T-shirt stared at the cops while his mother read the newspaper and felt for her coffee cup.

We drank coffee and Shanahan smoked cigarettes I'd gotten from a machine inside the front door while we waited for our food. He had to use two hands to get the cup to his mouth. "I broke a finger on fat boy," he said.

"Sure it wasn't that jab to the babe?" The thought of his punch smashing her face freaked me. In my memory it was like a powder puff exploding. Or one of those mushrooms in the woods that disintegrated when they were kicked.

"Naw," and he held up his wrapped hand and studied it and shook his head. He dropped it and looked out to the Galaxie. "How ya like that machine?"

"Beats thumbing," I said. He was staring at the car and smiling. "Drives like a log truck, but that's home right there. Been all over damn creation in it."

"Smells like you."

"What does?"

"Inside the car."

"Like me?" He grinned and said, "Yore normal hangout will take on your smell, dumb ass. You ever get a whiff of Big Ed? Imagine where he lives. And that greasy feller in the truck..."

"So Mic, tell me. How'd you get out? Who paid your bail? How's that work anyway." The questions took his eyes off the car.

"You won't believe it. Not in a month of Sundays."

"Try me."

The waitress—could've been Rennie ten years ago, blonde, tan and skinny—put down eggs and waffles between us. "All set?" And she looked at our coffee cups. Shanahan held his cup up with two hands like a beggar and gave her the gold tooth treatment. If she was bothered by his bandages and bruises she didn't show it. She chirped, "Back with a warm-up," and turned for the coffee station behind the service counter.

"Tell me."

"Sweet Lou did. Lou and Kathy. They come down in the middle of the night and started working it out." He sounded proud.

"No shit."

"Scout's honor," and he put his wrapped hand at his chest, took off his cap and stiffened his back. "Promise. And that ain't all." He put his hat back on.

"What?"

The waitress poured hot coffee. Shanahan said, "Thank you, honey." He watched her walk to the table where the troopers were. "She's cute as a speckled puppy, that one," he said. When he looked back to me, he took off his glasses and said, "They're runnin' off together." And he put his sunglasses back on.

"Whattaya mean?"

Fumbling with his fork, he looked at the food and said, "I shoulda got stove lids." Then, "Whattaya mean, what do I mean?" He chased egg and waffle across his plate with the fork wedged between his bandaged fingers and got it into his mouth. Chewing, he said, "They're runnin' off together. They're makin' like horseshit and hittin' the trail is what I mean. They got serious hot pants for each other. But they're in love." He used the back of his bandaged hand to wipe his mouth.

I leaned back and looked at Shanahan maneuver his food. If Lou and Kathy were leaving, among other things it meant two more good people were not going to be in the mix at The Mine Shaft. With only a couple hours of sleep, I couldn't get a grip on how that would play out. And Sweet Lou, was he really trying to disappear, or was Butcher in on it? I ran back over yesterday and everything that had happened and came up with nothing that made any sense. The memories of Sunday overlapped and were jumbled together like my collage. I ran my hand under the table and felt dried gum, like warts. I rubbed my pants leg. "What did it cost to get you out?"

"Bail was set at ten grand. Lou came up with whatever they needed. I expect he knows somebody."

"When you got to go to trial? There's a hearing or something, right?"

"Yeah. Two weeks. But I'll be long gone."

"Whattaya me—"

"What do I mean? Like this here. I'm curtin' out, splittin', ridin' off into the sunset, little dogie." He slurped his coffee then ran a piece of toast through a slick of egg yolk.

I looked over at the cops, who were trying to catch the attention of the waitress. "Be cool, Mic...the Man is over there."

Shanahan glanced at the troopers over the tops of his sunglasses and licked his lip. He didn't say anything about them, but he didn't lower his voice either when he said, "I've had it with this shithole."

"It's becoming a big club."

"What is?"

"The Tahoe's A Shithole I'm Getting Out Of Town Club," I said. He sucked his teeth.

"Never mind. Go on."

"Well, I'm going on up to Seattle and try and catch on at Boeing. That's where we was headed when we stopped here. The original game plan. Kathy was gonna make enough to go to junior college, but she don't need to worry about that no more. Sweet Lou's put her in the lap of luxury, son. She's gonna be fine."

I stopped talking when the troopers walked past our table. Both of them looked at both of us. I watched them in the window reflection as they put their hats on when they got to the door. They had flattop haircuts like Butcher, the little strap at the back of their Smokie Bear hats caught their necks where the hair was skinned shortest, where the skin was wrinkled thick. One of them looked over the Galaxie when they walked by, but they kept on.

I said, "Mic, Lou loses his bail if you split, right?"

"Get me a cigarette, will ya?"

I pulled one from the pack, and put it in his lips and struck a match. He drew on the cigarette and slumped in his chair. I dropped the match on my plate and doing it, did something I bitched about every night at the Hobart. And I wondered about the poor guy washing dishes here. I picked up the match and dropped it in the ashtray.

"Remember, Sweet Lou will be long gone," he said. "We're all gonna be history, son. Kinda jack Lou's got, he ain't gonna miss what it cost to spring me."

"You going to miss Kathy?"

He started studying his wrapped hand again, and said,

"Sure. Bet that." Then he said, "What time you goin' in?"

"Usual. Three. Couple of hours."

"Dandy. I'll give you a lift. Let's take a ride first." He nudged the check across to me and said, "If you'll settle this up, I'll catch you later."

"Lou didn't leave a little something for you, General?" He just stared at me. "Nevermind. Can do." And at the register he saw the money I'd won at Harrah's. He said, "Weeoo, buddy, is that a Jew bankroll or the real deal?"

Our waitress made change from a twenty and said, "Was everything all right?" Shanahan touched the brim of his hat and said, "Darlin', I'm doin' so fine I oughtta be arrested." He laughed, and said, "But I already done that," and he slapped my back and shouldered his way through the door.

I said to the girl, "Fine. Thanks," and handed her back a dollar for a tip. She smiled and said, "Have a nice day. Come back and see us," like she meant it.

We wound our way up to Heavenly Valley, the ski area on the mountain behind the casinos. Turner had driven me up there earlier in the summer. Shanahan had never seen it. There were switchbacks and overlooks along the way, and eventually, big empty parking lots, the locked-up ski lodge, and empty lift chairs and gondolas. They were quiet, strung along the cables far up the mountainside over scrubby grass and rock. Farther up you could still see snow on the mountain tops. We drove around the parking lot. The lift cables reminded Shanahan of the TVA power lines in western North Carolina and north Georgia. He told a story about his uncle helping to build the Hiawassee Dam. Then we started part of the way back down and pulled into a small turn off, looking over the lake, high enough that as we stood leaning against big boulders at the edge, the thinning stands of Ponderosa sliced the lake into blue sections. All the casinos and other businesses along the strip of South Lake Boulevard looked small and scrunched together from where we stood. From here it was all just a village or a settlement at the shore of a huge body of blue water. I never paid much attention to the lake going back and forth to the casino. Lake Tahoe was background music. But now we could see all the way to North Shore. It was so quiet. The racket from down there couldn't find us. "Turner and I got high up here once."

"Got any of that wacky weed with you?"

"Just the beer." We'd stopped and bought a six pack of Olympia. I remembered I had his knife. "Here." I gave it to him in his good hand.

"My frog sticker." He put his beer on the car hood. "Damn. Forgot they took it. Gracias, amigo," and he pulled it open with his teeth. "I traded up to this Case from a Barlow. I Jewed down a feller for it at a cold roll plant in Pennsylvania. Ol' boy name of Buel. He was from Wolfe County, Kentucky. That's a mean ass place, son. He ran the crane in the ceiling, that's kinda like one of them ski gondolas back there. Good view. Pay's better. You work alone. Sorta like a floatin' bass boat that hauled the steel rolls around. Buel ate onions whole like apples and was quick as shit with his hands. Saw him corner and catch a chipmunk in the parking lot all by himself once. Barehanded, fakin' and puttin' the moves on it." Shanahan made a quick move to his left, then winced and held his hand to his head. "Put it in his lunch pail and took it home to his dog to mess with."

"Cold roll?"

"Cold rolled steel is big coils of steel. Thick as a bank safe, thin as Reynolds Wrap, everything in between. Unroll 'em. Chop 'em, trim 'em. Stack it, bind it, ship it. Same boring shit every day. Just like that damn kitchen." He drank some beer, leaning against the grill of the Galaxie facing the lake, wiping the knife blade back and forth on his jeans. "It was work."

"Dangerous?"

"Nah. You just had to pay attention."

"What'd you do?"

"Worked at a shear. Big table with a choppin' blade across the middle that you tripped with a foot pedal. One feller slides a piece of steel through to the blade and holds it, the other feller trips the blade, and bam, the blade trims it. The other feller pulls it through and stacks it until the skid is full and banded up. Buel hooks it with the crane and moves it to the loading dock. Over and over. And over and over. Slide. Slam. Slide. Slide. Slam. Slide. Slide. Look at the clock. Slam. Think about a beer. Slide. Slide again. Worry about the rent. Slam. Look at the clock and think about stoppin' and gettin' a little tail on the way to the trailer. Slide. Hold this," and he handed me his beer and dropped the knife and it stuck in the ground. "I'm good at mumbley-peg," and he unlatched the car hood. He opened it all the way, looked at me, then slammed it with a bang. I jumped. He smiled. "Can't take it?" He opened the hood again and slammed it.

"Okay. I got it..."

He squatted and pulled the knife out of the dirt. "Whattaya think? Just like that. All shift long. Ten shears in a row. Slammin' and bangin' and waitin' for the dinner whistle. Money's decent but a reasonable man can't take much of that without going crazy. The sameness. Carpet mill, factory, assembly line, sawmill, cannery, steel warehouse. It's all the same sooner or later. But it ain't stoop work, at least. No sir. And I ain't never gonna dig up the first spud. I got limits. But it's all the same." He drank some beer. "That stinkin' kitchen ain't half bad compared, but I've had enough."

"Was there a Butcher?'

"There's always a Butcher," He said to the lake, "Yessir. He was the foreman. Had the place loaded up with relatives. Couldn't put your shoe down without steppin' on somebody he was related to. He was a pissant and he ain't worth drawing breath over. Specially up here where it's so clean." He dropped his can on the ground and said, "Let's do it again."

"Beaner got fired," I said.

"Cause of me, right?" I handed him another beer

"You and your blood. Couldn't get it out of the carpet."

"I shouldda kicked Butcher's ass too."

After a while I said, "You know today's a national holiday."

"For what? Gettin' my ass kicked?"

270

"Men on the moon."

"Shit, buddy, they deserve it. There's some fellas who know how to get a damn job done." He touched his ear lightly with his good hand. "Now, them boys had a view." He walked over to a boulder and said, "Good as this is, can you imagine what they was lookin' at? They're heroes. They're American heroes and they're lucky and they deserve a damn day of their own. Here's to 'em," and he tipped his beer up and drained it and flipped the empty can over into the trees. I opened the last two and handed him one.

"I could use some Fritos," he said. "Don't suppose you bought any with that beer, did ya?"

"Nope. No Fritos. Sorry." I walked up to the rock with him. "When you planning on taking off?"

He belched and made a motion with two fingers at his mouth. I gave him a cigarette and lit it, cupping the flame to the wind. He said, "I wanna bend your ear about that. Ask a favor. I need a little money to get goin'. I can always pick up some day work on the way to Seattle, but the quicker I get there, the better my chances are of catchin' on. I hate to put the arm on you, son, but if I don't get on the road, I'm gonna be in that hoosegow again. I can't be locked up."

The money in my pocket felt as big as the boulder we were leaning on.

"How much?"

"Couple hundred will get me down the road. I'm good for it. Give me an address, and I'll send it to you in a couple of weeks. There's lots of work up in that Seattle patch. Won't be no time."

I only made a hundred and twenty every two weeks. Until I got on a roll at Harvey's, the only time I'd seen that much was when Redding was buying dope. "Sure you can pay me back?" But I knew what I was getting into.

"Does a bear shit in the woods?" And he picked up a dead branch and squatted again, flat footed, and started to whittle and sing some song. Then he stopped but went on shaving the stick. He looked up at me counting bills off my roll. A car passed on the road. It was getting cooler. He said, "You know that's a song about a man watchin' a man beggin' for his life?"

I lost count. "How?" I started again. "What is?"

"Stagger Lee. Stagger Lee threw seven. Billy swore he threw eight." He looked back down and made a deep cut along the branch, and said, "Fuss with the wrong feller and you could get yourself killed."

I held out two hundred dollars in twenties.

On the way to The Mine Shaft, we stopped at a grocery store. Shanahan bought more beer, a big bag of Fritos, Miracle Whip, liverwurst, Vienna sausages and Wonder Bread. He told me he had plates, forks, spoons and glasses from the kitchen in the trunk. A block from the casino, in the parking lot of the drug store where I bought Lee's paregoric, I asked him to sign my two dollar bill.

"Bet that, college boy." And in big jagged letters, the pen

held best he could in his right hand, he signed his name. I got out and leaned in the window. I was about thirty feet from where he and Kathy had picked me up the day I'd applied for work at The Mine Shaft. "Who signed Fats Domino's name?"

"He did."

"You meet him in person?"

"Yep."

Shanahan said, "Weeeooo...Touch me."

"What do you want me to say to Lou and Kathy if I see them?" I asked.

He looked over his glasses at me. "You ain't gonna see 'em," he said, dead serious. Then he caught the gear shift with his right wrist and dropped it into drive and said, "And don't worry about your money, bet that. And don't let yore meat loaf. I'll see you around the bend." And he was gone. The Galaxie bucked when he drove off, and I knew he had to be steering with his wrapped-up right hand when he gave me the finger out the window.

Driving down from Heavenly Valley, he'd gone on and on about something that happened to him when he was kid. I watched the Galaxie go past The Mine Shaft and disappear toward Reno and thought about it.

As we'd pulled out of the overlook, he'd said, "College boy, we was dirt poor when I was comin' up. But whenever the carnival came to town, I'd muster every damn red cent I could git my hands on and I'd spend it on the Ferris wheel.

That's the only thing I cared a lick for. It was right in the middle of everything. Even when I didn't have no money, I'd hang around and pester the roustabout and make a nuisance of myself. That's another thing I done," he said. "I was a carny for a while back in the Fifties. And when it was slow, sometimes I'd get to ride for free. One year, I was about twelve or thirteen, they came back at the end of the summer as usual with the freaks and the crooked games and girly shows and raggedy animals. It was hot and dirty and smelly, but it was somethin' to do." He looked over at me, an eyebrow crooked above his glasses. "I'm a damn tulip compared to that..." He sniffed. "Smells fine in here."

"Go on."

"Well, this feller named Scoville was running things that summer and like I said, I stuck to him like a tick on a coon dog until he let me ride the wheel. I was the only one on it. Everybody was off watching some oddities bein' judged. I think a big hornet's nest some boy found in the woods won first prize that year. Maybe that or a two-headed snake. I can't recollect. Anyway he locked me in a rockin' red tub behind a chipped metal bar, and I was all set to go when I had second thoughts. I started worryin' that if I was the only one on the whole damn wheel, it might get goin' faster and faster and throw me off at the top when it got up a good head of steam. Well, college boy, all that was goin' through my head and I was still on the ground, frettin' and rockin' when Scoville leaned on that big handle and give me a wink and...this is something else I just remembered. How about that? I remember at that moment that I wanted to get some tattoos just like Scoville had. He had a dragon whose head started on his hand and it stretched all the way up to his elbow. He had a Bible verse on his other arm, but I can't

274

recollect it. You seen all mine?"

"Just Sugar Tit," I said.

"Hell, that ain't nuthin'." He was taking some of the curves down the hill pretty fast.

"Anyway, them gears started turning and I started up and goin' around, and I got my young ass woke up to some stuff that day that's stuck."

"What happened?"

"Well, first off it didn't stink up there and it weren't near as hot. There weren't no sweat and animal shit and cotton candy smells. And best of all, there was only me. I know I'd been ridin' that wheel every summer for years, but that summer things were different."

"Like..."

"Like things just look different when yore lookin' down at them. Sounds simple, but it ain't. They ain't the same they appear to be at all. But I only had a snatch hair's worth of time to look around because your only at the top for a second. Scoville just let me ride though. Round and round. I musta gone around a hundred times. But guess what?"

"What?"

Just when I was gettin' into a habit of thinking I was gonna keep goin' around, the wheel stopped. Stopped right at the damn top. Yessir. I was swingin' and rocking in the clean wind, wonderin' what in the hell was happening. But it was quiet. Peaceful. No gear noise and could hardly make out the tinny music. It was nice. But this here is what jolted me. Now that I had some time, some time to really look around instead of havin' to grab a quick look as I came over the top, I got pissed."

"About what?" And I could tell he was getting riled up, his face, even black and blue, was getting shaped into the mask he wore when he was about to go off.

"Well, two things. First, now that I could take my time and study everything, all around, it came to me that not only was the pissant little carnival even smaller than it seemed walkin' through it on the ground, I was able to see past the field it was in, past our sorry little town, I could see all the way down the highway damn near to the bridge at the river and that was a long ways off. And it was a cloudy day. About to rain."

"So why were you pissed?"

"Well I was pissed because I was a whip smart one, even at that age, and I realized up at the top of that wheel that I had never been any damn where, and nobody I knew had been any damn where and it shook me up and I swore as soon as I could I was gonna get out of that hick town. If I'd never got on that wheel that day, I might still be there. I guess I was pissed because I had to find it out myself. Didn't have no one cared to show me no different.

The second thing was that when I looked down, Scoville wasn't nowhere near. Run off somewhere. I sat up there and stewed for a long time. But I wasn't scared. Once, when I looked down, there was a girl walking by with a peppermint stripe balloon. Later, it must have got away. I saw it go past me and drift over toward the water tower, then it went higher and higher. I watched it until it disappeared into some dark clouds that were coming. And I didn't look down again until that drunk came back and brought me down. He was one sorry piece of shit excuse for a human being, but in his own dumb way, he helped me. I ain't been on a Ferris wheel since. But I seen a lot."

I had a half hour before I had to be at work so I walked back down the road to Harrah's. I went to the same table I'd won at last night and spread a hundred dollars in twenties on the felt at the Come Line. The croupier picked it up and handed me a chip. The name Harrah's was scrolled around the edges in flowery black and red speckled script. At the center was a dollar sign and the number one followed by two zeroes. I held the chip in my fingers, and for a second those three numbers strung together seemed as long as a cat walk, one I could run across and out of town.

"Bets down. We got a player. Coming out. Shoot 'em shooter..."

Chapter 14

One roll. Craps. Crapped out.

"Too bad, shooter. Tough luck." Words spinning in my head like a roulette wheel. I got back across the black and red carpet to the doors, down the steps to the road, numb from the lights on, lights off, throw of the dice. I thought about what a hundred bucks could get you. New boots or one of those cool Wyatt Earp cowboy hats Redding bought in Reno. Albums and wine and dope. Silver jewelry in Mexico if I ever got there. Drinks on Bourbon Street. If you had a hundred dollar chip in one hand and a hundred in cash in the other, no contest. Take the money. But all insight about value evaporated with the exchange. No wonder the casinos all over Nevada made so much bread. Hunsinger had been right. The house had the odds, even at the craps table. The pussy whipped loser guy in The Famous Smorgasbord line came back to me. I still wondered about him. But at least Wednesday, payday, my day off, was closing in. So I wasn't really in hot water yet. I didn't owe Turner rent money for another week. I could eat casino food and Redding always had extra cash and pot if I got in a pinch and needed something. I had a forty-eight hour survival plan. I kicked stones and flattened an empty beer can with my boot heel. I relaxed.

Someone in a passing car yelled, "hippie asshole," out the window and it took me a second to realize someone was taunting me. Pretty funny. But my sideburns at my jaw were thick enough to curl back in a wave. The breeze tickled them. And my hair had grown long enough to catch and blow in the wind. I had to keep pulling it behind my ears as I headed east up the road to work. If strangers were harassing me from car windows in California, I wondered what the reaction would be when I got back to Cincinnati. As I got closer to work, I rationalized the loss of a hundred bucks as a romantic, Bogart-like *Casablanca* moment. Something to tell stories and laugh about some day. By the time I got up to The Mine Shaft, I felt pretty good, cocky and independent even. Despite the gambling loss, this was one of those rare days and moments when I could convince myself things were and would be okay. Vic the survivor. I was pretty damn happy all of a sudden for a guy who just threw groceries and rent down a rat hole. My parents would freak. I looked up at the sky, one big clot of a cloud there, a bearing for me.

I came up The Mine Shaft drive, a tour bus idling and unloading. Charcoal-colored exhaust blasted my knees when I walked up behind, then along the side, cutting between excited passengers getting out, antsy to bet. A woman my mom's age stopped on the bottom bus step and gave me a look...could have been one of recognition. I was ready for a smile. Maybe I looked like their son? Instead I saw sourness and a familiar disappointment in her eyes and wondered what they saw. Maybe I did remind them of their son? Caught off guard, I pulled hair behind an ear. I had the thought that maybe their son was a Voorhees. Maybe they thought I should be over there avenging him. I turned before she stepped down.

I got to the parking lot and made for the back door. She'd upset me, robbed me of my new attitude and dumped me right at the same spot back where I'd crapped out. She'd reminded me of the damage from the last twenty four-hours. First, Rennie was good as gone. Shanahan had driven away a half hour earlier with two hundred of my dollars that seemed like two million right now. He was gone for good, I was sure. Lou and Kathy, they were history. Where the hell were they? Mexico? Hawaii? New York? Paris? In my mind, I wanted them happy together at the edge of pines on a secondary road not far away, behind the door of a rundown motel cabin. Under assumed names. Lou's big yellow Lincoln hidden around back probably, not in the weedy lot in the front driveway. He was too cool to call attention. I figured, based on what I knew about him, that Lou was one of those guys who, once he was discovered to have disappeared, would trigger a turnout of curious eyes at airports with international flights. At least that's the way I wanted him to be. A giggling country girl on his arm would be too obvious, and could mean trouble.

I would miss Beaner and his goodness and knew he would never be seen again. Those were five good people who a little more than a day ago were part of my life, and just like that, they were gone. I came up to the stoop and the back door, and Voorhees' funeral came back. His surprise death had sneaked up on us back then and changed our world. I had the same feeling about these five, but I wasn't going to have the chance to grieve for them. And that thought, somehow, made me realize why we had hurt so much at Voorhees' funeral, and finally it made sense why we felt the need to turn loose and get wrecked and party at Crow's. It was related, I realized. There was no need for the guilt we'd all ignored the next day, hungover. That was the way it was supposed to work around death and loss maybe. It was a discovery for me. As a kid, after a funeral for a friend or family member, besides church lady food at the house where there was some sober and quiet reflection, tears and regret, that was it.

I thought of the Dukes of Dixieland. Shit, where did that

come from? My first Dixieland record, the beginning of my long-distance romance with New Orleans. A funeral begins, and the preacher says over a slow dirge, *"Ashes and ashes and dust to dust, it's too bad the poor brother can't still be here on Earth with us....but since he's not..."* The snare drummer rolls into a setup for the band, and they pick up the tempo and march off in high-stepping, umbrella-twirling joy. That was the way it was in my mind. That was the way it should be anyway. I had to get there sometime and check it out for real. A New Orleans funeral for me.

But these five summer friends...eighty-sixed. There'd be no chance to really say goodbye and celebrate. Shanahan would have thought any fuss corny. To him and his hillbilly optimism, his life never had any endings anyway. It was one long series of starts. Rennie was the only one whose leaving I could still commemorate. And I decided I would do it. Whatever that might be. At least try. No matter what she said.

I missed seeing the Galaxie parked at the wall. As I walked into the kitchen, I knew I was going to miss Shanahan's bullshit and wondered how things would be rearranged, if they'd hire any new crew, who'd be doing different jobs. The smell of peppers and onions and olive oil hit me at the back door. That meant Tony was cooking for Butcher. The pot and pan sink was unmanned. It was piled high. Ed wasn't there yet. I got an apron from the stockroom and went to the Hobart. It was backed up, too. I guessed Shanahan hadn't been replaced. I cursed the day crew and knew it would take half the shift to catch up and there would be plenty of yelling along the way when things started to run out on the line. I was dreading this night. I wanted it over fast.

Tony was busy at the Vulcan. With the pots and pans piled up at the back, me and the Hobart hidden by a heap of full bus trays, a dirty floor that missed Shanahan's maniacal mopping, the kitchen looked messier than usual. As soon as I noticed, Tony noticed me. He said, "Kid. Give the floor a go 'round. How 'bout it?" It wasn't half bad to come in on the second shift after Shanahan had been doing the floor during the day, but without him, it was going to take some work to get it back to the way Tony liked it. I hadn't even filled one rack with dirty dishes.

"Sure, Tony."

He shook a skillet and shouted over his shoulder, "You're gonna have to use some elbow grease, kid. It's filthy."

"Right." It's what I got for getting in a little early.

The mop bucket in the alcove was half full of dirty, slate-colored water. The mop had been soaking for hours. Two bloated cigarette butts soaked on the surface. Half the strands of the mop gripped the edge like dried octopus tentacles. I could smell the staleness and dank as I rolled it to the back door and out into the sunshine. Turner and Redding were climbing out of Redding's VW, parked at Shanahan's usual spot at the wall.

"I picked him up thumbing down at state line." He jerked his thumb at Turner, who was wearing an oversized snap brim cap. He looked like the Dutch boy on the paint can label.

Turner said, "Shit, man, Victor, is it weird in there today?"

"No more than usual except that the day crew left a mess. And as you can see, I'm currently starring in the role of Tony's Mop Boy. God I hate this." I pulled the mop out of the water and let it drizzle onto the gravel. I waggled it back and forth and darkened a streak on the parking lot. "Maybe we could serve this, some cornstarch to tighten it."

"What about Shanahan? What's the deal?" Turner interrupted.

"Got bailed out."

"He inside?"

"Nope. He's gone."

"Gone?" Redding held up his hand to block the sun's glare. In the mask of shade, his blond, nearly white eyelashes, blinked fast as he asked his question. They rose and fell, flapping fast as butterfly wings just taking off. Somehow they projected intelligence. He stroked his almost visible mustache.

"Give me a hand," and I knelt to pick up the bucket. Turner lifted the other side and we carried it next to the Volkswagen and splashed it on the wall. The gray water ran into the gravel. The butts were curled like grub worms at our feet.

"Watch the car dudes."

I said, "He got bailed out. I gave him some money I won."

"For bail? You did?"

"No, someone else bailed him out. I gave him some money to get out of town. Then he split, and then I lost what was left. Spare me the gory details."

"With Kathy?"

"No. That's another story." I wanted to make sure when I told these guys what I knew about Lou and Kathy they understood how important it was. What was at stake, or at least what I thought was at stake. I started to tell them about Lou and Kathy when Lee's Calais made the turn into the lot and crunched over the gravel to where we were standing. Lee was at the passenger window, slouched, Skin behind the wheel. The right hand turn signal was still blinking. A baseball game was on the radio. Lee said, "Giants are winning. Beating the pants off the Pirates." Then he said, "How you cats doin? You meowin'?" I couldn't tell if he was drunk, but he was obviously in a good mood. He looked at Turner and closed one eye and slowly tilted his head to the side. Turner looked back with his nervous laugh and shoulder shake.

"What? Mr. Toodler."

"You look like an Italian condom salesman in that lid, babe." We all laughed.

"Careful what you say about Tony's people, Chef." Turner turned the hat around backwards and made a face at Lee.

"Oh my, yes," he sat up and Redding opened the door. Lee handed him his knife briefcase and Skin turned up a bottle in a brown paper bag, then he looped the lot and gave us a smile and a passing wave.

"Gas it up, pally," Lee yelled. "The good stuff."

"I'm going to tell this once and you got to keep it to yourself."

Redding said, "Sure."

Turner said, "Go ahead..."

Lee looked at all three of us with a cigarette hanging out of his mouth. He went face to face to face. He said, "What's up?"

I told them what I knew. I had to stop once again when Big Ed showed up. He wore his usual clothes. There was a magazine rolled up and sticking out of his back pants pocket.

"Hey..."

"Hi, Ed".

"What's happening, Ed?"

"Hey, babe..."

He grinned at the four of us standing off the stoop, at the mop bucket, and said, "You, also." He gave us the peace sign and went inside.

"Man," I said, and stopped and watched him go in. "Anyway, here's what I know."

Before we broke up, after I'd sworn them all to secrecy, I asked them what they thought it meant. For us. For everybody.

Sounding like he'd been there before, Lee said, "Shanahan may resurface. You can't tell with cats like that. They're always on the move. You never know. You just never know."

Turner said, "More of Butcher. Shit, man..." and he put his hands on his head, Kathy style.

Redding said, "More of Tony," and looked at Lee. Then Redding blinked a couple of times, looked at me and said, "Victor, I got a question. Why did Shanahan borrow money from you? Don't you think Sweet Lou would give him some road cash? If he was going to bail him out, you'd think he'd front him with some."

Lee said, "Good bet," far off, like he was straining to piece something together.

"Makes sense to me," said Turner.

It was the first I'd thought of that. It followed. But I wasn't ready to admit I'd been hustled by a friend. Not now. I'd written the money off in my mind anyway. I focused on Lee. I pictured the day I'd first seen him sitting with Sweet Lou at the bar, the day he'd been hired. I studied him now in the sun. "Well," and he shook his head sadly, "Sweet Lou was a noble cat...elegant," and walked between us. He had never looked more gentle and vulnerable to me. Could have been an old accountant arriving at the office. Then I got confused. Him talking about Lou in the past tense bothered me.

We got through Monday, and even though it was national holiday to celebrate the moonwalk, the crowd was the same, the food was the same, everybody did their normal thing. Rennie came to the alcove to smoke and tried to act the same but it didn't work. We talked and then she went back to the casino. On her break she must have gone somewhere else. I didn't see her the rest of Monday.

Butcher was around more than usual, but he seemed mellower. He wasn't slapping people on the backs and making jokes, but he was in the kitchen more. To me he was walking around lots trying to overhear something or catch a look in one of our faces. I figured he was trying to get at something.

Tuesday was a good day. The day before payday. The day before my day off, Lee's day off, Turner's too. It was our Friday night. The mood was always good no matter what was happening. It was good until Butcher called a meeting at three-thirty after everybody had come in. He had us all come out to his table, the house table, the booth in the corner of the dining room. He told us that if we didn't know it yet, Lou had left for another casino in Carson City and he, Butcher, would be taking over the job of Mine Shaft general manager. He might have looked at me when he said the part about Lou and Carson City, but I kept a straight face. Inside I vibrated. My eye got going. The girl and the busboy were, he said, "fired along with the hick who started the fight. You see any of them around here you call me or tell Tony." He made a back-handed wave at Tony, who was picking his tooth with the edge of a matchbook cover, standing next to Lee, who was straddling a chair turned around backward. The rest of the crew collected in a group, rocking from foot to foot or sitting in chairs at the end of Butcher's table. The house sound system was playing "Wichita Lineman". Big Ed was behind me and I could smell him. I could hear his soft, mindless humming as Butcher talked, but I think I was the only one it drove crazy. "We'll find another hostess. Tony can decide if he wants to replace the others." He nodded at Tony once more, who returned it, blinking, shaking his head in agreement. I could tell he was taking it all very seriously. "And so it's clear, Tony runs the kitchen. He says jump, you say how high and what color would you like me to be." I looked over at Lee. I figured this public statement was meant to embarrass him and remind Lee and me that he had caught us boozing. Lee's reaction was very composed and cool. I just stared and wondered if Butcher had that blackjack with him. "Any questions?"

None of us said anything as we broke up. Except Tony. He said, "Need anything, Butcher?"

Butcher said, "Yeah, but come here first," lacing his fingers on the table in front of him. And Tony slid into the booth as we went back to work.

"Hey," Tony yelled. "Put the chairs back where you got 'em. Jesus Christ."

Halfway into the shift, Tony came over with a new bus boy. He was older; looked Chinese, with a pigtail and a costume he could have stolen from Hop Sing on Ponderosa. But he was mostly bald on top and spoke good English. He had the phony smile of a cheat. I knew he was hired to spy on us, and I hated him the instant I shook his soft hand. Tony left him with me to get him an apron.

"Glad to meet you man," I said. "My name's Vic."

"Call me Sammy," he said.

Finally the shift ended. I looked for Rennie, but she was already gone. I thought about asking Redding to drop me at her place, but couldn't face it. So I took Redding's invitation to go by his place for a joint and some beers. He bought tacos at Tippy's. On the way I asked him if it made him nervous to drive around with drugs under the hood. He just said, "No."

His place was a real apartment, furnished more like a home than a crash pad and was always a nice change. He had real furniture and floor to ceiling curtains covering sliding glass doors that opened onto a small sitting area next to a swimming pool. There was a breakfast counter with stools. It was a pretty modern place. Shag carpet. Even had air conditioning. And he had a great stereo, the only thing that didn't come with the apartment. I never saw anybody else there except Turner.

We listened to music, drank beer and smoked some excellent hash. He told me he'd made at least one other run down to Berkeley to the house with the palm tree and the wind chimes to score opium. He said he moved it as fast as he could. It was very profitable. He reminded me he had a cool aunt and uncle who lived in North Shore, Twenty-One dealers at the Cal Neva Lodge. They and their friends were good customers.

"They have a very cool place. We can go anytime we want. Never anybody there during the day."

We both speculated on Lou and Kathy, spent some time on Shanahan. I moaned about Rennie leaving and how rotten I felt about it, even though I was starting to conclude what was happening was for the better. I was questioning my feelings.

Redding was cross-legged on the floor, his almost white hair seemed to glow in the room, his face picking up the light from a candle burning down on a low table between us. A wavy, soft pattern of candlelight slid around on the ceiling. He smiled. "I'll tell you about a girl," and he passed me the hash pipe and got up and turned over the Cream album.

"I went to Europe last summer on a charter. England, France, Austria, Spain..."

"That's cool."

"And Morocco."

"Wow. No shit. "

"Went over on that new jumbo jet. Three hundred and thirty-five kids from school. We landed in London and everybody scattered in two's and three's with backpacks and Euro Rail passes. After a month, the 747 left from London and went back to San Francisco. I convinced my parents it was an early graduation present. It was either Europe or camping in British Columbia. So I flipped a coin."

In Tahoe I was as far away from my home and parents as I had ever been. I had a hard time imagining trips to Europe and Canada. The distance and the money were out of the question. "Tell me about Morocco."

"Yeah, but that wasn't the plan. I'll get to that." He said, "You heard that new super group, Crosby, Stills and Nash?"

"A little."

"That song, 'Marrakesh Express'?"

"Part of it..." I hadn't liked what I'd heard. "It's not what I expected."

"Doesn't matter. I did it." He toked on the pipe. "I was there. Rode it."

"Cool."

"Anyway," said Redding, "I took this crazy route from London to Paris to Vienna, where it rained all the time and decided I wanted to see the sun, so with about ten days left, I rode forever to get back to Paris with the plan to go to Madrid. While I was in Paris, I left my backpack in the north train station and got locked out. Spent the night on the street, most of it trying to sleep on a bench next to a *pissoir*. Had to get up and walk around when two queers started fooling around in there in the middle of the night. I saw a robber being chased on foot by a French cop. That was cool. They both skidded when they rounded the corner. Like a movie.

"I left Paris from Austerlitz Station, the south station, early the next morning after I'd scored my bag from *Gare du Nord*. Drank rose wine and ate big sugar donuts for breakfast at a bar with some French guys on their way to work. Got a real buzz at seven in the morning. Since I have a Euro Rail pass, I get in a first-class compartment. They seat six, but I luck out and have the whole thing to myself. Wait a minute," he closed his eyes. "Listen..." and Cream is playing "Crossroads." Redding rocked his shoulders and head back and forth until the song ended. "Whew..." He drank some beer.

"Bitchin' song," I said.

"Anyway, we're moving down the tracks and I'm flipping through *Europe on Fifteen Dollars a Day*. After I'd been in a city, I would tear out the pages so the book wouldn't take up so much space in my backpack. But I stopped doing that after this guy I met in Salzburg told me some of the Spanish trains ran out of toilet paper. When that happened he used pages from cities he'd visited..."

"Long trip?"

"Overnight."

"Shit."

"Didn't have to..." and he smiled. "Anyway I'm trying to get an idea about where I'm going to stay when I get to Madrid. It's hot as hell, I start to drift off and the door slides open. There is this little man in a wrinkled black suit, beret, white shirt, no tie, he's smoking, and he smiles—has very few teeth—and he comes right in and sits down across from me. He bows and offers me a *Gaulouise*. The pack's blue. They all smoke them. No filters and smoke strong as this," and he waved the hash pipe in a figure eight in the room, "...and I say, 'No. *Gracias*,' and he says in English, 'Okay,' and shows me those bad teeth. He speaks decent English and he's pleasant enough, but after a while, I have to leave because even with the window open the smoke is killing me. And nice as he is, he stinks. So I get out into the aisle and stand by a window and watch the country side go by. But before I could leave, he told me a story about a Jewish cabaret singer he'd been friendly with who'd worked in a Parisian whorehouse after the occupation had ended. I don't

292

know how we got into that. I think I understood most of it. Anyway, it was pretty cool. Like one of Shanahan's stories. I wrote down notes in my journal later. Going to use it in a novel someday. And, he was about the size of that little Irishman you talked to who disappeared that came looking for Lee."

"Little Georgie."

"Yeah."

"Anyway, I'm at my window and this girl comes and stands at the next window. She's wearing the shiniest black boots. I still can see them. One ankle was crossed with the other like she was leaning at a bar. She caught me looking at her, but she smiled and we went back to looking out. It was a long train. The engine whistle was way off. You could barely hear it from up ahead when it blew. Like it didn't belong to us. There were others standing in the aisle, even though it was a first-class car. I stood there for a long time and eventually got into a conversation with the girl."

"Good looking?"

"Compared to what...who?"

"Anybody we know here? Rennie good looking?"

"No," he said after a pause. "But interesting. She told me she was an American living in London, about to be married to a South African lawyer who was there studying. She was travelling to meet her parents while her husband studied for exams. She got prettier the more we talked. Later there was the train and track change and customs at Perignan. I got my backpack from my compartment, the old man had nodded off. He had ashes all over his suit. He was snoring so I left him alone. The girl had a suitcase, and we walked to the Spanish train together. I don't know what happened to the little man, where he was on the new train. I never saw him again. So we walked with the others and kept talking. I told her I was worried the little man was going to miss the train and that maybe I should have shaken him awake. She said, 'He'll be fine' in a way that made me quit worrying. Victor, you know about the smaller gauge tracks in Spain? Why we had to change trains? Why they're like that?"

I didn't, but I said I did. Then, "Were you about to score?"

"No, man. Wasn't on my mind. She was really neat. Mesmerizing. Full of energy. So we found an empty compartment in a first-class car. Didn't want to get interrupted by little storytelling men in berets smoking bad cigarettes. But as the train pulled out, she went on to tell me that her father was a retired Foreign Service officer and her parents were vacationing with old friends in Madrid. She said she was hoping to persuade them to take a side trip to Marrakesh, where they'd lived for a year when she was a teenager. This was an interesting girl, Victor. A trip. We got very comfortable very fast. I told her I was touring around and had to be back in London in about ten days, that I had another year of college, then told her my plans to go to grad school, stay out of 'Nam, be a writer. That," Redding said, "made her frown for some reason, but I didn't ask why."

"School or Vietnam?"

"Didn't ask."

"For a while we just looked out the window and watched the small towns and villages fly past. She was wonderful to talk with. She said in Marrakesh there was this huge covered market, the souk, with fortune tellers and snake charmers and beggars and live geese and bright cloth and brass...anything you want. Even hash cookies. Dig that. They're legal. And you have to pay these little kids that speak about six or seven different languages to guide you in and out. Sounds amazing doesn't it? Another hit?"

I pulled on the pipe. Redding's stories were becoming vivid pictures in my floating head. My eyes closed, I climbed to a chair to sit and stretch my legs out in front of me. Being off on his trip was giving me a total escape from all the shit that had happened to me in the last few days. I was getting ideas, ideas about opportunities. I was high, but I was with him and the girl. "So go on."

He coughed, drank some beer. "On a siding, we were stopped for a long time. It's the middle of the night."

"You still in her compartment?"

"Yeah."

"Okay."

"Okay, so, while we were on this siding, sweating to death, after we'd hung out the window and bought ham sandwiches and warm Cokes from a vendor—I dropped some *pesetas* into the cinders by accident and the vendor guy crawled under the train to get them for me—she told me about this housekeeper in Marrakesh who was very special to her. She had to see her on this trip. It was very important. That was what was driving her. It was something she felt she had to do before she got married. She told me, 'We used to drink mint tea and whisper secrets back and forth in the walled tomato garden while my parents entertained.' "

That description lit my imagination in reds and greens and sandstone and blue. I could smell it all. "Did you tell her your dad was a big tomato farmer?"

"Give me a break, Victor..."

"What was her name?"

"Who? The housekeeper?"

"The girrrrl..." And I said it real slow, trying to tease him. But he didn't say anything for a few seconds.

"Helena. Helena was her name. After we ate, as the train picked up speed, she asked me to sit next to her."

"And nothing happened?"

"Here's what happened. We talked all night long. Almost all night. We crashed just before dawn and woke up when the train jerked into Channartin station and her head came off my shoulder. I had my arm around her."

"And?"

"And nothing. She was very cool. She gave me the name of the hotel her parents were staying in. Asked me to come by and shook my hand, got in a cab and drove away."

"That's it? What'd you do?"

"I watched for a second then got cornered by a guy who was an agent for some hotels downtown. He kept telling me he was, 'A personal friend of Arthur Frommer,' could get me a clean cheap room and a discount cab ride into downtown. I tried to ditch him, but he was so persistent I went along finally, got in a cab and drove off in the same direction I'd seen Helena go a few minutes earlier. They drive like crazy there.

"The cab left me in front of a small hotel on a narrow, cobblestone street downtown somewhere—it was more like an alley—it had a blue and plastic sign that said, *Hostal Matute*. It was crammed between a laundry and a bar. It was a nothing place across from some bigger buildings or apartments. Those had tall louvered windows and little crescent shaped iron balconies. The street was fucking crazy, man. Cars, all of them were small, were honking and driving up on the curbs to go around people. There was this old guy in a black suit pulling a burro through the traffic. Could not believe it. The burro had a mountain of straw on its back and the old guy was pulling clay pottery from inside the straw and selling doorway to doorway. People were hanging out upper story windows watching the street or leaning out and talking. Mothers were pushing carriages. Men and women were strolling like nothing was going on. People going in and out of the bar and dodging the woman with the broom in front of the laundry. It was madness, man. And it seemed like every corner there were the *Guardia Civil*, the cops, Franco's police, wearing their shiny three-cornered hats watching everybody. Sunny as it was, they always seemed to be standing in the only shade that was around. They had capes, too. They hid their hands in them."

I said without opening my eyes, hearing the lowness of my voice because of the hash, my words coming out slowly, "Sounds like they'd be perfect at The Mine Shaft."

Redding said, "Mean looking dudes."

"The *Hostal Matute* was simple except for huge double wooden doors with iron handles the size of big horse shoes. I mean big impressive doors. After seven p.m. the doors were locked, the driver told me, but each street had a *sereno*, a guy who hangs out and has keys to all the doors and all you had to do, he said, was to clap your hands and he would appear and open the door or gate. Any time of the night. 'He works for tips,' he said. 'Don't worry. He's trusted.' And that was it."

"Inside, it was dark and cool. The owners were nice in an appreciative way. Seemed like proud people. They didn't speak English, but when I mentioned the guy at the train station, they really warmed up. My room was on the third floor. The bathroom was at the end of the hall. It had two single beds. Each one had a different patterned spread tucked around the mattress, one chair and a table with a lamp. When I pushed open the wooden shutters above the street the heat came in fast, even though it was still morning."

"See anybody else there?"

"No, but I heard German, I think it was German, being spoken on the other side of the wall.

"I wandered around for a couple of days. I had every intention of going to see Helena and figured I had some time because she said they were going to be in Madrid for at least a week. Figured I'd made a friend. Found a good person to sightsee with."

"Nothing else?"

"I told you, Victor, she was just cool to be around. Besides, she was engaged."

"So what'd you do?"

"Went to the Prado, the museum. Took the subway to a bullfight."

"You're kidding."

"No, sat with some nice guys in the cheap seats, and they shared their white wine from a bota—goat skin thing, a bag, squirts wine—I brought one back. The first day I wandered into this big plaza called the *Plaza Mayor*, and I started to go back every day and sit and drink *Sangria*. I'd read up on it. The plaza used to have bullfights. Before that they used to burn people at the stake during the Inquisition." Redding got up and went to the bathroom. On the way he said over his shoulder, "*Auto-de-fe'. Auto-de-fe'* is what they called burning heretics at the stake." I lay on the couch and tried to visualize all the places he'd been telling me about. It all sounded so exotic and dramatic. I was jealous of his

299

opportunities and money, and for the umpteenth time asked myself why with all he had, and with parents who could afford to send him traipsing all over the world, he risked so much by dealing. On the way back from the bathroom, he put on a Paul Simon record. "It's the new one," he said. "The one with 'The Boxer'." He sat and relit the hash pipe.

"You think I'll be telling somebody about this summer sometime and making it sound cool?" I said. "At the moment there doesn't seem much to tell."

"I'll tell you what..." and he drew deep on the pipe and handed it to me as I lifted up off the couch. I pulled on it, my body humming. "I'll tell you what I think about memory and reality and especially history. If you want."

I exhaled and lay back down. "Sure. But hand me a beer first. Just don't forget the girl."

"It's simple, Vic. It's this: All history is, is what one generation happens to find interesting about the past. Got that?"

"Lemme think. I think I do...again?"

"Like 'Nam. Vietnam is going to be of interest to decades and decades of people. Sooner or later though it's going to be so far in the past that some historians are going reinterpret what it all meant, and change the way we are looking at it now. And they'll have other history and wars to evaluate.

"Okay...so..."

"So, next summer when you're talking about The Mine Shaft and all this shit, you will be doing it because you think it had some impact or you had some fun. In fifty years, you'll be telling other stories about other shit...your trip to the moon maybe. You might not even remember where Lake Tahoe is."

"Right," I said. "Let's get back to the Helen girl."

"Helena, dickhead. Well on the third day there after lunch in this little restaurant that smelled like olive oil halfway between the hotel and the Prado, I went to try and find the hotel where she was staying. It was supposed to be over on Jose Antonio Boulevard, which is one of the main drags, but I couldn't find it anywhere. I walked and I walked and I walked. Speaking of smells, if I get a whiff of any of these things now, it sends me right back to that day looking for that hotel."

"What things?"

"Hot asphalt, bus exhaust, cigarette smoke or sweat. They take me back to Madrid. On that day."

"Find her?"

"Finally. I mean I found the hotel. A big fancy place. Like an American hotel. Made the *Hostal Matute* seem like a dump. Even had air conditioning."

"She wasn't there?"

"They were there. They were registered. Had their names, but they were out. I left her a note to meet me at the *Plaza*

Mayor at the *Café Luis* at the top of the *Arch Cuchilleros*. Everybody knows where that is. Wrote that I would wait for her there by the steps at four o'clock, once everything opened back up after siesta."

"And?"

"And I went back there every day for the next five days. She never came. I went back to her hotel a couple of times and tried to call the room and I left more notes, but she never came. I couldn't figure it out. And it's funny, but, even though when we first met I wasn't emotionally attracted to her, as each day went by, I realized I had to see her more and more until after the fifth day I was really tripped out. Almost frantic."

"That's not you," I said.

"No."

"What'd you do?"

"What I did was drink tin pitchers of *Sangria* from four until seven every day. That cafe and those steep steps and the plaza became mine, man. Got to know it all really well. Got to know the sky and the weather vane that threw this thin shadow onto the cobblestones from the top of the cathedral. It would disappear and reappear as the clouds came and went. I got to be good…in Spanish…at telling the Algerian photographer who came by in his *fez* everyday with the drugged tiger cub draped over his arms that I wasn't interested in a photograph with me holding it. I started to recognize the faces of the school kids who knelt and played a card game on the stones in their uniforms. Some of the old

302

ladies in black who hunched together on the benches got so that once in a while they would actually give me a wrinkly smile. I read some more history about the plaza and I thought about the bleeding bulls, and the bleeding of the Inquisition victims, and the fear, Victor. I thought lots about fear sitting there. All the evil shit that had been carried out in that space. Once, when I started to get scared that I might not see Helena again, I traced a smiling face in the condensation on the pitcher and wrote her name below it."

"Bet you wished you'd gotten to know her better on the train, huh?"

"There was more going on in my head, but basically...yes. Anyway, the drunker I would get, the more I would dwell on how the plaza, now with children and shoppers and tourists and old friends and light, had once been so dark and violent. It was the only thing I could think about to keep my mind off Helena. It was freaky."

"What happened?"

"She never came."

"Ever?"

"Ever. You want to know what I did, don't you?"

"Yeah."

"I chased after her."

"Where?"

"Morocco. I went looking for her in Morocco," he said. "But it all came down to an artist and a game I made up."
"I don't get it..."

"One of the things I passed the time doing at the *Café Luis* was to flip through the postcards of the famous paintings I'd bought along the way at the museums. Like flash cards when you were a kid. Tested myself to make the time go."

"Like?"

"Like I'd just guess who the artist was. Study it. Guess. Flip it over. Test myself."

Then he leaned back in a yoga-like position and closed his eyes and spit out names: "Ribera, Breughal, Murillo, Valasquez, Rubens, Picasso, Braques, Goya, Van Gogh, Manet, Serrat, Miro, Bosch...I used to flip through the stack like baseball cards until I knew them by heart."

"What was the game?"

"Third of May. Third of May I called my game. I always got stuck on whether the painting was a Goya or an El Greco for some reason. Maybe it was the G. I don't know."

"Even I know El Greco."

"Good for you, Victor."

Anyway, when I went back to the hotel again, they had checked out. But there was a note at the desk for me. She wrote she was sorry to have been rude, but things got more complicated than she'd expected, and she was very sorry to have not been able to get together. *'But happily, my parents and I are going to visit Marrakech. I relish the memory of our time together on the train between Paris and Madrid and will think of you often and with fondness. Very warmly, Helena."*

"Well, I was surprised by how that made me feel, so I went back to the *Café Luis* and tried to decide what to do. Finally I decided I would go after her, try and find her, but only if I could get through the cards on one more try without missing."

"Wow...get 'em right, you're on the road...miss one, it's eighty-six on Helena. Pressure." I flashed on the night Lee got drunk and betrayed me, hiding in the pines from Turner, the car with the dome light on, trying to decide whether to quit or stay.

"Right. For one thing it meant I'd be risking making it to London for the flight back if I took too long."

"Man. Big time decision..." He didn't say anything. Paul Simon was singing about New York City.

Then he said firmly, "Well, I aced it. You ever seen that painting, Victor?"

"Maybe, somewhere, some survey course."

"There's more fear and pain in that painting than water in Lake Tahoe, Victor," and I think his voice broke and his face looked hurt.

"Third of May?" I asked. "Third of May?"

After some time Redding said, "Yeah. Goya painted The Third of May."

"You were going to go after her even if you guessed wrong, weren't you?"

His face cleared. "Yeah."

"I ended up back in Madrid at the *Hostel Matute*, two weeks later, sick as a dog. Missed the plane from London and had to wire my parents for more money to fly home."

"How sick?"

"If it wasn't dysentery it should have been. Hell if I know. It cleaned me out. When I took my clothes to the laundry next door, the lady held her nose and made a horrible face. Even after I felt better, I would get attacks on the street. One afternoon, back at the *Plaza Mayor*, I felt it coming and ran down the steps to the bathroom at the *café* and wasn't able to hold it. Before I could get to the hole in the floor they call a toilet, it let go. I walked all the way back to the *Hostel Matute*."

"With shit in your pants? In the street?"

"Yeah. Nothing else I could do. Just looked ahead and hoped no one cared. Stood in the shower with my clothes on. I was a mess. Red, white and blue bell bottoms. Ugh."

"Jesus..."

"I changed clothes and went out again. It passed. I felt better."

When I asked him what had happened in Morocco, if he'd found Helena, he told me he'd written a short story about it called *The Third of May*, and he went in back and brought out a small notebook. As high as I was, I might have drifted off at times and actually been dreaming, but whether I was awake or not, I didn't care. His story played in my stoned head like a movie and got under my skin.

"Ready to behold? Vic."

"Roll it man."

The Third of May

A slow, open train left him in Algeciras, down at the coast, on the Mediterranean on his search for her. To get there from Madrid the train clickety-clacked along in low mountains and scrubby but pretty countryside, through miles and miles of olive groves. It was dry and hot in a different way than northern California. He saw nothing but olive trees, row after row, scrolling up to him, round green plugs evenly spaced in khaki-colored dirt becoming taller and bushier as you gained on them and the train leveled alongside. He could almost reach out and touch the leaves. Then more green dots out in the distance, shimmering through the heat as the train climbed again. The air smelled like balsa wood. There were other American students on board, and the conductor didn't mind if they sat between the cars with their legs out swinging over the sides. He found the young people refreshing. They laughed and hollered over the hot wind and told stories about where they had been, traded food, drank wine.

He and a boy about his age from Philadelphia thought it would be cool and started speaking Spanish to impress some girls up in a seat near them. The Philadelphia boy, David, had broken his arm at Dachau, of all places, when he slipped off a bench he was standing on to take a picture of the barracks. He was a Jew. A German doctor set the break at a Munich hospital and put a cast on his arm. David attached huge significance to the whole episode, enjoying the irony. He was dramatic that way. He stood and leaned out, holding onto the rail with his good arm and told the girls in English that Cervantes had written *Don Quixote* about the region they were in. He held his broken arm outside the train like a mail hook as he gestured. He told the girls he was thinking about changing his name to Sancho Panza. David was funny and smart, and the girls liked him. He'd traveled all over. He told the California boy, Terry, a story about leaving his passport on the ferry passing from Copenhagen to Helsingbord, Sweden, earlier in the summer. He said he just might go to Morocco with Terry. He told him he had some friends who had been in Morocco and it was cool, but warned him to be careful about trying to bring any dope back into Spain. David said there was a sign as you left Spain warning that the penalty for smuggling anything...anything, no matter how much or what it was...was seven years and one day. And he yelled from out over the tracks as the train went by a crossing gate blocking a herd of yellowish goats and two boys waving at the train, "The day can be as long as they want it to be."

"What'd you do when you came back? Bring anything?"

"What do you think?"

"Are you Terry?"

"Wait."

David was going to be in Europe all summer, which is something Terry wanted to do sooner or later. And he was a talker. Terry could see how he charmed his way back on the Danish ferry. But when they stopped in Seville, one of the girls they were trying to impress was impressed it turns out, and invited him to stay there with her. And when she got off the train, David followed, waving goodbye with his broken arm to Terry, jerking it up and down like a pump handle and yelling, "*Adios, Hermano. Adios.*" Her friend seemed to like Terry, too, but he had to keep going. He had a mission. The girls were both from Quebec, school teachers out for two weeks on a scheduled tour. They had to be in certain places at certain times. It sounded like a drag to Terry. But they were really very sweet. The one that smiled at Terry over her shoulder was Jennette. He still thinks about her sometimes. She went on and on about how impolite Parisians were to her. How her spoken French dissatisfied them.

The train came through Malaga and dropped down to Algiceras, where Terry bought a ticket for the hovercraft to Tangier and killed time drinking beer and eating fried anchovies in a bar. They put them out in bowls, the *bocarona*. Little, tiny, salty things. He had a map and knew he first had to go to Tangier, so his plan was to get there, spend the night, then take a train to Marrakesh the next day. He guessed that Marrakesh was about two hundred and fifty miles from Tangier. Madrid was about two hundred fifty miles from Algiceras. All together it was about a five hundred mile trip. Like San Francisco to Los Angeles. When he thought about it like that, it didn't seem far.

The first problem was he found out too late his ticket on the hovercraft didn't go straight to Tangier. It went to a tiny province that Spain still controls at the tip of Morocco: Ceuta.

Border control is there. From Ceuta, the frontier, you still have to take a bus ride to Tangier. It wasn't a big deal. It just took longer than he expected.

"You with me, Victor?"

"I wish...yeah."

The Moroccan government was pretty tough on anybody they thought might be a hippie. Terry saw one Dutch freak get turned away at the frontier after a border guard yanked his hat off and hair fell down to his shoulders. If you had long hair, they weren't letting you in. That was that. He whined and begged, but that only made it worse. They sent him back. The bus to Tangier was packed with a few foreign students and tourists, but at least half the load were locals. Terry sat next to a Moroccan wearing a *jellaba* that looked as heavy as burlap. It was difficult for him to understand how you stay cool with those things. The Moroccan didn't talk or look at Terry, but kept his head bowed, praying or sleeping. Terry guessed he was sleeping. There was nothing along the way but sand and rock and once in a while a mud and stone one-room house or shed that looked abandoned. It was late in the day, and the light was different than it had been in Algeciras. By the time the bus got to the outskirts of Tangier, it was dusk and the sky was pink and blue with red smears, and it seemed the whole city was built right up into the sunset. He'd never seen anything so foreign. It was burning up on the bus and the flies were awful. It was good to get there though. He felt closer to her. The bus terminal was by the water, but it really wasn't much cooler. Irritating as the flies were, they weren't as bad as the boys that met the bus and crowded the door. The driver barked and shook his hand at them from his seat as the bus emptied. You literally had to jump into them. They were in a pack, all fighting and shoving to be picked as a guide for tips. If they thought you were an American, they got all over you. They yelled in French, then Spanish if you didn't understand that, then they'd switch to German, English or Arabic. It was amazing. It was impossible to lose them, so Terry finally just picked one who led him away. The boy wanted to carry Terry's backpack but he wouldn't allow it. He didn't trust him. Others followed them and wouldn't stop haggling after Terry. His kid finally picked up a rock and hit the biggest of the others in the leg and then they left them alone. Terry asked the kid what his name was. "Mohammed. Call me Mo," he said. He was about ten, caramel-colored skin and black curly hair, sweat beads around his neck, a confident little boy in an unbuttoned dirty white shirt and too short black pants gray from dust. No shoes. He kept looking over his shoulder at Terry like he might lose his meal ticket as they cut through the crowded streets. People were carrying live chickens tucked under their arms, dogs chased around in the dirt yapping. Most of the women except the tourists had their heads and faces covered. It was sweaty and smoky. The streets were dirt, packed hard, coated in dust as fine as gunpowder that layered your boots and legs and got up your nose. Walls and shuttered windows were everywhere. Soon as a shopkeeper or vendor spotted your back-pack or blue jeans, they started yelling and pulling you into their shops. Mo jabbered at them and pulled Terry in the direction he wanted. Unbelievable. "Where you taking me?" he asked, like it made a difference.

"A good place. A good place."

Terry followed him up narrow, worn, uneven stone steps into what he found out later was the Arab Quarter, a very bizarre old part of the city. Streets just end, no logic at all. Madrid seemed like an American city compared to Tangier. It was a maze, narrower streets than down below by the water, harder to pass by people. Packed. Terry stayed close to Mohammed, picked up some French words in the air, but for the most part all he heard was Arabic, which was impossible for him to understand. It sounded like throat clearing or coughing to his ears. Finally after what seemed like a hundred turns he left Terry at a small hotel that was part of a long tan wall. Terry gave Mo a Kennedy half dollar for a tip and thought he was going to explode he was so grateful. The desk clerk seemed jealous and shooed Mo into the street. Terry paid for the room in Spanish money and got Moroccan money, dirham, back as change. The room was adequate. And it was cheap. But no bathroom, no phone. And funky, slatted doors to the hall, high ceilings and a fan above the bed that turned so slow it didn't make a difference. Flies were all over. He stomped on two roaches. Bare walls without screens on the window, but it overlooked a mosque. Terry's window was level with a whitewashed tower edged in boxy blue designs. He stayed there for a long time and watched them coming to prayer and then the incredible eerie chanting as they prayed. There was a crescent moon out above the tower by then and it made Terry think of the vendor and the slivers of white coconut meat on the platter that had been shoved at him as he and Mo had climbed the steps to the Quarter. The vendor had yelled at Mohammed when Terry refused and said, "No, *merci*," but Mo shrugged him off in Arabic and asked Terry if he was from New York City. Mo was a cool little boy. He was hanging around in the street when Terry went out to find a place to eat later. Said he would translate and keep him out of trouble.

Terry got a train schedule at the desk and ended up eating

fish and chips and drinking lemon soda that was warm and watery at a desperate, fly-ridden cafe not too far from the hotel, still in the Quarter. All the Cinzano umbrellas were up even though it was night. It was next to a Moroccan restaurant called The Parisian. Mo said Terry would like the fish and chips place better, and he stuck around beyond the tables in the small square pacing while Terry ate and thought about her. There were weak electric lights at the corners of the rooftops that made bronze streaks on the walls and long dim shadows across the ground. There were candles in sooty glass bowls on the tables. A red-faced Englishman with a big belly in a sweaty undershirt shouted orders in Spanish to a woman inside and carried the fish and chips back and forth and grumbling, a towel over his shoulder. While he waited on tables, the cook—the man's wife, Mo said—worked a deep fryer behind a short counter, really just a shelf. He worked her constantly and very hard. The chips and fish came piled in a greasy cone of Arabic newspaper pages. There was a vinegar bottle and salt on all the tables but Terry's, and it was hard to get the Englishman's attention. When he finally got back from wherever, he smelled like gin, but he finally robbed the vinegar and salt from another table and said something in French to a tanned middle-aged couple in safari outfits who gave Terry indifferent looks.

He sat, ate and watched the scene, the constant movement of people passing through the square. The *jellabas* and the long robes gave the walkers a fluid, flowing look. No edges, if that makes any sense. It accented his difference. He wondered if she'd walked across this same square. The walkers were a stream that pushed him away and pulled him at the same time.

"This is incredible, man."

Redding was getting excited. "Let me read dude."

Terry thought of Helena and where he would start looking for her when he got to Marrakesh, her and that governess, them and their walled garden. He'd composed what he would say to her on the train. He knew he wasn't facing the reality of what he was up against yet. The outright foreignness of the Arab Quarter gave him an elevated sense of confidence somehow. But he was on his way and loved the idea that not a soul in sight had any idea who he was. Except Mo. And Mo knew nothing. And he was going to win. He would find her. Terry was in the frame of mind to will it to happen. No matter how long the odds, he knew that sometimes you had to put yourself in a position, let go and trust. Until you do that, you will die from the worry. You'll be frozen. And thinking those thoughts made him feel better.

Mohammed stood from a squat, slapping at flies as Terry got up. Mo waved at a young boy his age leading four, pale, spinster-looking women. They looked uneasy, but sat down at a table anyway after wiping off the seats. The owner had disappeared again. The other young boy said something to Mo in Arabic and they laughed. The man and woman in the safari clothes ignored everybody, smoking, elbows on the table.

Mo and Terry walked away from the square, in and out of shops and stalls and Mo haggled. But Terry couldn't tell if he was conspiring with the shop owners and vendors or not. He tried to keep the conversations in French or Spanish most of the time if possible. Funny, other Americans, the students you'd see—they stood out like sore thumbs—you could tell who they were, and they would make eye contact but never talk. It was as if they didn't want to acknowledge that someone else had discovered their little exotic spot. But an American accent stood out, and Terry thought, they probably didn't even know who Paul Bowles was. Terry's time was too valuable to waste on their silliness.

And late as it was, it was still hot, and the heat intensified the powerful odor of new leather that hung in the air. He had smelled it all day and night. It was the cured leather smell of a tack room full of saddles and riding gear. Wallets, bags, passport cases, satchels, vests, jackets, pants, stitched hats, gloves, purses, shoes—anything you could think of, all made of leather, for sale all over, hanging and piled inside and out of low-doored shops. He smelled cinnamon once or twice, and a whiff of flowers from somewhere on the breeze when it would blow over the walls and down the alley streets, but it wasn't often. Nothing overcame the leather. His shirt and that smell stuck to him. Finally, to shut up a vendor, he bought a spiral coin purse that you squeeze to open. But instead of leaving him alone, the vendor started trying to sell Terry a hat. It never stopped.

Mohammed led him to another restaurant that once you entered from a hilly lane through a double iron gate, opened onto outdoor terraces cut into the hillside with cafe tables and flickering candles in clay holders. Some of the tables were beneath arbors of vines, some were under the sky, but all looked out on the water, and on further until the lights of Gibraltar blinked way out. Terry had skirted Gibraltar earlier in the day in the hovercraft on the way to Ceuta. The view and the night were beautiful.

"Gibraltar as solid like Walter Cronkite used to say it was in the commercials?"

"Victor, c'mon..."

But in this cafe, Mohammed outside again, waiters in *jellabas* served mint tea and tiny oblong cakes of honey, almond and fresh coconut. There were no other tourists Terry could see. He needed Helena right then and there as he stared off at Gibraltar. Music was drifting in from somewhere. It was twangy, rhythmic with popping drums, maybe a sitar, but not exactly. He thought it might be a radio. While he was thinking of Helena, one of the waiters came by with a long pipe and what Mohammed told him later was Kif. Terry sat there, smoked and got high—had no idea what Kif was at that time—and felt like he was a million miles away from home. He was simply consumed and overwhelmed by a sense of adventure and at the same time he felt as if he was out on an edge somewhere. It was steep, the terraces were carved out of the hill over the water. And he was stoned and going to reward Mo with another Kennedy half. And find her.

In the morning it was incredibly hot again, hotter than Madrid at the same time of day.

And the light was different. Bluer, if that can be. Mohammed was waiting for Terry and led him down out of the Arab Quarter to the train station. On the way a street vendor with cameras dangling from his arms tried to sell one to Terry. His English was good. Terry held up his Pentax to show him he didn't need one, but he kept following them. Finally he gave up. Mohammed said they were all stolen from tourists. He said, "Be careful, New York."

It was not a fancy train that went to Marrakesh through Rabat and Casablanca, down along the coast. There were no compartments, you just grabbed a seat, which were nothing more than benches. It wasn't like a European train, and Terry's Euro Rail pass was of no use. He had to pay money. And it was at least three hours late in leaving. The train just sat there on the tracks and baked in the sun. No one was in a hurry. The car eventually filled up with people who seemed to know there was no reason to rush. Finally it pulled out at about ten in the morning, slow, jerky and squealing. Fifteen minutes into the trip, Terry realized he was in a fourth-class car, but by then it was too late. It was like riding in a horse stall compared to what he'd ridden in Spain, France and Austria. The interior was exposed wood, like barn board. The locals sat and clucked, almost gargling, waving their hands, boxes, bags and packages piled up around them. Somebody had two live chickens trussed up on the seat next to her. Another man had a whole watermelon. Terry couldn't believe the scene. The train lurched, the wheels grating; metal scraping metal, wobbling ahead. He could have walked as fast as the train was moving. The slow train from Madrid to Algiceras could have been an express compared to this. When the conductor came along, he and Terry made out good enough in French and it relaxed him. Terry settled in and tried to focus on Helena.

Occasionally the conductor would walk through the car and announce a stop in Arabic. Terry tried to figure out from his map where they were from time to time, and more or less could tell when they would be coming up on one of the towns along the line, like Asiiah, Larache, Kasar el Kabir, Souk el Arba du Rharb. He tried to memorize them for fun. It was a time-passing game he played.

But it was so slow and It gave him lots of time to think about Helena, their brief time together, the things they had revealed to one another, their plans, but worse, time to dwell on why she had run. Besides the stations, sometimes the train just stopped in the middle of nowhere. Nowhere. People would get on, get off and disappear. No tickets Terry could see, they just piled on. No system or order. Until dark he was able to see mountains out his window way off to the left broken up by palm trees.

It was after dark, they were somewhere out there, and he was very hungry and thirsty.

All around him people were pulling food out. All he'd brought was a piece of flat bread and a bottle of water and it was long gone. He wondered who Mohammed might be guiding around Tangier at that moment, leading them to fish and chips and Kif.

"Victor? Victor...you nodding?"

"Yeah. Yeah. Yeah. Yeah... Redding. What's Kif anyway?"

"One step before hash. Now stay with me."

There was a sing songy man in a *jellaba* and *fez* who came through the car selling food. He was tall and thin, with a big mustache and his *jellaba* was white and trimmed in red and gold. He was selling snacks from two big baskets. He had great balance. And the things he had for sale were wild. Nothing like it on a European train.

He sold hard boiled eggs, chocolate bars, bananas, oranges, hard candy, honey cakes, same watery sodas and Kif. And he had pipes for sale, too.

Terry gave him some dirham for a banana and an egg and some more lemony soda and probably over tipped. Then he ate and tried to sleep, wishing he could brush his teeth and trying to block out a woman in front of him haggling with the candy man about the price of something. They went at it forever.

Terry awoke in the middle of the night. His neck hurt. He was stretched across his bench with his head on his backpack. All the lights were out. It had gotten cold and looked like they were stopped in the middle of a desert. Silence. Nothing. From the dark about twenty Moroccans with their *jellaba* hoods pulled over their heads were picking their way across the tracks from a line of palms and gliding onto the train. He could see their breath clouds and heard them murmuring as they boarded. Only a dog barking from somewhere way out made a familiar sound. Some carried canvas rolls under their arms, still others, parcels with hairy twine. The coconut sliver moon from the mosque was still above and under it these people were just shapes. Watching them board the car from his window, they were as opaque as the trees against the desert night and he blinked awake as they came on and filled the empty seats around him. One sat on his bench and Terry said, 'excuse me'. He moved his feet and that man's face, all creases, worn, stony impassive, was the only face of theirs he saw clearly as he waited for him to slide over. Terry hugged his backpack and leaned on the window and tried to sleep. The car smelled like flint, burlap and wood smoke. And the train sat and sat and sat. He didn't know what the time was when the train finally pulled out on the way south.

In Casablanca the next morning, the railroad went on strike. The train just stopped.

End of the line. That was it, as far as it was going, but it took Terry a while to figure that out. He finally learned why from two college kids from New York who had been in a second-class car on the same train. He was growing a beard and had a controlling way about him. She was short with reddish hair and a big chest and, except for that, reminded Terry of Janis Joplin. They were headed for Marrakesh, too. Everyone else who'd been on the train when it arrived in Casablanca had just melted away. No one could tell them when the next train might come along or when the strike might be over. He tried to ask a man who was kneeling and praying on a piece of cardboard spread on the platform, but he ignored Terry. There was nobody at the ticket office either. They guessed that the strike had been expected. By everyone but the Americans.

But what they ended up having was an adventure. They walked to a hotel nearby and found a taxi driver smoking at an outside table. His name was Omat, a short bald man in a suit with skinny lapels, no tie and rope-soled canvas shoes. Omat drove a 1953 Chevrolet, and there aren't many American cars in Morocco. And they made a deal to take the three of them to Marrakesh. That was a trip. A real trip. Nobody can drive over there. They pay no attention to signs and signals. Before they could clear the outskirts of Casablanca, Omat had almost run over a Llama that a boy was chasing after with a stick. Soon as they got past that scene, he almost sideswiped another car, but kept going. The girl laughed and her boyfriend, who insisted on riding shotgun, braced himself and held onto the dashboard. It was better once they got to the highway and Omat didn't have to negotiate traffic. It was a hot and beautiful ride with the windows rolled down, but the girl talked the whole time. She told Terry her red hair had caused trouble in North Africa. In Tunisia some men had tried to break into their hotel room she said. She was convinced they wanted a white slave girl to sell in the desert. Terry could tell she loved the idea of it. At a roadside stop, Omat gassed up at an ancient Texaco pump and the American's sat under some palm shade at a table and drank cold Cokes. They tasted good but different, sweeter, with a lacy *Coca Cola* written in Arabic on the bottle. But being with the couple made him miss Helena even more. He was crazy to see her.

While Redding stopped and stenciled an Arabic *Coca Cola* logo in the air, I looked at him in amazement because of his story, a story about running after a girl he didn't even know, in a strange country, by himself. She was practically a ghost, but he had been willing to put himself in the middle of nowhere to be on her trail. For what? He swore he'd never even kissed her. And as I looked over at him, turning pages in the candlelight, going on and on, I guessed the ending. I knew where this story was headed. At least I thought I did. All that effort for someone he only shook hands with. Why? What do you get? And it was bothering me because it made me think of Rennie and what we'd done and said to each other. What about all the time and touching that had gone into our relationship? What did that mean? Why wasn't I fighting harder? Begging her to stay or promising to follow her? Look at tonight: I hadn't been interested in riding a mile to her apartment. What'd that say about me stacked up against Redding who'd been willing to go five hundred foreign miles after a dream girl?

My commitment was to run. I could park it in the "good time while it lasted" category. I hated to say goodbye to the best sex in my life, but I could split if I had to, let it go, be free and move on. But at the same time, I didn't want to feel that way. I didn't want to admit to myself we'd had nothing. That we'd probably used each other. And here's Redding, his character Terry practically singing about the scenery, the language, the strangers and the adventure he'd had on his impossible search for this girl. He had been all focus and determination and commitment. At least Redding tried. I looked at him through my bleary eyes and said, "Get it on, man. What happened in Marrakesh?"

Omat left them in the center of Marrakesh, a big open square, the Medina. He peeled out and almost clobbered an old man pushing a cart loaded with tomatoes. It was a sideshow. Food stalls and snake charmers and merchants and vendors—music, crowds, noise—madness, just like Helena described it. Jack, the guy, and his girlfriend, Jessica, and Terry stuck together to try and find a hotel, hostel, something, some place to stay that wasn't too expensive. Jack was paranoid about pickpockets. He got pissy with Jessica when she stopped to play a game of chance with a guy sitting on a blanket with three shells and a bead. That game. She won once, then lost three straight. Jack was full of, 'I told you so's,' as they walked away. Kids like Mohammed were everywhere again, and it really got to be a pain as they wandered around. They bothered you like the flies, and even though Terry told Jack about how well Mo had worked out in Tangier, he didn't trust them. He was convinced he could lead them to a place. And it was hot. No clouds, intense blue sky and a late-day sun beating down. Marrakesh is flat. No up and down like Tangier, no breeze. Finally Terry told Jack, who he could see was getting frustrated, that they ought to give up and get a kid to guide them. Like a pack of jackals, there were at least seven following them. Even though they were speaking Arabic, Terry knew they were joking about Jessica, so did Jack. He was getting intense. It was late in the day and Terry was exhausted and his back hurt, and he just wanted to lay down and sleep, so they finally picked a boy with a burr haircut, the biggest of them, and Jack gave him a few dirham. And then the kid just ran off. Jack went crazy. He started to chase the kid but Jessica held his arm and then he got mad at Terry like it was his fault. The others, who had scattered after their friend took Jack's money ran away, then came drifting back, but not too close. Terry fell back and told the next biggest boy he would pay him a Kennedy half. He showed it to him and his eyes got as big as the coin and he took them right away to a neat place close by they had passed in front of at least two times in two hours of walking around. It was down a side street off the Medina in a residential area. Terry heard *The Call to Pray* echoing over a loudspeaker from a mosque. The boy reacted the same way Mo did after Terry paid him but he didn't get the half dollar until they were checked in and after Jack had inspected the rooms. The boy ran down the street with the others clamoring after him to get a peek at his fifty-cent piece. Terry wished he'd brought a hundred of them.

From the street you'd never know it was a hotel. A red wooden door in a wall with a short stoop and no street number or sign. Sometimes it seems everything in Morocco is behind a wall. The hotel was small, three stories, all the rooms around an interior court-yard open under the sky. Tall palm plants in plain clay pots sat on the pink tile at pillars. There were red geraniums in the same kind of orange squat pots, and bushy plants, thick with small dark green leaves

323

flecked with bright, small white blossoms scattered around. It was radiant, cool and airy.

"You're a poet, man." I couldn't help myself. "I didn't know you had this side."

"You can't imagine. Like it so far?"

"I do. Keep going."

The sun had crossed over, and filtered, indirect sunlight washed over the courtyard. The sense of space was surprising since from the street you had no idea any of it existed. Birds dived in and out of the opening in the roof and chased each other off the railings. A bright yellow bird perched on the back of one of the chairs at a table and dared an old woman who was sweeping to chase him away. She ignored the bird, but he jigged his head and fanned his tail anyway. Terry couldn't tell how old the place was, but when he stood outside his room and leaned over the railing and looked straight down, he counted at least fifteen cracked tiles in the floor. The proprietor told them breakfast and dinner was included in the price of a room and the long communal table in the center of the courtyard was where they would be served. She spoke French and had deep dark eyes and seemed to give them the idea she approved of Americans in her hotel. She made sure they knew to leave room keys at the desk when they went out to shop or sightsee. You could tell she was used to how Americans behaved. Terry translated.

Terry was exhausted and didn't want to eat. Jack and his old lady had sex on their minds, so Terry said he'd see them later and went and fell out on his springy mattress with his clothes on. He didn't wake up until morning when someone was pounding on his door.

I said, "Tell me it was Helena coming to ravish you..."

"Jesus..."

"Sorry."

It was Jack. He and Jessica were going to the *souk*, the covered market, and asked Terry to go. He told them no, but to leave a message at the desk about where he could find them later. After the door closed, he stared at it and tried to decide where to start looking for Helena. He had no idea.

But he ended up doing what he had done in Madrid. He went hotel hopping. It was the only thing he could think of. When he asked the lady at the front desk about where to find the big hotels, she misunderstood for a moment and thought he was unhappy with his room. He was able to explain that he needed to find somebody, and she gave him a list and helped with directions. At the big table in the courtyard, Terry ate breakfast. He had figs and warm croissants with orange marmalade and strong coffee and sat with a farm equipment salesman from Amsterdam. The man wasn't unpleasant, but didn't talk much and was in a hurry. He told Terry not to leave anything valuable in his room. He was sweating through his shirt in the heat of the morning.

Terry went to four hotels, asking the same questions, getting the same answers. Feeling ridiculous, he decided to go to the Medina and wander around. He thought he might luck out and run into her there, but there was just more pestering from the kids. He wanted to enjoy the scene, but couldn't. He was watching the people. Searching.

Redding looked up. "Now that I think about it, it was like being one of the floor men in the casino watching the dealers. I, I mean Terry, was watching the watchers. Scanning for Helena."

Finally, to get the kids off his back Terry told one of the boys on his tail that he wanted to go into the *souk*, but he had to ditch his friends first, and if he did he was good for a big tip. Terry didn't know what the boy told the others, but they left him and his guide alone.

The *souk* was a combination beehive, ant hill, maze, all mixed up together. It was a city by itself. Rivers of aisles and stalls and haggling, shouting and grabbing, all under one roof. Terry felt like he was in a pipe or a tube the whole time. Perspiration and smoke, that leather smell and stale air was what you breathed. He was convinced if you didn't have a kid as a guide, you could get lost for days in there. Forget it if there was a fire. He wasn't planning on buying anything. He was watching the people, watching for Helena, obsessed. Then he spotted Jack and Jessica. They were looking over *jellabas* and Moroccan shirts at a stall. They had a kid with them who looked like he was doing the bargaining. Jessica showed off a big leather bag she'd bought earlier. She loved the *souk*. Jack tried on a long, striped *jellaba*, and said he felt like Charlton Heston as Moses. Terry thought he looked like the lead singer in Canned Heat in a dress but didn't say anything. Food vendors like the one from the train banged into you and shoved their baskets in your face.

The three of them each bought a *jellaba* and Jessica bought a white shirt with red and green embroidery for her sister and then they wandered the *souk*, stifling and claustrophobic. After a couple of hours, the dust and smell of heated canvas was oppressive, so when Terry told them he wanted to get going, they decided to leave as well and were led out. They paid the kid guides in the center of the square since they knew the way to the hotel. On the way Jack nudged Terry and said he'd bought some hash cookies in the *souk*. Terry was sure he'd been hustled. Jack winked at Jessica and got a big smile back when he suggested a nap. She winked at Terry behind Jack's back and smiled like she wanted Terry to go with them. At the hotel Jack said later, after supper, he wanted Terry to go to a cafe with them and get high. He thought that would be a real trip. Terry told them he would meet them at supper, and sat on a leather-covered stool in the lobby while they went to their room to screw, Jessica pouting back at Terry over her shoulder. He could hear the birds jabbering in the courtyard and didn't know what else to do and just shrugged when the lady with the nice eyes at the desk gave him a questioning look as she handed him his room key. And it was over right there. He knew it for some reason. Right there he gave up and wanted to leave.

Terry didn't really know why the realization that he had no hope of finding her came to him when it did. Maybe one side of his brain conquered the other, and the idiocy of doing what he was doing became too clear. Looking back now at the rest of his trip, time went by really fast. All the action compressed in memory.

They met for dinner in the courtyard. No one ate with them. The old lady they had seen pushing the broom the day before brought out *cous cous* and a patterned ceramic bowl of tomatoes with oil, salt, pepper and spices. They drank bottled water and watched newly arrived guests walking along the balconies to their rooms, but they hadn't come to supper by the time the Americans got up to leave. A father lifted a small boy up so he could see over the railing and he giggled and pointed down at them. They dropped room keys at the desk as they left and stopped at the first cafe they came to with outside tables. It didn't take all night and they did it without a guide. Terry was out of Kennedy halves anyway.

Jack and Jessica wanted to go to Fez after Marrakesh and asked Terry to go along. He told them he was way off track and had barely enough time to get back to London to catch his charter and that he was going to leave as soon as he could. Jessica said, "You haven't seen much of Marrakesh." He felt she meant something else and told her he'd seen enough to know he'd seen enough. That made her pick at her sunburned nose. So they sat and drank mint tea. Jack pulled the cookies from his pants pockets that were wrapped in wax paper. Six of them; just simple, crumbly sugar cookies. Terry told him he'd been ripped off. There was no way these things could get you stoned. Jack got defensive, as he expected. Terry could never travel with either of them, much less have a three-way. But they each ate two anyway and sipped the sweet green tea from little cups in silence. And after a while—and nobody was feeling anything—he excused himself to begin figuring out how to get back to Tangier, then London.

Before leaving the cafe he said he might see them in the morning, but if he didn't, good luck, safe travels and all that stuff. He'd tired of the two of them. At the front desk he found out there was an overnight bus to Tangier he could catch, and he calculated he had enough time to get back to Spain, then London if everything worked. While he was packing, the cookies kicked in. He had to stop and sit down he got so ripped. Then he tried on his *jellaba* and looked at himself in the full size mirror on the door of a standing closet. He thought about wearing it, but decided he would look like a fool. Then he got the munchies. All he had was a pear, so he ate that in about three bites and managed to finish packing. He found his way to the bus station which was in the Medina near where Omat had left them. And he was out of it. Everything seemed to jump at Terry. All the difference between him and his surroundings was enlarged, and for a time he forgot that Helena was the reason he was there. His sense of displacement was enormous and frightening. But he started to come down while he waited for the bus. Terry was the only American. He had the munchies bad, so he bought a burger from a vendor. It was sort of like an American hamburger, not sure about the meat, but wolfed it down anyway. He could have eaten dirt.

He tried to sleep on the bus, but only dozed. When it made a stop around midnight, he bought some chocolate, bottled water and a hard-boiled egg from a vendor and before dawn arrived in Tangier. It was four AM and he didn't want to waste the money and time on a hotel room because he was aiming to be on the first ferry or hovercraft in the morning going to Algiceras. He remembered from Mo that they didn't start until nine, so he wandered over to the beach near the port and waited for the sun to come up. He had his camera out ready to catch the sunrise, leaning against his backpack and was more tired from the trip than he knew and fell asleep.

When he awoke, the sun was high, his stomach was cramping and he didn't see his camera and thought he'd rolled over on it. But when he lifted his arm, there was nothing on the other end of the strap. It took him a second to understand that someone had cut the Pentax off his arm while he had been sleeping. Whoever it was could have cut his throat. Terry was really pissed, but had the cramps so bad all he could think about was a place to go to the bathroom.

He went into the bus station, but the bathroom was locked. The only thing he was familiar with was the Arab Quarter so he walked back up there. One of the kid guides started following him, but Terry was in such a state, all bent over, he left him alone without much hassle. He got to the square with the fish and chips restaurant and found the bathroom there, just a stifling hole, but got some relief, and didn't care that the owner cussed at him for not buying anything. All he could think about was that mushy pear and the burger he'd eaten. As soon as he got out in the street, he cramped up and had to go again. He felt like he was dying. There was no way he could get down to the waterfront. He was convinced he had dysentery.

He checked back into the same hotel he'd stayed earlier just so he had a place to shit. And Terry spent most of the night in a bathroom at the end of the hall with a rust-stained porcelain sink, dripping faucets and a cloudy mirror that made you look pasty and even worse than he felt. Once, someone came knocking and speaking Arabic and all Terry could say was, "Excusez-*moi*, Excusez-*moi*. Please." Of course he had nothing to take and wouldn't have known where to buy medicine or what to ask for. He might have lost five pounds that night. The biggest cockroach he'd ever seen crawled around his feet while he was sitting in there. He was so sick, though, he didn't have the strength to raise a foot to squash it. The insect seemed to cast a shadow big as a Volkswagen, and he simply stared.

The next morning he didn't feel much better and was really weak, but concluded he didn't have anything else left inside. So he toughed it out and made it to the ferry. He was on the water by ten. He curled up in a ball on a deck chair, hugged himself and tried to keep from throwing up or shitting his pants. The sea gulls sounded like they were laughing at him. And the waves were choppy. There were some preppy Americans on the ferry. He had his first laugh in a long time when at customs, because as rough as he must have looked, pale and dirty and smelly, the Spanish customs agents picked the two prepsters out of the line and took them to the area where they strip search people. Terry loved it. The brightest moment for him, especially because he had a lid of Kif in his pack and a pipe in his boot. He got to the train station and used his Euro Rail pass which was about to expire for a ticket to Madrid and bought three litter bottles of Fanta orange soda and in about an hour drank all three and never pissed. No one rode in his compartment the whole way, he smelled so bad. The *Hostel Matute* looked like a palace to him when he finally returned. Compared to Morocco, he might as well have been in his bed in California. He bought some stomach stuff, held his nose and drank it all down. He took a bath and slept for two straight days.

He didn't feel well enough to travel right away, and the London charter was long gone, so he bought a ticket from Madrid to San Francisco with money his parents wired to him at the American Express office on Jose Antonio and

331

hung around Madrid to get some strength back. There was one odd thing that happened to Terry before he left.

A tour bus passed by him on his last day while waiting for traffic across from the Prado, and as it went by, he looked up at the back window and thought he saw Helena's face looking out.

"This real or the story?"

"That's the story."

"Is it true?"

"You like it?"

"Yeah. But is it true?"

"Some of it."

"Did it all happen? All those people real?"

"Parts."

"Are you any of them?"

"I'm all of them or none of them," he said, "It needs work. Too many 'ands' and 'thats' and other problems. It needs an editor. Just my first try to tell a story that talks about something bigger. I don't know." Redding leaned back and stretched out on the floor. He was quiet and I think he went to sleep. The music had been over a long time. The candle was out. The hash, foil and matches, beer cans and pages to *The Third of May* were scattered on the floor and the table. As I fell asleep, I wondered if Helena had ever left Madrid in the first place. Or if he made it all up. And did it matter. Nothing he said gave me a clue.

In my hash dream Redding was at it again, but standing on the table, hundreds of Kennedy half dollars scattered at his feet, dressed in a red Moroccan *jellaba*, waving his arms like a preacher delivering a sermon, Crosby, Stills & Nash singing "Marrakesh Express" on the turntable. Redding's burning with passion about Helena, and he's going on and on about *'Her arid breezes and spicy bazaars and musky fragrances, her wailing mosques and flowing robes,* and he whirls in a circle that causes some of the coins to slide to the floor and the hem of his *jellaba* to rise and fall. He faces me again and goes on about, *'her candy Kif…and sexual African sky,'* he raises his open hands to the ceiling, *'a coconut sliver of moon in a dazzling field of sensual stars…a* backhand wave…*'a blush of palm shadow moving gently in the night breeze on her bedroom wall,* his fingertips at his nose, *'her scented body waiting for me in the night heat.'*

I saw it all.

Chapter 15

Redding shook me awake about noon, and we went to the waffle shop. Our plans were up in the air except for a stop to pick up our pay. We had a loose idea about going up to Redding's aunt and uncle's house at North Shore after that. I was just trying to wake up and chill out on my day off as best I could, hopefully away from Butcher and Sammy, away from The Mine Shaft.

At the front door the crisp air was a mix of pine and pancakes, maple syrup, bacon and coffee. We sat at the same table where Shanahan and I had eaten. On the other side of the window, Redding's VW was a space off from where Shanahan's Galaxie had been parked. The crowd was about the same, but there were no state troopers this time, and the cute waitress wasn't there, which was a bummer. I'd told Redding she was pretty neat and ripped off Shanahan's hillbilly expression, 'Cute as a speckled puppy,' to describe her. He said, "I'll miss that dude."

I wasn't quite sure what to make of Redding's short story about chasing Helena all over Morocco. But it was neat, and even if he'd made it all up, I thought he was a good writer. Bits of my hash dream about him reading were coming back in snatches, but they were out of order and mixed in with thoughts of Rennie. "Can I ask you about that girl and Morocco?"

He sniffed the milk in a small tin pitcher then dribbled some into his coffee. "Sure."

"What made you want to be a writer?"

"I like the idea of it."

"Can you make any money doing it?"

"Don't know. Doesn't matter. I can always deal."

"Does it come easy?"

"I just sit down and do it every once in a while."

I thought about that. One more example of his luck or talent or both. "Okay, do you miss Helena?"

He said, "I miss the idea of Helena."

A tall skinny waitress old enough to be the cute one's mother came over. I was really sorry the young girl wasn't working, and the thought of asking this one where she was ran through my mind, but the woman's height and her up-front bad attitude stopped me. She leaned on one leg and stuck a bony hip out while she scribbled on her pad. She sounded bored when she recited back our orders. She had a light mustache darker than Redding's, dull skin and wore a red sweater, I guess because of the air conditioning. You could see a trench of gray roots along a part in her brown hair when she tilted her head to write. Her name tag said, "Hi. My Name Is Nicole," and I told Redding after she walked away that it sounded like a little girl name and didn't fit with a frumpy older woman with no personality.

"Any more questions?"

"Yeah," I said. Knowing how serious it is to bring back drugs from Morocco into Spain, why in the hell did you risk smuggling that kif and pipe back in, especially knowing you might get searched like those preppies?"

Nicole was back with the coffee pot for refills, but we waved her off and that got us a look and she pivoted to the next table. Redding watched her pouring and said, "I'm lucky, Vic. I'm lucky and I get away with shit. It's the idea of it. That's just the way it is. I try not to overthink it." He looked back at me and said, "It's all about attitude." The way he said it, he didn't sound arrogant. It was just him.

"Jesus, you and Turner with that attitude shit. Where'd you get that?"

"I don't think you learn it, but maybe you do...or can." He made a face and said, "There's gum all over the bottom of this."

"I know. Hard as nails isn't it?"

His hands flew up, "Not the one I just felt. Shit," and he went to find the men's room. He stopped and said, "And I didn't bring anything over the border to Spain. That's fiction. What do I look like, a dumb ass?

He came back as Nicole brought our orders, plates of waffles and eggs. This time we asked for more coffee, and while she was putting our plates down answered flatly, "Coming up," then turned to check the room. She told a man with a newspaper in his hands at the register to, "Sit anywhere," and she reached behind and tightened the floppy red bow of her apron and walked to the coffee station. Later, when I wanted a glass of milk, she was at the register with a customer and wouldn't make eye contact. Shanahan wouldn't have stood for it. I missed the cute girl.

At the apartment, I could hear music coming from the windows as we pulled in downstairs. The dry heat on the back of my neck felt good, but I needed a shower and left Redding in the living room with Turner and Sara. The fat guy with the big beard who had snarled at me from the couch the morning after the fight at The Mine Shaft was still hanging around. Halfway down the hall to my mattress, I remembered the new *LIFE* was probably out and said, "Right back..." to the living room and went out and down the stairs to the market. Broke as I was, I still had forty cents for the magazine.

As I'd predicted, the cover picture was of an astronaut waving, and a caption in the upper right hand corner read, *Leaving For The Moon*. I flipped through it and took the steps two at a time, all excited about cutting it up and adding it to the collage. As I went through the living room, I saw the fat guy had his hand on Sarah's leg while he argued some point or another with Redding. I couldn't understand a word over the Bob Seger record that was blasting. Turner, as usual, was spaced out, sitting on the floor preoccupied with juggling a pencil through his fingers. He was agile with his big hands and could hold four eggs at a time with one of his mitts. He was king of the kitchen at that. But I was baffled by his relationship with Sara.

After a long shower, I sat on my mattress and looked through *LIFE* again. It was interesting, but the moon pictures reminded me of all the trouble that had happened at the casino. And even though I was anxious to get back to work on the collage, I started thinking about Rennie and worrying about how in the hell I was going to say goodbye to her. If I ever would. They were still arguing in the living room when the music, which had been really loud, stopped after a scrape on the vinyl, and I heard a different voice. A mad one. There was low talking to the voice and then I heard the door close and footsteps on the staircase. When I got to the living room Sara was giggling and Turner was standing at the stereo with his mouth open and his "Shit, man" expression on his face.

I said, "What's up?"

"Shit, man, Vic. That was the landlord, the market owner. He was bitching about the music."

"You have any shit out?"

Redding said, "No, but we were about to smoke a doobie."

Turner said, "We got to keep it down, and he started "Ramblin' Gamblin' Man" over again."

The fat guy said, "C'mon, man, give it a little more than that..." and Turner turned it up some, but nowhere near like it was.

Sara was sitting close to the fat guy on the couch. Her tie dyed T-shirt was bunched up between her legs. She had a big bruise turning the colors of her T-shirt on the inside of her thigh. She wasn't trying to hide it. "Victor, did you meet Paul? He's a friend of..." Sarah looked at Paul. He smiled at her in a big fake way and his eyes disappeared as his teeth showed themselves behind a thick, red brown mustache that hung over his lips. Sara touched his shoulder and said in a giggly way like she was high, "Who'd you say your friend was?"

"I didn't." Then he asked me if he could check out my *LIFE*. I hated to share but did. I did not dig this dude.

Sara said, "Oh never mind. It doesn't matter anyway. Paul's from back east and has been telling us about this monster music and arts festival that's going to be happening later this summer in upstate New York. We should all check it out. How groovy would that be? We've been tripping together. I'm ditching work again today. We're going to drop and go dig the beach. Want to? You guys are off, right?" She looked at Paul licking his index finger and turning magazine pages. She said, "He's got some heavy synthetic mescaline. I mean, it's really bitchin'."

I said, "I can't. Got to get to the casino. We're doing that, right?" and looked at Redding. I needed my money. He was pulling a joint out of his shoulder bag.

"Yeah, but let's do this first," and he lit the joint and we passed it back and forth. Redding closed one eye while he held his breath like the smoke could escape his sockets. Paul and Sara acted as if they were alone in the room and whispered in each other's ears. He tossed the *LIFE* to me like it was a Frisbee when he finished reading. When Paul exhaled, his face got into the same expression as his smile, no eyes, big teeth spraying smoke.

He said, "That's not bad shit." Then, "Any wine?" Sarah looked at the three of us on the floor.

Redding said, "There's a new gallon of Red Mountain in the back seat of my car," and started to get up, but Turner stopped him.

"There's some left in the kitchen. Hang on." While Turner was in the kitchen, Paul and Redding got into a technical discussion about the merits of synthetic versus organic mescaline. They sounded like they knew what they were talking about. Sara listened close to everything Paul said, nodding, mouth open, folding her legs up under her. Then she interrupted them. "It's simple for me. I hate to barf..."

Redding said, "Synthetic mescaline doesn't make you do that."

Paul had his arms folded like he didn't agree and said, "Puking before an organic mescaline rush is a spiritual high," then he smiled that big fake smile like he'd just made some world-shaking pronouncement.

Turner said, "Thanks, Carlos Castaneda," as he flipped his pencil in the air. If Paul thought he was being mocked it didn't show. He just smiled that shit eating smile. I thought he might be getting to Turner after all.

Sara said, "I still hate to barf, but I love to do mescaline. I'll sacrifice." She pulled a leather head band off, shook her hair then pulled it back through her hair. She beamed at Paul and said, "I'm a simple girl."

"Is it like acid?" I asked.

Redding said, "It's different."

Paul chimed in. "It's not as intense, man." He turned his attention down to me as Sara drank from the bottle of wine Paul passed her. He said, "You smoke weed, right?"

"Yeah. Sure."

"Hash?"

"Yeah..."

"He did opium in Berkeley," Redding said, like I was a prize student.

"Excellent." He smiled at me. "Okay, mescaline, synthetic or organic, is just like an intense, longer hash high. Simple. No hallucinations...get ripped to the gills, my man. You got to do it." He pushed me with his jack-o-lantern smile. "You owe it to yourself. It's not a big deal. Your day off, right?" I looked at Redding.

"I'm in no hurry." He was clipping surgical scissors to the roach, right in front of his nose.

"Turner?" I said. "You doin' any?"

"Nope, but don't let me hold you back boys and girls, if you think you can handle it."

He flipped his pencil in the air and tried to grab it with his teeth.

"Whattaya mean?"

"Can you handle being really spaced out?"

"You just stay wrecked longer. Right?"

Paul said, "Do a half tab. Not to worry. It's just like being good and stoned."

I didn't see any reason to not get high on my day off. "Solid, I'll do a half."

Redding said, "I'll split it with you."

"Then we're going to the casino, right?"

"Yeah," he laughed and looked at Turner. "That'll be a trip."

Sara giggled and put her arm across Paul's back and said, "This is so bitchin'. You guys can drop us at the beach. Far out." Then she jumped up and said, "Let me go find my jeans."

We all crammed into the VW and dropped Sara and Paul at the beach. On the way, Sara sat on Paul's lap in the front seat and made out. They both reeked of clove incense and sweat, and I punched out the side window as far as it would go to let in some air. It had gotten breezy and cool out, and when we let them out, they went skipping off together holding hands toward the lake's edge like silly flower children, long hair blowing. A barefoot freak sitting on a picnic table playing a blond guitar looked up and smiled at them as they ran past. We watched him turn and watch as they ran in circles around a pine tree like it was a May Pole, dancing barefoot in the pine needles with their faces turned up. He stopped playing and pulled a cigarette from the neck of his guitar and dragged on it.

"He's a fat fuck," said Turner out of nowhere as we pulled onto South Lake Boulevard.

Redding shifted into second, wound the engine, clutched and shifted to third, got some speed, and in the pause of the clutch between third and fourth gears I finally said, "They're just ballin' buddies, Carl," trying to be funny. Then Redding turned on the radio. The Youngbloods were on again. Turner kept time with his fingers on the unopened half gallon of Red Mountain by his side and didn't say anything.

I was waiting to get high.

Later, just before we crossed into Nevada at Stateline, we got directed into a traffic checkpoint. A California Highway Patrolman stepped into the road and waved Redding over through a temporary lane of orange traffic cones along the curb. The VW whined like a blender as he backed down through the gears. We slowed and pulled up behind a yellow Chevy Bel Air with California tags. Another cop ahead of us was leaning into the window and talking with the driver. They passed some things back and forth.

Redding said, "They're just checking licenses. It's routine. Be cool."

All I could think about was what he might have in the trunk. My heart started to pound and I felt the first lightness of the mescaline." Redding, what if...?"

"Be cool," he said. "Just be cool. Don't do anything stupid that'll get him curious. He's just checking to see if licenses and plates are current."

"What's in the trunk?"

"You don't want to know."

"You holdin'?"

Grinning and looking straight ahead. "You could say that."

"Shit."

Turner said, "Do you think this gallon of vino is a red flag?"

"Yeah, hide it," I said, very conscious of carefully and slowly turning to Redding, who was blowing dust off his sunglasses.

"No," he said, almost without moving his lips, slipping his glasses back on. "Don't start jumping around. It'll look suspicious. There's nothing illegal about unopened wine. I'm twenty-one. Reach in the glove compartment and hand me the registration, please, Victor."

Turner seemed like he was over his funk about Paul and Sara. He said, "Let's see, underground radio on, a dollar-fifty-nine jug of Red Mountain on the back seat, three freaks in a Volkswagen, pigs got us penned up, enough dope in the trunk to get all of Tahoe stoned...Shit, man, I'm thinking we could be seriously fucked. This could be eighty-six, boys."

Everything he said was true, but for some reason I laughed. I was nervous and my heart felt like it was about to jump up my throat or through my chest and splatter on the windshield. My mouth was dry, I felt my cheeks flush, and I moved up to a high where I'd never been. This was not a hash high. My hands kept floating up like they were being pulled by strings. I sat on them. Every color in my field of sight was getting brighter.

"You feel anything yet, man?"

Redding said, "Shhh, maybe. C'mon. Don't laugh. Be polite. And get off your hands, Vic. Look normal. Jesus Christ."

I licked my lips, and fidgeted and pulled my hair behind my ears. The Chevy drove away and the cop waved us up to a point at his boot toe. Redding turned off the radio and drove to him. The cop cocked his head. His reflective sunglasses were the color of the mercury I'd once broken from my mother's thermometer as a kid. They were puddled pools of silver on his face. The moving car they reflected made them liquidy and runny.

"Officer..."

Looking past Redding, looking us over. I felt his eyes stay on me.

"Your license and registration, please." Redding handed them through the window. The cop walked to the front of the car and looked at the license plates. I couldn't take my eyes off his sunglasses. I just stared and hummed. He walked to the rear and came back and said, "Those prescription?" and pointed to Redding's sunglasses.

"No sir."

"According to your license you're required to wear prescription glasses."

"Yes sir. I wear contacts."

"Got 'em on?" and he leaned on the door and looked at me and Turner for the second time. I wanted to laugh, this was suddenly becoming hilarious, but I held it.

Turner said, "Hi."

"Step out of the car, sir," at Redding.

"Something wrong officer?"

"Step out, please. I need to check your eyes for contact lenses. Then you can be on your way."

My mood shifted again because I figured this could lead to no good. The wine in the back seat had blown it. It was as big as a lake buoy back there, begging for attention. It was like having *Drug Mobile* painted on the doors. He had to be suspicious. This would go over big with my parents. I wondered if I could be drafted with an arrest record for drugs. Was there a silver lining here? What a way to get out of going to Vietnam. Then for an instant all the surfaces surrounding me softened, or I thought they did. Then as fast the dashboard regained its form, the police cruiser at the curb quit pulsing, and my seat gave back its support. I blinked the feeling away and didn't want to feel it again. Then I wondered if anything had actually happened at all. I wanted to ask Redding if he was positive we'd dropped mescaline and not acid or some other crazy shit, but the cop had him tilting his head up to catch an angle on his eyes to spot the contacts. I hoped to hell he was wearing them and was starting to scare myself and wanted to get out and run. My eyes were alternating with flutters and I twisted the rearview mirror and looked. In the reflection I saw Turner staring at me, eyes wide and his goofy smile. Beyond him a car was pulling up to our bumper and the driver was staring at me and grinning. I was sure of it. I looked at my reflection and thought I caught my whole face pulse, loosening and sucking in on itself. I shook my head and twisted the mirror away. It felt like an hour had just passed, and I was afraid to talk or turn and look at the person behind us whose stare was scalding the back of my neck. I was sweating and even though the car was turned off, my feet vibrated like my boot soles were on top of a beehive. I wanted to break away, run across the street, make it for the lake, dive in and swim away. Solid gone.

Redding got back in the car.

I stared straight ahead as he cranked the ignition and said out the window, "Thank you, officer." I wanted to feel the back of my head for blood from the boring eyes of the other driver. I knew my hair and collar would be soaked. I said, "Let's gettafuck out of here. Take off."

Turner said, "Shit, man, this is a trip."

Redding pulled into traffic and said, "Come down you guys..." and we were thrown forward as he clutched between first and second.

Redding had dropped the same amount of mescaline as me. I watched him. But he still looked like he was able to drive, function, and was acting normal. At least it seemed like it. On the other hand, I was beginning to feel different than any way I had felt in my life. After I snuck a look back to see if the evil staring driver was on our heels, I calmed down and tried to think. This was not a beer high, or a dizzy, loud, puking, purple passion, stumbly bum, frat party drunk. Whatever, this was not a dumb, slow motion, get stoned and get the munchies and pig out on Oreos pot high; and it wasn't the gooey rounded feeling I'd experienced with hashish, or going to sleep after red wine and sopers. I went through the out of control moments of my life and could come up with nothing that compared to this feeling. And as if I needed proof, I was losing a fight against a mounting physical sense of light headedness and numbed detachment, although at the same time and—strange to me—I was getting to a point of sharp awareness. I had the ability, ripped as I was, to comprehend and understand everything and everybody around me as if I had a super sensitive nervous system wired into the universe. It was as if the walls, barriers, defenses and signals usually thrown up to confuse, deflect and steer a person one way or the other were suddenly stripped away. I dissolved in the essence of things without the help of words or body language. I experienced buildings, didn't need the doors to be inside or the signs to define purpose. I could tell by the way the couple in front of Harvey's was standing that their conversation was about him losing all their money at roulette. A pretty girl looking up into the face of her boyfriend said, "Let's go back to the hotel and get it on." A dog on the curb yanked his head up from a candy wrapper and pointed its nose at me and made eye contact as we drove by and I got it. I understood...I was feeling. Totally feeling, connecting, understanding all around and near me in flashes of insight computed in my brain with unbelievable speed. It was very cool. I was reading Redding's and Turner's minds, anticipating their words and thoughts. All the casinos, buildings and tourists along South Lake Boulevard made perfect sense to me for the first time all summer. We floated through it all, the VW purring.

We had a huge laugh about the traffic stop and our incredible luck. We laughed our asses off to the point we cried. I stomped the floor saying, "I know. I know. I know." Nothing was melting or pulsing now. I wasn't edgy and was even brave enough to look in the rear view mirror and saw a big smiling me looking back.

In the back seat Turner said, "You boys high or what?" That sounded like the funniest thing I had ever heard. We laughed and went back over the whole traffic stop in every detail and laughed some more.

"I was weirded out for a minute," I said, "But if this is what this shit does for you, I'm all for it."

"It's pretty bitchin', isn't it," Redding said. "But I've got some mescaline psilocybin that's even better. Wait and see."

I said, "Far out."

Even though we only had a few more blocks to The Mine Shaft, we stopped and picked up a long-haired hitchhiker. As soon as he was in the car, he pulled a baggie out of his jeans and asked us if we wanted to, "Score some awesome mescaline." That broke Redding, Turner and me up so bad the hitchhiker got scared and asked us to pull over and let him out. We were hooting and laughing about that as we pulled around and parked close to the grease barrel and the back door. I stared at the barrel and had never seen anything as dense and sturdy in my life.

At the cashier's cage, we picked up our pay and drink tokes and started to leave by the front door so we wouldn't risk being grabbed by Tony to work on our day off. I flashed on Sweet Lou and Kathy. There was a lunch time line halfway down the hall to the smorgasbord, the casino about a third full of lazy, daytime gamblers, every one of them ugly as sin. They were all losing. Danny looked at me funny as he wiped down the bar. But he looked strange to me, too. His long face had become even longer and thinner and he reminded me of a ferret. His eyes seemed redder, his shoulders weaker. I turned away. I didn't see Butcher, but my eyes found Rennie at work even though it was her normal day off. For once she wasn't focused on the players at her table. She was staring over our way. I hadn't seen her except for a minute earlier in the week when she'd come into the alcove to smoke. Her stare made my mood shift again. I couldn't interpret her expression and it bothered me and it was intense. Turner and Redding were at the red double doors by Danny's register calling me, but their voices sounded far away. Then from across the room, a slot bell started clanging, and the casino suddenly bubbled into a molten swirl of rougey red. The ghosts of cigarette smoke drifting in the air smelled like sulfur. I flinched and became nauseous from the crunch of Shanahan's fist on my jaw and at the same time cheered him in his madness as he cold-cocked the floozy. I realized I was standing at the place where the blood had been scrubbed from the carpet. I felt Beaner's trembling fear of Butcher, the sick slap of the blackjack to Shanahan's head and the knee in his chest. It all boiled up under me. In my head, there was an astronaut hopping in long slow leaps across the moon's surface. The trace of his jumps stitched what I was feeling together in a quilt of terror. But the strangest and most unsettling phenomenon was that Rennie's face, that beautiful face and that blonde hair, suddenly looked old and fearful and my feet wouldn't budge, and I thought I might be sinking into the lava the carpet had become and couldn't fight off her stare. I felt a hand on my shoulder and it was Turner, but his face was wobbly and blurred like a nightmare clown. I stumbled backward and went through the red double doors with him and Redding, being dragged like the soldiers had dragged their friend. I experienced the spitting girl and the name calling. But I did risk one last look back at Rennie, who was still staring. And even at that distance she looked gray and witchy and tired. And lost.

In the brightness outside, white bright like a flashlight to dilated pupils, I heard Redding say, "You all right, dude?"

Turner said, "Shit, man, Redding. Did that fat ass say anything about lacing that shit with acid or something?"

Redding said, "I don't think so. I'm trippin' but I'm okay. Victor, my man. You cool?"

I heard myself say, "I'll be all right. Let's split. C'mon. C'mon. Let's split. I'm really messed up." I was talking very fast.

Redding said, "We're outta here." And we kicked gravel as we walked around the building to the car and I felt incredibly lucky to be with friends. I was disconnected, jittery and scared. I looked up and saw the grease man riding the shaking tail lift up to the truck bed with a barrel and I felt good and reassured that another nice person was nearby. But when I tried to say hi and horse around like we did, he ignored me with a frown of what looked like disappointment or disgust, hugged the barrel and wrestled it onto the truck with the others. I looked at Turner and Redding. I looked all over their faces for an answer.

Turner said, "He's having a bad day."

I swear to God I had the feeling I had let the grease man down somehow and wondered what he was seeing in me today that was different. I felt a vague, queasy guilt. I felt like an exposed liar. I was dazed and bewildered. Just then Sammy, came out the back door with an armload of crushed cardboard boxes. He looked us over and said, "You guys want to work? We're short today. Tony's looking for help." I didn't trust Sammy. I hated the way he pimped as Butcher's spy. I'd only been around him a short time and my first sense of him as a sneak was holding up. But in my freaked out state of mind I felt trapped by him, helpless and off guard. Sammy walked closer with his armload of boxes. "Whattaya say fellas? Why don't you come in and give us a hand?" His question was loaded with borrowed threat and it pissed me off. He blinked and waited for us to say something. He read the silence. "You fellas high, huh? Taking a trip?"

Turner said, "Sammy, listen man, it's our day off. We just got paid. We're gonna lay low." The grease man's truck rumbled to a start, made a loop of the lot and left. He looked straight ahead as he drove. The smell of oily rags left out in the rain stayed where the truck had been parked. Splotches of spilled grease stained the gravel.

"Be a big help to us. We're backed up," he said, and turned to walk to the dumpster.

He threw in his load. Over a shoulder he said, "That's okay, though. That's okay. I won't tell Tony I saw you."

I was having trouble holding on. We looked at each other as Sammy walked to the back door. He spit in the new grease barrel and turned. "You sure, guys?"

Turner said, "Hold on," and walked to the stoop. Sammy looked past Turner at Redding and me the whole time they were talking. Beyond them, I could see into the kitchen. Like everything at the moment, it seemed like a different place. The grease and steam and leftover food, boiling sauces and thievery, bullshit, meanness, greed and cheating poured out of the door and layered me in a soot of revulsion. I almost puked at the thought of another tray of baked chicken and looked down at my hand and stared with dread because it had started to breathe. Then both hands were undulating, rolling with small waves, and my skin had become chicken skin, pale and dimpled. When I clenched them they became blobs. I held them at my back. I snapped my head up to check the other's reactions. Redding stood next to me waiting for Turner to finish with Sammy. Sammy wiped the crown of his head with a handkerchief and wouldn't take his eyes off me. "Redding," I grunted. "Redding, my hands. They're melting...breathing...doing something. Let's get the fuck out of here." I tried to hold my voice down. I saw a pink splotch reflected in both of Redding's sunglass lenses. I worried up the image of the guy who had freaked from bad acid earlier in the summer at the apartment. I was him.

Redding said, "Don't panic. It's just a bad trip. Don't panic." A police car went by on the road in front and I was sure it would turn in and bust me. It took forever to go by. Turner finally came over and said, "I'm going to work. Sammy'll screw us if we don't help out. I don't mind. You're both too ripped to do anything anyway." Turner looked back as Sammy went into the kitchen. Then he said to Redding, "Get

Vic somewhere where he can come down, man." Then to me, "It'll wear off, Victor. Give it a couple hours."

I said, "Thanks, man." I loved Turner at that moment, felt he and Redding were the only buffer between me and insanity.

Turner said, "Hey, Ed..." and Big Ed showed at the back door bouncing on the balls of his feet, doing his hopping dance. He had a dirty towel over his shoulder, his usual slick, dirty clothes. His shirt rode up onto his hairy belly and he smiled a silent hello. I felt he was speaking straight at me in his looniness. Instead of looking like the human gargoyle I knew, at that moment, in his wide-eyed leer, I sensed all his torment, betrayal and remoteness, and felt sympathy and understanding settle on me. Silently I asked his forgiveness and began to cry. Redding looked over his sunglasses at me.

"C'mon let's go," he said. "Christ."

Sammy came to Ed's side as we started to leave and I slid into blackness again. I heard him say, "Inside you crazy shit." Then to Turner. "I'm glad you can help out. Smart. Get an apron. Let's go."

I could hear Tony yelling in the kitchen. I said to Redding, "I hate this fucking shit. I'm going crazy."

Redding said, "Be cool. Let's go to North Shore. It's very mellow up there. Be cool."

"How do you maintain?" I asked as we drove away. I slid my palms up and down the front of my jeans to wipe away the sweat. My heart fluttered as fast as my eyelids.

"I just do" he said. "Or I've done more. Got tolerance."

"It's scaring me," I said. I swore to never do it again.

"It can open you up," he said as we drove past the turn off to Zephyr Cove. "You can find things. Things find you. It's like dreaming out loud. Subconscious mail delivery." Dreaming out loud. He told me that was one way to look at tripping. The Stones came on the radio again with that song that seemed to be playing constantly. What did I want? I wanted to come down.

Things, the disturbing images and thoughts didn't get any better in North Shore. His aunt and uncle lived in a small house surrounded by tall Ponderosas, a cabin, really, at the end of a short gravel drive off a quiet road. The house backed up to the edge of a steep bank over a cove surrounded by trees that looked like a blue thumb stuck out from the lake. As we pulled around to the side of the house, I counted ten short docks with small boats tied up that jutted into the cove about every fifty yards. From the docks steep, switchback stairs climbed up into the trees, where I guessed were more houses. The docks and stairs were the only evidence of other homes because I couldn't see any except one on either side of his aunt's and uncle's house. Those two were partly blocked by pine trees and ratty bushes and looked identical to the one where we were. Except for a far off chain saw, maybe it was a motor boat engine, and a squirrel or a bird rattling around in the dry pine needles somewhere close it was as quiet and serene as the overlook up at Heavenly Valley. I hoped the calm and lack of people and noise would help me get it together. Redding said his aunt and uncle probably had just left for second shift at the

Cal Neva. "Nobody's here," he said. "We're cool. Want to get high?" and he laughed and said, "Sorry dude."

When he asked me if I was feeling any better, I wanted to answer yes, and only anxiety and strain and unpredictable hallucinations stopped me from saying anything but, "I have to come down. I have to come down." I realized I was repeating myself but couldn't help it. If I stared at anything too long, it began to move, breathe, pulsate, become something new and threatening. I had to continually roll my head on my shoulders like a blind person to stop conjuring up demons.

A yapping poodle clawed at the storm door with its forepaws at the back of the house while Redding looked for the house key. The dog's nails clicking on the door and the yapping only intensified my edginess. Old scratches on the window glass and dried drool fogged my vision. "The dog's all right," said Redding. "He won't bite."

"What's his name?" I stood and waited for him to unlock the door. I stared at the last four feet of a green garden hose unspooled from the galvanized wheel attached to the house. The nozzle at the end of the hose was the kind with a squeeze handle, like pliers. It was in a bed of fuzzy new grass trying to grow in the shade of the pines. I stared at the nozzle and watched it turn into a snake. The barking and Redding's voice trailed away and I watched, couldn't pull away as the green snake raised up into a spirally coil then somehow elongated and turned. Screws became eyes and the nozzle metamorphosized into a hissing snake head with darting tongue and it weaved in a slither, flattening the grass on its way toward me. Water dripping from the nozzle became venom from a wicked mouth. I was conscious of this madness, but I couldn't shake it away. I couldn't move. From somewhere though I was finally able to summon up the will to shake my head and I fell back. I looked down to the cove and saw a boat at the top of an upside down V heading out to the lake. I wanted to be on it. I looked back at the snake. It had become a hose again in the new patch of lawn, innocent. I knew Redding hadn't seen anything, and by now knew it was useless to even mention my delirious visions to him. My terrifying conclusion to it all was that I was somehow projecting my flawed makeup onto and into things and people. What else? And it upset me. I started to worry that before this horrible experience ended, I was going to be forced to discover something hidden in me that would have stayed buried except for this mescaline trip. A psychedelic hand was pushing me into a dark, deep, well of my being, and I had no resistance. I wished Sara had never brought that slob Paul to the apartment.

I heard Redding say, "Frank, the dog's named after Frank Sinatra. My aunt and uncle love him. They've met him at work."

The dog freaked me out, and all I could think about was how Frank reminded me of a bat. I think it was the redness that rimmed his eyes, or his incisors. I thought of the snake and tried not to stare at the dog. Frank jerked his head back and forth as he yapped. He slobbered on the door and his body arced as he leaped. I didn't want to be around a poodle named Frank Sinatra. To get away I walked to the landing at the boat steps and looked down over the edge. I imagined flying to the water.

When Redding opened the door, Frank tore around the yard in overlapping circles between the trees, stopping at one to piss, raising his leg, fixing on me and panting while he did, then ran in my direction but veered away when I hopped back and said, "Fuck off, Frank." He had a red leather collar, and I wondered what the real Frank would think about this faggoty little dog named for him. Redding got Frank back in the house with a whistle. The dark stain of Frank's piss on the pine tree became a gooey slug before I could look away.

"Eat?" yelled Redding from the door.

Food was the last thing I wanted. My appetite had been dulled to zip by the dope. If I was drunk I would lie down and try to sleep, but I was so hyper and freaked, I couldn't sleep if I wanted to. Anyway, I didn't want to close my eyes because I didn't know what I would see behind them. I looked down at the lake and thought about flying again. I decided, though, that if I could focus on the sky I might be able to wait out this trip and not be hassled by any more terrible images. I decided to try to lie down in the small front yard, under the sun. Looking at clouds as a kid had been fun and I remembered it as a nice thought. I needed pleasant thoughts. I told Redding I was going to crash in front. I hoped it would help.

But it didn't. My hands behind my head, stretched out, trying to breathe evenly, the very first cloud I stared at became an angry, bubbling head, furious at me and I went in the house. I tried to drink a beer, but it tasted flat and salty. When I put headphones on and lay down on the living room floor to listen to Crosby, Stills & Nash, lost for a second, eyes closed, no threatening pictures in my brain, Frank surprised me with a jump onto my chest that panicked me into a ranting, cussing, and eventually, a crying spell. Redding tried to calm me down, and although I appreciated his attention

358

and friendship, I was overwhelmed with the partially formed vision of the bloody, bony essence of my being, stripped and flayed, howling at the exposure, uncovered, deep inside me and fighting to bore back under.

We drove back to Tahoe after dark. I tried to sleep on Redding's couch but just tossed and turned. I was nervously exhausted and felt it, but I couldn't relax. I didn't eat or drink anything except ice water. Even though I quit hallucinating, I was as strung out as I ever had been and could not shake one image. A bloody, sinewy, shaft or pole. I saw flashes of it when I was tripping. I don't know what it was or what it meant. I would never do that shit again, but I knew I was going to have to live with that image for the rest of my life.

Redding and I went by the apartment the next morning and found Sara curled in a blanket on the couch in tears with a swollen face and a cut on her lip. She said her legs and arms were bruised, too. She told us Paul hit her because she wouldn't go to San Francisco with him. Turner had walked in on them. Redding and I looked at each other. "What happened?" I asked, sitting on the edge of the couch. I wanted to touch her but didn't.

Sara looked like she wanted to smile, but in gulps as she cried said Turner had beaten the shit out of Paul and threw him down the steps. "He hit him so hard with the croupier stick he keeps in our room, it broke. Told Paul if he didn't leave right away he was going to stick the broken end down his throat."

"What'd he do? He split, right?" I saw some clothes of his in the corner.

"No, not right at once. He tried to make a joke, believe it or not. That's when Carl threw him down the steps. He probably ran to San Francisco." And Sara put her head in her arms and shook. She said, "I just wanted to get high."

Redding said to me, "You okay, now?"

"I'm fine."

I looked over at Sara.

Redding asked me if I needed a ride to work.

"I'll get there," I said. "Thanks," and I walked to my mattress and stared at the ceiling.

At two I took a shower and thumbed to The Mine Shaft. My last ride was a guy about my age, not a freak, who said he was a waiter at the Sahara full time, but to me he didn't seem to have the personality for it. He said, "See you around," like he meant it when he dropped me, and it made me risk a look up to the sky for some reason. I was happy not to see a cloud.

Chapter 16

Rennie came into the alcove for a smoke a couple of hours into the shift. And even though I felt better, I was walking around dog tired, wasted from no sleep and nursing a psychic hangover, but today she looked pretty as ever. The glimpse under the surface—the only way I could think to describe what had happened—had done its damage though, scarred me, maybe forever. Who could tell? It was as if the experience had burned a coating off me, like I'd molted a protective layer. Either that or I had added something forever that was heavy and a burden, slowing the forward motion of my soul. I couldn't do anything about it now. I had seen things and I had been changed, and I wished the whole day had never happened. And worse, I wondered whether or not to be afraid of myself. But I thought, tough shit, and sprayed hardened mash potatoes off a plate and put it in the rack and wished I could blast yesterday away as easy. It's over, I got through it, I said to myself. I will never do anything stronger than hash again. I swore it.

Rennie looked as tired as I felt. Up close I saw big half circles under her eyes. Her makeup didn't hide the puffiness at all. "I packed all night," she said. "The car's loaded. I gave notice. I'm leaving after this shift. I'm settled up."

I leaned on the wall. "We gonna have a chance to say goodbye? I can see you later, right?"

"You want to?"

"Well, yeah..." I wondered what she was thinking, whether she might be willing to have one more big time together, but I knew she was gone. She was so tired it made her easier to read.

"I tried to get your attention yesterday when you came in."
She looked for an ashtray and stepped over to the other side
of the alcove and dropped the butt in the mop bucket. It
hissed in the gray water.

"Caught you, I said. "So you're the one who does that."

She waited for Sammy to slide between us carrying a
porcelain urn filled with peach-colored salad dressing. He
gave me a knowing look or something like it I hated. "I've
wanted to do that all summer," she said, and looked into the
mop bucket like she was waiting for a pot to boil. "Yesterday.
What was wrong with you guys?" She looked up and tapped
my nose with her index finger. "And you look as I tired as I
feel."

Yesterday's Rennie, haggard and old, flapped like a slow
motion stingray through the ooze of my freaked memory. It
jolted me but the feeling passed and I leaned into the
protection of her perfume smell and smoky hair.
"I...we...Redding and me, we did some mescaline. It was just
a half tab. When we were here, it was starting to really kick
in and got very strange. I don't want to think about it," I said.
"And I didn't sleep a wink. Been up all night too."

"You should have come by." I wondered if she meant for
sex. "I could have used your help packing." That answered
that and I wondered again how and why she could shift
gears so fast from passionate and willing, to practical and
distant.

"Can I see you after work at least? Before you take off? We

can take a ride. Go to Tippy's or get some waffles."
Sammy's constant snooping had stopped our pilfering food,
even though Lee didn't care.

"Sure. I have to eat. I'm pregnant, remember? If I don't eat
something every five minutes, I feel like I'm going to up-
chuck."

"You drive?"

She opened a compact and dipped her head to catch her
face. "Can't." She put on new lipstick, puckered her lips and
said, "I crammed it. Every inch, even the passenger side."
She patted her cheeks with makeup, whisked hard under
each eye and snapped the compact shut, dropping it in her
purse. "Well?" I didn't know if it was a car question or a
demand to comment on her makeup job.

"I'll figure it out," I said.

"How do I look for a pregnant lady?" She patted her
stomach, turned in profile and looked at me across her
shoulder. "Well?"

She looked the same to me. "You're the only one I've ever
known."

"Victor..." She half smirked, half smiled, pecked me on the
cheek, and said, "See ya."

"Here we go. It's already started," I said. "That's the kind of
kiss old lover's give each other," and she smirked and didn't
smile and I watched her turn the corner into the restaurant.
But it was the first time she'd ever touched me at The Mine

Shaft.

Redding yelled from somewhere, "Victor, we're eighty-six on plates. Need 'em. On the double."

As I got back to the Hobart, Sammy came in with a full bus tub and dropped it on the counter. "Chop, chop, Romeo. Chop, chop," and he walked away laughing his greasy laugh and wiping his bald head with a handkerchief. Big Ed walked up on the way to the rack above the Vulcan with a stack of sauce pans and pots. Yesterday came back and I remembered my softened attitude toward him, but he was talking to himself or his voices or whatever, and I didn't want to catch his eye. Anyway, I didn't know what I would do or say if I had the chance.

The whole kitchen and everyone in it felt different, had changed over my day of tripping. Now it glared in my face. It was like seeing the filmy, stainless and dirty tile and leftover food for the first time, understanding finally what a hole it was. Why now? The trip? Like, why before had I never bothered to look up to see the twisted strip of fly-paper, thick with a coat of dead flies, that dangled over the swinging doors, blowing at a tilt by the exhaust fan? And what about all of us, the crew? Did anyone ever look up in this place? Were we all here, trapped and doomed like those flies? What about Lee over at the chopping block with his back hunched over, trying with all his might to keep from carving up a finger on his shaking hands, hiding from Sammy's prying. What about Redding, a guy with everything, thawing chicken parts in the sink, dealing and charming his lucky way through life? What was he doing wasting his time in this cesspool? And how did Turner get fulfillment slamming lettuce heads and breaking handfuls of eggs and making

Tony's gooey sauces when he had at least had the guts to stand for something? On the other hand, I guess you could make a case for some sign of nobility for every damn one of the pitiful crowd, come and gone, including the ones on the sideline who hovered and dropped in, then out, like Little Georgie, the grease man, Shanahan and Kathy and Beaner. Even Sweet Lou. But what about me?

What did I see when I peeled back the surface and examined my circumstance as a member of this crowd. What had happened in the last two months that would help me sort out the future? What had I gained? It wasn't money. Was this adventure helping or hurting, or worse, just a distraction? Tonight seeing this place so plainly, the one thing that still wasn't answered, was where I would be, what I would do at the end of the summer? That was still out there. I was no closer to an answer than I had been when I had ridden with Suicide Dave. Jesus Christ, I thought, I hoped I wouldn't still be in the kitchen of The Mine Shaft until my physical.

And what about Big Ed? Where did he fit? Why was he such a point of focus for me all at once? I wiped steam and sweat from my face with my shoulder and watched him carry an armload of black roasting pans to his sink. Same clothes, same detached, far off insane smile. Same lope. And I decided he symbolized every damn one of us. Big, crazy, Ed. He was the pure distillation, the richest reduction, the absolute essence of us all. Either he was the noblest or the most vile, but he was us, and we were him and that made me laugh out loud. I surprised myself and it must have shook Sammy, because it made him stop and stare with his mouth open trying to think of something surly to say. But I went on laughing over the disposer sink, right in his confused, slitty face, and he walked away from me and the dirty dishes in a hurry.

I needed to borrow a car. I had two choices. Redding's VW or Lee's Calais. The No Reverse Volvo wouldn't start. I didn't want to risk the VW and the drugs in the trunk, but if this was a normal day after the Moonlight Ranch for Lee, and judging by his hangover it looked like it was, the Calais could be anywhere and I didn't have the time to go looking for it. But when I asked him at break time, he said he'd managed to "negotiate" it all the way home. "Moored her on the wrong side of the street, babe, but navigated her back just peachy." In a lower voice he said, "How we gonna get a belt with that porky little chink sneaking around?" His face was paler and looked chilly, his lips were the color of liver. Ashes dusted the front of his chef's jacket, which wasn't right given his vanity. His after-shave didn't hide the booze sweating out of his skin. I caught a whiff of Listerine. The lettuce head he had been chopping was in ribbons.

"I'll work on it. So how you going to get home if I take the Calais?"

He took a deep breath and looked at his feet like he was trying to control something. He swallowed and brushed the ashes from his jacket, surprised to find them there. "I'm some toodler, eh? I look like a hobo, for Chrissake."

"So how you going to get to your apartment?"

"Yeah. Good question...oh, I'll get ahold of Skin. No problem."

"I could ask Redding..."

"Nope. I don't look dignified in that little kraut tin can. Don't worry about it. Keep her and pick me up tomorrow on the way in. And ignore the back seat," he said. "It looks like Fibber McGee's closet. Karlene threw some stuff in last night. I didn't see it until this afternoon."

"You sure?"

He closed his eyes again and then said, "I'm sure, babe." He held back a burp while he handed me his key, by itself on a ring in a snap leather case the size of a razor blade and rubbed shiny black.

"Thanks."

"Where you going anyway?"

"Gonna say goodbye to Rennie."

"That's a shame," he said. "She's a doll. She got a new gig or just going over the wall?"

"She's going home. She's had it here. She has a daughter in Tucson."

"Imagine that. Hmmm. Yeah," and he tapped his French knife on the block, "she's a doll." He pinged the knife tip in a tinny nervous way and it reminded me of a drummer riding a cymbal on one of his jazz records. "A real dish."

I said, "Thanks again for the wheels. I appreciate it. I'll pick you up about two-thirty tomorrow. Okay?"

"So you pining away, babe?"

"What?"

"Pining. Sad. Blue. In the lake for her. You need to listen to some Gil Evans."

"I guess." I didn't know who he was talking about. I didn't want to get into it.

A grin changed his face. He stopped pinging the knife. "I'll tell you. I'm taking you with me and Skin to the Ranch. That'll cure what ails you and—" Sammy interrupted with an obvious gape into Lee's coffee cup. He moved around the kitchen and did it wherever there was someone with a glass or a cup. Turner saw him coming and faked a gulp and belched in his face. Sammy patrolled around like a cop with his hands together at the small of his back. "Just a busboy and he struts around here like a yard boss, the bandy legged Charlie Chan prick," said Lee, and he rubbed his stomach where his apron string was knotted. "Listen, kid," he winced, "do me a favor before you get back to the Hobart. I'll cover for you. Hustle down to the pill roller and pick up some paregoric. If I can't get a drink, I'm going to need something to straighten me out," and he started to reach under his apron for his pocket. "I got to get this body to start accepting fluids."

I said, "I'll pay for it. Don't worry. Thanks again for the Calais." I grabbed Turner so he could sign the book at the drugstore. I was afraid I'd bought too much of the stuff.

On the way to the bathroom, Lee yelled across the kitchen, "Gas her up, you toodlers. High test."

Big Ed was bent over the grease barrel as we went out the

368

back door. Turner said to his back, "Drop something in there, Ed?" Ed didn't turn or answer, "Hello to you, too, Ed."

We heard him say, "You also," as we walked to the Cadillac. His words echoed inside the half full barrel.

Turner said, "Maybe he thinks Apollo II splashed down in there."

I said, "My heat shield about burned up yesterday."

****

Rennie and I were at the overlook in Heavenly Valley. It was cold and even though it was almost one in the morning, it wasn't pitch dark. It was like the fake night of low budget movies and television shows that use lens filters to shoot night scenes during the day. Elaine knew all about the process: Day for night. The moon light threw shadows. The big rocks Shanahan and I had drunk beer and whittled next to faced us through the windshield. They were less impressive now and could have been props of *papier-mâché*. They lost their heaviness in this half light. The front seat of Lee's Calais was wide as a couch, and between Rennie and me were orange stained taco wrappers from a torn bag from Tippy's. The smell of chili powder bit into, but didn't block the spice of Lee's after-shave stewing in the upholstery. The casino lights and the lake were below, but from the car all you could see were some lights at North Shore, where, in my mind, I knew demon snakes, menacing clouds and a sinister dog lived. I felt protected in the big car behind the rocks. Even though she was leaving, I felt good to have Rennie with me.

"This is a great spot," I said. "Can't believe you've never been up here."

"Victor, you know I've never been anywhere."

I said, "You want the rest of this taco?"

"They're not my favorite."

"Sorry."

"Don't be sorry. I'm just not as hungry as I thought." She leaned on the door and pulled Coke through her straw.

"What?"

"I'm just looking at you. I can do that. Remember?"

"Yeah. Right. Go right ahead." Then I said, "Well, what's your plan?"

"I don't know. I'm going to drive as far as I can tonight and get to Tucson when I get there. I'll see what happens after that. That's my plan."

I stuffed the taco wrappers into the bag and dropped it over the back seat. "Can you believe how big this car is? It's a boat." The dash top looked as long and wide as a surf board.

"Huge," she said. "What's all that stuff back there?" and she twisted to the back seat.

"Lee's girlfriend gave it to him. Who knows." The seat was

covered in boxes, more on the floor. A lamp shade poked out of the top of one, a plastic magnolia blossom out of another. "You want to smoke a joint? I got some beer, too."

"Victor..." it wasn't quite a whine, but I could tell it was the new Rennie. "Victor, I have too good of a time with you when we do that. I don't trust myself."

"So, I'm supposed to take that as a compliment?"

"No, I just can't. I know what we'll end up doing."

"That's the idea."

She said, "I know me and I have to be going soon. Please...You have to be as tired as I am. You said you hadn't slept much either."

"Is this the part where I act mature and say I understand, and we have an adult conversation, instead of getting high and dragging each other into the back seat? We can move that stuff."

"Please..."

"The back seat's bigger than my mattress," I said. "Or the back seat of your Nova. Remember that?"

"Of course I remember that." She slid away from the door. There was still plenty of space between us. She leaned at me defiantly, arms folded, dipping a shoulder, the way she did when she wanted to make a point. "You know what, Victor? I really do care about you, and you have been one of the most important people in my life whether you want to believe it or not, and I am never going to forget you. And, if you want to, I'll do it with you. If you really want, if you really—"

"You will?"

"Yes I will. You mean that much to me. I'm here, aren't I, instead of being on the road where I need to be." I thought I could hear her getting close to crying. But every moment we'd had together unwound like a film in my head. I saw us in her apartment. I heard White Bird.

"I'll move the boxes," I said.

She brushed her hand across the seat space between us. "Let's do it here."

"In front?"

"In front," she said firmly. "There's room. Just turn on the heat. Once my teeth start chattering I can't stop. Just like when I cry," and she reached for the buttons on her blouse.

And then I realized what it would be like. It would be even worse than the last time we were together at her place. The night she told me all the news. I knew she wouldn't really be into it. And if she wasn't into it, the sex would be business like, dutiful and whatever passion she could get up would be manufactured. I would feel it and it would be no good.

"That's okay." I held up my hand, surprised at myself. "It's okay. Don't worry about it. I give. I get it..." I decided against giving her my reasons. "You're right," I said. But she read my mind.

"It wouldn't be any good…"

She pushed down on the seat, palms flat and I saw a tear. It came down her cheek, picking up the night light until she rubbed it away with her fist.

"You all right?"

"I'm all right."

"Sorry."

"Like I said. No need to be sorry." She scooted over to me. "Let's listen to the radio."

"Sure." I turned the ignition. The dash board lit up and Rennie held her watch in the greenish light and checked the time. When I turned the radio on, the station was playing the Stones record I seemed to be hearing everywhere. "I can't believe it."

"What?"

"That song. It's all over the radio all summer. The last two months, it's all I hear. What do you think it means?"

"The song? The words?" She was tapping her front teeth with her nails. "Or the fact that you hear it all the time?"

"What are they singing about?"

Rennie said, "I think it means what it says. You get the basics no matter what you wish for. Like dealing cards. Everybody wants to be dealt twenty-one, but when the dealer hits you, you get whatever the card is. To me it's about the difference between dreaming and real life. Something like that. I didn't wish for a crummy marriage and chiseling husband, but my hand is my hand. I didn't wish to get pregnant again, but I am." She looked down and patted her stomach. "Maybe I'm supposed to be, oh I don't know. I don't like the Rolling Stones anyway," she said. Then, "I'm cold Victor. That's my reality. I know I need heat." She tapped me on the nose and I turned up the heater fan. Then she said, "I need to get going soon."

We made out like high school kids, steaming up the windows, and then after she signed my two dollar bill, I drove her back to my apartment, where she'd left her car.

On the way I'd said, "Speaking of dreams, you have any?"

She said, "Dream, dreams? What I wish for or what happens when I sleep."

"What happens when you sleep?"

"Oh, I don't know. The ones I can remember are the usual, I think—"

"Like what?" I thought of my flying fantasies, my reinterpretations and transformations of daily events and happenings into bizarre and sometimes scary nightmares. And other ones I couldn't remember specifically, left me frustrated, tight-chested, with an uneasy vagueness after I was awake.

"Can't remember the way to class, forgot I had a test, forgot my locker combination," she said. "Loose teeth, falling, I give birth to a monkey, being chased, naked in public..."

"I've had all those. Except for the monkey." She cocked her head and smiled weakly.

"The other night I dreamed I was at The Mine Shaft at my table and I was stark naked. When I realized it, I went running all over the casino for a place to hide. Butcher was chasing me. Sammy and Danny were pointing out all my hiding places. Oooh," and she shivered and snuggled into me. "I know where that one came from. I called and called for you or Lou to help, but you didn't come."

"You glad to be out of there?"

"You can't imagine." I took a corner, turning the wheel all the way with one finger. The power steering belt yelped then quieted as we straightened out. "I'm just going to try and kick start a new life at home. We'll see." We didn't talk for a while, but when we came to the Y and started to turn left, she said, "Victor, I just remembered. What do you think of this one?"

And she went on to tell me she had been having a recurring dream, about her house in Tucson, the one she lived in when she was married. In her dream she would regularly discover the house had a third floor she knew nothing about. The dream was brand new every time. With curiosity, and then delight, she would open a door she'd never noticed that led to a staircase up into a complete new floor with bright shafts of sunlight, tall ceilings, scrubbed wood floors, and "tons" of space that ran the length of the house. Nobody knew about the floor but her. It was her secret. On the window sills were crystal vases of cut flowers that threw pale silhouettes on the white walls. In the dream she would waltz around the undiscovered room, touch the walls and lean out the windows and get dizzy with happiness planning how she could put all this new space to good use, how welcome, how joyous the discovery.

She said, "So naturally when I wake up, I'm sad because it seemed so real, but the real joy I feel in the dream is stronger and I get over feeling bad," she said as we pulled up next to her car. "I love that room. I love that dream. I ask for it when I say my prayers. What do you think it stands for?"

"Are you pregnant in the dream?"

She paused. "I don't know..."

"When did you start having it?"

"Right after I came to Tahoe."

I said, "I really don't have any idea unless that's the wish part of you."

"The wish part of me?"

"The part...where you're at...where you're at in the instant before the dealer hits you with the card. The moment before you're faced with reality. A dice in the air moment. When you still have hope. That part of you. I guess it could mean anything," I said. "I've never had that one. Sounds nice."

"It is."

She said she would call me with her number when she got to

her mom's house in Tucson. But as I watched her drive away, packing boxes blocking the rear window, no way to see me waving, I realized she'd never called me at my apartment. I'd never given her my number. She had no way of getting in touch with me unless she called The Mine Shaft, and that would never happen. I was so damn tired and everything seemed so trivial all of a sudden. But upstairs at the apartment, for a change, there were no strangers sleeping on the couch.

The next day, Friday, Turner told me he was worried about Sara. The episode with Paul had her freaked out, he said. It had made her afraid to leave the apartment, and she had no intention of ever going back to her job at Harrah's. When she came out of their room she looked very sad and her bruises were still ugly, yellowing and spreading. She slid her feet as she walked to the couch. Turner and I were at the kitchen table eating cereal at noon.

"How'd it go with Rennie?"

"It went fine."

"I thought she was cool."

"She is." I said. "She's pregnant."

"Shit, man...you? You get her in trouble?" I said no and explained the whole story and told him I figured she was gone for good. I had to admit a fantasy that she would come back, or that I would track her down at the end of the summer, but knew it was me being horny. And stupid. The phone rang on the table in front of Sara. Sara's monotone words were the first noise other than the scraping of her feet

I'd heard her make all morning.

"Hello. Uh huh. Okay. Yeah. Yeah, he's here. Really?" Really was the first word to have any energy. "Sure." even more. Then Sara said, "It's for you, Victor."

Turner pushed on the table and rocked back in his chair. "It's her. She can't stay away, Victor. Shit, man. She hasn't been gone twelve hours and she's calling. Sure you're not the father?"

"I'm sure," I said, positive it wasn't Rennie, but for some reason nervous. I wanted it to be her and I didn't. I felt my heart bumping in a conceited way as I reached for the phone.

Before I could get it to my ear, Sara said, quietly, "It's a girl named Dew. She's in Carson City and wants directions."

"It's Dew?" I had the phone in my hand at my waist like it was a dumbbell. I curled it to my ear. I said, "Dew?" one more time into the receiver.

Dew was on the road. She'd set out from Cincinnati three weeks earlier on the sourthern route headed for San Francisco driving Palmeri's VW bus and burning a quart of oil every five hundred miles. She bought it from him for four hundred dollars. Along the way she'd camped, slept in the bus at truck stops and on the road side, stayed with "shirttail" relatives in Tennessee, worked for a few days for her meals in a commune in New Mexico, and put herself up in a Holiday Inn "for a night or two" for a change of pace and a shower. To have someone to talk to, and trying to be helpful, she'd picked up a dozen or so hitchhikers, including an out of work Oklahoma laborer, his wife and baby ("Pitiful and sad. Can't get over it. Gave them milk money for the baby. Broke my heart."), a religious wacko, a migrating pipe fitter, and one "aimless freak" who wouldn't get out when she came to the little town, Piersall, Texas, where he said he had been headed. Dew said she tried to be polite but firm with him, but when he said he wanted to go all the way to San Francisco with her, she'd had to conk him in the head with a full can of 10W-40 Quaker State and roll him out at a picnic site by the highway. "I just stunned him. I had the feeling that he wanted to fiddle around. I had to do it. I'll tell you about it when I see you." I smiled at Sara, who looked back, dejected, hollow eyed.

"You want to stay here?" I looked at Turner with the repeated question. He was draining milk from his cereal bowl. He gave me a thumbs-up, put his bowl on the table and wiped milk off his bare chest. Sara stared at the Zodiac poster on the wall at my back.

"Can I?" The familiar pitch of Dew's voice sent me back to the day she'd stormed out of Palmeri's to buy rice. It linked me to something. It was unexpected but a good feeling anyway. I couldn't define it, but it was nice to hear her again and wondered what it would be like to have her around. I wondered if she'd keep her clothes on. I put Turner on the phone to give her directions and could tell right away by his side of the conversation they connected. Didn't surprise me. Before we hung up, I asked how she got the number. She said, "I looked up your parents in the book." I'd left the apartment number with them in case of an emergency when I'd first got to Tahoe. If they'd called, I'd missed them. I hadn't called either. She said, "They say, 'Hi.' They'd like to know when you're coming home."

A little past two, after a talk with Turner and a few wordless nods out of Sara about Dew sleeping on the couch, I left for Lee's apartment. There I grabbed one of the boxes from the back seat and went to his door and knocked. I could hear jazz coming from inside, and as I was about to knock again, I heard Lee say, "It's unlocked, Skinny." I could still smell paint, but it wasn't as strong. The only other odor was stale cigarette smoke. The room was humid. Lee was shaving over the sink in the small kitchen to the left in his white pants, undershirt, no shoes.

"Hey, man." I put the box against the wall, next to the knife briefcase. "What are you doing shaving in the kitchen?" He tilted his head up and drew the razor under his chin from his Adam's apple. He looked at himself in a small oval hand mirror propped on its side on a shelf next to a Mine Shaft bar glass half full of what I guessed was watery scotch and milk. He reached for the glass and turned to me. I could see a patch of shaving cream under his left ear. I pointed. "You missed a spot."

He took a drink and said, "Hey, cat. You meowin' today? Thought you were Skin. What's happening?"

"Came to get you for work. Brought the Calais back. Thanks again." I pointed to the spot of shaving cream again under his ear. Then I touched the same spot on my neck.

He turned and said to the mirror, "Oh, my," put the glass on the shelf and instead of using the razor, wiped away the shaving cream with a towel. "Can't be a distinguished cat looking like that, now can I?" Then he got his glass and walked into the room and said, "What about the Caddy? Did you find it?" He sat on his bed and lit a cigarette. "Where'd we leave it this time? Skin and I hunted all over. He was going to give me a lift."

I thought it over. "It wasn't lost. You let me borrow it to see Rennie. Remember?" Lee leaned over and poured scotch into the glass then held the bottle out to me. I said, "Nah," and walked over and leaned on the wall across from his bed. I could see him working over in his head what I had just told him. He sipped at his drink and put it on the box with the ashtray next to his bed. He flexed his left hand and looked at it.

"You had it? It wasn't lost?"

"Yeah, we talked about it yesterday afternoon by the chopping block when Sammy was sneaking around. Remember? I went and got paregoric for you..." He drew on a cigarette and looked in the direction of the record player on the small kitchen table.

"That's Monk," to the record player. Then, back to me, "Man. I'm buffaloed. Noggin's an empty vessel. I don't know what...Thought it was eighty-sixed for good." He smiled, "So we're in the pink, huh? You like the way she handles?" He coughed into his hand. "Sorry."

"It's big."

"Holds the road," he cleared his throat. "Makes a statement." He took another drink. "It's coming back now. Yeah. So how was the goodbye to the gal?"

I said, "She's gone. I got to say goodbye. That was it. It wasn't much. She signed the two dollar bill. I didn't feel like talking about her. "So, tell me why you're shaving in the kitchen? You didn't say." I heard a bird chirp, close, like it was on the ledge outside.

"I didn't?"

"Nope."

"The bathroom mirror got broken somehow."

"How?"

"Don't know. Can't tell you. This ain't the Mark Hopkins in case you haven't noticed." He pointed to the box by the door. "You bring that?"

"Yeah. There's more on the back seat. Want me to bring 'em in?"

"That's all right. Karlene, the old dear, wants me to make this place more homey." He looked around. "Ain't that something." He started to laugh, then began coughing.

"Can I take a leak?"

"You know where it is?"

"Yeah." And I walked through the closet. The three suits were still hanging. A bale of laundry was cracked open. Starched, folded kitchen whites slid along the shelf. And in a cage on the shelf was a green and yellow parakeet. It walked along a shit coated perch and chirped at me as I walked into the bathroom. The medicine cabinet mirror was mostly gone except for a triangle piece of it in the lower left corner. It showed me my shoulder when I stood in front. Brown cardboard backing with streaks of hardened glue were where the rest of the mirror had been. I shivered when I turned and my boot scraped a piece of mirror into the tile. The parakeet chirped again.

In the room, Lee was on his knees bent over the box I'd brought in.

"There's a parakeet in your closet."

"Yeah, man." He spoke down into the box.

"Where'd you get it?"

"Skin. Irma La Douce gave it to him. He's trying to get back on her good side. The bird was driving her crazy."

"Why didn't he keep it?"

"It drove Skin crazy. He hates little noises."

"Does it have a name?"

"I don't know. I call it Bird."

"What kind of a name is that?"

"Charlie Parker's nickname." He was digging in the box.

"Who's that?"

"I'll tell you sometime. Remind me."

"What are you going to do with it?"

He didn't answer. He said, " 'Straight, No Chaser'," in the direction of the record player.

"Yeah, babe. Look at this," and he turned and straightened up. He was holding something that looked like a coconut, but bigger, and shaped differently.

"What'd you just say?"

"What? Oh. That Monk tune right now. That's, " 'Straight, No Chaser'." He's a serious toodler."

He walked over to his bed and sat. After he lit another cigarette and sipped his drink, he held the gourd or whatever it was in the palms of both hands in front of his eyes like it was a crystal ball. He said again, "Know what this is?"

I started to worry we were going to be late for work. "No idea."

He held it up to his nose and closed his eyes and smiled like he was remembering something. He held it out again and said, "It's the sweetest fruit, pally."

"Looks sorta like a coconut."

"It's a *Coco de Mer*. You're close. It's from The Seychelles islands, off Africa. It's the coconut of the sea."

"Cool. Hey we ought to be moving..."

"But it is much finer than that. Look." And he turned it around and held it out for me to see. I wasn't sure what he was showing me.

"Check it out close, babe. It's in the shape of a woman's lips."

"Lips?"

He smiled and said, "The sweet lips…"

And then I saw what I thought he meant. "Well, it does sort of look like...a pussy?"

"Jackpot. And these come from only one place in the world, the Seychelles. I've carried this around with me for years. I lost it for a while, then Karlene had it for safe keeping. Means loads to me. I'm glad I got it back. Thanks." He stared at it with a deep look then over to me gratefully."

"I just brought the box in. It was in the car. And we should get—"

He interrupted me with, "You feeling bad about your girl leaving?"

"Well, yeah. I guess."

"First time you got screwed like that? Dumped?"

"Yeah…"

He was still looking at the *Coco de Mer*. "If that's the worst thing that ever happens to you, you're going to have a fine life. Be a lucky toodler. You know that?"

I didn't know what to say, so I just said, "Yeah, I know."

And he started up in the same intense way he had done about his cooking in the kitchen that time and I kept saying, "Yeah, yeah," and, "Yeah, I know," or, "I know," to all his questions and the things he was going on about, and all of a sudden he yelled at the top of his lungs, "No you don't. Jesus Christ. You have no idea and you have no business saying you do. Where do you get off..." And he got up and walked into the closet. And I heard the bathroom door close. Then water running. The parakeet was making a racket and I'm sure he had been ignoring it. The *Coco de Mer* was on his bed and the record ended.

I put the Calais key on top of the knife briefcase and left and walked to work. I was at the Hobart when Lee got in. He wasn't too late. He came over and said, "Sorry, kid. I'm meowin' again. I'll make it up to you. You're a toodler." He walked over to the chopping block and brushed some scraps on the floor and put his briefcase down. Tony came over with a clipboard, waving his hands about something and they walked together through the alcove into the restaurant.

The next morning at eleven, just jeans on, barefoot, emptying ashtrays and picking up empty beer cans and wine bottles in the living room, between two songs on a Joe Cocker record, I heard the bus pull in and stop at the bottom of the steps. Looking down from the landing, the bus top was scorched from the sun and looked like the bottom of an old sauce pan. The paint was burned away in splotches. Blue curtains with flowers were stretched along the windows. The big yellow peace symbol Palmeri had painted on the side door was faded and streaked by a rooster comb of mud. I smelled hot motor oil. Dew got out and paraded to the front

386

of the VW and stopped, feet apart, her hands on her hips, and looked up at me. It'd been only two months, but this was not Palmeri's Dew. This Dew, with the big smile, seemed a milder version, somehow, but unchanged at the same time. When she said, "Hey, Victor, you long-haired freak, you've lost weight." I realized what was going on. What was happening. As we measured each other's changes, I felt a turnaround coming for the first time in days.

"Welcome to Tahoe, Earth Momma."

"Far out," she yelled. "Come down here and hug my neck, dude."

I left the bag of cans and bottles on the landing and went down the stairs, already hot from the morning sun, where she met me and we hugged. And I was not only surprised by the affection she showed, but felt great when she released me, and at arm's length, her hands on my shoulders, looking me up and down, said, "Victor, you look splendid, honey. You're giving off great vibes."

I said, "You also," using Big Ed's words for some reason. She had her hair pulled back into a bouncy pony tail. She undid it and shook her wiry hair into an Afro, and it glowed in the sun. She was wearing a western shirt with pearl snaps and jeans that made her long legs seem longer than I remembered, and cowboy boots.

She picked at a necklace of beads around my neck with her fingertips. "These are nice. And so are your bums." She grabbed my shoulder to turn me. "Lemme see that hair." She spun me back. "Little Victor, out here doin' it..." Then she said, "Can I borrow your bathroom?" And she gave me a killer look.

Behind her, going up the steps, I asked her if she'd had trouble finding the apartment. I remembered her butterfly tattoo.

"No. But the traffic back by those casinos was the pits. Bad kharma..."

"You see The Mine Shaft?"

"Where?"

"Just as you come in, on the left."

"I don't think so."

"Figures."

Turner met us at the door and said, "Helloo, Dew," and shook his head and flopped his hair. I already felt possessive of her and could sense the chemistry between her and Turner, but decided to let it go, boosted by the confidence she'd brought to me. But we had lots of ground to cover and catch up on. And I decided then and there to start wearing my hair in a ponytail.

"Nothing has changed in Cincinnati. Does it ever?"

"No antiwar stuff. No protests?"

"Some. Playing at it."

"Heard any music?"

"Paul Butterfield came to Coney Island, the frat boys didn't get it. Moody Blues and Van Morrison were at Cincinnati Gardens. That was cool. Let's see, the only other people I've seen are Janis Ian and the Grass Roots."

"There's some super music out here. Heard Santana?"

"Nope."

"Quicksilver Messenger Service? Dan Hicks?"

"No. "

"Wait till you get to the Haight." I let her believe I'd been to San Francisco.

I was surprised to find out about Palmeri. "He's history. He was really starting to bring me down. I got sick of the hustling and dope selling and his dumb store and the pseudo hippie crap that he was all about," she said. "He thought he was such a hot shot, nonconformist. Phew. And I caught him at the apartment with two teeny boppers crawling over him. I got fed up with the whole scene. I bullied him into selling me his bus cheap. I knew what I was doing. I think he was afraid I'd tattle on him about the little girls. He was giving them sopers for sex, the pig. Good riddance."

"Where are you living?"

"Back there? The Queen City?" and she laughed. "I'll figure that out when I go back if I ever do." Dew said all she saw when she closed her eyes were roads. "And I think that means something, so I'm staying out."

As we told stories, I watched her looking around the apartment and I noticed for the first time what a real dive it was. Not a rat trap really, but beat up and temporary. Dirty and disorganized. And Turner was getting off on Dew. That was clear. But she was hard not to like with her sense of humor and the way she showed interest in whoever she was talking to. She also had tremendous energy and strong opinions she wasn't afraid to talk about. Her body language even underscored her personality. On the floor, cross-legged, her back straight as a board, shoulders back, chin up, Dew was dynamite. You had to listen to her. Even when Sara managed to get out a few words to describe what had happened to her, Dew was sympathetic and it was real. You could tell. "Aw, honey, bless your heart. It'll be all right," and she touched her knee gently. I had forgotten how much power Dew could bring to a scene. She was a one-woman happening.

Turner convinced Sara it would be good for her to get out and go with him across the road and do some laundry. Sara hadn't been outside since the day she and Paul tripped at the lake, the beating day. I don't think she'd taken a bath either. When they left, Dew said, "Show me your pad, Victor."

I said, "You've seen most of it," and I walked her into the kitchen, then Sara and Turner's bedroom, the bathroom, my mattress.

"You sleep here?" She looked over my collage. "You doing this?"

"Yeah. It's my thing. I'm going to work on it until I leave. It's really been the only constant since I've been out here."

390

"You put lots of time into it?"

"Yeah. Much as I can. It means a lot to me."

Dew said, "Sara is a pitiful thing."

"I know." Saying those words reminded me of Lee's blow up.

"This place is the worse," she said, still looking at my collage.

"Yeah, but it's cheap."

"There's lots going on in your collage. That boy's eyes..." and she stepped on the mattress and touched the face of the LIFE soldier like she was trying to close a dead man's eyes. She faced me and said, "There's lots going on, isn't there, Victor?" And she put her hands on her hips like she did by the bus and stuck her chest out and said, "Help me bring in my things. I'll start cleaning up."

"You don't have to do that," I said.

"Phew," she said. "I'm going to help you get it together." She stepped off the mattress and went down the hall dragging a finger along the wall as she went.

Chapter 17

I really didn't want her to go, but Dew left at dawn with the parakeet in the middle of September, the mini-bus popping five smaller and thinner clouds of oily exhaust as she went through the gears, finally on her way down to San Francisco. She'd asked me one more time to go with her, but for some reason I couldn't.

"Victor, it's the right thing to do," she'd said, and told me she would let me know when she got to the city. She hugged me and whispered in my ear, "We're evolving to a new way of relating."

I watched while she disappeared from the bottom step under a milk orange sky. "The color of a melting Creamsicle," she'd christened the morning, her face turned up into it as she pulled the door open. A chilly, familiar, empty feeling wrapped around my neck and made me shiver and I remembered Rennie's leaving on this same road, but she had left at night, and driven off in the opposite direction. I wondered if that meant anything. How many more women in my life would I be waving goodbye to who didn't wave back?

On that Saturday in July when she had driven in from Carson City, we'd all immediately felt her energy and presence, but none of us knew or were ready for what it would be like to spin in Dew's orbit.

The first thing she did was to rescue the parakeet from Lee. When I'd mentioned Bird—the bird—to her, and that Lee was keeping it in his closet, she looked at me and said, "Phew," and insisted we go to his apartment before we did anything else, except for first putting one more quart of oil in the bus. When I opened the engine door at the back, I could see splatters of burnt oil spots thrown all over the engine walls like modern art, like De Kooning or Pollack, or whoever did that kind of stuff. Elaine would've known. And that was the first time I had even thought of her in who knows when. When we drove, we left a trail of blue fumes. Dew had hung a brass wind chime from the ceiling above where the middle seat should have been and it jangled as we drove, accenting each gear shift with its tinkling. The odor of sweet incense filled the van, even with the windows rolled down. Dew called the mini-bus her "Rolling Temple of Love and Truth."

Lee wasn't home, but the apartment door was unlocked and we went in and took the bird. Dew stood for a second with the bird cage in the middle of Lee's room and said, "I thought your place was messy." Karlene's boxes from the back seat of the Calais were scattered around. Dew hoisted the cage and said, "You're such a pretty boy," to the parakeet, and that became his new name. She put a finger up to the cage and let Pretty Boy peck at it. "You're such a pretty boy," she said again. "We're gonna spruce up your little home for you, you pretty boy," her nose almost touching the cage.

I said, "Lee drinks."

Dew lowered the cage and looked away from the bird. "Phew. It smells dead in here," she said, not like the smell scared her, but like she was reporting a fact.

I pointed at the double coconut resting on its side on the box by his bed. I said, "That thing comes from the Seychelles islands. That's the only place they grow. He loves it. Really attached. He knows a lot about the place somehow," I said. I wondered if she would see the woman in it like Lee did.

Read the sexual part.

"How? Has he been there?"

"I don't know. Didn't ask." Dew turned a slow circle in the room. The bird bit the cage bars and chirped. "He says most of the people there don't get married. They just live together and raise kids. Sorta like a hippie commune, I guess."

"Well that's groovy," she said and stepped into the kitchen holding the cage in front of her like it was a lantern as she inspected, then turned back around, touching a stack of album covers next to the record player with her free hand. "What did you say you call that thing?" She gestured with the cage. Pretty Boy balanced on his perch and bobbed his head.

"The coconut? *Coco de Mer*, I think he said. Coconut of the Sea."

Dew picked up an album from the stack and while she was looking at the cover said, "It needs a pair of undies." Pretty Boy chirped again and strutted along his dirty perch, twisting his head back under an aqua green and yellow wing to get at something.

Then she started cleaning. And the cleaner and more organized our apartment became, the better Sara seemed to get. It was like Dew considered Sara one more project to take on, another corner to sweep, another kitchen cabinet to line with paper. One more rescue. The two of them got close and pretty soon Sara started to get most of the way back to the way she was before Paul beat her up. And she quit taking drugs and you even had to coax her to have a beer.

And she started working again, this time as a Keno runner at the Sahara. Dew also taught her how to make rice and vegetable curry and other vegetarian stuff. It was goo to me, but Turner loved it and swore off meat forever. There was never middle ground with him. He would have pushed a peanut up the middle of South Lake Boulevard with his nose if she had asked. Dew knocked him out, knocked us all out. We were all ready for her to become our queen bee.

She even got to Lee. She charmed him enough to let her dye his hair one day, the fringe he had. She tried to match the color of his real hair to the walnut color of a toupee he wanted to try out. It was his dumb vanity. Turner and I told him being a bald guy was no big deal, but he wouldn't hear any of it. Lee saw himself with a "modified Duane Eddy look" and came back from Reno one day with the hairpiece in a Florsheim shoe box. Karlene arranged to get Lee a discount from a regular customer of hers who called himself Motell, who owned and operated Monsieur Motell's Hat and Wig shop in downtown Reno. Lee drove the Calais to our apartment for the dye job because Dew said there was no way she was ever going back to his "dead smelling place." As he came in, limping and complaining about a gout attack, wearing his whites, his fedora on, the shoe box under an arm, he saw Pretty Boy in his cage hanging from the ceiling in front of the Zodiac poster. He said, "Whattaya say, Bird..."

Dew said, "His name is Pretty Boy now. It's a better name than Bird for a parakeet," as she smiled, stuck a finger into the cage bars and let Pretty Boy peck.

"I just think Bird is more of a toodlin' name," he said, and tapped on the shoe box and said, "Wait'll you check out this rug, doll. I got a deal. That cat Motell gave me the good customer discount and cleaned and blocked this in the bargain." And he bapped the underside of the brim of his fedora with a flick of his finger. When Turner asked to see what the toupee looked like, Lee wound up with an exaggerated closed fist and said, "Not in a million years, Alice." And he made all of us leave except Dew.

When we came back in an hour, there were a couple of wet towels hanging over the outside railing, and inside the apartment a smell of shampoo and vinegar. Lee and Dew were at the kitchen table by the window. Someone had tried to lower the venetian blinds and they were stuck at an angle. She was drinking tea and leaning on her elbows. One of Dew's Merle Haggard records was playing. He was singing about trains. Lee gripped a water glass of red wine and was staring at the table like there was a chess piece waiting to be moved. Another towel was draped across his shoulders like a boxer between rounds waiting for the bell. Except in his apartment, I had never seen his head uncovered. At an angle it made me uncomfortable, like he was a different person, not just Lee with fake hair. Sara, Turner and I stopped in a line in the middle of the living room. Dew faced us and nodded with her mouth tight and her eyebrows scrunched. Lee was more in profile. I could tell we needed to be careful about our reactions. I saw a red line behind his ear that dripped into his collar. He swiveled sideways and said, "Whattya say, toodlers?" while he reached back for his cigarettes and lighter on the table.

Turner, as usual, was the first to answer. "Shit, man. Lee. You look great."

"Really bitchin'..." said Sara.

Lee lit a cigarette and said, "Can it. It's rough. I know. I feel like a fat Sal Mineo."

Dew said, "Leeeeee," stretching out his name, and reached across for his hand, "it'll just take some getting used to, honey. What'd I tell you? It's a big change. It'll take some time," and she looked hard at me.

All I could think to say was, "Cool. It's cool." But he really looked awful. Against the redness of his hair, his skin looked more pale than normal. Dew had even done his eyebrows. Now they matched his lips. I thought he looked like a Dracula clown. The yodeling country song, Pretty Boy's squawking, Dew's will, the window blinds hanging unevenly, and Lee's new look...all of it combined to choke the room with a stupid, sympathetic tension. I suffered with him and said again, "Cool," and felt like I was in a scene from a Fellini movie.

But he cut me off with, "Hold on, Kingfish." And he picked up a mirror on the table and stared at himself. Then he played with a hooking, stiff curl that dipped onto the right side of his forehead, and said in a flat way, "Just eighty-six it, doll. I crapped out on this one," and he ordered us out again.

We hung around the laundromat laughing at two really stoned freaks wrapped in blankets watching their clothes tumble. When we came back up to the apartment the Calais was gone. Towels were hanging over the railing again, three this time, wet and splotched with hair dye, and inside Dew was sweeping. She stopped and said, "I told you I clean when I get anxious. I got most of it out though. He's back to normal," and started back to sweeping. Then she stopped again and leaned on the broom and said, "I worry about that man." She said she told him the Chinese ate cherries to cure gout. "And I fixed the blinds."

What caught me off guard was her instant hate of Redding. But the more I thought about it, it made sense. She thought he was lazy and dangerous, a spoiled little rich kid taking his good luck for granted. "Wasting God's gifts and whatnot," is how she'd put it. "He's got more blessings than he can say grace over, and he's flushing it all down the toilet." Redding picked up on her vibes and stayed out of her way. While Dew was in Lake Tahoe, the only time I saw Redding was when we were at work, and there, things were fine. But one Wednesday, Dew was with me when I was picking up my pay at the cashier's cage and we ran into Redding. It was strange and uncomfortable. The last time I remembered feeling the same way was when a high school buddy had ditched me and the guys for a serious first romance with a cheerleader. I felt like I had deserted Redding when I saw he was reluctant to talk or hang out while Dew was around. But I got over it. Dew's pull was magnetic. I think she scared the shit out of him.

And we started sleeping together. After her first week there, she had come down the hall one night after work. I was cutting and pasting on the collage and thought she had been asleep on the couch in the living room. She wore nothing, and I could think of nothing to say. Her hair was all wild and spiky and she kissed me on the forehead and said, "Don't worry. This is the natural thing to do." Then she straightened up and said, "I forgot to cover Pretty Boy's cage," and she walked back down the hall, and I saw her butterfly tattoo for the first time since Palmeri's apartment. It wasn't as big or as colorful as I'd remembered. And I didn't feel any allegiance to him. After, she propped her chin on her hand and looked me in the eye and said. "What are you going to do, Victor?"

While Dew was in town, there was a slide towards routine and calm. One day I realized my eye had not quivered in weeks and things had become as normal as possible in the kitchen and at the casino. Butcher wasn't being a pain in the ass and even Sammy wasn't bothering anyone, but I think that just came from the being used to them and knowing what to expect. And Tony was Tony. I figured he just was pissed at life and brought it to work with him. I knew he had an old lady and wondered how she put up with him. Actually, knowing what to expect from people was the key to getting along, I figured out. But deep down, I gave Dew's presence the credit for all the good vibes and kharma that were around. I scared myself when I thought about her moving on. Compared to Dew, my time with Rennie was a date. Elaine, a hand shake. I saw that now looking back, lots of things were more clear. It was the unknown stuff ahead of me I couldn't make out. When I tried to look for clues, all I saw were the dead soldier's eyes from the collage. His stare blocked me. I felt like I needed to be on one of the roads Dew said she saw when she closed her eyes.

The only thing weird during Dew's reign were the couple of times rumors floated through the kitchen about Sweet Lou and Kathy. Somebody had checked out the Carson City casino Butcher had said Lou was supposed to be at, but he wasn't there. Somebody else heard Lou's car was blown to bits in a motel parking lot in Los Angeles, a mob hit. Somebody else said they heard Kathy and Lou had gone to Seattle, picked up Mic and were somewhere in Canada. I didn't know what to believe and realized it didn't matter anyway. They were history, like Rennie and Elaine. They only existed in memory and on my two dollar bill.

But at least the grease man was back to treating me nice. Big Ed, who Dew loved to hear stories about, was still acting paranoid and talking to himself, but he hadn't bumped into any waitresses lately. Lee's Moonlight Ranch hangovers were as bad, but he got to work. Once in late July though, it took us three days to find the Calais. It turned up again at the Zephyr Cove Marina parking lot like it had once before. The windows were down and it had cat paw prints all over the hood.

I marked the weeks Dew was at the apartment by *LIFE* covers. When she arrived in July, I was starting to cut up the issue about the Apollo II astronauts. Her farewell gift to me when she left for San Francisco six weeks later was a special $1.25 issue on the Woodstock Music Festival, the Happening in New York Paul had told us about. In between those issues, Senator Kennedy had been in a car accident and a girl with him had drowned, there were two covers in a row about the moonwalk like I'd guessed, one about taxes and inflation that was boring, one about London, England, with a sexy girl in a mini-skirt walking to the camera. The next, at the end of August, Norman Mailer's big head filling up the page looking intellectual, and one of my favorites the first week in September: a cover with the pop artist, Peter Max, his head floating in clouds and colors and rainbows like the "Sergeant Pepper" album. His head, with white, green, yellow and purple stars under his chin was as big as Mailer's on his cover page, but Max was smiling. All teeth and Fu Manchu. Mailer had the same big, wide, Welsh-looking face of my Dad, and it reminded me of Dad's brooding. On the collage I put Mailer and Max side by side and loved how Max's eyes and all the color of the page contrasted with Mailer's grimness. LIFE said Peter Max was vegetarian who didn't smoke or drink or do drugs. LIFE didn't say anything about Mailer doing drugs, but I knew he thought of himself as a tough little dude who wasn't afraid of fighting and was a big drinker. I could see him in the kitchen of The Mine Shaft. He'd fit right in.

The Peter Max issue was really good. Besides neat psychedelic pictures of the artist and all the stuff he was into, there were the usual evil pictures of Nixon, and Haldeman and Kissinger sitting around dreaming up trouble, a stupid vodka ad that had a drink for each astrological sign and an address to mail away for the drink that matched your sign. In the ad, a James Bond-looking guy in a white suit and a sexy girl with tall white plastic boots and white lipstick were picnicking in the middle of an astrological calendar with a vodka drink on each month. I put Nixon's head on the man and Kissinger's on the woman. A Viceroy ad reminded me of one of my uncles, and I used the whole page because I liked the brightness of the red. In it there was an arrow going through an apple and the headline said, *Never Misses, Never Quits.* On the back cover there was a woman with an L&M up to her lips looking very sexy, and I cut around her hair, and took out the head of the male model nuzzling next to her and fitted her onto the collage next to the staring soldier. I wanted him to be next to something soft, smoky and beautiful. Permanently.

Dew found a picture of Haldeman and Ehrlichman wearing swimsuits and fooling with a sailboat in a story about Nixon's western White House. She said they reminded her of a dangerous Spin and Marty, and she pasted that picture next to a napalm victim somewhere in Vietnam. I cut the General Electric logo out of a washing machine ad and pasted it upside down near Norman Mailer. From a story about Roy Cohn, there were a series of pictures of him I used because I thought he had Lenny Bruce's eyes. I just used the eyes, six sets of them in a pinwheel. I cut the word Canadian out of a Canadian Club whiskey ad because I was starting to think I might end up there. There was no logic in what was going up on the wall, but I felt it was starting to mean something. At least to me. And Dew was into it.

She wanted to know everything about the Moonlight Ranch. She was fascinated for some reason. When I told her I had been dodging Lee's pressure, she surprised me and encouraged me to go with him and Skin.

"And take me."

"You?" We'd been cutting up the London, England, *LIFE*. "What for? It's a whorehouse in the desert." Dew was sitting, leaning back against the wall at the end of the mattress. She was topless and wore cut-off jeans. I was past the stage when I had to have her every time she took her clothes off. She was in synch with her naturalness, and you just accepted whatever she did because she could pull it off. I wasn't even embarrassed anymore for her when she paraded around naked in front of Sara and Turner. "You're all evolving," she'd complimented us one night late, listening to music and eating rice. "It's a natural evolution." I'd almost forgotten her real name was Helen and never brought up northern Kentucky.

"Why do you want to go?" I asked her again. I told her Rennie had wanted to know all about it, too. I said, "Rennie said she was just curious."

"Well I'm curious, too," she said. She picked dried Elmer's Glue off a fingertip. Pretty Boy was strutting in his cage on the floor next to the mattress. She liked to have him around. He started cracking seeds. She thought I was silly when I asked her to cover the cage when we were in bed. "And I want you to go with one of the girls."

"You've got to be kidding…" I said. "Get real, Dew."

"Oh, I'm real, buster," she said, and looked up at the collage. "I just want to know how it all works, that's all. I'm very real. And I'm real curious."

I shook my head, watched Pretty Boy eat and wondered what made girls want to know how whores behaved.

The Moonlight Ranch was a series of connected trailers clustered together by an asphalt parking lot off the highway outside Reno, ninety minutes away. It was just like Turner had described it. The plain mailbox where the drive met the highway had a route number on it and could have been a mailbox in Cincinnati. Lee drove with Skin riding shotgun, and Dew and me in the back seat. Lee and Skin shared a fifth of Cutty Sark on the way. The sky at dusk changed from blue to slate blue to gray for a second, then to pink to rose to a blue-black, "like crushed velvet," said Dew, to full black as we pulled into the parking lot. Lee and Skin hadn't seemed fazed at all with the idea of Dew going with us even though I'd told them I thought it was a goofy plan. They loved the idea. Skin said it was "tasty."

Dew had leaned over the seat as we'd driven, bugging the old guys with questions, some about the Moonlight Ranch, some about other stuff. Skin remembered the Gaiety Burlesque House in Cincinnati. He'd been there with Tempest Storm. He talked about Newport and Covington,

Kentucky. He said he had known a twenty-one dealer there with the tip of the bone of his little finger on his right hand exposed, "And polished," he claimed, "to help him cut the deck." The wind ripped through the open windows and Lee had to screw his fedora down tighter once or twice, and I had another flashback of riding from the airport earlier in the summer with Suicide Dave. Lee and Skin snorted and laughed. They reminded each other of funny stories and passed the bottle back to us a couple of times. Dew reacted with "phew," and looked over at me when they told a dirty joke or replayed one of their escapades. But I was nervous and pulled at my ponytail and my eye fluttered for the first time in weeks. When we pulled in and parked next to a pickup, Dew said, "It's not what I expected." Music came from behind the door that seemed to be the main one. Down a short walk, through a metal fence, there were three steps up to the door covered in phony grass, a flimsy metal hand rail on both sides.

Skin rolled his head to the back seat, his hand on the door handle. "What'd you expect, dear?" He waited with his mouth open and his eyebrows arched. Lee was already out of the Calais, pulling at his belt, humming, buttoning his suit coat.

Dew dipped her head and surveyed the area through all the windows. "More cars, maybe," she said. Then, looking at the front door, "Pillars maybe?"

Lee adjusted his fedora and said, "Chop, chop, pally. It's post time." He could tell I was fidgety. When Skin and Dew came around the front of the Calais, Lee opened the door and said to the others standing at the headlight, "Skinny, did you tell Sportin' Life here that they measure your willy on the first visit?"

I said, "Yeah, right." They both clapped their hands, enjoying themselves. They loved it. Skin gave Dew a soft punch in the shoulder. She looked like she might believe him and turned back to me. When she turned her head, Skin's eyes tracked down her back to her butt and he gave a silent whistle.

He looked up and said, "Yeah, the tape measure hangs on the back of the front door. Karlene does the measuring. "Don't panic, kid. Girth counts."

Then they all started laughing again. Even Dew. She said, "Phew. Calm down, Victor."

The inside of the main trailer was like a lobby with three separate hallways that spoked off to somewhere. They glowed red. The low ceilings and tightness of the walls made me think of the *souk* in Redding's Marrakesh story. The air here seemed just as close with the smell of flowery perfumes and something like soap. I remembered Turner's description and the story about his pecker shrinking then swelling. I wondered if the girl he'd been with was still here. I'm sure they had their share of college boys. The music playing was the kind you heard on the Lawrence Welk Show. The saxophone section was competing with at least one grinding air conditioner. Five girls lounged on a few stuffed chairs and a short couch, legs crossed, reading, playing cards or filing their nails, but not talking. They wore lots of makeup and were dressed in lacy slips and Playmate-looking underwear, and one of the girls had tall boots on. Lee said, "Karlene, baby," to an older woman in a long, Hawaiian patterned, shift of a dress. She stood from a rocking chair and up with her, the five girls. "We've got company, ladies," she said. "Time to party."

Around the rest of the room were floor lamps with fringe on the shades and ashtrays on stands. Against one wall was a piece of dark furniture with doors that looked like it belonged in a Victorian parlor. There were bottles of booze set up on it as a bar. The walls were dark knotty pine paneling broken up by heavy red curtains that hung to the floor, hiding windows. In an uneven row at eye level were old saloon pictures of cowboys with droopy mustaches with their arms around the shoulders of manly looking women in big dresses and bustles. The floor gave as you walked like it was made of plywood and was layered in thin, worn rugs that overlapped, making ridges that made it easy to trip if you dragged your feet. When Lee introduced me to Karlene with a big bow and a wave, the vibration from my footsteps rattled glasses on the bar. I caught my boot heel on a bunched rug, and fell close enough to her to get a strong whiff of her perfume and powder.

I said, "Hi." She touched my cheek.

Karlene had orangish red hair teased high and was puffy and older than I expected. She had a big mole at the corner of her mouth. I guessed her around fifty-five. She'd probably been pretty when she was younger...what Lee called "formerly a looker," but had on heavy makeup, and veiny hands that were thin and looked weak. On one finger she wore a ring with a large green stone, rimmed in gold. Her boobs were big and the high waist of the dress held them up. Lee made drinks, and before I finished mine, Lee and Skin had disappeared, cackling and pawing down different hallways with two of the girls. Karlene didn't seem to mind. I guess she was the Madam. She talked to the girls with her eyes before she said anything. She ran the show. The other three girls in the room kept looking over at me then back to

Karlene. Dew said to Karlene, "I worry about Lee."

Karlene said as she rocked, "I used to worry about him. But that was then. Now is too late for that."

"Meaning?"

"Meaning there was a time when I fell in the lake for him..."

"Meaning?"

Karlene dabbed at the edge of her mouth with her little finger. "Was really turned on. That's what I mean."

"Oh honey..."

She said, "It's not a problem," and got up and walked over to the bar and poured herself another drink from a bottle that looked like Crown Royal. "I'm not supposed to do this. State law." There was silence except for the air conditioner and the music and Dew looked at me like I was supposed to be doing something. Karlene crossed the room, the glasses on the bar rattling. She breathed heavy and lowered into the rocker. She scooted it back to where it had crept from. A big fake flower rose and fell between her boobs. She looked at me. I said, "What?"

She said, "My young friend, coming all the way over here and not having a date is like taking a shower with your clothes on. What's Lee say, it's like eating salmon without Hollandaise."

I felt like I was ten years old. Dew smiled her easy smile at me, which was irritating. I looked across at the girls and to me they seemed confused with her being in the room, but it wasn't getting to Dew. The girls went back to whatever they had been doing. I had no idea what to say.

Karlene spoke. "Well take your time. Your pals are here for a while. I can tell you that."

Then she turned to Dew again and said, "No woman will ever be as important to him as his freedom. And if a woman thinks she can be, then she's just fooling herself." She smiled, a beaten kind of smile, licked her lips and squinted like she'd just tasted something bitter. She went on, "You see, I was raised as the special one in my house. I was the bee's knees. Got everything I wanted, all the time, and I expected it to last. But I finally gave up trying to get from him so I'm giving him my things. Giving them away. I'm looking ahead. Planning."

"Honey," Dew said. "You're giving yourself away."

Karlene ignored that and it made Dew stop mid-reach from touching Karlene's knee.

Karlene said, "Can I offer anyone else another drink?"

I said, "No, but I'll get you one."

"How sweet," she said.

Dew said, "Not me."

Then while I was pouring, I heard her behind me saying to Dew, "He's so adorable."

I finally went with a girl named Sheila, who looked like she was about my age. It turned out okay, but before we did anything she wanted to know all about Dew. "She's your girl, right?" she'd asked.

"Yeah."

"Does she want to party with us? I don't, but there are girls here that will do that."

"No," I said. Then I wondered a second.

"So why would a girl want to come to a place like this with her boyfriend then?" She said, "Don't you think that's strange?" Sheila reached behind and undid her bra. She had a blue tattoo of something on the inner thigh of her right leg. It had the opposite effect of me than Dew's butterfly.

I had no way of explaining Dew. "She's curious, is what she said."

"Well, I'm a curious person," Sheila said. "And personally, I think it's freaky. But to each his own, I guess." Then, with her hands on her hips she said, "Well, what do you want to do?" I could still hear the Lawrence Welk music from the lobby. There was a drum solo going on.

Now I understood better how they could lose the Calais. Lee, Skin and Karlene got totally smashed. I drove back to Tahoe with Lee and Skin in the back passed out. Karlene got so drunk she'd started talking about planning her funeral and how fat and old she'd become. Dew did her Dew thing and tried to comfort her, but Karlene wouldn't stop drinking. When Lee finally came out of the room with his girl, Karlene tried to muscle him back down the hall and they fell on the floor. It was terrible. It would have been funny if it weren't so sad. I felt sorry for both of them. Dew said, "You know when people start talking about death and giving things away and drinking so much, they could be depressed." Skin was snoring.

I told the Suicide Dave story about the guy in Vietnam who gave away the Purple Hearts then shot himself in the head. Dew was quiet. I wondered if she was glad she had come along. Suddenly, Lee said, "Pull over, I'm gonna heave." And when I skidded to a stop, just off the road, he opened the door and rolled out.

I said, "Hey Dew...still curious?"

She said, "Help him, Victor."

The night before Dew left, I volunteered to work late and prep for the morning. I didn't want to be around the flurry of packing and organizing. Dew was all business when she had her mind focused on a job. And just as bad, I had the growing feeling things were about to slide again. For the worse. So when I got off I walked down South Lake Boulevard to the Sahara to play the slots, drink some beers and see who the free entertainment was in the lounge. I definitely didn't want to go back to the apartment. Dew had announced to us that afternoon she was leaving to get on the road to San Francisco. Sara cried and hugged her. Turner got all excited for her and volunteered a list of places she could crash. She'd told me it was the natural order of things and the time was right. I was okay for a while, but now I was back to feeling deserted and confused. If I went to the apartment, I'd have to help her pack and check things off her list. Sex would be out of the question. When she was fixated on something "naturalness" only included order and attention to detail. I felt like another loose end that had to be checked off. But I didn't want to give up so easily. So I planned on avoiding her.

The main floor of the Sahara was scattered with lost, late-night gamblers, the kind who wander back and forth, between tables and slot machines. I'd noticed through the summer people in casinos always had something in their hands, either drink glasses, Keno slips, cups of quarters and dimes, chips, cards or...sometimes...folding money. It made me think about winning and losing and what your hands had to do with it. If you kept them in your pocket, you couldn't win. But you couldn't lose either. Lee said money was just a "conversation." I watched a man put a coin in a slot and pull the handle. He was committed. Maybe that was it, I thought. He reached in the cup. He put the nickel in the slot. He pulled the handle. His hands made commitments for him. I felt a tap on my shoulder.

"Hey, man. Remember me?"

When I turned, it took me a second, because even though I recognized the face from somewhere, I didn't know who it was at first. He was about my age but was dressed like a preppie and he needed a shave. We shook. He introduced himself as Robert and reminded me he was the guy who'd picked me up hitching on the way to work the morning after my bad mescaline trip. I remembered that at the time he'd said he was a waiter at one of the restaurants at the Sahara. He seemed friendly enough and pulled some Sahara drink tokes out of his jacket and offered to buy me a beer, so we went to the lounge. We drank and caught the last part of the last act. It was four girls with identical blonde wigs who looked and sounded like the Lennon Sisters. They sang close harmonies, swayed and snapped their fingers in front of a three-piece combo of black guys who had frozen smiles on their faces. When they finished, Robert asked me if I wanted to smoke a joint. Late as it was, as tired as I was, I didn't want to go to the apartment. I said, "Sure."

Robert hopped up and said, "Cool, let's get out of here. I got a car."

We talked as we drove and he told me he hadn't been waiting on tables for a few weeks, and he was looking for work. He said he had a job as a security guard lined up but he was making a living at the moment gambling. Still, Robert said, he felt he might have to hang on a few more weeks until after Labor Day when all the college kids went back to school. He said, "When are you leaving?"

School started in the middle of October, but I had no idea where I would be then. My answer to him was, "I'm I-A. I'm supposed to be taking my physical then." But he didn't seem to want to talk about Vietnam.

He told me what I had already learned about the tourist season, how things were still busy after Labor Day. After that he said, you could have your pick of jobs until things slowed down later in the fall, until ski season then it picked up again. We compared secret spots to smoke pot, and for a second, with all the driving around, I felt like I was in high school with a girl trying to find a private place to park and make out.

We finally ended up at the overlook in Heavenly Valley, the same place I'd come with Rennie, the same spot Shanahan had hunkered and whittled. When Robert passed me the joint, as I looked toward North Shore, I had the thought that on this spot I'd lost a girlfriend and money, and wondered what made me keep coming back to an unlucky place. I felt uptight and couldn't put my finger on the cause but figured it was the memory that this was where unhappy stuff had taken place. Or, maybe because I was facing north, that the hallucinations and demons from North Shore were winding up to skip like a flat rock across the lake, and smash through the windshield and come alive again.

While I had smoke in my lungs, Robert said, "You know Proverbs? The Bible?"

I grunted, "Unh unh," then exhaled, and said, "No, not really." Shit, I thought. A Jesus freak. I got ready for a lecture and started searching for the least insulting way to cut it short and get him to take me back to the apartment. I felt hustled and stupid. I passed the joint back and looked at him real close a second then looked away. He was turned in the seat with his left elbow resting on the steering wheel. He pinched the joint in his right hand as he talked, his palm open to me as if he were making the, "Okay," sign. His eyes were wide.

"It's about the end of ignorance," he said. "The questions it asks are the engine of truth." I waited for the rest of his sermon. The pot was good. It hit me instantly and started slowing everything down. Then I was able to understand the tension in the car, parked up here, just the two of us in the cool, dark, empty turnout just down the switchback from the locked and deserted ski resort, high up over the lake. I figured it out before he gave himself away. He wasn't a Jesus freak, and I was trapped with him on this thin-air Lover's Lane. I was shrieking inside. He blurted, "Can we make love?" and drew back against the door quick.

It all made sense. I tried to control myself and wanted to play it just right, not freak either one of us out. I needed to get through it. My ears rang. I could feel his nervousness. I listened to his breathing. His fear and jumpiness were bouncing all over the car. I said, "Listen, man, I'm not into that. It's cool if you are. But I'm not." I felt like I'd been through this before, but I knew I hadn't. Still, it felt familiar.

He stared at me and breathed short, quick breaths through his nose. Then Robert said, "Okay." He rolled the window down and dropped the joint on the ground outside. He said as he started the car, "You must be happy with your life." It sounded weak and sad.

I didn't know if I was. "Maybe," I said, "I think I am. I want to be. Can we go?"

I got scared again when he took a dark road I didn't know to get to the Y. Neither one of us talked as he drove back down into the tree line, no buildings or houses or lights, the stars blocked by pine trees. I was only conscious of my heart my eye and my breathing. He dropped me and peeled out, which I read as frustration. But I felt relieved, and I felt sorry for him. I felt foolish and certain now the slide was about to begin, and Robert was the sign that confirmed it.

It was three in the morning. Upstairs, Turner and Sara were in bed. Pretty Boy's cage was covered, but Dew was in the kitchen making chocolate chip cookies. She'd told me she always had them with her when she traveled. Her hair was wet, drying into spikes, and she was wearing one of my Penney's T-shirts, the green one. It hung to the top of her thighs. I told her about Robert.

414

She touched a cookie on a sheet and pulled her finger away. "Phew," she said. "You're kidding..."

I fell into a chair at the kitchen table and started eating cookies. "Nope."

She said, "How did it make you feel?"

"What?"

"Being hit on by a guy."

"I didn't like it. These are good cookies," I said. "I've really got the munchies."

"Eat all you want. There's nothing bad in them for you."

"I ended up feeling sorry for him."

Dew slid cooled cookies off a sheet onto a plate. She said, "That's a decision you have to make. You make yours, he makes his. I make mine." Dew told me she was going to stay up all night. Before I crashed, she kissed me, hugged me tight and said, "This has been a trip, Victor. Do I get to sign your two dollar bill?" And I let her check me off her list.

That night I watched myself in a dream. In it, I was being pulled out into the ocean, fighting with all my might against the current. What I was fighting for on the beach was a message written in the sand. I was desperate to read it. But at the same time I knew the message was nothing more than a tangle of bird tracks, the hieroglyphics of sea gulls, and they were moments away from the next wave erasing them. But I kept swimming. I was pulled so far out the dunes disappeared. When I woke, Dew was carrying her stuff out to the mini-bus and the sun was coming up.

Chapter 18

Redding was the first to leave. He wanted to drive across the country and back before he started grad school. He had never been east, even though he'd taken that cool trip to Europe and Morocco. When he was really little, his family had taken a Thanksgiving trip to New York City. All he remembered was the airplane and the Christmas camels at Radio City Music Hall. That and the smell of burnt chestnuts on the street. For all he knew, he said, there were still stage coaches and Indians and buffalo in between the two oceans. He wanted to get on the road and keep a journal, maybe get some material for a book or a short story. And he told me if I wanted to, I could catch a ride back with him. All I had to do was be in Susanville at his parent's house by October 10.

Leaving The Mine Shaft, unless you got fired or taken away in handcuffs like Shanahan, or plain disappeared like Lou and Kathy, was about as exciting as getting hired. You just told Lee or Tony you were leaving. They tallied your hours, and so you couldn't steal anything, Sammy walked you to the cashier's cage and then all the way out through the front or the back door. It was legal of course to come back into the casino once you weren't an employee, but you knew you weren't welcome. When you were gone, you were gone...unless they needed workers and you were stupid enough to come back. Redding left halfway through a shift one night. When he shook hands with Lee, he palmed him a joint. Lee, who was already hammered by then, closed his hand and said, "Oh, my," as Sammy watched. "Keep it in the road, pally," Lee said, and slipped it in his pants pocket.

Redding said, "Later," gave us the peace sign then walked with Sammy to the back door. His wispy little mustache was as blond and fine as it was the day I met him. Just in case the trip back east fell through, I had him sign the two dollar bill. He wrote his name on the front in the margin at a corner behind the 2.

I said, "See you in Susanville on the tenth."

He said, "Peace, brother..." to Ed when he went by the sink at the back door. Ed grinned to the water and said, "You also."

Both shifts were losing the college kids, and the ones who could stick around worked longer hours and more days. I did a couple double shifts and worked straight through two weeks once. The money was nice. But there was a trade-off. Because help was so hard to find, guys like Tony became grudgingly nicer, less of a pain in the ass to be around. He had to, or he was going to have to end up mopping his own floor. I also got bumped farther up the chain and got off the damn Hobart machine and started helping Lee and Tony cook. I liked learning to cook. Besides something new, I felt creative and was getting a practical skill. But Tony still liked the way I mopped floors, so when I was working with him, even when I was cooking, I had to mop. I caught him being nice to me a few times and he taught me how to make some of his special stuff like his bean and noodle soup, "*Pasta e fazoo*," he called it, one of the only times he smiled. Big Ed got promoted off the pots and pans and took my place on the Hobart and he actually did pretty good. The repetition and sameness of the work Shanahan couldn't abide fit fine in that scary tunnel Ed lived. But working the Hobart put him in closer physical range of the waitresses and other girls who came into the alcove. I tried to keep an eye on him.

All the work was good because it helped me get my mind off Dew, and I was able to save some dough. The OT was there, and I didn't piss it away at the tables because I was so tired when I got off work all I could do was work on the collage and crash. The September 12 *LIFE* had a sad picture of Coretta King on the cover.

I finally had to talk to my parents. Redding was planning on going down the coast of California and wanted to go as far into Mexico as he had time. He'd told me we needed passports or birth certificates. Besides New Orleans, one of the cities he planned on getting to, Mexico was one of those places I'd always wanted to see, so I was forced into the call. And I dreaded it. I didn't want to make the call from the apartment with Turner and Sara around. I had no idea what to expect, so I used the pay phone at the laundromat.

I called collect and it got bad fast. They had been officially notified I had flunked out. They wanted me to come home right away and demanded to know, "What are you going to do? What are your plans?" Dad did his best to control himself and said my time would be better served trying to get my II-S status back by applying to a junior college somewhere other than, "...roaming around the country." That was a joke. Once the Selective Service had you, they had you. Everybody knew that. Then he zoomed right through to the end of his fuse when I said I might go to Canada or stay in Mexico instead of dealing with any of it. I knew that would make them crazy. Dad said what he always said. "Son, It will follow you around for the rest of your life."

I told him what Turner had done in Oakland and that stopped him in his tracks a minute. Mom started yelling at Dad on the extension, "Do something. Do something." like I was eight

419

years old sitting across the kitchen table from them pushing my cauliflower away. I could see her pacing and sitting on the edge of her bed and standing and rubbing Jergen's lotion on her hands with the receiver pinched between her ear and shoulder. I knew before she said it that I was going to be accused of being the cause of a migraine. When she said, "Look what you've done. I feel it coming on..."

I yelled, "Will you please just send me my birth certificate, or I will never come home." A woman sitting along the wall under a sign with step-by-step instructions on how to use the washers and dryers looked up from a *Reader's Digest*. Mom dropped the receiver and I listened to her thin, faraway crying in their bedroom. I could see her thrown across her bed. Since anger was the only emotion she and Dad had ever shown me and my brother in my twenty-year memory, it sounded odd, unusual and phony. And self-centered I guess. I should have felt pity, but it just made me mad. I said, "Sorry, Dad." I was sorry I was a disappointment. I was sorry I had let them down and cost them money. I was sorry I had projected a migraine onto my Mom from three thousand miles away. And I was sorry he was going to have to deal with it, the dark room, cold wash rags and vomit. I felt sorry for my brother, who was still in the middle of it all. My head was spinning like the washers and dryers, and the detergent smell burned my nose and eyes.

The last thing Dad said, his clipped words singed by the static of my Mom's crying, was, "Where do you want it sent?" I gave him Turner's post office box number. Then he said across the line, "Be careful."

I said, "I will," and slammed the phone down so hard a cat that had been sleeping in the sun on the low ledge at my feet by the front window snarled, jumped up and took off out the door. I had to walk, and started down the road away from the apartment in the direction of the summit and San Francisco fighting for breath. I waved off, without looking up, offers for rides, and I wondered if I would ever live long enough to have the strength to overcome the regret and anger I had inside me about two people who said they loved me. They kept saying it over and over, but that's not what I heard.

Sammy came into the kitchen early one shift while I was thawing chicken parts in the sink. Lee hadn't shown up for work again, and no one had heard from him. He was missing more and more shifts. I'd left work a couple of times to get him. If he was at his apartment, which he was some of the time, he was either too sick or I couldn't wake him up.

Sammy came over to the sink and said, "Sinclare, the health department man came to see Butcher and almost closed us down. The whole shooting match. That would be very bad for you, college boy. Very thick glue."

I dried my hands on a towel and looked at him. I hated the way he emphasized the *ing* when he said shooting. I said, "Why? What? What the hell are you talking about?"

"He did not get his money. Someone took his money. The slicer money. He was very mad. It cost Butcher twice as much and he's pissed. You don't want Butcher pissed at you. Trust me." He ran his hand over his head. "I think your friend Lee took it."

"No way. He's not even here."

Sammy scanned the kitchen with a hand over his eyes like

he was searching for something in bright sunlight. "Yes. You got that right. I can see that." Then he narrowed his eyes at me. I didn't know how he could see. "No matter. He's in on it. I can tell. You too, maybe. You better watch your ass..." and he turned and walked away through the doors to the line. Sammy was scary. His connection to Butcher gave his threats weight. A boring and tiresome wedge of customer noise, food smells and music from the sound system came in when the door swung open and closed. I went back to prying the pieces apart, the frost clouded the water and made it cold. It numbed my fingers. The chicken parts separated and floated. I swore one more time I was never going to eat chicken again, and wondered what had happened to the inspector's bribe. The money, always two new fifty dollar bills in a paper clip, waited for him on the radial slicer blade like a free piece of rare roast beef. The slicer always got checked first. When he made his regular tour of the kitchen—Lee called it a, "Fly by," and Turner always made sure to pick his nose in front of him—the inspector would halfheartedly stick his head in the walk-in, stab the ham and roast beef with his thermometer, kneel and look under the racks for rat shit, lift and smell something from the reach-in, and go out through the line, poking and scooping. Then he filled out a report on a metal clipboard with a cheap-looking ball point pen at a booth while he ate a free lunch. It took about five minutes from the slicer to the smorgasbord line. He took his time at lunch. But the money was not there on his last "surprise" visit, and Butcher had been shaken down if you believed Sammy. I didn't know how or who, but I knew it couldn't have been Lee. Sammy was up to some shit, and we had to watch out. I was afraid of who he was after.

Lee was back the next day. He was still drunk but managed

422

to function. Even I couldn't figure out where he'd hidden the booze, but he had a drink going all night. I told him about the missing slicer money. We were standing on the back step taking a break. It was getting dark earlier and earlier and the air was getting cooler every night. Lee was smoking and drinking vodka from a coffee mug. Big Ed was muttering back at the pot and pan sink. We were short. Lee had asked him to wash a couple of roasting pans. More guys had left. Even Turner was making noises about taking Sara up to Alaska or Mendocino. Lee held the cup out to me. "Belt?"

"Nah," I said. I looked back over my shoulder into the kitchen. "You better be careful. I think Sammy might be on your ass...up to something."

"Too bad, toodler. Let Charlie Chan come gunning."

"What do you think about the slicer money?"

"I think the little chink took the C note." Then he said, "Let's get going, pally. Let's eighty-six this night." And as we turned, Sammy was at the pot and pan sink, his hand on the corner of it. Lee took a slow drink from his cup and poured the rest of the vodka in the grease barrel.

Big Ed looked down at Sammy then muttered back into the pan he was scrubbing.

Sammy made an ugly face at Ed then said, "Chop, chop, Chef Lee. No more rapping. Butcher wants a steak. Pronto." And I knew he thought he had caught us. He spun, strutted away and yelled, "Lickety split," into the kitchen.

"Nice job with the vodka," I said.

"It killed me," he said, and he ducked into the stockroom.

Hitching to work the next day, just at the Y, a car slowed and I reached for the handle, glad to get a ride so fast. At the rolled-down window the driver was startled, shock all over his beard stubble face, and he sped off while I was still leaning into the road. It gave me the creeps. It was Robert, the sign of the slide, the queer prophet of the end of ignorance. I walked the rest of the way in.

When I got to work one day just before Labor Day, the only two people in the kitchen were Turner and Big Ed. Ed was humming and policing his area behind the Hobart counter. Turner was making a roast beef sandwich over by the double sinks. I said, "I thought you were a vegetarian now."

"Shit man, Victor. Dew would be disappointed, wouldn't she?"

"I think so." It felt weird. "Where the hell is everybody?"

"Got me," and as he said that Sammy came through the alcove. Turner tucked the sandwich under his apron and walked back around to the saucer. Sammy was smirking and it freaked me out.

"Butcher would like to see you, Sinclare. In the office please."

"When?"

"Now, please. Lickety split."

"What about?"

Sammy said, "Please come, college man. Butcher is waiting."

I walked with Sammy through the casino and down the hall past the cashier's cage on to the manager's office. I went in first. Sammy closed the door and stood in front of it. Butcher was at my left behind his desk with his hands folded in front of him, fingers interlocked. He had a toothpick in his mouth. He'd just had a haircut and the flat top had been cut to the skin on top of his head. His turtleneck sweater seemed like a golf tee for his huge head. Facing him to my right, sitting, was Tony in his whites, legs crossed, smoking, his face saying nothing. But even blank it was already on its way to a scowl. Standing next to him against the wall in front of a crowded bulletin board facing Butcher was Lee. He was a mess. He was dressed in his gray suit and wore a tie, but everything was wrinkled as if he had just gotten out of bed. But he wasn't wearing his hat and that was strange. His fedora was clinched at his crotch. He was sweating in the small room, made hotter by Sammy and me heating up the air, taking up more space. Butcher sucked on his toothpick and said, "Go on, Lee." Out of the corner of my eye, I saw Sammy shoot me a quick glance.

"After we prepped and closed, I met my pal Skin, you know him, and we went to Harvey's and had a few belts, hit a couple of tables. Irma joined us when she got off and we went back to her place for drinks. The three of us. Just having a few laughs." Lee shifted his weight. I could tell he was in bad shape and was dying for a drink. He probably needed some paregoric. Lapels of sweat streaked his shirt alongside his tie. I was able to make out the sugary smell of the old booze on his skin even from where I was. I could tell he was hurting to read Butcher. But Butcher just looked him back. I knew Lee wanted to sit, but he was in a bad spot. I wondered if it was about the slicer money, or if Sammy had finally cooked up some other way to screw him. Lee was cornered and his disadvantage added the heat of another person to the room.

"Go on," Butcher said again, his only movement, the toothpick rolling to the other side of his mouth.

"Well, you know how it goes, Butcher," Lee started. "Irma La Douce gets all blubbery about her gung-ho son-in-law. He just re-upped for his third tour in Vietnam. Her daughter's a mess because of it all. You know, we try and cheer her up. One thing leads to another—"

Butcher interrupted him. "Do I need all this dope?" Then, "You want to sit, Lee?" Tony was in the only extra chair. He looked at Butcher, then back at Lee. He made no effort to stand. It was a joke.

Lee said, "That's okay."

I looked at Sammy, who was smiling his slitty little smile.

"Smoke?" asked Butcher.

"I'll take a smoke," said Lee.

"Sure." Butcher slid a pack of cigarettes across the desk.

Lee's hand shook one to his lips. Tony raised a lighter and flicked it without turning and Lee bent down and got the cigarette into the flame. He inhaled and hacked, and got a thanks out between his fingers.

Butcher said, "Go on." I had no idea what was happening. I held my eye.

"Well we juiced till about dawn. Got her calmed down." Lee stubbed out the cigarette in a Mine Shaft ashtray on the desk after only two or three puffs. He looked over at Sammy. But instead of hate, it was a pale, pleading look and it made me sick. Lee jittered like spit on the griddle. He looked like he might be ready to puke. There was quiet except for muffled casino sounds on the other side of the door. Tony looked at his watch. Sammy just kept smiling. Butcher played over the toothpick with his tongue. Lee filled in the silence. "Butcher..." he said, running the brim of the fedora around through his hands like he was turning a steering wheel, "...Butcher...don't eighty-six me. Please...I am so sorry I was AWOL yesterday. I know I've been out some lately, but I always call in. I'm sorry about yesterday, really."

I looked around the room. All these guys...all of them...had seen Lee at work the day before. I was confused and scared.

He went on, "We just flopped at Irma's. I musta had the flu or something, but when I woke up, I'd missed a whole day. I came right over." He slipped into his normal voice and made a play for Butcher. "Whattaya say, man?"

Butcher yelled, "Stop it. I can't take anymore. Fucking stop." He looked at Lee with stunned disbelief. "Jesus H fucking Christ. Just can it, Goddammit. Lee, my friend..." he started, "you were here yesterday. You prepped and you worked dinner and you closed. Shit," he said, and looked at everybody in the office one at a time, twitching his head. He and Sammy shared smiles. Without looking, he ripped a strip of paper off an adding machine on the desk and rolled it into a ball. He cranked the handle again. He finally leaned back. His chair creaked like a beam about to break. I could see the realization begin to break across Lee's face. I wondered if he was remembering we'd spent the whole shift together yesterday. He and I had had a long conversation about his time cooking on a cruise ship.

He had been drunk, but he'd pulled it off like he usually did. Earlier in the summer, he had told me about the lost days that happened to him sometimes. Complete blackouts that most of the time eventually returned as gauzy memories. He'd said it was a whiskey ghost on the loose that stole memories from him. He'd laughed about it then.

"Butcher, I..."

"Don't start, Lee," Butcher spit out the words like one. "You're gone. Get out. I got enough damn drunks and rummies around here to worry about. I don't need another one in the kitchen, and a thief on top of it."

I said, "Wait. It's not fair..." before I knew it. Tony winced. Lee was staring at the floor. Sammy looked at me like I'd pulled a gun from my apron.

And just as fast, Butcher said, "What? "He back-handed the air. "You get out to."

"Sammy, eighty-six them both," and Butcher stood up and stared at me. Something reckless in me made me not look away. I challenged him.

Then Tony said, "Butcher, I need the kid. We're short." It was the first time Tony had spoken.

Butcher stepped at me and I got out of the way so he could get out the door. He stopped and said to Tony while he looked me in the face, "Do what you got to do. Just get the alchy out of here." Then he turned to Lee. "It was a great tale. Very moving. Drop bread crumbs the next time so you'll know where the hell you been. Now go wait in the restaurant." Then he said, "Sammy, keep an eye on him. I'm going to go see if he owes us anything," and he left. Cool air rushed in.

Tony said, "C'mon, kid. We're behind. Sorry, Lee," he said. "I gotta couple names. I'll write 'em down and give 'em to the kid. See ya' around." Then he said to me again, "C'mon, kid. Move it."

With Sammy just outside the door and Tony already down the hall, I said, "Lee. You don't remember yesterday? At all?"

He put his hat on and picked up the crushed cigarette from the ashtray. He stroked the wrinkles out and put it in his mouth and patted his pockets. "I thought I did," he said. "But I guess I got it mixed up with a different one."

I said, "I'll come see you after I get off."

He said, "Don't worry about me, pally. I'm a toodler." And he pointed through the door and said, "Me and that little Chinaman there are going to grab a table and settle my accounts."

****

It was crazy busy over the Labor Day weekend. I didn't do anything but sleep and work. We were short, and without Lee I got to do more and more of the cooking. Tony started to depend on me. And because we needed all the help we could find, the little bastard Sammy was doing real work instead of busting our balls for Butcher.

There was some excitement when Big Ed bumped into a waitress and caused the usual scene. Tony's fuse was short and when Ed tried to defend himself with his usual, inane defense about her bumping him first, Tony backed him all the way back against the Hobart and said the next time he pulled a stunt like that he was going to fire him. Ed acted like a child who'd been sent to his room and sulked and mumbled, but got back to washing racks of dishes and pots and pans. I kept my eye on him. All the extra work seemed to be knocking him off whatever balance he had. I sensed he was in for a big blow, and I didn't want to be around when it happened.

The Wednesday after Labor Day I bought the new *LIFE* with Jerry Koosman on the cover then finally went to check on Lee. He was pretty good for him. He was drinking but seemed all right. His apartment looked exactly the same. The bathroom mirror wasn't fixed. There was a razor above the sink with the shaving cream can. The boxes were still unpacked.

"So how are you doing?"

"Hunky dory. Skinny has a line on a grill job at the Sahara."

"What are you going to do?"

He said, "Quit asking questions. You want a drink?"

"Sure."

"You know where it is. Go make one."

I went into the kitchen and rinsed a glass. "Got any ice?"

"Look in the ice box."

The ice trays were empty. The freezer compartment needed defrosting. It smelled tinny. "Nope."

"Sorry."

There was nothing to drink in the kitchen or the refrigerator. I took the glass back into the room, and Lee poured scotch into it.

"How many fingers? Say when."

I said, "When," when there was an inch of scotch in the glass. "Who's playing?"

Like he was answering a different question he said, "Keely Smith. Don't you think she's a doll?" Then he said. "What?"

"Who's on the record player." It was piano.

He sniffed and raised his eyebrows and cocked his head to the record player. "Bud Powell."

"Who's he?"

"Quit asking me questions, pally."

We listened to the music a while then I said, "Tell me again what kind of job Skin's working on for you."

He didn't answer my question. Instead he said, "What are you going to do about that Vietnam thing?"

I sipped at the scotch. "Don't know." I told him about the conversation with my parents.

He said, "Too bad." Then, swishing his glass from side to side like a metronome, he said, "They're just doing their thing. You know. What they know how to do. It's just the way it is. That's all." And he took a sip.

We listened to the Bud Powell record. Lee sat on the bed, his back against the wall. I leaned on the other wall sitting on the floor. After a while he said, "Want some advice from an old toodler who's rung every gong in the temple?"

"Sure."

"About all your stuff. You know what I mean..."

"Vietnam?"

"Righto. And the other things."

"Parents?"

"Bingo."

"What?"

"Do something."

"What do you mean?"

He said it again. "Just do something. Get off this hill. Quit stalling."

We talked off and on and said we'd stay in touch, and he promised me we'd have a "big boy" dinner before I was gone. We shook on it, set a date and listened to more music. I felt a real rush from the scotch. My face warm. He went to the bathroom a lot. One time, he came back through the closet from the bathroom with a wooden box in his hands. He eased himself down on the floor and set it between us. He said, "Take a look at this. I've actually been off this hill before." And he lifted the lid and started to pull things out and arrange them on the floor around us. "Now you can ask all the questions you want. Except for that," and he pulled a card, the King of Hearts, from the box and put it on his bed. "Can't talk about him. Still hurts too much." He stopped my question with his eyes and said, "Go on. Ask away."

"What's that?" It was small coils of what looked like black wire.

"Elephant hair bracelet from Kenya. Cost me a Marlboro."

"What's that?"

A silver rosary from El Salvador."

"That?"

"A *mate* pot from Argentina."

"Mate?"

"Tea."

And we lost track of time. Before I had draped an old army blanket over him, passed out, and hitched back to the Y, he'd signed my two dollar bill and shown me a silver, Aztec calendar pendant from Mexico City, the queen of spades, his favorite, from a deck of Wolf cards, an ashtray from the Tropicana Club in Havana, Cuba, a switchblade, an alligator claw from New Orleans, a mini bottle of pink sand from Bermuda, dog tags, an ivory ring from Cape Town, a whale tooth from Victoria, British Columbia, a one dollar chip from Caesar's Palace in Las Vegas, a jade sculpture of a fat, laughing Chinese guy with an enormous penis, a menu from Sardi's with some autographs, an old black-and-white photograph of a young couple in front of a cafe in Paris, a golf tee, a Derringer, a pair of women's red panties, Chinese fish pliers, ticket stubs from a New York Giants game, a black beret, a smooth flat stone, polished, with a natural groove for your thumb, a ukulele pic he said was from Arthur Godfrey, and an eagle feather. And he had a story for every one.

Before he passed out, he gave me a circular ivory carving of a water buffalo, the size of a quarter, set in dull silver. He said Cape Town was more beautiful than twenty San Franciscos. The last thing he said to me was, "Find the gal that took Bird."

I wrote my parents' address on the back of a Keno slip and left it on the box by his bed.

Turner gave his notice and left The Mine Shaft. He and Sara

434

were going to take the Volvo to Mendocino if it would start, then after a while go to Alaska. "Then maybe Ibizia, Vic." He told me the rent had been paid through the fifteenth of October. I told him I would be in Susanville with Redding by then. He gave me a big lecture about Vietnam and the army. "Shit, man, Victor. Don't let them do it to you. You can't. It's immoral and you're not," he'd said. Sara said if I saw Dew to give her a big hug. I said I would, but I knew I wouldn't.

It was slower after Labor Day, but Tony kept bugging me to stay. There was no good help around. And we had established a pretty okay relationship. It was amazing to me to look back over the four months I had been there and to think how far I had come with him. I'd even met his wife. Tony had picked me up hitching to work one day, and we'd stopped by his little house just off South Lake Boulevard. She was quiet and nice. Smiled at him as he gruffed around. They fit each other.

While I was loading a steam tray with baked chicken one night, I heard an explosion of plates on the kitchen tile. When I came through the swinging doors, a freckled little waitress was picking herself off the floor, screaming and crying. She backed up into me, shaking, her hands on her neck. Ed was standing at the alcove, at least a dozen shattered plates at his feet, one not broken in his hand. He was hopping and jigging, looking as scary and crazy as I had ever seen him. He was all pulsing neck and gibberish, and I could see he was somewhere way off. I walked around the girl and stood in front of her. Ed's eyes were black. I said, "Ed, what the hell...?" and he came right over to me and smashed the plate on the floor at my feet.

He yelled over my shoulder at the waitress and said she had

been watching and waiting for the chance to bump him and, "She finally did it and I am sick of her intrusions and spying and plans to attack me." He took another step and I pushed him and it took all his attention away from the girl. Ed grabbed me and threw me back toward the alcove so hard I knocked over the stack of booster seats, fell on top of the mop bucket and turned it over. Dirty water ran across the tile. My shoulder felt like it was broken and as I rolled to my back he took huge quick steps and stood over me. I could see the roof of his mouth as he gulped air. There was a gurgle coming from his throat. His Adam's apple pumped like a piston, and I scrambled backward, slipping in the water. I said, "C'mon, Ed..." Then he looked past me and I heard Tony.

"Motherfucker..." He was behind me with a napkin at his neck. "You big dumb motherfucking ape." Tony came past me and as he did he pulled a gravity knife out of his pocket and shook it into the locked position. "What'd I tell you? Huh? What'd I tell you?" He held it in a relaxed way at his waist and started at Ed, who was backing up now, surprised and afraid, meek, his hands cupped at his mouth like a squirrel. Tony stopped and looked down at me and said, "You okay, kid?" I nodded. I was shaking and scared shitless. My pants were soaked in mop water.

The Hobart cycle had just ended. Vapor leaked from the hood, Ed backed up through it. Tony marched on him waving the knife in circles over his head, cutting tight halos in the steam. He backed Ed outside, and I heard Tony say he would cut his balls off if he ever saw him again.

The waitress was still crying but I pushed up and went right to Butcher's booth. He was eating and reading a newspaper.

I was shaking and wet. My shoulder was killing me. I told him I had been attacked in his kitchen and so had a waitress. I asked him what he was going to do about it. He kept his eyes on his paper and said, "Send Tony out here."

I walked out of The Mine Shaft and never went back.

I spent the last few days in Tahoe working on the collage. One day I knew it was finished. I backed up down the hall and tried to take in every little piece of it. Then tried to see it as a whole. But whatever I did, however I looked at it, I kept returning to the dead soldier's eyes for some help. But he always just looked back with his stare. I did write my parents a letter. In it I asked them to try to understand. I said I was sorry about a dozen times. I went to Lee's apartment to say goodbye and maybe go to dinner like we planned, but it was empty. Trash and empty boxes were in the hall. The Calais wasn't on the street. On the morning of the tenth of October, I mailed the letter, bought a cheap journal to make some notes in on the trip back across the country and stuck my thumb out on the road in front of the Tahoe Sierra Market. I stood a while next to a pile of dead pine limbs someone had trimmed. The needles had dried into a rust color from green and hung straight from the dead limbs like fringe from uniform epaulets. There was still some scent of pine, but it had dulled, too.

Diary

October 10

Takes all day to get to Redding's house in Susanville. Stand for a long time near the summit. Beautiful but starting to get really cold. Get to his house in time for supper. He wants to know what's been happening. Tell him. It's a big tomato farm. Tells me that when he was a kid he used to sit in the field with a salt shaker and eat tomatoes like apples. Have dinner with his parents. They're real normal. Eat so many tomatoes I get the shits.

October 11

We pick up a friend of Redding's. A guy who has been drafted and is leaving for Vietnam in three weeks. He's never been back east either. He wants to blow it all out before he goes. His name's Barry. We're crowded in the VW but we plan on taking turns driving and sitting in the back. We split for San Francisco to check it out.

October 12

We go to see the new hippie movie, Easy Rider. Why do they always make southern people look so dumb and violent? Cool bikes. Far out music. Hang around Haight Ashbury. Redding says we need to score some pot. He doesn't have enough in the car. Think of Dew. Wouldn't know where to look. Blow too much money on a motel in Mountain View. We decide to camp the rest of the way. See posters for anti-war demonstration in Washington, D.C., later in the month. Buy the new *LIFE*. The cover is about the history of revolt. Look around.

October 13

Drive to Santa Cruz. Check out the beach. Go along the coast past Big Sur. Unbelievable! Seals! Can't find a place to camp and have to spend more money in a motel. Pissed. Drink lots of beer and smoke lots of numbers. One of us sneaks in later to save money. Flip a coin to see who gets the floor. Barry is funny but is really bummed about Nam. Convinced he's going to get killed. Obsessed with getting laid. Hear on the radio they arrested some cult people for the Tate LaBianca murders.

October 14

Drive to Mexican border, but stop first at a Navajo Indian rummage-sale in San Diego and buy an old blue denim Navy ensign's shirt with stripes on the sleeves. Cross the border at Tijuana. Hot and smells like shit. Find out I don't need the birth certificate to get in. Dirty dry and dusty. Hustled constantly. Lots of junk for sale. We figure out how to find the road south and head for Ensenada. Sign in TJ says 79 miles. On the map it looks like we can make it by night. We do. Trip is kinda scary because the landscape is so desolate and empty. Unfamiliar. Hot as shit. Miss the Tahoe air. Miss Dew. Afraid to camp. Find a real cheap motel. Go to bar, hookers all over. Can't deal with it. Redding and I go back to the room. Double beds. I lose toss. Sleep on floor between wall and bed. Wake up in middle of night. Look over Redding who is sleeping through it to bed by window. Watch. Woman is on top of Barry. In silhouette from moonlight coming in window. They're getting it on. She screams when her wig comes off in his hands. Barry screams. Redding wakes up. Woman cries. We calm her down. She's got pink spoolies in her hair. We stay up and talk. Get to know her. Take her to breakfast at dawn. Drive her home. Meet her little kids. Dogs everywhere. We're all big pals. Barry starts worrying as we drive back to TJ that he has the clap.

October 15

Drive all the way to Las Vegas. Check out the big casinos. Sick of gambling towns. Lose money at craps. Camp at Lake Mead. Get bad cramps. Beg drugstore guy to give me something. It works.

October 16

Go through New Mexico and Arizona. In Tucson I think of Rennie for the first time. Eat huevos rancheros? Eggs and beans. Redding is starting to figure out how far away New Orleans really is so all we do is drive. Drive through downtown Houston at night. Humid, hot and scary. Black dudes all over. Later that night I sleep on the grass in a field off the highway with my head next to the front tire. Barry is wedged in the back seat. Groans in his sleep. Redding's on the ground on the other side of the car. We get high and compare our trip to Easy Rider movie. I wonder what Elaine made of the movie. Redding says he could write a better story, but I haven't seen him make any notes. Barry's worrying about the clap and Vietnam and he's getting to me.

October 17

Still in Texas. Thunderstorms. Hot. Boring. Can't wait for Louisiana. Lots of Dr. Pepper and cheeseburgers. At Louisiana border have first sense of being back near home even though I am still a long way away.

October 18

Nothing to say. Sick of the Volkswagen. Wish the back window would open all the way. Barry is constantly checking his pecker.

October 19

Get to New Orleans in the early morning. The streets are being hosed down. Humid. Drive around. Redding and Barry say it's time to head back west. Give me a chance to change my mind and go back. Want to. Don't want to. I call the airport and figure I have just enough money to fly from Memphis to Cincinnati. Will have to hitch from New Orleans to Memphis. Say good-by to the guys. Redding is loose as ever. Barry buys a case of Dixie Beer to drink in the car. I tell him good luck. Don't worry. Right! Eat cheap at an Oyster House. Go to voodoo store on Bourbon Street. Scary clerk asks about my ivory. Panhandler harasses me for blocks. Pay fifty cents to have my Tarot Cards read on the street. I hope her predictions are half right. Music everywhere. Drink a bunch of Tom Collins'.

October 20

Have to walk way out Canal Street before I get a ride. A semi hauling show horses to Jackson, Mississippi stops. Young guy driving says he will give me a ride and pay me ten bucks if I will help him unload when we get there. It's cool being up in a big truck. Do the work. Buys me two bottles of Coke. I try and get a ride outside the Fairgrounds in Jackson at dark and get picked up by three frat guys from Ole Miss who turn out to be nice. They don't mention my clothes or ponytail. They want to talk about the World Series and ask about the easy sex in San Francisco. They drop me in a little town called Tchula at midnight, about a hundred miles from Memphis. I doze on a table at a piknik site by the road. Raccoons keep me awake digging through garbage cans. Mosquitoes eat me alive. Fingering Lee's ivory around my neck like a rosary.

October 21

Under a sign that says Next Exit, Duck. Writing this. Have been thumbing for fucking EVER! Sitting on my duffel. Every bit of suede is gone from my boots. They're brown greasy and dark. No rides. Rerunning the entire summer through my head. I make a decision. And I finally feel some peace. For now anyway. Was it that simple?

October 22

Do it.

October 23

October 24

October 25

The End

About the Author

William Gerald Hamby lives in Richmond, Virginia. His travel notebooks on Cuba and Thailand, and a variety of articles and essays have been published in the *Richmond Times Dispatch*, music journals and magazines. He has an EMMY from the Washington, D.C. chapter of the National Academy of Television Arts and Sciences. This is his first novel.

For more information,
william.hamby1@gmail.com

Find more books from
Keith Publications, LLC
At

www.keithpublications.com

CPSIA information can be obtained
at www.ICGtesting.com
Printed in the USA
LVOW03s0100300917
550531LV00001B/12/P